The Chronicles

Of Dreams and Nightmares

S. J. Coates

The Chronicles of Pylisya: Of Dreams and Nightmares
Copyright © S. J. Coates 2020

Cover and map illustrations © 2020 by S. J. Coates

The moral right of the author has been asserted.

All rights reserved.

Except for brief quotations in printed reviews, no part of this publication may be reproduced or transmitted in any form or by any means (electronic, mechanical, photocopying or otherwise) without the prior permission of the author and publisher.

Of Dreams and Nightmares is the first book in the youth fantasy fiction series, *The Chronicles of Pylisya.*

ISBN-13: 9798609303066

The Chronicles of Pylisya

- Book One -

ACKNOWLEDGEMENTS

To my parents, for always supporting me and encouraging my creativity. You've constantly been there, and I couldn't ask for anyone better to walk this journey with me.

To my sister, Lucy, for listening to all my weird and wonderful ideas, and letting me bounce them off you. This story would not be what it is today, without your willingness to hear me out.

To my various English teachers over the years: thank you for encouraging the shy student reading in the corner, and helping me to believe I could do this.

To Luke Jeffery, for giving me advice and guiding this book in its final stages. I'm so grateful for the help that you gave me.

Lastly, and most importantly, I thank you God, for giving me the ability to do this, and being with me every step of the way. Pylisya would not be possible without You.

- Pylisya -

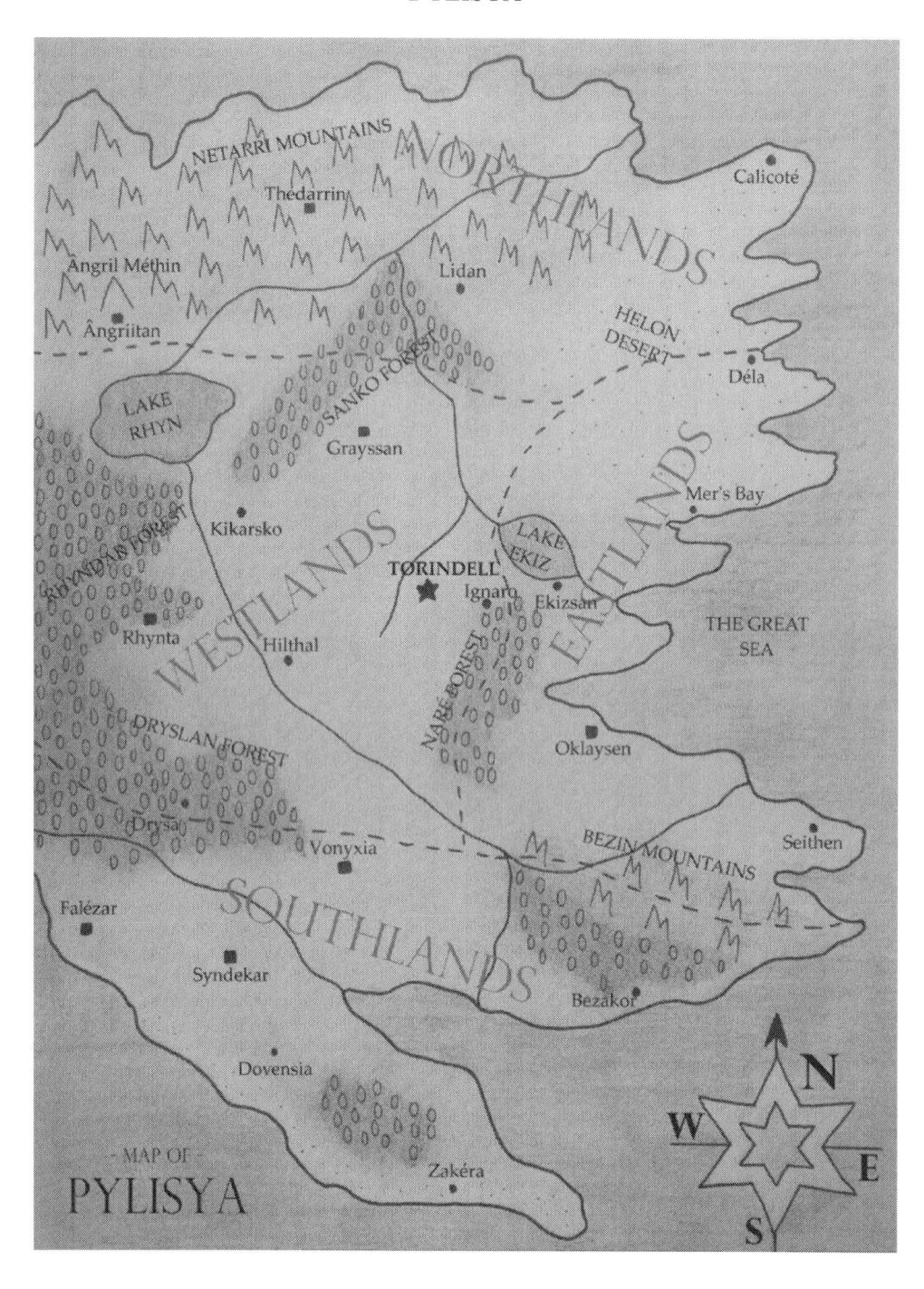

- PART ONE: DREAMS -

Chapter One

- Benji -

Westlands, Pylisya. Summer's End, 5964 PY.

I used to think that everyone saw the colours, but it seemed that this realm of vision was unique to me.

Every living being had their own shade, pulsing with the rhythm of their spirit, encompassing them in a tone that reflected the being's inner workings. The correct term was souls, my brother told me when I tried to explain it, but he didn't understand and that was why I was hiding from him.

That's not exactly true, my twin, Kalic, unhelpfully supplied through our rather frustrating mental bond.

I sighed. *Just keep quiet, and stay out of my head!*

We ducked down behind the dresser and I stared in the direction of the door, where the soft green of our brother lurked. Darkness surrounded and my breathing hitched, the steady in-out-in-out threatening to betray my location. Our backs pressed against the dresser, hearts pounding in perfect rhythm, using the shadows to our advantage. We would be safe here, unless the lights along the wall were lit. I clutched Kalic's hand as the glow of a torch flickered in the corner of my vision, moving to ignite the various candles across the stone wall. Footsteps drew closer and closer, matching the drumming of my heartbeat, until-

"Found you!"

I screamed as strong arms lifted me out and away from my sanctuary, then the sound turned into a giggle when the dark eyes of my older brother, Turvo, met mine. He discarded the torch to better hold me in his arms, grunting slightly with the motion.

"Which one are you again?" he teased, ruffling my hair. I clung to his shirt, feeling the thrum of his green beneath my fingers.

"Kalic," I giggled.

"No, *I'm* Kalic!" my twin protested, stepping out of the shadows. Turvo smirked.

"Found you too, then," he laughed.

Disapproval rippled through Kalic's colour, mixed with a bitter green taste of betrayal as he put together my deliberate actions.

"Benji, you-!" The pointed tips of his ears turned bright red and I knew he would've run at me if I wasn't safely in Turvo's arms.

"You still won, Kal," Turvo pointed out.

"Huh," my twin grunted, but already the scarlet anger was fading.

I stuck my tongue out at him. "Can we play another game?"

"Yes! And this time, I'll beat you, Benji," Kalic grinned, his feet tapping in anticipation.

But Turvo, ever the spoilsport, exhaled loudly and shook his head. "Sorry, but Mutti wants you to get ready. We've got visitors coming."

"Oh," we said in unison, and I beamed at Kalic. His warm red gained a tinge of yellow that merged with, and overcame, the blue of sadness.

Perfect timing, he commented, his thoughts blending with mine.

Indeed. But Turvo's hiding something. I shared the view of our brother's slightly mottled green, but Kalic frowned, unable to comprehend the colours displayed.

I'm sure he'll tell us, my twin then supplied, before we gently extracted ourselves from the shared mind-space.

I wriggled and lightly punched Turvo's firm chest, telling him I wanted to be put down. He relented with a slight sigh of relief, then started walking away.

"What visitors, Turvo?" Kalic asked then, ambling after our brother. I followed, moving to tread in the invisible footprints he left.

"Important ones, so you'll need your best robes," Turvo replied mysteriously, holding the door open for the two of us to trot out. Once in the light of the hallway, we exchanged looks - and thoughts - of equal confusion and disgust. Turvo's attempts at being secretive usually didn't last long, so I wasn't too concerned about what he was hiding. But was it *really* necessary for us to wear our horrible, itchy robes?

Apparently so, as Turvo soon handed us over to Mutti, who instantly fretted that we would not have enough time for a proper bath. I sniffed, long and hard, but as far as I could tell we did not smell bad. Kalic was fiery and metallic as usual, and I smelt- well, like me.

"Turvo, you must get ready as well!" Mutti exclaimed, agitation lacing her tone. I reached up and patted her arm gently, trying to soothe her like Atti did. It didn't seem to work much though.

She took our hands and hurried us into the bedroom we shared, quickly undoing the ties of Kalic's tunic. He swatted her hands away, pointing out that he was ten and more than capable enough to dress himself.

"What about you, Benji?" she asked.

Yes, what about you, Benji? Kalic echoed mentally in a teasing tone.

I scowled at him. "I can do it myself, Mutti," I declared, though my clumsy figures were already fumbling with the various laces and ties. I could tell by the darkening of Mutti's lilac that she was growing exasperated with my slowness, but I wasn't going to quit just because my hands were a little clammy.

By the time my clothes lay in a jumbled heap, Kalic was already layered in his best robes. They were a deep purplish-crimson, with little yellow leaves and flowers embroidered around the cuffs, collar, and bottom hem. A white belt clutched his waist, matching the pale breeches and undershirt that were only slightly visible beneath the thick outer robes. With his dark hair torn from its usual ponytail and brushed so it sat neatly upon his shoulders, he looked as regal as a grandson of King Myranis should. He made a face when he caught me staring, embarrassment and pride both threading through his colour.

Mutti turned her attention to me, wasting no time in assisting with my own robes. I wanted to complain - Kalic hadn't needed any help and I was more than capable of dressing myself - but for the sake of speed I let her. My undergarments were a soft orange, bordering on yellow, as I could not be trusted to keep white stain-free. The last time I'd worn white, the fabric had ended up every colour but the one it started as. It had been Mutti's fault for giving me a white tunic when I was having one of my painting days, but she didn't see it that way.

I squirmed as the heavy outer robes embraced me, the underside of the embroidered cuffs already itching my wrists terribly. I quite liked the deep blue, but it was not *me*. Blue was my brother Fírean's colour: who, for some reason, was always dressed in pale blues, greens, and browns. Mutti got the colours wrong and I pointed this out to her frequently with no understanding on her part.

"You look lovely in blue, Benji."

"But it's Fír's! Not mine!"

"No, this was made especially for you, little shadow."

I huffed as she tied the matching orange-yellow belt around my waist, the colour of which annoyed me. Was it orange? Or was it yellow? Why couldn't it make up its mind?

"Ouch!" I cried as Mutti attacked my curls with a brush. I barely held back another cry as it caught on a knot, snapping some of the bristles and tearing a clump of hair from my sensitive scalp.

"Mutti, stop," I whined, trying to wriggle away from her. She threw the brush down after a few more painful failures, resorting to combing with her fingers, working the knots out gently but firmly.

"How is your hair so much thicker than your brother's?" she muttered.

I glanced over at Kalic, sitting on the edge of his bed, fiddling with a wooden carving he had recently started. Mutti would be mad if she saw the dust and splinters falling onto his robes as he chipped away with his pocket-knife, grumbling each time a wisp of hair blew across his face.

"There. All done," Mutti declared, and the three of us sighed with different levels of relief. I stood and clasped my hands together to refrain from scratching.

"Ah, my beautiful boys," she smiled, kissing each of us on the forehead before stepping back to admire the robes we wore. "I really must get in a painter sometime," she mused.

My ears drooped. *A painter?* That would mean sitting around in my horrid robes for most of the day!

Kalic echoed my movements, grumbling again as he slipped his pocket-knife into his belt.

"Straighten up, both of you," Mutti chided, "Benji, don't let your ears do that. It's most unbecoming."

My brow furrowed as I concentrated hard on getting them to point upright again, but it was no easy task. They didn't just move when I willed it and Mutti knew that, so her request was silly.

She started rambling again but was quickly interrupted by Turvo bursting into our room like a hurricane. He, too, wore his best robes - a lovely deep peridot - and I giggled slightly when I noticed the brown mud-stains already gathered around the bottom.

"Come on!" he yelled, "They're here!"

I jumped to my feet, Kalic close behind me. "Who's here?" we exclaimed at once.

Turvo smirked and glanced at Mutti. "Come see!" he urged.

Mutti sighed loudly as the three of us tore down the hall, a winding passage that bent and curved at every span. The stark white walls were almost a sickly shade and I grimaced at the lifeless colours present in the paintings lining each one. They were cold and unnatural: not the warm, bright shades that coated each person I knew.

Suddenly my feet slipped and I found myself skidding on the recently-polished marble floors, nearly knocking into Kalic.

"Aye, watch it!" he cried, repeating the words mentally with more force.

"Sorry," I mumbled, managing to stop without falling flat on my face.

Turvo halted too and I realised we'd almost fallen down the stairs that led down to the front door. He turned to scrutinise our appearances and I squirmed as he adjusted my robes slightly.

"Now, no more running in these, okay?"

"Since when did he become our mother?" Kalic muttered grumpily, and I laughed.

Turvo glanced in the mirror, checking his blond ponytail was in its usual immaculate high position. Another laugh escaped my lips, purely because it was amusing how my brother could fuss so much over his hair and face, yet pay no heed to the state of his clothes.

Mutti soon caught up to us, also dressed in one of her best dresses, a deep purple velvet that complimented her colour nicely. As customary, Turvo held the door open for her to exit first, then we followed hot on her heels, Kalic and I struggling to balance looking regal with our desperation to see who our mysterious visitors were. Clearly they were people of some importance, or we would not all be dressed in beautiful, suffocating robes.

Mutti stopped and curtsied gracefully. We moved either side of her, but I was so excited by who I saw that I forgot to bow.

"Fírean! Lanny!"

The family either side of me shot me a dirty look, but I only had eyes for those in front. Our brother, Fírean, stumbled as he climbed off his horse, flushing pink with embarrassment. Turvo broke our line and approached coolly, though he couldn't hide the relief and joy in his colour from me. The two barely managed to exchange greetings before Fírean had wrapped his younger brother up in an embrace, blue and green merging into a loving aqua.

But my attention was drawn not to Atti sitting astride his grand white stallion, nor the two elves beside him that I did not recognise. The one I wanted to see the most stroked the smooth palomino coat of his elegant mare, almost the same colour as his curls. Another cry escaped my mouth and he turned just as I ran into his arms.

"Lanny! Lanny!" I exclaimed, laughing as he scooped me up. His warm gold embraced me gently, with the care and love only the eldest brother could possess. I breathed in his scent, all scrolls and wood mixed with Brina's equine and some other scent I didn't recognise: metallic? I frowned. Metallic was a scent that belonged to Kalic, when he worked with our onta in the forge. It did not belong to my gentle eldest brother.

Lanny set me down, pausing only to hand Brina's reins to Turvo before he took my small hand in his much larger one, leading me over to Atti and his two elvish companions. All were dressed in fine robes, with Atti looking the part of heir to the throne, for once. The elf on his left was the most regal, clothed in white and gold that highlighted his pale complexion, and as my eyes ran up his body I registered who he was: the crown resting upon his silvery-blond hair only confirmed it.

"Y-your Majesty!" I stammered, clutching Lanny's hand tighter in my nervousness. My grandfather let out a low chuckle, much to my confusion.

"Ah, young Benji, yes?"

I nodded rapidly.

He smiled, his dark eyes sparkling like his son's - my Atti's - did. "No need to address me so. 'Anatti' will do just fine."

"Yes, Anatti," I whispered, the familial word strange on my tongue. His colour was a brighter orange than Atti's, more of a yellow like the colour of my belt; yet it contained deep pools of blue that confused me and turned it a little green in places.

I closed my eyes so all I could see were the colours. Lanny's gold enveloped me, but the colour that caught my attention was that of the third elf. I had not seen a colour on him before, but I perceived him now as a lovely, soft silver. Opening my eyes again, I was confused to see that his silver did not encompass him like the colours of everyone else around us did; in fact, I could only really see it when my eyes were shut to the mosaic of the world around. I chewed on a strand of hair that had trickled into my mouth, watching him curiously. His grey eyes seemed distant, but when they focused they did so on me, and I instinctively tried to hide behind Lanny.

"Who's that?" I mumbled into his cloak, the twitch of his ears telling me he'd still heard me.

"He is Ethlon, one of Anatti's advisors," Lanny explained, gently nudging me out from under his cloak.

I sneezed. "Lanny, you smell funny," I complained, completely ignoring his answer. I didn't want to meet an advisor-person. He sounded old and boring.

Lanny glanced down at me, his blue eyes momentarily clouded. "Do I? Hmm, best take a bath then," he chuckled, but it sounded forced.

I frowned at him, then at Ethlon, who was still staring at me. He blinked slowly, his pale eyebrows turning down towards his nose, then whispered something to Atti. Atti's colour flooded with grey anxiety and his face visibly paled at whatever Ethlon said. My free hand curled into a little fist and I decided then and there that I did not like Ethlon, despite his colour being nice and soothing. He kept staring at me in a rather uncomfortable manner and he was making Atti stress and worry. Plus, his hair was a peculiar colour - a pale, golden-orange - and it was cropped very short, exposing his pointed ears fully, a style that was very frowned upon amongst elves. I tugged on Lanny's hand.

"Can we go?" I asked.

"I can, but you can't. Anatti made this trip specially to see you."

I pulled my hand from his and crossed my arms. "Don't want to see him."

Lanny actually scowled, his features temporarily losing some of their natural beauty. "He hasn't seen you since your second birthday, Benji! I know he is the king but he's also Atti's father. And it's important to spend time with family, yes?"

"Yes," I sighed, staring at the little bug crawling over the toe of my boot. Lanny and strange Ethlon were still looking at me, I could feel their gazes locked on my face, but I knelt down to retrieve it anyway. Its shell was a bright green, rippling with tinges of orange as it scurried around my palm.

The pulse of its colour was faint, yet I had no doubts about its existence; it was as alive as me and the elves around us.

"Benji?"

Lanny reached down and tugged on my hand, interrupting my thoughts and clearly trying to pull me up. I wanted to resist and sit in the dirt with the colourful insects instead of making conversation with the newcomers, but Mutti would be mad if I did so. Reluctantly I straightened, still cupping the bug in my hand.

"Look," I said, holding it out. The little bug's wings emerged and it buzzed lightly, taking to the air with an innocent joy that thrummed through its colour. I smiled as I watched it leave, yellow flooding through me too. Lanny's bright eyes followed its movements for a moment, then he led me back over to where my grandfather and Atti were deep in conversation, their colours merging. Atti's orange still held too much grey anxiety for my liking, seeming to grow when he noticed me again.

"Arlan," Atti started, "Benji and I need to talk." I frowned at his use of Lanny's full name, then shook my head rapidly.

"Lanny, don't leave me," I pleaded, clutching my brother's hand tighter. Honestly, he'd only just returned from a season away! We had so much to talk about; I didn't want to lose him again so soon.

Atti sighed. "It's nothing bad, Benji," he said, the flicker in his colour telling me he was lying.

I clenched my fist and shook my head again. "No! Your colours are weird," I cried, trying to hide behind Lanny, "I don't want to talk!"

Ethlon stiffened. "Colours?" he repeated, his unnerving eyes bearing down on me.

I nodded slowly, not liking the way he seemed to take in my every movement, feeling exposed to his scrutiny.

"Colours," he muttered again, this time barely coherent. Lanny's hand untangled from mine and rested on the back of my head, gently urging me forwards, but I held my ground.

"Is he going to hurt me?" I asked Lanny, tentatively looking up at him. His light brow furrowed.

"No! Of course not. I know Ethlon well, he has talked often with me and Atti. He won't hurt you. At least, he'd better not," he added, shooting Ethlon a glare laced in red.

My eyes darted to Atti for confirmation.

He sighed. "We just need to talk, Benji. That is all." His orange was still clouded but the warm tone reassured me enough. Something definitely wasn't right, but if I wouldn't get hurt, what harm was there?

Don't do it, something within me urged. I ignored it.

"Okay," I relented, cautiously padding over to Atti and extending my hand to his. He accepted, his orange pulsing and thrumming against my palm, nearly as soothing as Lanny's gold.

"Arlan, take your grandfather to the back lounge. Ask the chef to prepare a meal and..."

I zoned out as Atti gave Lanny various tasks, which I thought rather unfair as Lanny himself had only just returned home. Nevertheless, my brother obeyed without visible complaint, heading inside accompanied by the king and my other brothers. As I refocused, I felt Ethlon's gaze on me again - *what is his interest with me?* - but somehow managed to return it this time, concentrating on keeping my expression straight and unimpressed. At least, I tried to mimic Atti when he was annoyed at Fírean for incessantly playing the lute past dusk. However, it did not invoke the reaction Fírean gave Atti; rather, Ethlon remained as stone-faced as he had been the whole time he was with us. His strange silver did not even flicker.

How can he be so monochrome? I wondered, but did not voice my thoughts.

"Benji, Ethlon, walk with me," Atti commanded, starting off towards the gardens. I trotted after him as best I could, but my short legs had to work thrice as hard to keep pace with the two older elves.

"Atti, slow down!" I whined, nearly standing on a snail in my clumsy hurry.

"Ah, sorry Benji," he said, though his tone and colour were far from apologetic, "We just need to go somewhere private. Come on." He stopped and scooped me up, carrying me on his hip the rest of the way, with much less protest or strain than Turvo would've given. I stretched out my arm to caress the bold emerald leaves of the various hedges we passed, my fingertips meeting the occasional soft petals blossoming within, still growing strong despite the waning season. Closing my eyes, I let the colours of life thrum and buzz around me, until a sharp pain in my finger caused me to cry out. Atti's colour flared with surprise and he almost dropped me.

"Aye! Benji, what is it?"

I didn't know, my eyes were leaking down my cheeks and I couldn't see, but my hand was hurting, all nasty and white-coloured, and Atti's flash of red annoyance was *not* helping.

"I don't see what you want with him," he snapped, "He's a child, and a babyish one at that. How many ten-year-olds do *this* when they prick themselves on a tiny little thorn, hmm?"

Ethlon's cold voice cut through my hurt, grounding me to the moment "He is still very young, Arazair. Perhaps you are being a little too harsh?" he suggested.

I roughly rubbed my eyes with the cuffs of my sleeves, my cheeks heating up as I realised what had happened; it was just a small cut, the shock of which had caused me more distress than the injury itself.

Atti glanced down at me, as if contemplating why Elohim had given him a son like me. I didn't blame him. I *knew* I was weird; the other elves thought I wouldn't hear their whispers, but my ears were keen. I tried to block out the nasty comments in my direction, though I was unable to ignore the horrid colours coating their words. Only Lanny held no malice towards me and that was why I loved him the most.

Well, Kalic, too, but I could never truly tell what he thought unless we were standing close together, something which was both a blessing and a curse.

The silence from Atti continued and I squirmed out of his arms, landing somewhat awkwardly on the soft grass. My robes were almost suffocating so I pulled off the outer layer, setting it down on a nearby stone bench. Then I glanced up at the two adults, both with immobile faces.

"What do you want?" I asked quietly, forcing myself to sit on the bench. My muscles were screaming at me to put them in use and run, away from creepy Ethlon and disappointed Atti, but I forced myself to stay. Ethlon ran his eyes over me again.

"You can see the colours, can't you, Benji?"

My stomach twisted and I suddenly felt very sick. "I, uh, yes, like-" I looked around somewhat frantically "-the green of the grass and the orange of those fading leaves. But everyone sees those, right?" It wasn't the answer he wanted, but I couldn't tell him the truth; my family always told me to not mention the colours to everyone.

Seeking reassurance, I looked to Atti, but his lips were pursed, his the solid orange of his colour not betraying any emotion.

"That is not what I meant, and you know it," Ethlon said, slightly harsh. I clenched a fist and shook my head.

"No, I don't," I huffed, "Can I go and see Lanny now?"

Atti sighed and knelt down in front of me. "Benji, please. Ethlon only wants to help. You can tell him the truth," he whispered.

I shook my head again.

Atti huffed rather irritably. "Listen, Arlan and I are both concerned about you. You have to be truthful with Ethlon. Because if what he thinks is true, that you are a Chr-" He paused momentarily, "If you truly *can* see colours, and it's not just an attention-seeking act, then we need to know. The ability could put you in danger," he finished, his tone surprisingly steady.

"In danger?" I repeated, my eyes widening as I glanced back at Ethlon. He nodded slowly.

My pulse quickened. Of *course* I could see colours, I wasn't desperate enough to make it up. And I didn't want to be in danger, either, but what would that mean for me?

Somewhat absentmindedly I glanced down at my hands, only now registering the crimson liquid trailing down from my aching finger.

Oh, no. Blood... I can't stand blood! I gagged, barely holding back the acidic liquid rising in my throat as my stomach somersaulted, feeling dizzy all of a sudden. I swayed and pitched forwards, everything starting to blur.

"Benji. Benji, answer me!" Ethlon demanded. I tried to open my mouth but the words didn't come. Something was holding me back, choking me, stopping the words from forming on my tongue. I fell further, the colours shifting and morphing, blending into a dark mess that descended upon my mind.

And for a brief moment, I saw nothing.

Chapter Two

- Jackie -

Wales, Earth. September, 2004 AD.

"Benji!" I gasped, sitting bolt upright, the blankets sliding off my bed with the motion. The echoes of the foreign world still danced through my mind and it took me a few minutes to reconcile where I was. Across the room, my adopted sister Hazel stirred, her furrowed brow illuminated by the wisps of moonlight creeping through the blinds.

"Can you quit the sleep talking? Please?" she mumbled sleepily.

"Sorry," I replied, swinging my legs around, "But I keep having those dreams." I got up and padded across the cold floor, ignoring the chills surging up my tired, protesting legs. Hazel watched me with dark, narrowed eyes peeking over the top of her duvet.

"Again?" she muttered, curiosity and tiredness mixing in her voice. I smiled slightly and ruffled her rich hair, wanting so badly to talk with her about it, but she was still only eleven.

"Nevermind me. You should get your sleep," I instructed, and she complied, whispering something before turning over and shuffling even further down under the covers. I seized a torch and flicked it on, carefully treading across the wooden floors, watching my step to avoid any creaky boards. Once by the door, I set the torch gently down on the desk right beside it, sitting on the firm stool almost immediately. My hands worked systematically, seizing my favourite fountain pen; despite the availability of ballpoints, I found it easier for the words to come when I wrote with ink. And come they did, as I slipped in a fresh ink cartridge and pressed it to paper, the details of my dream re-emerging. Its vivid qualities made it seem more of a memory than a dream at times.

I chewed on the tip of the pen after the entire dream had passed through my head. *This should be enough*, I thought, gently setting the pen down in its rightful place. At the children's home where I volunteered, each Friday afternoon was the teacher's time off and it was part of my job to keep the children occupied. To do that, I began relying on the strange and fascinating dreams of mine. It was as if a world was building in my head, full of characters with lives that I enjoyed watching unfold like some sort of movie. I only hoped that my words could capture some essence of the cinematic atmosphere that my mind wove each night. The dreams were strange and followed no trend other than a focus on a family of elves. Usually each ended in some sort of peaceful resolution, but last night...

My mind puzzled over the ending of the dream, which had been complete darkness. I'd never had a dream end that way; for some bizarre reason I feared for Benji. But why? Wasn't he just a character conjured by my weird imagination as I slept?

With a groan, I switched the torch off and grabbed my coat, slipping out of the room before Hazel could wake again. The heavy snoring from the room opposite implied that Mum was still asleep, so I made it downstairs with no unwanted incidents. It was only five in the morning, but I just could not get back to sleep, not with the uncomfortable feeling creeping down my spine.

Perhaps a walk will help?

I pulled my boots on and snuck outside, wincing as the door shut with a loud *click*. It was folly to go into the woods when it was still dark, Mum had drummed that in to me many times, but this morning I felt a strange and irresistible pull to enter the woodlands not twenty metres from my house. Besides, I was almost an adult now, and it wasn't *that* dark. Dawn could not be any more than an hour away. I'd be fine.

Soft leaves crunched underfoot as the canopy of trees grew ever thicker, their wide leaves preventing even a small glimpse at the sky. I traced the smooth bark of a nearby tree, stopping for a brief break. *Surely the sun would have risen by now?* I glanced at my watch, only to discover it was not there. And I was still wearing my polka-dot pyjamas. *Great.* I'd been in such a hurry to get out of the house that I'd forgotten everything essential. Even my phone was absent from my coat pocket. Had I put it on charge? I couldn't remember. The woodland air was musky and thick with the scent of pinecones, making me feel rather drowsy. My body ached from days of limited sleep and the gathering mist was doing nothing to help keep my focus. I wanted to curl up and drift off...

No! My eyes snapped open again and I slapped my cheeks. What was I doing? Something felt wrong in these woods, something I'd not felt before. *But then,* I glanced back at the curving path, *I don't think I've ever wandered this far.* Why had I come to the woods again? To clear my head, I thought, and it had done quite the opposite. I felt so disorientated and muggy; I couldn't tell what direction I was headed.

Something rustled in the bushes behind me and I tensed up, instinctively reaching for the inside pocket of my coat, which held a small penknife, left over from my Girl Guide days. *At least I have something to defend myself with.* But it was not a wild animal that emerged from the bush: rather, a small, copper-skinned girl.

Hazel.

"Jackie!" she cried, running over to me. I embraced her tightly.

"What are you doing here, Zel?" I exclaimed, glancing around for any other signs of life. Her tiny body trembled in my arms.

"I followed you, but then this wood felt weird and I wanted to stop but I kept going... I want to go home," she sobbed. I gently ran my hand through her thick, brown-black hair, untangling the strands somewhat absentmindedly.

"It's alright, Zel. We'll just retrace our steps, okay?"

She nodded swiftly. I let go of her and turned to go down the path, but stopped.

"What is it?" Hazel tugged on my hand, but I remained frozen for a while longer.

"It's gone," I finally whispered, "The path's gone."

"We're lost?" she shrieked. I sensed another creature approaching us and clamped my hand over Hazel's mouth before she could say any more. Then I seized the penknife with my other hand, gripping it with the blade facing down, my thumb resting on the top of the handle.

"Stay back," I warned, trying to keep my voice from trembling. Hazel clutched my arm, her eyes wide.

Someone to the left of us laughed and I pivoted in that direction. "So, this is Sachiel's spawn? She doesn't resemble him much." The voice was masculine and held a sneer that I'd grown to associate with the jerks that liked to harass my family in the streets. Thanks to Hazel's ethnicity and my East Asian ancestry, we were often subjected to harsh comments that were entirely unnecessary. I'd stood up to the bullies enough times to know what to expect. But why would they follow us into the woods? And who was Sachiel? One of Hazel's birth parents perhaps?

"I don't know who you're talking about," I said harshly, "Now leave us alone."

The speaker moved into our limited vision and I gasped. He was not one of the pale-faced jerks who I'd met before: in fact, his skin was darker than Hazel's, but unnaturally so. It was a bluish-black, almost navy, and seemed to be stretched thin over his stocky body. His eyes fixed on me, glowing with unholy fire, and his red lips parted, revealing perfectly white pointed teeth. I pushed Hazel behind me, raising the knife protectively, though I could not stop my hand from shaking. *God, please,* I prayed silently, *Help us!* I didn't really know *who* I was praying to - I wasn't much of a religious person - but Mum had enough faith to drum into us what to do when in trouble. *Don't panic. Pray.*

"You have his eyes," the creep hissed, staring right into them and bringing my thoughts tumbling back down to reality. Confusion mingled with my fear. Mum had always said my eyes were like my father's, but I'd never met him. He was dead, she said. Died shortly after my conception.

So why did this creep talk like he knew him?

"Whose eyes?" I asked innocently, starting to assess the situation. There was a narrow gap between the trees on our right. If I could distract him long enough...

"Sachiel's, of course. Don't you pay attention, girl?" he spat. I tapped Hazel's arm and pointed at the opening without taking my eyes off our attacker, hoping she'd understand what I meant.

"I don't know a Sachiel. You've got the wrong person," I said, trying to sound sassy or at least just a little confident, "And yes, I have my father's eyes, but he's dead. Motorbike accident. Sixteen years ago." The painful words lingered in the air, threatening to break the fragile patch in my heart that still ached for the lack of a father, but the soft sound of young feet grazing the mud and grass anchored me to the moment.

"He's dead? Really? That's funny, because I'm certain I saw-" He stopped midsentence, suddenly noticing Hazel's absence. "Where did the dwarf go?"

I clenched my fists. "She's not a dwarf!" I yelled, infuriated by his insult.

He laughed, the high-pitched sound sending shivers down my entire body. "How little you know," he sneered, "Get her!"

Five other creatures emerged from the bushes, each identical in colour and stature to the first creep. I considered fighting for a moment, but the swords they carried deterred me from that option. Instead I turned tail and fled, running down the same narrow path I'd instructed Hazel to travel. As I ran, my mind could barely keep up with the strangeness of what I was witnessing. Human-like creatures with bizarre skin and wielding swords- *swords!* Who carried swords in this day and age? They were like something out of my dreams, except I'd never dreamt of anything that horrible. And who on Earth was Sachiel?

I caught up to Hazel in no time. She stood as if transfixed and only responded when I turned her to face me.

"Don't stop! They're just behind us," I gasped out.

Hazel trembled. "But... the trees..."

"You're scared of trees now?" I looked ahead and could hardly see anything; the mist was so thick. "I'll guide you through. Don't worry, just hold my hand, okay?"

She took my hand with a grip stronger than her size and age would imply, and we broke into a run together, barely avoiding the protruding tree roots. I doubted I could see any clearer than Hazel, but it was better to run into the mist than to be killed by the creeps pursuing us.

The mist grew thicker, blinding me to anything but its slightly-purple glow. I slowed to a jog and frowned at that observation. *Purple?* Since when-

"Jackie!" Hazel screamed as her hand was torn from mine. I surged forward instinctively and found myself falling, though I could not see anything around me. The mist rippled and tightened around me, solidifying as it touched my arms, and though I was falling still I felt secure somehow.

God, is this You? What the heck is happening?

My mind cleared for the first time since entering the forest and the pull to its depths ceased, as if I'd reached the point that had called to me. I tried to glance behind, but there was no sign of our attackers. Vaguely I wondered how far I'd fallen and if they had some sort of enhanced vision - or maybe just common sense - to stop them running right off the edge as I had. But as far as I was aware, there were no cliffs anywhere near us. Rolling hills and valleys, yes, but cliff edges? Short drops that led to rivers perhaps, but never anything that would lead to me falling this long. A hand extended towards me and I grasped it, finding it to belong to Hazel. We clutched each other, neither saying a word, both uncertain as to what had happened, yet I was strangely unafraid. Perhaps it was the odd security I felt, as if I was *meant* to encounter those creeps, *meant* to tumble into this sudden abyss. That somehow, everything would work out.

After what seemed like hours but was probably minutes, even just seconds, the mist began to clear and my vision strengthened. I took in a shaky breath, previously unaware that I'd been holding it in, and the sweetest scent flooded into my nostrils. It was full of warmth and peace, if those things could actually *have* scents, like chestnuts in autumn and pansies in spring. I glanced down at Hazel, still in my arms, intending to speak to her but no words would form. *Strange*. We didn't seem to be falling so fast now, which confused me: nothing had been done to slow our fall, had it? At least, nothing that I could deduce logically.

As if logic could be applied in our situation. Nothing was making any sense at the moment.

"Jackie, look!" Hazel exclaimed suddenly, her grip on my arm tightening. I followed her gaze and nearly threw up at the ground rushing towards us. *I don't want to die...!* But my earlier observations were correct, we *were* slowing, and the calm rippled over me again, some sort of assurance that we were going to be okay. I tried to glance behind, but could see nothing except the parting mist. How far had we fallen? Why was the grass below such a strong green? And where was the cliff edge we'd supposedly rushed off?

Ah, child. So many questions. In time, you will come to see the answers.

I started and looked around frantically, but there was no-one else in sight. "Did you hear that?" I asked Hazel cautiously.

She shook her head. "Hear what?"

"Nevermind." *Must've imagined it.*

My feet hit the grass and I braced myself for the painful shock that would surely follow, but for some reason it was nonexistent, as if I'd jumped on the spot, not fallen for who knew how far. Hazel slipped out of my arms and touched the ground cautiously, her feet clad only in thin socks that were torn and muddied. I looked down at my own boots, covered in dirt and torn leaves, suddenly aware of small pains on my legs. Evidently our journey through the woodlands was not without attacks from silently cruel tree branches, whose whips had left multiple shallow cuts on my cheeks as well as the legs. I shivered, though the sun shone brightly on the incredibly vibrant grass. My coldness was no surprise, really. After all, I was clothed in naught but my pyjamas and a tattered coat.

"Where are we?" Hazel asked tentatively.

I stopped and took a look, a *proper* look at our surroundings. The sky was a gorgeous blue in every direction and the green grass stretched as far as the eye could see. To our left a cluster of trees stood, their dark leaves beautiful and inviting, but I refrained from heading that way. If I strained my eyes, I could just about make out the form of mountains in the distance, the brilliant sunlight bursting past their peaks. A movement on the right seized my attention and I stared in disbelief as a herd of horses trotted into view. They were nothing terribly unusual - all the normal colours - but they were roaming free and I'd never heard of horses running wild in south Wales; at least, not those strong, well-bred horses. Little mountain ponies perhaps. But the equines I watched were definitely horses, their sleeks coats shining as they broke into a collective gallop. Beside me Hazel gasped in wonder, seemingly transfixed by the horses as well. It wasn't until I turned to glance at her that I realised she was focused on something else: something above us.

"Jackie!" she breathed, too excited to speak. I followed her gaze and was immediately convinced I was dreaming again.

How else would I be seeing a dragon?

"This is nuts," I breathed, still staring. I blinked. Pinched myself. Blinked a little longer, hoping for the images to go away. But they still remained. The vibrant colours. Wild horses. A freaking dragon!

Seriously. A dragon? I knew my country's flag displayed one of the mythical beasts, but that was what they were: *mythical*. There certainly should *not* be one flying over my head, exhaling a gentle stream of smoke. Part of me wondered if it was mechanical, but the movements were far too fluid and natural. *So, dragons are real.* I supposed it wasn't the strangest thing I'd seen. Not much different to seeing those creeps-

Oh! I stiffened and realised I was still clutching my penknife. Where *were* those creeps, exactly?

"Zel, you didn't see anyone follow us, did you?" I asked warily.

"I didn't see anything," she retorted, a little harsher than I'd expected. I frowned.

"What's wrong?"

"I don't know," she admitted, "I think it's this place. Messing with my head." Her brow furrowed. "We're not in Wales, are we?"

My heartbeat accelerated. "Wh-what makes you say that?" I stuttered, though deep down, I wondered the same. This place seemed... *different*. I had no other words for it. Yet it also seemed familiar, somehow, which was strange, as I'd never-

I gasped suddenly as the truth crashed down on me with such a force that I stumbled backwards, barely able to keep myself upright. "Oh, gosh... This... this is the place from my dreams!"

Chapter Three

- Benji -

"Benji! Benji, are you alright?"
"What happened to him?"
"He passed out, I think."
"Vaznek!"
"Ah, language, Arlan!"
"Sorry. But what did you do to him?"
"We were just talking, and then he collapsed."
"Yeah. Sure. Like *that's* what happened."

I groaned, trying to bring myself back to consciousness. Slowly the colours of the elves surrounding me became clear: Lanny's gold on my left, the lilac and orange of my parents on the right, and Ethlon's stone silver straight ahead. All were tainted with blue-grey concern, even Ethlon, which surprised me. But what I didn't like was the red churning through Lanny's usually placid colour. *Why is he angry?*

I forced my eyes to open, staring right up into Lanny's face. "Please don't be cross," I whispered, though my voice sounded rather strained.

Lanny tensed slightly. "I'm alright. But are you?"

I nodded slowly and sat up, not looking in Ethlon's direction. I still wasn't sure if I could believe what he said or not. It frustrated me that I couldn't see his colours properly. Unless, of course, he just didn't feel any emotion. But that was too weird.

"Benji?" Mutti's soft fingers caressed my cheek, her lilac rippling with worry, and instantly shame flooded through me.

"I'm sorry Mutti," I exclaimed, "I got my best robes dirty!"

Someone laughed and I sensed Turvo's green rippling with yellow in the adjacent room. Lanny frowned, his anger growing, but Atti reached across me to take my brother's arm, as if restraining him.

"You're worried about the robes?" Mutti asked, incredulous.

No, I'm worried about creepy Ethlon! You're the one who is always concerned about our clothes, how we look. Can't you just stop and help me, for once?

"You are," I muttered, turning my head away.

"Oh, Benji, I'm not worried at all." She ran her hands through my tangled curls and pulled me close to her. I settled into her arms as she kissed my head tenderly. "And you really don't need to either. Tulia is already cleaning them, alright?"

I nodded again, my head still feeling quite dizzy, and I wasn't convinced I was seeing the colours correctly. I wanted strange Ethlon to go, I wanted the red to leave Lanny's gold, I wanted my brother to hold me tight and tell me that everything would be okay and that all the scary, secretive things Atti and Ethlon had babbled about were not true. I didn't want to be in danger. My family was safe, I'd always thought. Anatti was the most powerful elf in Pylisya. Why was it different now?

My breathing sped up and I started to panic, a hundred scenarios flashing through my mind. Cold-hearted faeries looming over me, their colours black and red, holding swords dripping with blood- *how did my thoughts turn so dark? I've been listening to Turvo too much.*

"He's freaking out again."

"Arlan, get Fírean. Now."

My brother left the room and I tried desperately to stop the flood of violent images but could not banish them from my head. I felt sick, so sick, like my entire insides wanted to explode from my mouth. My heart pounded like Turvo's did after his afternoon runs and sweat trickled down my face, mingling with the frightened tears. Mutti's soft breathing soothed me slightly but I was too tense, ears pricked, as if I expected the danger to come to me. *Ridiculous.* I glanced up at Ethlon, his face stone-cold. No change in his colour, either. I just couldn't understand how he was so stiff and oblivious to everything that was going on. After all, he was the one who was putting me in this danger! I still didn't fully understand what the 'danger' was, exactly, but the colours of my family and the images it brought to mind implied enough.

Soft, gentle music crept into my quivering ears, whispered notes of calm and happiness. I followed the direction of the tune to Fírean, stood in the doorway, his pale hands holding a wooden pan flute, whistling a beautiful melody. A smile spread across my face, peace replacing the panic inside of me; I loved it when Fírean played. His songs were almost always joyful, reciting the stories of springs past, nature's secrets, and other happy memories held in my brother's gentle mind. I closed my eyes, adoring the way Fírean's blue blended with Lanny's gold. It was a blissful union of colours, but as with Lanny, there was something different about Fírean. My nostrils flared, trying to identify it. Metallic, again. Too much like Kalic. The scent was weird on my oldest brothers.

"Lanny, where did you and Fír go?" I asked, staring at them.

Lanny's gold flickered. "We spent time with Anatti, Ethlon, and Atti. Remember? I did tell you that before we left."

I frowned. "So is there metal at the castle?"

Fírean paused in his playing. "Why are you asking, Benji?"

Lanny exchanged glances with Atti that made me uneasy. "It doesn't matter," Atti interrupted, "How is your finger?"

"Fine. And it *does* matter."

"Benji, enough," Mutti chided, getting to her feet, "Your brothers and Atti have had a long journey to get here. I think it's time we let them rest, yes?"

"But I'm happy to play," Fírean protested.

Mutti gave him a look and he quickly left the room.

I slid off the sofa where I'd been lying and moved to leave as well. Lanny's gold darkened and he placed his hand on my shoulder. "I think it's best you stay here, Benji."

I huffed. "Why?" It really wasn't a big deal. The sight of blood *always* made me dizzy. Though the fact I'd passed out in the garden and woken up indoors was a *little* worrying. Still, it wasn't cause enough for concern, and I continued to frown at my eldest brother.

He looked to Mutti for help and she sighed. "You fainted. It's best for you to just sit down and rest a while, okay?"

No, it's not okay. You're hiding something from me. Stop lying and faking it. Things are wrong. There's danger. Why won't you just tell me?

But something happened to the words on their journey from my brain to my mouth and all that came out was a mumbled "m'kay".

"Good." Lanny smiled, ruffled my hair, then left.

I stared at Ethlon, trying to make sense of his colour whilst desperately attempting to hide my own. I was turning blue, splashed with red, and if anyone else could read my colours I felt certain they'd figure out my intentions. But if Ethlon really could see colours he made no comments about mine; his silver remained completely monochrome.

It was time to play shadows again. I just had to get the room clear.

Thankfully, Atti's actions played in my favour for once, as he decided to have a private discussion with Ethlon. I ignored their departure, focusing on keeping my expression relatively flat. Then I grimaced, looking down at my finger. It had a small strip of cloth wrapped around securely: Mutti's work, I guessed.

"Does it still hurt?" she asked.

"Yes," I admitted reluctantly.

"Hmm, some fruit should help. What would you like? Apple?"

I sighed. Mutti was all about the natural remedies sometimes. "Yes, that sounds nice."

"Alright, just wait here a moment. You'll be okay alone, won't you?" She couldn't stop the worry from creeping into her tone and colour, and I felt guilty for a brief moment.

"Yes," I said again. I feared that if I tried to speak in longer sentences, the words would fail me, as they often did. She smiled and kissed my forehead, and I turned away to hide the grin spreading across my face.

Once Mutti had gone, I snuck out of the room, pleased that I'd been dressed in a plain grey shirt and dark brown breeches. Pausing, I reached out with my senses to locate my targets and found them with relative ease, thanks to the familiarity of their colours. They were in the dining room, so I headed there, being careful to avoid any awkward encounters. Mutti's lilac was still in the kitchen, tinged with slight distress, but I didn't want to go investigate.

The door to the dining room was ajar, yet I hesitated. Red churned in all of the colours of the elves within, most prominent and terrifying in Lanny. His colour was a whirlwind, streaked violently with scarlet and cerulean and other shades that blurred together too fast for me to make any sense of them. Why was Lanny so... so...? I couldn't think of the word. But it was not like Lanny at all. And that frightened me.

Inhaling deeply, I slipped through the doorway, immediately ducking and half-sliding, half-crawling across the marble floor. The dresser was high enough off the ground that I could slip underneath; it would be a bit of a squeeze, but at least I could listen in to their conversation. Lanny and Fírean had been joined by Turvo and the king, and I sensed Atti making his way to us, clearly displeased at the conflict that was occurring in the presence of our monarch. I wondered how the situation had escalated so quickly. Weren't they fine a few moments ago?

"He's going to figure it out, Arlan. You can't protect him forever."

Red surged faster through Lanny. "I don't want them taking him!" he yelled, "Who knows what they'll do?"

Turvo's green darkened dangerously and I tensed up instinctively, even though from my current position he could not get to me - nor I to him - unless the dresser was moved. "I don't get your connection with the darn kid. He's got to grow up someday."

I imagined Lanny's blue eyes burning as if on fire. "Grow up? Seriously? He's still a child. *You're* the one who needs to grow up. Look at the situation as a whole!"

"None of us mean any harm to Benji," Anatti said softly. I stiffened. *They're talking about me?*

"Oh, vaznek. *Sure* you don't," Lanny replied sarcastically, dragging out each syllable.

Atti burst into the room in that moment, his colour burning. "Arlan. Outside. Now."

Turvo sniggered despite his fury, kindling Lanny's scarlet.

"I'm going outside, but *not* to talk with you," Lanny spat, his uncharacteristic viciousness terrifying me, "And if you even want me to listen to you, you won't do this to Benji. Or *any* of my brothers."

"Not even me?" Turvo chipped in.

Lanny's colour flashed but he managed to restrain himself. "Not even you." He stormed out of the room, muttering curses under his breath, his colour so conflicted it was painful for me to try and follow his motions.

Atti turned as if to follow, but stopped, his colour glaring at Turvo. "What did you say to him?"

"I was defending you," Turvo replied, his voice shaking imperceptibly.

Anatti stood, moving between them. "Don't start this. Please."

The scarlet pulsing through them did not cease, but it stopped its growth. Only Fírean was relatively unaffected by the anger that was seizing my family, his colour a sadder blue than usual. I felt blue, too. They had been arguing about me and I really wasn't worth all the strife. Before I'd thought my actions through, I shuffled out from under the dresser, coming to stand between Atti and Turvo.

"I'm sorry," I whispered.

Everyone in the room jumped. Atti recovered first. "What are you doing here, Benji?" he exploded.

I cowered away. "You're all unhappy," I cried, "and angry and it's my fault!"

"Arazair, he could tell," Anatti breathed.

Turvo scowled. "Doesn't take a genius to work that out. We *were* yelling."

Atti shot a glare at Turvo, then he and Anatti both turned their attention to me. "Did you sense the emotions, Benji?"

"Colours," I corrected, then froze. "You won't danger me?"

"Danger you? At least speak some sense!" Turvo snapped.

"Enough!" Atti shouted, spinning to face Turvo, "Get out! If you carry on with this darn attitude I'll... I'll...!" He didn't finish the threat, but if the anger in his expression was even a tenth of what I saw in his colour, Turvo would be scared stiff. My brother said nothing, exiting without a sound, but the white bursting into his green confirmed my theory. I suddenly noticed Ethlon's silver again: silent, standing just inside the doorway, observing like I had been.

"Your son didn't seem too afraid," he said, approaching Atti.

I frowned. "You're wrong."

"Am I?" Ethlon cocked his head and raised one perfectly arched eyebrow.

"Y-yeah," I stuttered, not liking the expression in his eyes. *Did he just trick me into saying that?*

"I'm interested," he continued, "in what colour you saw. And don't lie to me, Benji. I know you see them."

Blood rushed to my cheeks and I suddenly found my feet very interesting. Was that a speck of green paint on the largest toe of my left foot?

"White," I muttered, "White on his green."

"Interesting." Ethlon's calculating eyes danced across the room. "What colour is your Atti?"

"Orange," I answered instantly.

"Anatti?"

"Yellow."

"And who is blue?"

"Fír." I peered up at my interrogator through my fringe, noticing too the expressions of those around me. Anatti's mouth hung open in a very un-royal manner, his dark eyes wide in disbelief. Atti stood as a frozen statue, his features sculpted to abnormal blankness. Across the room, Fírean's lips ceased their movements, his colour fluttering with confusion. Only Ethlon maintained some air of composure.

"Am I in danger?" I whispered lowly, hoping that my words would come out coherently, but only he would hear.

He hesitated. "Depends," he replied in a similar tone.

"On what?"

Ethlon glanced at Atti, who was still unmoving, then returned his gaze to me. "Come," he said gently, extending a hand to me. I took it cautiously, wondering at the sudden change in his attitude. Earlier on he looked like he had bad intentions, but now I wasn't so sure. Lanny seemed to think they would do something bad to me, but his anger had been more directed at Atti.

This is all far too confusing.

Inhaling deeply, I let him lead me out of the dining room and into the hallway, taking the opportunity to brush the dust off my clothes as we walked.

"Why-" I started, the look he shot me almost freezing me in place.

"In a moment. Keep walking," he interrupted harshly. I obeyed, letting my mind wander a bit. Who exactly was Ethlon? And could I really trust him?

No answer presented itself.

We came to a rest out in the garden again and this time I made sure my hands were well clear of any plants and shrubbery, lest they had nasty thorns too. Ethlon paced back and forth, running a hand through his short hair as if he were deeply conflicted, but I knew from his lack of colours that it wasn't the case. My fingers twitched, desiring to hold something. I didn't mind the silence if I had something to do, like painting, but all my brushes and paints were back in my room and I was out in the large gardens with a strange elf and thousands of little bugs. I focused then on their colours, mostly yellow, the innocent joy that their short lives were full of. Out here, the only red I saw was the natural colour of the roses and the small pulses of a group of ants that were annoyed to find my boot in the way of their path. I shifted my position, trying my best to not squash any of them, and made a mental note to never harm any of these fascinating creatures. Not even the littlest bugs.

"What makes you say that?"

I jumped and nearly stood on the ants. "Say what?"

"Your comment. About the creatures." Ethlon's intense gaze made me flinch.

"I was just thinking," I said, stumbling over the words as they spilt from my lips. Clearly my thoughts had not just been in my head. *Unless...*

No. That was ridiculous. Ethlon couldn't read my mind, or he'd know what I thought of him and would be very cross. Only Kalic was able to get inside my head and that was because we were twins.

"I don't want to hurt you, Benji. Or put you in danger. And that's why I came." He crouched down so that we were eye level and I wanted to believe him - I really did - I just couldn't see the glimmer of truth in his grey eyes.

"You see the colours. That isn't a bad thing, it just..." He bit his lip, trying to find the right words, "It might cause problems. But I can help you, Benji. I can help you to control those powers. And then you won't be in danger."

I blinked. "Powers?" I echoed, then frowned. *Can Ethlon see the colours too? Am I not the only one?*

"What else would they be? You have a unique gift." He smiled and my frown faded, a warmth spreading through me, more at his words than his expression, though both played a part.

"A gift," I whispered, staring at my hands. *A gift that will put me and my family in danger. Unless...*

I could see then, the options in front of me; no matter what I did, my 'powers', as he called them, would not disappear. It was my choice to let them be, or try to control them and stop the danger they possessed. The concepts were difficult to grasp, but I knew in my heart what had to be done, no matter how I felt about it. Because, honestly, the whole situation terrified me. I wanted nothing more than to turn and run, far, far away. But I forced my jaw to set firm, controlling my posture and tone like Lanny did.

"Teach me."

Chapter Four

- Jackie -

I stared at the blades of grass quivering gently in the breeze, the unfamiliar scents threatening to overwhelm me. Hazel lay beside me, far too relaxed for someone who'd fallen through a weird mist and ended up in a land that I thought I'd imagined.

Apparently, that wasn't the case. So what did my dreams mean, then? Were they real? Or was I a psycho who wouldn't wake from yet another dream? I didn't think I was dreaming – I kept pinching myself and it hurt like it was real – but the situation was too strange to comprehend any other way.

"Jackie, look!"

I sighed. Hazel's enthusiasm was beginning to irritate me, as she seemed to point out anything and everything that she saw, from regular-looking birds to strangely coloured bugs.

"What now?" I huffed, unable to keep the emotions from creeping into my voice. Thankfully, Hazel didn't notice.

"There's a girl riding towards us, look!" she cried excitedly.

I glanced up at the gorgeous palomino mare thundering across the field, her pale mane streaming out behind her as the powerful legs propelled her onwards. The rider's sandy blond hair flowed freely in elegant curls and I stared, mesmerised, at the fluidity and grace of their movements. My fixation did not last long, as I soon figured out their path of travel.

"Zel! Move!" I gasped, forcing my muscles to respond. They did so stiffly, pulling Hazel to her feet with robotic motions, my feet dragging the both of us out of the immediate danger. Thankfully, the rider slowed, and as they drew closer I discerned that, despite the long hair and flowing garments that had induced Hazel's opinion, the person was, in fact, male. His pale face was quite round and babyish, with a small nose and angelic features that I'd seen before on photo-shopped models. Eyes like sapphires met my curious gaze, equally as fascinated and bewildered as I was. He looked like someone straight out of a medieval history book, clad in a soft blue tunic and peanut-coloured breeches with high boots to complete the look. Had I seen him anywhere else, I would've thought him to be a cosplayer. But in the alien land we'd found ourselves in, I supposed anything was possible.

"Greetings. I did not expect to find any maidens so far from the town. Are you alright?"

I blinked, my brain slow to process his melodic words. His voice was soft and lilting, with a slight accent, and each syllable he pronounced with incredible precision. My breathing quickened and I struggled to think of an answer, glancing across to see Hazel was even more hypnotised by this stranger than I was.

"Y-yeah," I managed to stammer, "Though we're actually, uh, a little lost."

"Ah. You have wandered far." It was more of a statement than a question and I nodded in response.

"We fell," Hazel corrected, snapping out of her trance.

"Fell?" The stranger's perfect brow furrowed slightly.

"It's really hard to explain," I said, before Hazel could open her mouth again.

"I see." His confused eyes told me quite the opposite, though he seemed too polite to pry. Before I could blink again, he'd dismounted, leading his mare the last distance between us, who I noticed now only had a bridle on. Had he really galloped *without* a saddle on?

"I can take you back to the town, if you want," he offered.

I hesitated. Part of me screamed yes, fascinated by the beautiful stranger, but I didn't want to let my stupid emotions get the better of me. *What if this is a trick?* I wondered, *what if he's some sort of creep?* He smiled at Hazel, but it was genuine and there was no malice or ill-intent in his expression. Besides, he was polite, and after staring at him for a few minutes more I had a strange sense of familiarity, as if I'd seen him before. Which was impossible, of course. Perhaps I'd seen someone like him on TV, or in a magazine. He certainly looked like a celebrity.

"That would be very kind of you," I finally replied, "though we did not come from the town. We actually have travelled from another land, I believe, and quite by accident too." As soon as the words were out, I clamped my mouth shut, hoping I wasn't going to weird this guy out.

"Another land?" he repeated, frowning again, "I am not quite sure what you mean, though I must say, your clothes are strange."

I looked down and blushed upon the remembrance that I was wearing polka-dot pyjamas, which were hardly modest. "We are in need of new clothes," I admitted.

"Do you have anything to trade?"

"No, we have naught but what we wear," I replied, lowering my voice so it would appear sad, letting my face droop. Hazel caught on to what I was doing and manipulated her expression into a melancholy exhaustion.

The stranger's face softened. "In that case, come to my home. I am sure we can sort you out with something."

"Thank you," I breathed, struggling to hide my excitement and hoping he'd read it as gratitude.

"And get those injuries seen to, as well," he added, gesturing to the abrasions on my face and legs.

"Is it bad?" I asked anxiously, dropping my earlier act of 'sad, poor traveller'.

His eyes flickered with something indistinguishable. "Nothing that won't be healed with natural creams. They won't scar, I'm sure of it." His gaze then darted between us, as if trying to figure out my connection with Hazel. "Is she your... niece?"

"What?" I spluttered, "No! She's my sister!"

How old do you think I am, seriously?

He backed up, slightly awkward, though I couldn't really associate 'awkward' with him. "My apologies, I thought not. Though you don't seem much alike."

"Why did you think that, then?"

He dodged the question. "My apologies," he said again, then turned to Hazel. "Brina is ready for you. May I?" She nodded and he scooped her up with relative ease, setting her on the horse's back. All my anger at his misjudgement faded and in its place, terror clutched at my heart, increasing its palpitations.

"We're riding?" I screeched, startling the horse. Hazel barely held on and it took the stranger a minute or so to soothe his mare.

"You don't ride?" he asked, shocked. I nodded. When I turned twelve, Mum had given me the option of learning to drive, or ride horses. I'd decided on the former, waiting patiently for my seventeenth whilst she continued saving. Of course, neither of us had factored in Hazel at that point, so I then let Mum spend her savings on our new family member instead. I didn't mind, but sometimes I wished I'd said yes to the horse-riding initially.

Never had I wished that more than now.

"I'll lead, don't worry," the stranger was saying, and I realised I should probably ask his name, though I was a tad too shy. Instead I nodded and climbed onto the mare's back somewhat reluctantly, wrapping my arms around Hazel's waist. I told myself it was to secure her, but in truth I was holding on for my own benefit. Honestly, I could face up to creepy navy-skinned men, but when it came to horses, I was strangely terrified. Not of the beasts themselves, but of the act of riding. The unfamiliarity was frightening, though I'd never admit it to anyone.

He took the reins of the horse and urged her into a walk, then a steady trot. I tightened my grip on Hazel's waist as he jogged along beside us, his movements inhumanly fluid. At some unspoken command the horse sped up, yet he still kept pace, running in perfect rhythm with the mare's cantering. When I wasn't fighting back the nausea that bouncing on a horse's back induced, I marvelled at the endurance he displayed, able to keep at our speed over quite a long distance. I didn't know quite how far we'd travelled, but the sun was steadily moving across the sky and soon I could not see the mountains. The forest kept going, a constant green mass on our left, though the trees began to thin out, changing shape and size the further we travelled. Beneath the mare's sturdy hooves, the grass was as vividly green as the patch where we'd landed, its colour never fading, not even when boots and hooves trod on it. The clarity and brightness of all the surrounding colours made me feel like I was in a primary school child's painting, with the typical yellow sun, blue sky, and green grass. No words had been spoken on our journey, but it wasn't silent; my breathing and heartbeat were almost deafening combined, trying to compete with the storm created by the horse's hooves. The stranger seemed to move almost silently, his feet barely making a sound, but the other noises were so loud I doubted I'd hear him unless he was really stomping on each step. A loud trill sounded from the skies and I risked a glance up just as a flock of small, baby-pink birds flew overhead, calling each other with high-pitched notes that quivered in the air. I watched as they spun and looped together, creating a pattern with their swift movements, before spiralling off towards the beckoning trees.

When I finally tore my eyes from the fascinating little birds, a gasp escaped my mouth at the signs of civilisation that had seemingly appeared from thin air. Wooden shacks dotted the landscape and a low stone wall ran around the perimeter, a meagre attempt at defences. The scent of freshly baked bread wafted up my nose as we drew closer, and people buzzed through the streets, all clothed in similar fashion to our guide. I expected us to ride into the little town, but at the last minute he changed direction and led us around it instead, making the first eye contact with me since our journey had begun.

"My house is on the outskirts," he explained, breaking the silence. His words ignited the air between us and heat rose unbidden to my cheeks.

"What's the name of the town?" Hazel asked brightly.

"Kikarsko."

Any last doubt that we were still in Wales vanished from my mind and I dared to voice the one thing I'd wondered the most.

"What is the name of this land?"

He stopped and glanced up at me, rather baffled. "These are the Westlands, though that is not what you mean, is it?"

"No," I breathed, my eyes tracing his smooth jawline.

"Well," he continued, seemingly unaware of my shameful scrutinizing, "this world has many names, though we call it Pylisya."

"Pylisya," I echoed, tasting each foreign syllable on my lips. *So this place has a name, and a strange one at that.* I still had no idea how we'd ended up here - the name gave me no clues at all - but I found some comfort in the information I was acquiring. Piece by piece, I would assemble a picture of this 'Pylisya', determined to unlock the mysteries its existence presented.

The stranger urged his horse on again, but I managed to find my voice. "Wait," I blurted out, "You haven't told us your name."

Something unidentifiable flashed in his blue eyes. "You haven't told me yours."

I recoiled slightly at his harsh retort. "Jackie. I'm Jackie," I said, struggling to keep my tone steady.

"My name is Arlan," he smiled slightly, his face resuming its calm composure. I, however, was the opposite of calm, and not just because the sound of his voice sent shivers through my body. The gears of my mind churned, processing his name, searching to find where I'd heard it before, why it was so familiar...

I gasped, my heart pounding with renewed ferocity. *Arlan*: he was one of the elves I'd dreamt about! My eyes fixed on his face again, touching on the pointed ears that protruded through the fountain of curls. How had I not noticed them before? What concerned me more than my lack of observation, however, was that what I'd dreamt was suddenly coming true.

"Your brother," I spluttered, "Benji." I meant it to be a question, but my words came out funny, pitching in bizarre places.

Arlan's eyes narrowed. "What about him?" he challenged.

"Oh, dang it," I whispered, "This... this can't be happening." I was going mad; I was sure of it.

His expression grew dark. "If you're here for my brother-" he half-growled, the words laced in threat.

I tensed up further. "No! I just, I-"

How do I say this without sounding crazy?

"-I dreamt about him. And you. And your family."

So much for not sounding crazy.

Arlan blinked, his turn to be awestruck. Though how someone like *him* could be awestruck at *me,* I had no idea.

"You're a dream-prophet?" he murmured, partly to himself.

"A what now?" Bewilderment flooded through me, my muzzy brain failing to comprehend his words.

"Unaware as well," he carried on, in the same muttering tone.

I stared at him dumbly as he took a few deep breaths in, collecting himself, then resumed his jog, the horse matching his pace. Forcibly I turned my head away, renewing my interest in the landscape whilst our conversation churned in my mind. Why was he so calm upon hearing my insane chatter? I would be majorly creeped-out if someone told me *they* had dreamt of *me*. Were 'dream-prophets', or whatever he'd called me, common in Pylisya? I rolled the word across the tip of my tongue. *Prophet*. It just brought to mind a bunch of grey-haired, bearded guys in long robes from Biblical times. I barely stifled a laugh at that image.

Ridiculous, the rational side of my mind chided, *this is all ridiculous. Dragons and elves and prophets! What next, unicorns?* For a moment the doubt crept in, but I shook it off. Everything felt too *real* to be a fragment of my imagination, or some sort of drug-induced hallucination. Even if it had been drugs – which was absurd, as I'd never go anywhere near those toxic killers – the effects would've worn off by now. Thus, I came to the same conclusion: that I was in a foreign world, which I had somehow glimpsed in my dreams.

But that only brought up another major question: *how* did I get here? Seemingly through that mist-stuff, yes, but *how*? And why? I frowned, an unfamiliar thought crawling into my brain. *Did God bring me here?* Inhaling deeply, I opened my eyes and gazed at the too-blue sky.

"If it *was* You, Big Guy," I whispered, "Give me a sign. Or something. Please," I finished lamely, shooting a glance at Arlan, who thankfully hadn't noticed my failed attempts at a prayer. I wasn't entirely sure that someone was actually listening, but the events that had transpired were just too crazy to have happened coincidentally. No, I was certain that some supernatural force was involved: whoever or whatever it may be.

Our pace slowed then and I looked up, nearly choking in my effort to hold back the gasp building in my throat. A grand building towered above us, more of a mansion than a house, with walls of the softest stone-grey. Windows were spaced regularly on each floor, symmetrically orientated around the magnificent double-doors that were the building's centrepiece. Columns of a dazzling, crystalline material rose either side of the doors, morphing into an archway that provided a shelter for whoever stood on the doorstep: like a porch, though 'porch' seemed too small of a word for the majestic architecture. Exuberant hedges rose immediately in front of us, dotted with blossoms ranging in colour, from pink taffy to deep cobalt. The shrubbery wrapped around the mansion, creating a large perimeter that left room for a vast lawn between the hedges and the building itself, a mass of green broken only by the central path. Arlan reduced his speed to a walk but continued to lead us on, starting down the cobbled, grey-cream path. As we drew closer again, a couple of side buildings caught my eye: to the left, an ornately decorated greenhouse, leading into a maze of more hedges and greenery; and to the right, a block of dusty-brown brick stables. I stared at Arlan in disbelief.

"This is... yours?" I whispered.

Hazel yawned and stretched in my arms, her bizarre silence now explained: she'd fallen asleep. Her yawn swiftly morphed into a gasp as she, too, took in the magnificent sight befalling us. I kept my gaze fixed on our beautiful - and evidently rich - companion.

He turned to me and smiled slightly. "My family's, really, but yes. Welcome to my home."

Chapter Five

- Benji -

"Focus," Ethlon commanded. I sighed and closed my eyes again, trying to block out the colours I sensed with no success. Kalic's metallic red still shone as bright as before, playing with Fírean's blue in a pattern that was giving me a headache. I huffed and snapped my eyes open again.

"It's no use!" I cried, stomping my foot in irritation. Both Fírean and Ethlon frowned at my childish behaviour and I immediately stopped, face heating up in embarrassment.

"No point in stopping it," I added grumpily. I meant to ask - *what is the point in stopping myself from seeing colours? It's impossible!* – but, as usual, the words jumbled and half of them didn't even make it out of my mouth.

Fírean and Kalic exchanged frustrated looks. "Can I go now?" Kalic grumbled, "I've got other things I need to do."

Sorry, Benji, he added mentally, but I ignored him.

"Me, too." Fírean shot a worried glance my way, his cheeks flushing pink. "I mean, I really have to work on my new composition..." His tone was anxious, afraid of hurting my feelings, but Kalic had already done that. I sighed and looked at Ethlon.

"None of you are going anywhere," he said stiffly.

Kalic pouted and folded his arms. "But Benji-"

"I don't mind," I interrupted quickly, forcing a smile in my twin's direction. I was glad that he couldn't see the blue threatening to overwhelm my colour. Besides, I really wanted to go and do some painting. The way Fírean's and Kalic's colours mixed had given me a new idea.

"No. Your brother is coming, and I believe he desires to see us all." Ethlon's cold eyes surveyed the room. "We should meet him here."

I stood and ran over to the door, thoughts of painting pushed aside, my breathing quickening as unfamiliar smells crept up my nose. More metallic, combined with a strange floral scent and a few other things I could not recognise; some were quite appealing, others horrific and terrifying. One smell stood out above all else; it was a toxic odour, damp and coated in evil, yet I could not put a name to it. My eyes darted to Ethlon.

"What's going on?" I whispered, flitting my focus from Ethlon to the dimly-lit hallway.

"I don't know entirely," he murmured, his eyes clouding over. I closed mine to perceive his colour, expecting no change, but for once his silver was misted: a clear indicator that he was deep in thought. Fírean and Kalic were as confused as I was, the latter rather irritated too. I didn't understand why he had such a burning desire to get away from me. We were usually so close; did he fear the danger I had inadvertently summoned? Guilt flooded over me but I pushed against it, reminding myself that I'd chosen to do the right thing. Ethlon was going to help me control my powers. So far, though, 'control' simply meant 'suppress'. And that just wasn't working.

I snapped out of my thought stream as an unfamiliar colour entered my vision. It was a soft, pale cerulean, pulsing weakly as if newly formed. Ribbons of moss-like confusion wavered throughout, tinged with the bold amber of curiosity. Beside the newcomer, Lanny's gold thrummed, the furious scarlet now barely evident. I opened my eyes and smiled at him as best I could.

"Lanny!" I exclaimed, "You're back!" I paused, realising that he probably didn't know I had witnessed his argument and subsequent departure. Or that I'd agreed to Ethlon's wishes.

I don't want them taking him! he'd yelled in fury at Turvo. As far as I was aware, Ethlon wasn't planning on taking me anywhere, but had I gone against what Lanny desired for me by complying with him?

"Lanny," I began again, somewhat sheepishly, "I decided, Ethlon will-"

He raised a hand, silencing me. "Not now, Benji. There is someone I want you to meet," he added, addressing the rest of us. It was then that I noticed the girl standing behind him, the source of that lovely cerulean. She was relatively ordinary in appearance, shorter and paler than Lanny, with hair as dark as mine bouncing off her shoulders. Her clothing was strangely familiar and hung loose on her slim frame. The one feature that stood out, made her more unique, was the deep, vibrant colour of her eyes. They were a strong green, almost like emeralds, an unnatural shade I'd never seen on a person before. And, as usual, they were locked on my eldest brother. But as I scrutinised her further, I noticed her focus was not the typical adoration, rather confusion, accompanied by a desire for understanding, both palpable in the faint colours winding around her. She tore her gaze from Lanny after a few moments, surveying the rest of us, though her eyes kept flickering back to me.

"I'm Jackie," she said, "It is nice to meet you." Her accent was strange, stressing each word in the wrong place, and she spoke rather quickly.

"Uh, hello," Fírean stammered, pink flooding his colour. I took a glimpse at my other brothers and was surprised to see that both of them had red cheeks. Ethlon looked as amused as a dead rat; I shared that emotion partially. Fírean was sensitive, I knew that, but why was *Kalic* – steadfast, independent Kalic – embarrassed? He blocked me from his mind so I couldn't attempt to pry.

"I'm Kalic, but you can call me Kal," my twin then introduced himself a little too eagerly, extending a hand to the newcomer. She regarded him with curiosity, but no trace of the emotions that I saw coursing through him were reflected even minutely in her colour. That was no surprise: she *was* at least five years his senior, if not more. Fírean, however, was closer to her age and as aware as I was of that fact. He stumbled over his own introduction, refusing to make eye contact with anyone, and quickly excused himself afterwards, almost tripping over thin air as he hurried out. I suppressed a giggle, exchanging glances with Kalic, whose face now held some of the humour I felt.

"And you are?"

I blinked, feeling the girl's gaze on me. "Benji," I said, my voice quivering as it always did when I first talked to strangers. Surprise and some other emotion I didn't catch flickered in her eyes, but she quickly composed herself.

"You have a cool house," she smiled, clearly trying to make conversation.

"Cool?" Lanny frowned in confusion. "It's quite hot today."

"Oh, I meant it as a synonym for nice. Great."

"Ah." Clarity flooded his colour. "Thank you, then."

Kalic coughed. "So, is she your girlfriend?" he asked casually. It was Lanny's turn to do a tomato impression.

"What? No!" he spluttered. She blushed and looked away as well. My eyes narrowed. *Girlfriend?* Where did Kalic get that notion? The girl didn't hold any love in her eyes, at least, none that I could see. Frowning, I looked into the depths of those emeralds again, searching her cerulean at the same time, and found that she *did* feel something for my brother. *Ugh. Of course.* What the emotion was, exactly, I couldn't tell, other than it was positive. But did Lanny reciprocate those feelings? His face was bright red still, gold tinged with rosy pink, which could simply mean that he was embarrassed but I wasn't so sure. Why else would he have the girl brought to meet us? Her eyes darted to Lanny but he looked away, the twitch of his mouth indicating he couldn't think of a suitable response. Thankfully – for him, at least – the girl intervened.

"My sister and I were lost, but Arlan found us and brought us here," she explained, putting a little too much stress on my brother's name.

Kalic perked up immediately. "You have a sister?"

Lanny and I groaned in unison. "Kal, really?" Lanny chided. Kalic shrugged, a crooked smirk on his face. I tried to imitate him and only succeeded in making him laugh. But at least he wasn't desperate to leave me anymore.

Ethlon cleared his throat, startling the girl, who clearly didn't notice him there. Not that he was easy to miss, with his imposing figure and bright hair.

"Arlan," he said, his voice relatively calm, "If you don't mind, we were in the middle of a lesson."

"Ah, of course." If Lanny wondered why we were having a lesson in the back room, he didn't voice it. "I'll take Jackie to see the others," he added, before the two of them exited.

I watched his disappearing back sadly, all the momentary joy at my twin's antics fading until I could barely feel it. For the first time in a long time, Lanny had left without promising when to make time for me. I knew he couldn't always talk to me – often, he was busy studying, or working with Atti – but even if that was the case, he would kiss my head and reassure me that we'd talk later. But this time, there was nothing. I saw what would happen next. Lanny would have even less time for me and our brothers, and more time for that girl. I supposed that I was foolish to ignore the inevitable; he was, after all, the most handsome person in the Westlands, according to everyone but Turvo. And one day he'd meet a girl and they'd hold hands and marry and then Lanny would move out and have children of his own and forget about me.

My bottom lip trembled and I clenched my fists, refusing to let myself get upset over a silly thing. I was likely overreacting; Lanny had only just met this girl, he was unlikely to be marrying her any time soon, if at all.

It still hurt that he'd hardly acknowledged me, especially after spending so much time away.

Benji? What's wrong? Kalic asked gently. I roughly shoved him from my mind, pivoting on my heel and abruptly running out of the door, my bare feet finding very little traction on the marble floors. I ran and ran and ran, marble turning to stone and then grass as I found myself out in the gardens again, still going despite the lack of footwear.

The colours inside were too *much,* their confusion and concern colliding in an ugly mess, and I needed space to think. Was I being a little silly? Yes, probably.

But for some reason, I couldn't shake the fear that the new girl was going to tear my family apart.

I didn't want her to steal Lanny away, to place more strain on the threads of our family. In fact, I didn't want to see her *ever* again. She would have to stay away from my Lanny or I would never go back.

But what if he doesn't want her to go? Would Lanny let *me* go? Panic bubbled in my throat and I failed to suppress it, unleashing itself as a strangled scream. What if Lanny didn't want me anymore? What was I to do then? Lanny was the *only* person in this world that I felt truly wanted me. If he adopted the opinion of everyone else...

I grit my teeth, my hands forming tiny fists. If the worst happened and Lanny didn't want me anymore, then what did it matter if I was in danger? I could just run away, far away from my family to keep them safe, and no-one would care.

It would just be me. Me and my stupid colours.

I closed my eyes, frustrated that I could not see further. If only I could see Lanny's colour right now! Then I'd be able to figure out how he was feeling about me and that girl.

Ethlon did say that I have power. And can't power be expanded?

I inhaled deeply, trying my best to concentrate. All around me the colours of little bugs thrummed, merging with those of the singing plants to create a beautiful, multicoloured kaleidoscope. But I pushed past that, focusing on keeping my breathing steady, and my heartbeat slowed as I extended my mind. The kaleidoscope now blurred into an ugly brown monochrome, easier to ignore now, and the other colours became evident. Kalic's metallic red was the first I sensed, still in the back room. He was accompanied, I thought, by Ethlon, though his silver was difficult enough to see even when in sight of him, so I couldn't be completely sure. On the second floor the colours of my parents hummed, both streaked with a grey anxiety. Fírean's blue shone through too, though I had yet to find any sign of Lanny, or Turvo, now I thought of it. In fact, I had not sensed Turvo's green for a while. Perhaps he'd gone out riding?

I shook my head, drawing my focus back to my family. I had to find Lanny. If I could just get a glimpse of his gold- ah! I gasped audibly as I found him, up in the attic. *What is he doing up there?* I wondered, *aren't we banned from the attic?*

To make matters worse, he was not alone. The faint cerulean, grown stronger now, was entwining itself with his gold.

My eyes snapped open, pain spiking in my heart, and I forced myself to breathe before I could do something stupid. Lanny was with the girl. Of course.

But did that mean he'd stopped caring for me?

I wasn't entirely sure.

With a sigh, I turned to leave the gardens, but froze as Ethlon's silver suddenly appeared within my field of vision, followed by Anatti. Heart pounding, I dropped to my knees, peering at them through a gap in the thick bushes.

"Do you think the faeries will come for him?" Anatti asked softly.

Ethlon's silver flickered. "I'm not sure. They have one already, but Benji-" I barely suppressed a gasp as he said my name, "- he's the most powerful I've seen."

Powerful how, exactly? I glanced down at my hands which still held their slightly-chubby, babyish shape and frowned, not seeing how I could be powerful in any way.

"But you can help him?" Anatti pressed, yellow streaked with deep grey concern.

Ethlon sighed. "I hope so. It might be too late, though; they may already have caught onto him. We must be alert, for danger is imminent."

I physically recoiled, head spinning. *Someone's after me... I'm putting my family in danger!*

Standing as quietly as I could, I slipped away from the two adults, not wanting to hear any more of their conversation. Tears of fear welled in my eyes but I managed to hold them back, trying desperately to think up a plan of action. I could lie; pretend that I was going back to the capital city with Ethlon and try to lose him whilst on the road. But I was a terrible liar and Ethlon's quiet but thorough observance would make it nigh impossible to achieve.

Or I could just leave. Sneak away in the night. I couldn't ride by myself yet, but I had legs, so I could obviously just walk. The nearest town was Kikarsko and from there I could try and find someone who could give me a lift to somewhere much more remote. The Northlands, perhaps; they were far enough away that I shouldn't bring any danger to my family. I couldn't help but smile despite my dismal situation, because what mattered was that my family would be *safe*. Plus, I was actually quite good at the whole planning thing. Normally someone else would make plans for me – Mutti, usually – but I couldn't tell anyone else my current desires or they'd try and stop me. And *nobody* was going to stop me from keeping my family safe.

Nightfall came far too leisurely. I had a single rucksack all packed before mid-afternoon, shoving it under my bed in case Kalic started poking around my half of our room. I kept my distance from him as much as I could, focusing my mind on everything but my plan, so that no stray thoughts would creep his way. Our day continued as it always did, except Lanny traded with Fírean for our lesson, so we had music instead of reading. I didn't mind, though. Hearing Fírean play always helped to calm me down, but it didn't change my decision. If anything, it only served to fuel my determination to succeed.

Fírean was strong, but he was an artist, not a fighter. If danger came, I wasn't sure how well he'd hold up. And I couldn't risk him getting hurt.

After returning back from my enlightening walk in the gardens, I'd apologised to Mutti for running off and leaving grassy footprints around the house, then gave each member of my family an extra-big hug. I hoped they'd realise, after I was gone, that I *did* still love them, no matter what they thought of me.

Now I glanced across at my twin, sound asleep, his ears quivering as he dreamt: of what, I had no idea. His familiar colour pulsed lightly and for a moment I was tempted to just stay, or at least get Kalic to come with me. But he was unlikely to leave – he was happy here and would likely tell our parents about my plan – and even if he *did* decide to leave with me, then he'd be in danger too. And I couldn't allow that.

Slowly, I slipped out of bed, my hands fumbling in the darkness to grab the straps of my rucksack. Then I crept past my brother, pausing only to pull my cloak off the hook and shrug it on. I'd gone to bed fully dressed, in some of my favourite robes, so I wouldn't have to fuss with clothing in the dark. The door was left ajar – another preparation by me – so I snuck out and down the hall, staying on the tips of my toes to make as little noise as possible.

Shadows rose up at every corner, some stretching their black arms out to grab me, urging me to stay. I shook them off, digging deep inside me for the courage I hoped was there. Everyone else in my family was so brave; surely I had some of that in me, too? I resisted the urge to light a torch, knowing that it would only bring attention to myself. As it was, I had to pass Fírean's room; my brother was a light sleeper, if he even was sleeping. It wasn't unusual for Fírean to be up well past dusk, scribbling down new compositions he'd dreamt of. And if he saw me, I definitely would not make it out.

Thankfully, his blue remained calmly pulsing in his room and I did manage to make it outside, slipping my feet into the waiting boots before trudging out into the cold night. The faint breeze brushed against my cheek and I shivered, instinctively pulling my cloak tighter around me.

I shouldn't be out here. Just turn around. Go back inside.

My heart pounded rhythmically and I hesitated, doubt churning through my mind. Was I being too radical? Perhaps. *But it's better to be safe than sorry, right?*

Taking a deep breath, I took one last look at my home, its pale walls illuminated eerily by the foreign moonlight, then turned and ventured into the unknown.

Chapter Six

- Jackie -

I fiddled with the hazelnut-coloured sleeves of the unfamiliar yet rather comfy tunic I'd been dressed in. Arlan had been loath to give me 'boy's clothes', as he dubbed them, but having no sisters meant they had no 'female' clothing in my size. I was glad; the dress that Kalia – his mother – wore was quite hideous, in my opinion. Purple bows and frills and lace. *Yuck*. Not that the tunic and breeches were any better, really. They were another extreme: dull, plain, and boring. At least I could move in them; I sincerely doubted she could jog, let alone run, in that dress. Though, despite the garish clothing, Kalia had been kind to me so far, applying soothing cream to my minor injuries and taking Hazel on a tour so Arlan and I could try and find a reason behind the madness of my new reality.

My attention diverted back to the present, watching my elven companion sift through the various boxes and crates clogging up the attic, in an attempt to find information on the 'dream-prophet' stuff he'd babbled on about. A collection of cobwebs glided past my face as another crate was disturbed. I sighed. If Mum were here, she'd freak out at all the dust and disorganisation-

Mum!

All the blood rushed out of my cheeks. In my bewilderment and wonder at this strange new place, I had completely forgotten about the one I loved the most. How was that even possible? Guilt and anxiety churned within me.

"Oh gosh," I muttered, "She'll be so worried..." I doubted 'worried' would even cover it.

"Worried? Who?" Arlan paused in his searching. I stared at him with wide eyes.

"My mum! She doesn't know we're here, it was an accident and-" I froze, another horror growing in my mind- "Dang it!" I screeched, "Those creeps! What if they traced our tracks and went back to-"

I choked off, knowing I was becoming hysterical but not caring. "Don't let them find her! Please, God, don't let them find her!"

My thoughts were wild, jumbled, filled with the worst-case scenarios: the navy skinned creeps breaking into my house, seizing Mum, holding those deadly swords to her throat...

A bizarre noise like a dying animal reverberated around us and I registered Arlan was now beside me, his warm hand resting on my shoulder.

"Shh, Jackie, it's okay," he soothed, "We'll work this out, alright? You just need to be calm, so I can understand." His angel's voice comforted me and I inhaled shakily, finding that the strange noise had been my odd combination of sobbing and screaming.

"H-hazel," I stammered like a drunken fool, "She can't find out, can't suspect, I... I won't..."

"Hazel's fine. She's safe with my mother still. Don't worry, we'll work this out," he whispered again, his breath lightly brushing my ear. I froze. He was so close!

Arlan pulled back then and examined my face. "What's wrong?" he asked, his deep eyes studying me. "Are you...embarrassed?"

I prodded my cheek, feeling the heat there. Of *course* I was embarrassed; I'd just had a complete breakdown in front of the cutest guy I'd ever seen. I had to hand it to him, though: he'd dealt with me very well. Most guys I knew would've just left me screaming by myself. Then again, most guys I knew did not wear their hair almost down to their hips, nor dress in pristine white tunics. For some, being dressed in anything more than sweatpants was a miracle.

Arlan continued staring and I blushed more, irritated that I'd let my mind wander whilst my body displayed all the typical female reactions. Since when did boys make me blush? *Ugh.* I had to work this crazy thing out. And fast.

"Arlan, I really appreciate your hospitality, but I have to go," I blurted out, not liking that something in me ached to say those words. *Seriously, girl? You hardly know the guy. And he's an elf. Something out of an old fairy-tale. Really.*

"Go?" His pale brow furrowed elegantly. Combined with his babyish face and large, bright eyes, it gave him a look of childish confusion that was quite adorable. Not that I'd *ever* openly admit that to anyone.

"Yes, I need to go," I affirmed.

"But you said that you were from far away, and lost."

Observant, too. More points.

"I am, but my mother is in danger. And I need to help her, I just... I don't know how to get back to her." I lowered my head, hoping my words didn't sound too weird.

His gaze bore into me still and I suppressed a shudder, focusing instead on thinking of possible responses. Half of them involved me getting into some sort of bother; well, more bother than I was in at that moment. If that was even possible.

"You're not from around here." He said it as a statement, assuming he was correct. He was, of course, but that didn't stop my annoyance.

"No, I-" I paused, trying to determine the best way to explain my situation. If I said I was from another world entirely, would he think me mad? Burn me at the stake, or whatever they did to crazy people here? Arlan didn't seem anything like a medieval savage, and neither did his parents or siblings; they were a little weird, but not anyone who'd be for that sort of thing. But they *did* seem rich. Maybe they left the gory stuff to the poorer people.

Arlan continued rambling at me, though his rambling sounded more like softly-sung music, not the randomly pitched mess of my speech. I blinked, trying to focus on the individual words and utterly failing.

"I'm sorry," I muttered awkwardly, "I didn't catch a word of that."

"Ah." His pale hand extended and rubbed the top of my ear before I could flinch away. "Of course, your hearing is not like mine." His own ears twitched, alerting me to their presence. I leant closer and tentatively reached out my hand.

"May I?" I asked cautiously, my voice barely above a whisper. He nodded, his mouth quivering in his attempt to suppress a smile. I stroked the length of his ear, surprised at its smoothness and flexibility. The tip was pointed, as I expected from an elf, but it was longer, the muscle structure more complex than that of a human's. His ears seemed to move independently: they perked up now, tensing into a position that was akin to mine. But when I touched the base of his ear, the place where it joined his sculpted face, the muscles relaxed and it flopped, the tip turning downwards now.

"That's so weird," I breathed, slowly drawing my hand back. His ears drooped more.

"Weird?" he echoed, his voice almost hurt.

"Fascinating," I smiled, "Weird in a good way."

"Ah." I watched with curiosity as his ears perked up again, seemingly by themselves. "I forget, some of your speech is unfamiliar to me," he continued, "And though you look like a fairy, you don't talk like them."

I frowned. "Fairy? Aren't those just little things that live in flowers?"

He laughed, the sound like bells tinkling in the summer air. "Ah, no. *Faery*, with 'ae'. Also known as fae. The other type, those are a myth."

"Oh." I felt tempted to add that in my mind, *he* was supposedly a myth, but decided against it. "I'm not a fairy, though. I'm a human."

He blinked. "A human? But those are just a myth too!" he exclaimed.

I laughed, partly in disbelief. "You think *I'm* a myth? Where I'm from, your kin are the subject of children's bedtime stories. No-one thinks elves are real."

"Curious." He tilted his head slightly, a crooked smile forming on his lips. "So, it appears that we think each other to be a myth. But I can tell that you're not." His hand touched mine lightly. "You're real. Flesh and blood, as I am."

"I know," I whispered, my heartbeat accelerating. What else was I supposed to say to this fantasy creature? *Of course* I was real. Though the dizziness in my head and the rapid pounding in my chest weren't exactly natural for me. I did wonder if I was dreaming still, even though everything else pointed towards this being reality. Perhaps that's why he said that, to reassure me that I wasn't dreaming, that everything I was seeing and feeling was real.

"So, where are you from?" he asked gently, breaking the silence. I avoided his probing gaze.

"You're not going to accuse me of madness, are you?" I asked gingerly, internally annoyed at myself for letting the walls fall down. *So much for trying to keep the truth hidden.*

"Of course not." His tone was genuine and it was all the reassurance I needed.

A torrent of words flooded out of me, explaining everything that had happened. From the dreams I'd started having after my thirteenth birthday, to the most recent events in the woods, with the creepy humanoids. He didn't seem to know anything about those creatures, or Sachiel, but was very interested in every other insignificant detail. Mostly about my mother and the general human way of life. I never thought I'd have to explain to someone the texture and taste of pizza, or the function and appeal of cars, but he took the information well, asking question after question. Many things he was surprised at, from the concept of continents and countries, to the lack of fantastical creatures.

"No," I laughed after another stream of questions, "We definitely do *not* have dragons."

"Oh," he said, rather disappointed, "I thought that since they were disappearing from here, perhaps they were going to your world instead."

"Nope. No dragons, only in legends," I explained, still grinning.

"Well, I must say, your world seems most interesting," he concluded, smiling as well.

I shrugged. "Interesting is one word for it, I suppose. There's a lot of bad that happens too."

"Evil is everywhere," he stated solemnly, "But at least we have Elohim's light to help us overcome it."

I blinked. "Elohim?"

His face turned into that wide-eyed, babyish look of surprise that was becoming increasingly familiar. "You've never heard of Elohim? He is our Creator, the One who shaped this world: and others, I had always assumed."

I frowned. The name did seem familiar, somehow. "He's just called God in our world, though different religions have different views on Him," I explained.

Arlan shook his head, incredulous. "Different *religions*? Hah. That is a term we do not use. There *is* no religion. It is simply the truth."

"Hmm," was all I could manage in reply, my mind buzzing. That what Arlan said was true, I had little doubt; at least, it was what he believed. And maybe that was what applied here, in Pylisya. But for the grand scheme of things? I wasn't sure. Something supernatural had definitely happened in my coming here. But what it was, I didn't know. Could it be this Elohim he spoke of? Was Elohim the same as the God my mum had spoken fondly of? *My mum!* Arlan had been so successful in distracting me and cheering me up that I'd forgotten all about Mum, again! *I'm such a terrible daughter. She must be worried sick!* I glanced outside and gasped. It was night-time, but not night as I'd come to know it. I turned and stared at Arlan.

"How long have we been up here?" I asked, my voice trembling imperceptibly.

"All afternoon." He smiled wryly. "Time flies, doesn't it?"

I nodded slowly, exhaustion suddenly overwhelming me. The slices of bread we'd ate earlier - something remotely *normal* in this world – weren't satisfying my hunger anymore. I was surprised I'd even gone this long without thoughts of food.

Food. I wonder what else they eat here.

"Do you want to go outside?" Arlan enquired softly. I realised that I had been staring blankly out of the small attic window. My tired eyes refocused on the beautiful sight outside, and despite my weariness, I *did* want to see if the sky I was viewing through that window was the actual sky hanging over us, or just some distorted image.

"Sure," I replied, hoping I wouldn't fall asleep in front of him. He smiled, extending his hand to me, and I took it. His customs were slowly becoming more familiar, though they were different to what I'd come to see as normal. Here, holding hands was just something people did when walking. It didn't mean anything relationship-wise, which I'd quickly grasped. In fact, it made sense to take someone's hand, especially when walking in the dark. For a place full of mystical beings, there was an incredible amount of logic in the workings of Pylisya and the actions of its people.

Arlan took us down the winding stairs and through various hallways that all seemed identical to me, with pale walls and marble floors. Our way was lit by a single torch he carried: the sort I'd seen in films, consisting of oil-coated cloth burning a steady flame, not the battery-powered one we had by the backdoor at home. It cast strange and fascinating patterns on the walls, distorted reflections of the two of us and other shapes that I couldn't quite make out. One looked like a dragon spreading its wings; another, a human-like figure with a fishtail. I voiced this to Arlan and he laughed softly.

"Yes, there are merfolk here. I didn't realise so many of our people were seen as mythical in your world," he grinned, his expression barely illuminated. The harsh lighting from the flames highlighted the structure of his cheekbones and jaw that were not so evident in the daylight. They were slightly angular, and not as rounded and childlike as I'd first assumed.

"How old are you?" I whispered.

"I turn twenty next spring," he answered, turning his head away. I ducked mine, ashamed at the heat flooding to my cheeks. He was only a little older than me and I was surprisingly delighted at that. *Silly Jackie*, I chided.

I didn't respond - of course, I could've just told him *my* age - but I didn't trust my voice to not betray me. We continued through the mansion in silence, pausing only to sneakily open doors. I got the impression than Arlan was used to sneaking out and well-practiced at it; that, or he was just incredibly skilled at moving without making any sounds. I was just thankful the physical symptoms of tiredness had temporarily left my body.

Eventually, we emerged into the open and I gasped involuntarily. The sky hanging above us was a heavenly navy, tinged with crimson in some spots, like blemishes on a canvas. Stars glittered in unfamiliar constellations, their lights varying from the usual yellow-white to soft pink and even bright green in some places. It was as if someone had taken paints of various colours and flicked spots onto the canvas of the night, letting those spots evolve into little bright lights of their own. The most prominent light came from a slightly oval, bluish object, much larger than the other stars. I presumed it was Pylisya's moon, though it made Earth's moon seem tiny and pitiful in comparison. The moon illuminated the gardens around us with a soft blue glow, banishing the darkness with its tender light. I sat down and stared at the grass beneath my bare feet, now a vibrant turquoise that caressed my toes gently as a pleasant breeze rippled over us, then quickly turned my attention back to the tapestry in the sky.

"It's breath-taking," I managed to say, completely in awe.

"Aye, it is," Arlan whispered in agreement. I glanced at him and blushed immediately; his eyes were not fixed on the beauty of the night. Rather, the miniature oceans washed over my face, making me wonder what colours my skin and hair would seem in this light.

"Your eyes are such a mesmerising shade," he murmured, "I've never seen any like them before."

"Is that a bad thing?" I gasped out, my heart running laps around my chest, it was pounding so hard.

His crooked smile returned. "Fascinating," he replied, "Weird in a good way."

I blushed harder, if that was even possible. "You stole my line," I accused, though I didn't sound very mad. Quite the opposite, actually.

He chuckled lightly. "Borrowed, more like," he corrected and I laughed too. My stomach fluttered and launched into a series of somersaults, though I wasn't feeling that queasy. A little hungry and light-headed perhaps, but the emotions surging through my veins were something else. Something I was entirely unfamiliar with.

A low rumble arrested my attention and a light blush spread across Arlan's cheeks as he glanced at his stomach, the source of the noise.

"I guess skipping meals has its side effects," he commented sheepishly. I smiled.

"I'm pretty hungry too. I don't know how I've coped, after having only that bread to eat today," I confessed.

His face paled. "My mother didn't offer you anything else?" he asked, aghast. I shook my head. "Vaznek! Jackie, I am sorry!" he continued, distress etching into his words. I placed my hand on his shoulder gently.

"It's alright, Arlan. You and your family have already done much to help us. Besides, I haven't been that hungry today," I added with a shrug, hoping my casual tone would disguise the lie.

"Still, I think we should get something now," he said, elegantly standing. I echoed his movements much more awkwardly, then froze as anxiety crossed his face.

"What is it?"

"Shh," he urged, his ears perking up as he turned slowly. I looked around as well, too amazed by the beauty of the moonlight to notice anything amiss.

"Someone just passed through here," he muttered.

I blinked. "How could you tell that?"

"I heard them," he said simply, as if that was going to explain everything. I frowned. Sure, his hearing was superior to mine, but *that* superior? And if someone had passed us by, wouldn't we have seen them?

"Look." He crept over to the main path, the grey stone now a deep blue itself, almost the colour of his eyes. I knelt down, but couldn't see anything different. Then I leant closer.

"Footprints?"

"Yes." His voice was becoming more stressed with each syllable.

"They're quite small footprints, though," I added. *I wonder whose they could be?*

Arlan stiffened as realisation dawned on him. "Benji," he breathed, "Oh no, I completely neglected him today! He probably saw me with you and thought..." He turned away from me, running a hand through his long hair. I didn't need him to finish the sentence to know what he meant. As strange as it seemed, I'd been inside Benji's head: or at least, dreamt as if I was. I knew how much Arlan meant to him. And I knew his fears.

I raised my eyes to meet Arlan's frightened ones. I didn't think him as one who would be scared, but the terror within them was for Benji, not for himself. If it was Hazel who'd ambled off in the dark... My teeth ground together and I turned back towards the mansion.

"Come on," I urged, "He can't have wandered far. We'll get your horse and go find him, okay?" *And put on decent footwear first,* I added mentally.

"But you don't ride," he pointed out.

I suppressed the shudder that arose at the thought of riding a horse again, pushing it down with the unwanted feelings of hunger and exhaustion. "Doesn't matter," I said firmly, "Your brother is out there, and I'm going to help you find him."

CHAPTER SEVEN

- *Benji* -

My breath came out in laboured gasps as I stumbled through the smouldering darkness, the canopy of leaves above preventing the moon from lighting my path. I tried my best to keep the panic at bay, but the colours all around me were unfriendly, belonging to strange creatures of the night, or others that were rather disgruntled at my heavy footsteps awakening them. Despite the temptation, I did not turn back or slow my pace, but kept on, though I knew not where I was going. I shifted the weight of my rucksack to my left shoulder, already tired and exhausted in every way. But the forest wasn't a safe place to rest; I had enough sense to not try and lay down amongst the dark, damp leaves.

A sudden snuffle in the bushes alerted me to the danger I was in and I immediately scrambled up the nearest tree, clinging to its creaking branches with fervour as I tried to identify the source of the sound. Green plants and yellow bugs dominated the rainbow of the woods, but there was a sudden blob of orange, smaller than a horse but still large enough to deal some damage if I aggravated it. I held my breath as a rugged, hairy snout peeped out from the undergrowth, followed by narrowed, piggy eyes that glanced around with a fear almost equal to mine. Fascinated, I leant forward as much as I dared, glimpsing the spindly legs capped with chestnut hooves that struggled to bear the weight of its rounded body and the pointed ears that twitched like mine, sensitive to even the smallest motion. I knew from the paintings I'd seen in some of Lanny's scrolls that the creature before me was an urthet. It would not harm me deliberately - it was prey itself for hunters both elven and animal - but if I were to get in its path when startled, I'd be run over and trampled. With my legs trembling and weak as they were, I couldn't even hope to outrun it.

So, I waited up in the tree, fighting the darkness that clutched at my colour until the ruddy, orange urthet vanished out of my sight. Cautiously, I half-climbed, half-fell out of the tree, wincing as white flashed through my feet upon impact with the ground. I needed to rest, to sleep, but I *had* to get to the village first. *Surely, it's not much further?*

Just when I thought I could not go on any longer, the soft amber glow of torchlight entered my vision, accompanied by the flickering colours of various peoples. The boldest were elves, their clouded colours signifying most were still asleep. But I could also see the predominantly-brown auras of a few dwarves and the uncomfortably grey pulses of faeries. The latter made me shudder. I didn't like the faeries; they were far too strange. Only when their emotions hit the extremes did a flicker of colour show, or that was my theory, anyway. One time Turvo had gotten into a fight with an older faery, both of them screaming and shouting, but the faery only showed a tiny bit of red. It was very confusing.

I shook my head to clear my thoughts, suddenly noticing I'd wandered past a few small houses. The architecture was a little familiar; I'd definitely been here before. The moonlight barely lit up the streets, fading now as dawn was fast approaching. I ducked into a narrow street, setting my rucksack down and curling up into a little ball. Now I'd stopped, the tiredness caught up to me fully and my legs protested at all the walking I'd made them do. My feet were sore, too, so I pulled my boots off, feeling dizzy as a sickly stench forced its way up my nose. Small crimson splotches dotted the skin near my toes and I sickened further. *Blood.* Why were my feet bleeding? I hadn't stood on any of those nasty thorns, had I?

Please don't faint, please don't faint, I chanted, immediately looking away from the crimson evil.

"Are you alright?"

I gasped and scrambled back, eyes darting around furiously for any sign of danger. But all that was in front of me was a girl.

She was a little older than me, but younger than Turvo. I couldn't make out her face very well, though her hair glinted bluish-silver in the fading light. Her colour was very peculiar; at first, I thought it to be black – which was impossible, as black meant *no* colour – but on further scrutiny I realised it had a red tint to it: a lovely burgundy.

"Your colour is pretty," I breathed.

"My... colour?" She frowned and the warnings I'd heard most my life rushed through my head. *Colours. Danger. Power. Not safe...*

I ignored them. My family were relatively far away, so what did it matter if *I* was in danger now? At least they weren't in danger with me.

"Colour. Pretty," I said again, words failing me. Her eyes, a shocking amber, traced the dark skin on her arm.

My brow furrowed. Why was it that when I talked about colours, people thought I meant their skin tone? That was not the case, though her skin *was* a pretty colour.

"Thanks, I guess," she mumbled somewhat awkwardly. Then her voice grew louder. "Say, what are you doing here? Aren't you a little young to be out so early?"

I glared. "Not that young!" I exclaimed.

"Huh. You can't even form a coherent sentence." She rolled her eyes and I shuffled back. No matter how pretty her colour seemed, her attitude towards me did not reflect it.

"Words don't like me," I huffed, trying to shove my boots on. A strangled whimper broke out at the action and I threw the boot away as if it were a hot iron. My feet felt like they were burning, white shooting through my colour.

"Shh!" the girl hissed, "You'll alert the guards!"

I clamped my hand over my mouth to suppress the strange noises it was making. "Guards?" I whispered in confusion, after gaining control over myself.

"Yes, guards. Vaznek, you're not a regular here, are you?"

My cheeks felt warm and I shook my head. "Thought no guards in Kikarsko," I muttered.

"You thought wrong." She straightened up and lit a torch that had seemingly appeared from nowhere. "Come on. Those blisters look nasty, you should get them seen to."

I panicked. What if someone saw me and recognised me? The girl seemed to catch on to my emotions.

"Or not," she added quickly, scrutinizing me. Her eyes flickered from my cloak to the rucksack I wore. "Hmm," she mused, "You won't be able to walk far, though, if that was your plan."

I sighed. "Need to get out of here."

"Why? Where are your parents?"

Her questions were starting to irritate me and a flush of red invaded my colour.

"Home," I snapped, "I'm running away." The words stained the air between us and I suddenly felt terrified with them out in the open. *Running away.* Did I *really* want to run away? Away from the home I knew?

Yes, I told myself, *I need to keep them safe. I have to get further away.*

The girl's eyes lit up at my words. "Running away? Wow. You're tougher than I thought." She extended a dark hand to me and I took it, awkwardly struggling to my feet. They hurt when my weight was forced on them, my left foot especially, but I managed to ignore that little bit of white threading up my leg. The girl's words sent a little orange pride through my colour that warmed it throughout.

"Can you help?" I looked down at my stained feet, admitting that she was right on her earlier point. I couldn't walk far; I could barely stand. I needed to get fixed up and then I could leave, go far away and take the danger with me.

The girl just blinked and stared at me like I was a complete idiot. "I already said I'd get someone to help you," she huffed, "So just wait here."

She darted off, her burgundy melting instantly into the shadows. I stared up at the brightening sky. Dawn was going to be soon. I vaguely mused on whether my family would miss me when I woke up, but refused to dwell on it too long. After all, no matter how they felt, *I* missed *them*. And I couldn't let my feelings control me.

Something small, ginger and furry brushed against my leg. I started and glanced down in shock, then instantly relaxed. It was just a little kitty. I stroked its smooth back, feeling the soft turquoise thrum against my own colour. Not for the first time, I wondered what my colour was. How did the kitty's turquoise mix with mine? Did we compliment? Contrast?

"Ah, I see you've met Mali."

The girl was back. Already. I frowned up at her. "Mali?"

"The cat," she explained, but I wasn't really listening, because there were more colours with her. The first was a soft, chocolate-brown that made me feel safe, until my eyes flitted to the other three, who were all the same cold, hard grey. *Faeries.* I shuddered slightly and wrapped my cloak tighter around myself.

"What happened?" the non-faery asked. As he drew nearer, I discerned he was a dwarf, not much older than me. His skin was very tanned and his dark hair was cropped short. Already a little stubble dotted his chin, just below the friendly smile on his face. I smiled shyly in return.

"I walked a long way," I said, my voice barely above a whisper, "And now my feet hurt."

He grimaced. "Blisters. Pretty bad, too." He turned to look at the faeries behind, as if asking something, but no words were passed. "Can you walk a little further?" he asked again, reverting his attention to me.

I tried. White flashed through my colour again but I managed to take a few, clumsy steps. The dwarf took my boots in one small but sturdy hand and scooped up Mali with the other.

"Come, this way," he said, turning a corner into another narrow alley. I followed gingerly, trying to block out the pain from my injured feet as they fell on the cobblestones. The faeries following us were making me nervous, so I concentrated on slowing my pulse, not wanting them to see my fear. I didn't remember Kikarsko being so cold and hard.

Maybe coming here wasn't such a good idea.

I sped up as much as I could, so I was now beside the dwarf. "What's your name?" I enquired, desperate to break the silence.

"Thorn," he replied in a whisper.

"Who's she?" I pointed to the girl, who had now overtaken us.

"Amatria." The name sent shivers down my spine, though for what reason I couldn't tell. She stiffened slightly at the sound of her name, but did not slow.

"What's yours?" Thorn asked.

"Benji," I smiled, then froze. *Silly! They'll know who I am now!* But Thorn showed no visible sign of recognition, so I forced myself to relax and carried on walking with them.

Eventually we came to a stop by a small house that had a musky smell rising from it. Some of the windows were boarded up and the roof was patched and breaking. Amatria continued straight on in and I couldn't help but grimace slightly. It was very crowded inside: at least five more faeries and one other dwarf. I suddenly wanted to turn and run away, but Thorn had already taken my boots in and the faeries were pressing up behind me, their greys beginning to pulse against mine, so I fought back against the terror rising up inside, and stepped through over the threshold.

"Welcome," a cold, masculine voice crooned, "Any luck tonight, Tria?"

Amatria's colour flashed but she thrust a small sack into the hand of a tall faery, and I assumed he was the one who'd spoken. His skin was almost as dark as hers and he had a cool yet caring demeanour, one that confused me greatly.

"That, and a potential recruit," she said quickly, gesturing towards me. I froze again.

"Recruit?" I echoed, swaying on my pained feet.

The faery frowned, his violet eyes scrutinising me. "He's quite young. And injured. Get him seen to, then I'll consider," he commanded, turning his attention to Thorn.

The dwarf bowed in a rather jerky manner. "Of course, sir. This way." He took my arm and led me away from the faeries, much to my relief, into a small room at the back, empty save for a wooden bed and a shelf of peculiar-looking herbs. A flash of turquoise darted past us, settling into Mali, who nimbly leapt onto the bed and looked at me as if to say, *what are you waiting for?* I sat next to her and breathed a sigh of relief at the pressure alleviated from my feet.

"So, who exactly are you?" I asked Thorn, gently stroking Mali's silky fur.

He ground a couple of herbs into a nasty-looking paste. "We're street kids. Orphans and runaways, mostly. The people no-one wants," he answered bitterly, his colour flashing crimson.

"Your family didn't want you?"

Thorn stiffened. "Not exactly. I... didn't chose to come here." I cringed as he rubbed the paste over my blisters, but the stinging soon gave way to a small throb that was much more manageable.

"What happened?" I whispered.

He glanced at Mali, then at the ajar door, and sighed, chocolate-brown turning blue-grey. "I was visiting Torindell with my parents," he murmured, "but on the way back to the Northlands, we were ambushed. I tried to run, but the faeries caught me, and dragged me here. My parents, though..." Thorn's voice broke and his eyes grew moist with the pain of the memory. I gently touched his shoulder, feeling his colour latch onto mine, filling me with the blues and greys it was brimming over with. Water threatened to fall from my eyes, too, but Thorn seemed to brighten up at my touch.

"I'm sorry," I managed to say.

"I've been here for three years, now. There's not much to be sorry for," he answered gruffly, but the gratitude pulsing throughout his colour could not be hidden from me.

"But you," he continued lowly, "You have to get out of here, Benji. Return home, to your family, before the faeries enslave you too."

I shook my head. "I'm a danger to my family, Thorn. And they don't care for me much."

"Nonsense," he scoffed, "I know who you are, Benji Zeraphin. And if the faeries haven't figured it out yet, they soon will. You'll be much safer *with* your family than running away from them. *Of course* your family will want you. You're special, Benji. And royal. A *prince*, for Zeraphin's sake! Pun intended," he added with a slight chuckle.

I stared down at my feet, with their bloodied and swollen skin. "I have to stay away, to keep them safe," I whispered.

Thorn cocked a bushy eyebrow and I explained my situation as best I could, mentally cringing every time words skipped my mouth or syllables fell in the wrong order. The dwarf seemed to follow on, though, his colour shifting with each sentence I finished, eventually landing on a disapproving olive.

"So, you ran away, partly because your brother has a new friend? Is that it?"

I blushed. "No, I'm a danger-"

"No, you're not. You eavesdropped, Benji; you didn't get the whole picture." He sighed, pinching the bridge of his nose. "Seriously, though. I think you should go back and actually have a conversation with that Dethan elf, or whatever his name is."

"Ethlon," I corrected.

"Yes, him. You've got to figure this out. Plus, your brother is probably just getting to know his new friend. Doesn't mean anything is going to happen," Thorn stated rather matter-of-factly.

I sighed, trying to run through yesterday's events, but exhaustion was tugging on my brain and making it more sluggish than usual. Was Thorn right? Part of me hoped so, but if he was, then *I* would be *wrong* and I didn't like the thought of that. My conclusion was sound, or so it was until Thorn gave a different perspective on the matter. But then, what did *he* know? He didn't see the colours, didn't fear that he'd endanger those he loved, didn't have the curse of seeing all the greys and browns and gold-

Gold.

I gasped and almost fell off the bed, as the familiar colour crept into my vision. "He's here!" I choked out, staggering to my feet, pain and exhaustion dismissed for a moment.

"Careful!" Thorn chided, then, "Who's here?"

I opened my mouth to reply, but was silenced by a loud explosion that shook the rickety frame of the building. Then I cringed back at the sudden amount of white flashing in the room next door, clamping my hands over my eyes in an effort to shut it out. As Thorn called my name in concern, the door was torn from its hinges and gold flooded my vision, wrapping around me in a consuming manner. I gasped for breath, my fingers grasping at the crisp folds of the tunic, tightening around familiar curls.

"Lanny," I cried into his chest, taking a moment to lose myself in the beauty of his colour and his scent. When I dared to look up, Thorn stood frozen next to the cerulean girl, who I examined quickly. She seemed more relaxed now, though her tunic was dotted with specks of crimson which puzzled me. Lanny sensed my gaze and turned in that direction.

"Jackie helped me find you," he said softly.

I blinked. "She... you... looked?"

"Of course," Lanny replied, confusion tainting his gold.

"I told you they'd come," Thorn said, folding his arms. My cheeks flushed and I nodded slowly.

"You were right," I murmured, hoping he wouldn't hear, but the shock of yellow to his chocolate-brown suggested otherwise.

My brother then turned to the dwarf. "Were the faeries keeping you here?"

He hesitated, but nodded.

"Then I suggest you leave now, while you have the chance. You may come with us, or return to your home." Lanny's voice was firm, but I sensed an underlying care.

"Thorn helped me," I inputted. *Doesn't that mean he can stay?*

"I know." His tone did not waver. "What will it be?"

"I think I'll go," Thorn said hastily, "Back to Northlands."

"Very well." My brother tossed some coins to him and he caught it with surprising speed. "That should be enough to get you a ride out. Take care, young dwarf. And thank you."

With that said, Lanny turned and left, out of a back door I hadn't noticed before. I wanted to say goodbye to Thorn too, but we were soon running through a different set of streets, away from the horrid faeries. I clung to my brother, barely daring to breathe as we raced towards an exit from this scary town. The stench of burning assaulted my nostrils and I cringed into Lanny's chest.

"Don't look back," he mumbled, though to himself or to me, I could not tell.

Jackie's cerulean was struggling to keep up with us, streaked with ribbons of fatigue. I knew it was daytime now; the sun's rays beat down on my back. So why were both my – *rescuers*, I supposed – why were they so tired?

Lanny ran on for countless moments, his gold growing more and more clouded. I had the strange sense that we were being followed, but I didn't trust myself enough to voice those concerns. Eventually, we stopped, and he half-collapsed on the ground, me tumbling out of his arms. I lay in the soft grass, panting, trying to collect my thoughts together. I was tired, too, barely able to *think*, let alone think *straight*.

Should I really go back, if I was going to be a danger to my family? And did Lanny still care for me, or was he going to be distracted with the new girl, like I feared? Was he tired because he'd been searching for me? Was he tired because he'd spent the night with *her*?

I raised my head just enough to see Lanny talking to Jackie and ignoring me. Immediately my eyes grew damp and I growled in frustration, cursing the stupid doubts and fears that refused to leave me alone. At that peculiar sound, Lanny's head snapped up and he quickly closed the gap between us.

"Benji, are you okay?" he asked gently, his voice full of love, not pity.

I shrugged, turning to curl myself against his chest, letting his arms wrap around me. He stroked my hair, caressing my scalp and lifting the curls, patiently waiting as I wrestled my thoughts into words.

"Am I a danger to you?" I whispered.

His fingers froze. "No! Benji, you're not, okay? Ethlon's just paranoid," he grumbled, his colour flashing with irritation.

I pulled away from him, my eyes narrowing. "But I have this stupid ability and it's just going to hurt you," I blurted out.

Lanny groaned. "I am seriously going to have a word with Ethlon," he muttered, then his tone softened, "Listen, Benji. Your ability isn't stupid, it's incredible. You've been blessed with such a gift-"

"It feels like a curse!" I yelled suddenly, "It's a mistake, like I am!"

"What?" my perfect brother spluttered, momentarily lost for words.

"Everyone thinks I'm a mistake," I whispered, staring at the little insects jumping around in the grass by my feet, ignoring Lanny's conflicted gold and the curious cerulean only two spans away.

"No, we don't. That's a lie, Benji. You are most definitely *not* a mistake," Lanny said firmly, pulling me into an embrace again. I locked up my muscles, refusing to relax, and he sighed.

"Elohim gave you those gifts and put you here for a reason," he continued, his voice calmer.

"Elohim?" I echoed, the name tasting warm on my tongue, bringing to mind a soothing mix of colours. Gold and orange, like the best parts of Lanny and Atti, mixed with warm white and yellow.

"Yes, Elohim," Lanny managed to smile, his colour returning to normal, "Elohim has a plan for every one of us. Especially you, little one. And it does *not* involve you running away; you are much safer with us than going alone, okay?"

"Okay," I nodded, finally relaxing into his embrace. The feeling of danger didn't disappear, but it faded for now, trapped by the love of my eldest brother.

I'm not a danger to my family. I'm safe with them. Elohim will make sure of that.

If only I could truly believe those words.

Chapter Eight

- Jackie -

We rode away from Kikarsko at a steady pace, fast enough to cover ground but not so fast that I would be thrown off. As it was, I bounced up and down in the saddle with no control, my hands gripping the horse's reins so tightly that my knuckles turned white. I was beyond the point of exhaustion, my eyes drifting shut every half-minute, despite the glaring sun beating down on us. My body ached, muscles I never knew I had protesting at their sudden use.

The events that had just transpired spun around my mind and I shuddered, still trying to make sense of it all. Somehow, I'd known exactly where Benji was. It had been purely instinctive, something I didn't understand. And the fight against those cold-faced faeries was, again, acted out by instinct. I'd only an elven dagger with me – one that Arlan had given to me before we left the house, *just in case* – and already I felt guilty for using it. Wielding it as a weapon against a foe intent on killing me was not something I'd ever anticipated. Our fight was so rapid I barely took in what was happening until he stumbled away from me, crimson trailing from a slash in his abdomen.

A wound I'd given him.

Arlan reassured me he wouldn't die from it, but I wasn't so sure. I'd watched my fair share of action movies; a wound like that was often fatal and I'd delivered it by accident.

My stomach growled, not satisfied with the three apples I'd managed to scoff on the journey, though they were probably the three best-tasting apples I'd ever had. They were with the horses' feed in the stables, and I'd wondered why something so delicious was going to be given to animals. Arlan had shrugged when I voiced that.

"The horses like them. And if it's good enough for Brina, it's good enough for me," he'd replied, stroking his mare's mane.

"So you eat hay?" I'd joked, like an idiot, ignoring the sobriety of our situation.

He'd laughed too, seizing a piece of hay and chewing on it, much to my disgust. I'd grimaced as he swallowed and concluded that the last time he'd eaten hay, it was much nicer.

"Jackie!" Benji's unfamiliar trill broke through my reminiscing and I started, accidentally halting the poor horse. Both elves regarded me quizzically, their pointed ears adopting the same drooping pose. It was comical, really, but I was too tired to even laugh.

"M'kay," I mumbled, struggling to stay on the horse.

Arlan's delicate brow furrowed. "What's wrong?" he asked, concern tinting his words.

"She's tired," Benji pointed out matter-of-factly, "And me too." He yawned for emphasis, eyes closing with the motion, and I couldn't help but stare. His eyelids were translucent and a gentle silver in colour, unlike the healthy cream of his freckled skin. I glanced at Arlan, scrutinising the slither of lid above his bright eyes, but they appeared normal enough. *Hmm.* Maybe I was imagining it?

We kept moving, coming swiftly upon the mansion they called home. With great struggle I dismounted the horse, gratefully passing the reins to a waiting elf: one of Arlan's brothers, I guessed, though I couldn't tell which one. I was barely able to stay upright, yet I forced myself onwards, led by Arlan to the room that had been prepared for myself and Hazel. I didn't stop to change my clothes, let alone check how Hazel was faring, my eyes drifting shut the second I hit the downy pillows.

When I awoke, the sun was still beating down, uncomfortably so now. My body felt drowsy still, but I forced myself out of the bed, not wanting to abuse their hospitality.

Then the smoke hit me.

I gagged as it curled around me, gasping for clean air, my vision swiftly deteriorating until I could no longer see any potential exits. A hand extended towards me, cutting through the smoke, and I took it without thought, gladly being led away from the smothering atmosphere.

As my vision cleared, I realised it was Arlan who had come to my rescue, *again,* but there was something different about him. *Of course,* the logical side of my brain suggested, *his home is on fire.* Though I was tempted to agree, I could not see or hear any flames.

And suddenly we were outside, in unfamiliar territory.

Grey stone columns rose up around us, like old Greek architecture. They formed a slight oval shape, though it looked like the two nearest were slightly out of alignment. The grass was not green, but rather a muddied, yellowish shade, dried and bleached by the burning sun. Slabs a darker shade than the columns broke the grass at various points, scattered with no clear correlation. I inhaled cautiously, finding the air to be much too still and very bitter on my tongue. Confusion churned within me and I turned to face Arlan, questions bubbling on my lips, only to be silenced by his expression. He looked older, paler, lips tight together in a harrowing look.

"I have to go," he said, in a cold monotone.

"Go?" I echoed. *And leave me alone in this strange place? Besides, aren't I the one who is supposed to leave? I have to get back to Mum...*

He nodded, his eyes now a polluted ocean, all brightness sucked out of them.

"This can't happen," he whispered, gesturing to the two of us. I blinked. When had I given him the impression that I *liked* him? Sure, I thought he was cute, but any other girl would feel the same. Plus, he probably had a girl here, didn't he?

I registered that my mouth was hanging open like a goldfish and hurriedly worked my jaw to correct it.

"You're breaking up with me?" I gasped out, then blushed and clamped my hands over my mouth. Where had *that* come from? I doubted I knew him enough to call him a friend, let alone-!

To my surprise, his expression softened and his hand moved from mine to caress my cheek, as if we had an intimate relationship.

"I'm sorry," he breathed, all honey and cinnamon; then he was gone.

I shot up with a start, frightening Hazel, who was sitting across the room, in a similar setup to what we had back home. No smoke was in the air and it was growing darker outside – near dusk, I reckoned.

"Jackie?" Hazel asked cautiously. I blinked, rubbing the sleep from my eyes, and nodded in acknowledgement.

"Sorry if I woke you," I apologised, stretching as I got up. Hazel shrugged, her little bunches bobbing with the motion.

"I've been sleeping for hours, I think. Only recently woke up myself." She glanced around, eyes shining with curiosity. "I thought I'd dreamt of this place, but it's real, isn't it? We're really here!" Excitement crept into her tone and I resisted the urge to roll my eyes. *Trust Zel to take delight in being stuck in an alien land.*

"Here, with elves and dragons and the wonders of your stories!" she marvelled, continuing babbling to herself.

I froze. *Dreams. Stories.* My heart pounded faster and my mind raced, struggling to comprehend. I half-wondered if, by sleeping in Pylisya, I would dream of home. Instead, I'd had a weird dream about Arlan, where we were – I stopped that train, physically shaking my head. It was just a silly dream. Fantasies conjured by – well, by this fantasy that I found myself in.

But didn't Arlan call me a dream-prophet?

I sighed. He hadn't been able to find anything in the attic on the matter and I sincerely doubted it was even a real thing. Prophets were things that only existed in the Bible. And all the ones I could recall were male, so why would I-

My thoughts were interrupted again, this time by a screech as the door was thrust open, its old hinges complaining loudly.

"Jackie! Are you awake?"

It was Arlan, and I stiffened instinctively, eyes darting, nostrils flaring, trying to detect any trace of smoke. Nothing. I fixed my gaze back on his face: bright, flushed, and perfectly at ease. Excited, even.

I managed a smile. "Well, I'm awake now," I replied, slight sarcasm creeping in.

His expression fell minutely. "Ah. Sorry. I'm not used to this. Visitors." It was strange to hear him stumble over his words, as if he were a socially awkward human. "But come!" he continued, the elation returning. His enthusiasm leaked into my mind, fully awakening my body.

"Sure, just – can I change first?"

"Of course." He smiled brightly and stepped back out, shutting the door with much more care than his entrance. I frowned. Where was I supposed to find a change of clothes?

"There's spare tunics in that trunk there," Hazel said, as if she'd read my mind.

"Thanks." I got dressed quickly, glad to discard the sweaty, bloodstained clothes. The new set of tunic and breeches were much nicer colours: soft green and deep brown, respectively. I didn't mull over the clothes for long, running a hand through my knotted hair as I glanced in the mirror, checking that I would scrape a pass at being presentable. Then I darted to the door, opening it for Arlan, who was still jittery with excitement.

"I finally found something!" he declared, moving past and flumping on my borrowed bed, his action somehow still graceful. I shot a glance at Hazel.

"I'm going to see Kalia," she said quickly, before padding off. I let her go. It went against my instincts, but she seemed safe enough here. These were our hosts; they would not hurt us. That alone was barely enough to convince me, but I had that strange sense of peace wash over me again, like it had when I was falling. Hazel would be safe; I just knew it.

Arlan's pleasant voice cut through my thoughts, scattering them like dust in the wind.

"I'm sorry I didn't find anything when you were with me, but I do have two points of interest now!" He flourished the scrolls that had made their way from the crook of his arm to his hands in less than a second.

"Have you been searching since we got back?" I asked.

He grinned. "Not straight away, but, yes."

I blinked and stared at him, incredulous. "You didn't sleep? Aren't you tired?"

"A little," he confessed, with a casual shrug. I scrutinised his face, but could see no trace of the coldness present in my dream; only slightly dark circles below his eyes hinted at his tiredness.

"Nuts," I muttered under my breath.

He bounced slightly on the bed. "Don't you want to hear what I found?"

"I suppose." I settled for a casual tone, knowing that if I tried to sound enthusiastic, the fear gathering within would break into my words. His face fell ever so slightly, but I sat next to him, adjusting my posture so I'd appear more interested than I sounded.

He took it as an opportunity to start.

"Dream-prophets," he started, like it was some sort of announcement, "were those who saw visions of the past and future – usually the latter – when they were asleep. And some even saw into other worlds." He met my gaze in that moment, his eyebrows twitching, and I concentrated very hard on keeping my expression interested, refusing to let the words sink in. I had to hear the whole story first.

"There hasn't been a dream-prophet in Pylisya for centuries. The last known one was last seen in the Eastlands, three hundred and six years ago," His voice rose with elation, "And listen to this! He wrote that his successor would be female, instantly recognisable by her eyes. Green eyes." Arlan grew solemn and I shifted uncomfortably under his scrutiny.

"Quite a lot of people have green eyes," I muttered dismissively.

He shook his head, almost cautious as he spoke. "Maybe in *your* world. But nobody has green eyes in Pylisya. *Nobody.*"

I gaped at him. "Nobody?" In an entire - world, nation, whatever this was - not a *single person* had green eyes? I knew mine were quite a unique shade, but still! Not even brown-green, or blue-green? I voiced this to Arlan and he shook his head again.

"We elves have brown and grey eyes, mostly. Blue is quite rare." He gestured to his own dazzling sapphires. "Faeries sometimes have redder eyes, and dwarves are mostly brown-eyed. The merfolk's eyes range from lilac to dark blue. I've even seen some people with amber eyes. But never green."

His hand extended towards my face and my breathing hitched, the dream flashing through my head. Thankfully, it changed direction, resting on his knee, now clad in a deep lavender.

"Does it say anything else?" I choked out, irritated that my emotions were screaming and forcing their way into my words. If he was concerned at my behaviour, he neither voiced or showed it.

"Yes. Lethan – the last dream-prophet – was pursued by those we call cobrai."

I stiffened. "Snakes?"

Arlan laughed a little, the sound echoing awkwardly through the frozen atmosphere. "No, though their mannerisms are rather serpentine. They are similar to us in body shape." He gently flattened out a portion of the scroll on the bedding between us, his fingers resting on an ancient-looking painting. I peered closer and gasped.

Blue-black skin. Glistening white teeth. Fiery eyes.

"Those... those *things*," I whispered, quivering, "They confronted me and Zel in the woods. At home. They talked about that someone named Sachiel..."

I trailed off, the terror finding a gap in my defences which it tore down eagerly.

"Did the cobrai target Lethan's home? His family?"

I barely held in a cry as Arlan nodded.

Mum is in danger! I knew they'd try and get her too... Oh gosh, I have to get back, but how? Can I even get back? What... what if I'm too late?

"Jackie," Arlan urged, staring with concern as I hyperventilated, fear tightening its chokehold on me.

"Jackie," he repeated, his lyrical voice making my name sound like it was something to be treasured. I struggled to calm my breathing.

"That's what the other scroll is for. It speaks of portals, to other worlds. We can get you home."

"Home?" I echoed hoarsely. The word tasted sweet on my tongue.

Arlan stood and ran a hand through his long hair. "Of course, I can't send you alone," he added, "We'll have to get some knights, especially if the cobrai are after you. I didn't recognise your description at first..." He continued muttering to himself, far too fast for my ears to catch on to any more.

Suddenly my vision dipped and something else, something not of this room, flashed across my eyes. A humanoid figure, trying to get through the mist in the forest but stumbling back, as if he'd hit a brick wall. He turned towards me and I dimly recognised his features as elvish before my sight returned to normal.

"I don't think you should come." The words were out of my mouth before I'd had time to fully think them through. Hurt darted across Arlan's face, making him momentarily seem like a scolded child.

"Really?" he whispered, an uncharacteristic harshness coating his tone, "So you're just going to take off on me, like Benji did?"

I recoiled. *Of course.* He was hurt that Benji had left, believing that it was partly because of him. And now he thought that I was *using* him?

I needed time to think.

"Maybe you should check on Benji," I murmured, refusing to meet his gaze.

"Maybe you should get something to eat. Kitchen's on the ground floor. Can't miss it," he retorted in an almost-monotone. I waited until he had left the room before standing, reaching for the second scroll. It contained words that I could not decipher – some sort of elvish language, I guessed – but the diagram beneath was clearly a map. Thankfully the author had labelled it in English: albeit swirly-hand, Shakespearean English.

I searched for Kikarsko, the one place I knew, and located it in the region named Westlands, a term I'd heard Arlan use. To the south-east, right in the centre of the map, lay Torindell, the capital of both the Westlands and the whole of Pylisya. I studied the map carefully. *Northlands, Eastlands, Southlands, Westlands.* The former, where the dwarf had promised to go, was dominated by mountainous terrain, with deserts crowding the more eastern areas. As they neared the coast, in the region aptly named Eastlands, the deserts turned to beaches that led into the sea. The Southlands had plenty of green plains, but it was drawn and annotated in less detail than the others, as if the author had not ventured much into those lands. The majority of the detail was focused on the Westlands, clearly the largest region, and I deduced that it was where the author was from.

I scoured the map for anything that would clue me towards a portal, and found it: a forest, forming the border between Westlands and Southlands, annotated with the note;

'*Dryslan Forest. Many disappearances occur. Reports of strange mist attacks. Do not travel at night.*'

I grinned, because that was *exactly* what I was going to do.

But not this night.

I still wasn't sure of the scale of the map, so I couldn't risk setting out only to find myself lost in the wilderness all night. I sighed. *Best to find Arlan again. But first, food.*

I shoved the scroll between the bed and the dresser, slipping my elven dagger into the folds of my tunic as a precaution, then headed out into the hallway. It was light enough to see without needing a torch, but the walls around were illuminated with a bluish tinge, hinting at the peculiar moonlight that was soon to come. The sheath of the dagger rubbed against my skin – not painful, just uncomfortable – and I made a mental note to sort out a belt so I could wear it properly.

The marble floors were smooth under my bare feet, the passage curving elegantly as it brought me to the stairs. I followed them down, continuing at a steady pace, trusting that the kitchen would be as easy to find as Arlan had implied. Sure enough, the smell of loaves baking shot up my nose, igniting my stomach with a roaring, crippling hunger. I gasped, physically doubling over as pain lurched within me, but forced myself to stagger into the large, open kitchen, clenching my jaw in an attempt to stop the nausea. Three cooks lined against the far wall, each dealing with various ingredients that were mostly foreign. A couple of other servants dotted around, ferrying bowls and saucepans between the large worktop and the ovens to my left. A small table with high stools rested in the centre, its wooden top doubling as an extra workspace. I staggered towards it, trying to slow my brain down enough to get the words out.

One of the cooks paused, taking in my curled posture, and immediately trotted over.

"Oh, dear, you look starved!" she exclaimed.

"Do you have any to spare?" I managed to gasp out.

"Of course! Come, sit," she rumbled, taking my hand. Her weathered face and firm grip reminded me somewhat of my grandmother. Maternal, of course; I'd never met any of my father's family.

The pangs of my stomach were forcing me to the edge of consciousness, but I resisted long enough to devour the thick soup set in front of me. There were hints of cheese and thyme, plus some other pleasant herbs I could not identify. Small chunks of meat swirled amongst the base, moist and soft with the taste of chicken. All too soon the bowl was empty and a satisfied burp escaped my lips. I blushed as someone across the room laughed, then realised it was just Hazel.

I turned to the cook, grinning. "Thank you, that was delicious!"

She smiled, eyes twinkling. "Can't have our young prince's rescuer going hungry now, can we?"

I blanked. "Prince?"

Immediately the kitchen staff burst into a chorus of laughs, whilst I looked on, confused and very self-conscious.

"Ah, dear," the cook gasped out, struggling to compose herself, "You're really not from around here, are you?"

I continued to stare blankly at her.

"Love, your expression is priceless," she said, as if it was an explanation for their outburst.

"I don't get it," I whispered, in the same moment that my brain made the connection. *Very large house. Servants. Wealth.*

"Oh!"

Benji was a prince. And Arlan. How did I not see it before?

Well, duh. Their grandfather is *the king.*

I wanted to just feel stupid, but instead panic gripped me. Because I'd finally seen it; the nightmare. The first time I'd dreamt of Pylisya.

It hadn't happened yet.

And I couldn't stick around to watch it unfold.

Chapter Nine

- Benji -

I lay on the downy grass, eyes closed, watching the colours dance all around me: Kalic's red and Fírean's blue – much deeper than usual – combined with Ethlon's illusive silver. It was such a beautiful picture; I *really* wanted to grab a paintbrush and my paints, to spend the rest of the day painting my family and Ethlon. The colours of various insects splattered onto my imaginary canvas and I inhaled as serenity settled over me. Thankfully no-one had discussed my running-away; I overheard Lanny telling Atti it was too 'sensitive' to go over at the moment. Of course, everyone knew about it, but-

"Focus," Ethlon commanded, interrupting my thoughts, "Reach out. Feel their emotions."

I cleared my mind and tried, I really did, but I could only *see*, not *feel* like I had done with Thorn in Kikarsko. My breath escaped my mouth with a rather loud huff.

"No good," I complained, sitting up.

Kalic swatted at Fírean. "Can you *please* stop with that now?" he grumbled.

Fírean set his lute down. "Sorry," my gentle brother whispered, his blue deeper than usual, "That song, it makes me sad." I peered closer at the curious glistening on his cheeks.

"Well it makes *me* annoyed," Kalic said, jabbing his finger at his chest, like I'd seen Turvo do. I wasn't sure Kal was quite doing it in the right context, though.

I am! he protested, intruding on my thoughts. I stuck my tongue out at him.

"That was the point," Ethlon explained coolly, "I wanted to test Benji, and needed you two to both feel strong emotion."

"Why always us?" Kalic continued to moan, "I mean, why can't you ask Arlan or Turvo or some of the servants to help Benji instead? Sorry, Benji, I just-"

"Shh," Ethlon hissed, interrupting my twin's rant, his eyes focusing on something on the horizon. Instinctively I turned that way as well, the ugly grey approaching us making me cringe back. Fírean's blue moved to my side, his arms wrapping around me protectively, which confused me greatly.

"What's-" I started to say.

"Fírean, get the twins inside. I'll alert your father," Ethlon commanded, and I suddenly saw him as the elf that was worthy enough to be the King's most trusted advisor. I was scooped up none-too-gently by Fírean, who also seized Kalic's hand, and ran with us back into the house, almost colliding with Turvo in the process.

"What's going on?" the younger exclaimed.

Fírean set me down, a frown crossing his pale face. "You can't go out riding, Turvo. Stay here."

Turvo bristled. "You can't tell me-"

"Turvo. Come back inside. Now!" Atti shouted, his orange still pulsing with red and grey, though the anxiety was much more prevalent than before. Turvo obeyed somewhat reluctantly, a flash of annoyance ripping through him, accompanied by something else I could not identify.

We carried on down the hall with Fírean, up the stairs to our bedroom. I hurried along as fast as my sore feet and short legs would allow, wondering how Kalic was faster than me despite us being the same size.

"Fír," I panted, my still-healing blisters throbbing, "What's going on?"

His deep eyes met mine. "I think you know, don't you?" he whispered, and my mind flashed to the faeries and the strange girl named Amatria.

"Followed?" I asked quietly.

He shrugged. "I'm not sure. Might be the same group, might be a different one – oh, don't give me that look, Benji!"

I clenched my fists, a deep scowl etched on my face. This was *my* fault! If I hadn't run away and found those stupid faeries, then they wouldn't have come here to endanger my family! Or would they have come anyway? It seemed that I *was* a danger, despite Lanny telling me otherwise.

"It's my fault," I groaned, "I should go-"

"No, stay here," Fírean urged, "We'll protect you; I promise."

Kalic snorted at the thought of Fírean protecting us. "What with?" he laughed, "A song?"

A laugh crept out of me too as he shared that mental image and Fírean flushed red. "I could use a sword," he retorted indignantly.

Kalic smirked, clearly unconvinced, but we didn't have much time to laugh over it, because Lanny burst into the room, his eyes seeking me.

"It's the faeries' king," he said, "Just paying a visit, though I suspect it's more than that." He glanced at me again and I almost cowered back, having to remind myself that it was not Lanny who I was really afraid of.

"He wants to see us?" Fírean enquired. Lanny nodded solemnly.

"Help the twins, would you? Kal, swap clothes with Benji. And both of you, tie your hair back," he added, his attention turned to us.

Kalic and I both frowned and eyed up each other's garments. He was wearing a scruffy crimson tunic, with tan breeches that clung to his slim frame. And it stank of metal and fire and, well, *Kalic*.

"Why?" we protested in unison.

Lanny sighed. "The faeries might be able to sense your... *ability*, Benji," he replied slowly, "And we need to make that as hard as possible for them."

I wrinkled my nose, understanding the logic of what Lanny was saying, but I still didn't want to wear Kalic's smelly tunic. Before I could protest again, Fírean was already grabbing at my clothes, trying to unlace the front of my tunic. I pushed him away, my fingers fumbling with the ties, yet I managed to undress myself in record time. Kalic snatched the clothes from me and roughly tossed his smelly ones to me, which of course I did not catch, and relented to letting Fírean help dress me in them. My twin looked very strange in my light blue tunic and orange-yellow breeches, and his colour was strange, too. A more faded red.

I turned to Fírean quizzically. "Kal's colour is wrong," I grumbled.

"That's the point," Lanny stated, then he turned and left the room at some hidden signal.

"But the colour looks all horrible now," I complained after him, even though he was probably out of earshot.

"Colour? Benji, listen. You have to stop with the colour thing," Fírean said anxiously as he combed my unruly hair, "Especially not around the faeries- oh!" He stared at yet another brush that had snapped in half. I sighed.

"Just ponytail it." I gestured at Kalic's hair for explanation and Fírean obeyed, tugging my hair into an uncomfortable restraint. I didn't understand how Kalic *liked* having his tied back. It was much nicer hanging down, wild and free.

No, it's nicer tied back, out of my way, he retorted.

Suit yourself. I pulled a face and he chuckled.

Fírean left the room in a hurry, presumably to get himself ready, so Kalic and I sat on our beds, thoughts flickering between us. I was beginning to lose track of where his concerns ended and my concerns started, when a sudden turquoise brushed against my legs. I yelped, sending the source of the turquoise running back.

"Aye! Benji, what is it?" Kalic exclaimed, staring at me.

I scanned the room frantically and caught a slither of ginger fur. "M-Mali?" I stuttered, staring as the little cat trotted back over to me, "Uh, how?"

"You know this cat?" Kalic scrutinized Mali, his colour making me feel uncomfortable. I bent down and scooped Mali up like I'd seen Thorn do, and she purred, her turquoise thrumming against my shaking fingers.

"Yeah. I saw her, uh, in the gardens," I lied, quickly faking a memory in my mind, in case he was still looking. I didn't know why, but I thought if Kalic knew Mali was from Kikarsko, he might cause her harm. Especially since she'd been in that place with the creepy faeries. So I pretended that she was a stray I'd found one day a few weeks ago, but as I stroked her, I rubbed my hands in the smooth fur, checking that there was nothing hidden – no message or threat or anything – and her colour was so *pretty* I deemed her perfectly safe.

Suddenly Fírean rushed in again, his hair a mess. "They're here," he gasped out, at the same time that I sensed the horrid greys just outside. Atti's orange mingled with them, surprisingly cool despite the air of danger around. I slipped my hand into Fírean's as we made our way back downstairs, my brother explaining that we *had* to see the faery-king, but he would make sure it was for as little time as possible. I nodded, conscious that my ears were drooping, and struggled to think of something that would make me happier with no success. We were walking into the jaws of danger, I sensed it, but what could I do?

The five of us lined up in the hall, in order of age, as if we were antiques at an auction. I didn't like being separated from both Lanny and Fírean; I felt safe with either of them, more so with Lanny, but it was Turvo who stood on my right, his solid green not doing anything to soothe my worries. Atti let the faery-king enter, playing the part of the diplomat, though he couldn't hide his concern and fear from me. I physically recoiled as the faery-king's colour assaulted me, stopped from falling only by Turvo's firm hold on my arm. It was worse than the usual dull grey: ugly browns and greens and some streaks of red that made me nauseous surged amongst the grey base, and I realised that he was not exactly what he claimed. No faery would have that many colours, but I couldn't think of what other race he could be; something in my gut urged me to remain silent, so I did.

Atti introduced the faery-king to Lanny first, momentary pride lacing his colour. I couldn't help but smile too at the elegance and grace my best brother possessed.

"It is a pleasure to meet you, Arlan," the faery-king said and my smile faded, replaced by a grimace: both at the sickly tone and the use of my brother's full name.

He's Lanny, not Arlan, I wanted to argue, but again I did not let the words escape my lips. Lanny answered the faery-king's questions perfectly, talking about the histories he was currently studying and the scroll he'd written on them. I listened too, my ears naturally perking up, curious to find out more about what exactly Lanny did with his time away. But my brother did not disclose much else and I was left feeling disappointed, the emotion echoed in two other people: the faery-king and the cerulean girl, Jackie, who was just outside the door, eavesdropping. I was tempted to sneak a glance her way, but it might've revealed her and I didn't want her to be in danger too.

"And what is your skill?"

I jumped slightly, panicking, then calmed down when I realised Fírean was the target of the question. The faery-king's judgmental eyes fixed on my brother and he shifted uncomfortably beneath their piercing gaze. He swallowed nervously, his colour flickering, and suddenly found his hands very interesting to look at. I frowned; such behaviour was not natural of Fírean. I wondered if he was ashamed of something – which was partially reflected in his colour – but what did he have to be ashamed about?

"I play," he finally muttered.

The faery-king's eyes ignited. "Oh? What game?"

"N-no, I play music. Sing, harp," Fírean corrected lamely, his hands doing that weird gesture thing they did when he was agitated.

Immediately the interest sparked out. "You sing? Is that all?"

My eyes narrowed, a sudden surge of scarlet accelerating my heartbeat as I observed the faery-king's disgusting colours again. I really wanted to throw some bold colours in there. Red, make him feel angry. Or a harsh, bright green of jealously. My brother was amazing and I wanted him to see that. Before I could stop myself, my foolish tongue wriggled and the cords of my throat vibrated, spewing words from my mouth that really should've stayed in my brain.

"Fír is really talented!" I blurted out, "He can cook and sew as well!"

Fírean's colour immediately faded to a pale blue, with grey anxiety charging throughout. Across from me someone cursed; the faery-king burst out laughing.

"Cooking? Sewing?" he scoffed, "Those are all girls' jobs!"

Fírean ducked his head in embarrassment, crimson hurt lacing his colour, and outside Jackie huffed rather loudly. I could tell she didn't appreciate those being branded as 'girls' jobs'.

Thankfully the faery-king swiftly turned his attention to Turvo, though not before he'd got a good laugh out of my brother. I wanted to sink into the floor, or maybe turn back the time. All I'd wanted was for him to see how wonderful Fírean was, but it seemed I'd only just made things worse. Maybe that was why Fírean snuck down to the kitchens late at night when he thought none of us would be watching, or why he hid his sewing equipment under the loose floorboards in the music room. Of course, *I* knew. I'd eaten a lot of his cooking and it was all delicious. I'd also asked him to fix my clothes sometimes, so I wouldn't have to inconvenience Mutti.

Still, why were those skills to be ashamed of?

I couldn't mull over it long, though, as the faery-king was now asking me questions. I stared at him blankly, then looked over to Lanny for help, because I didn't know what he'd just said.

"It's okay," Lanny said, "You can tell him what you like doing, yes?"

I made a mental note to give Lanny a massive thank-you later and nodded. "Painting," I said with a smile.

"Oh," came the unamused reply and the faery-king moved on to enquire of Kalic's interests. I exhaled, relieved that he had not probed me further. There was definitely something I didn't like about him and I was glad that he'd completely overlooked me. Though, upon focusing on the faery-king again, I noticed there was something else in the room. Another presence, another colour, whoever it belonged to not visible to my eyes. But I could still sense it: a faded, yellowish colour, warm despite its transparency, hovering between me and the faery-king. I wondered if it were protecting me somehow, but that was absurd, wasn't it? How could an ethereal being protect me from the physical? And why would it want to protect *me*, anyway?

Mali curled around my legs, her soothing purr distracting me from the chaotic whirlwind my mind was turning into. I considered scooping her up, but to do that I'd have to pull my arm free of Turvo, which would no doubt would bring unwanted attention to myself. The faery-king was nearly finished speaking to Kalic; I had not caught a word of their conversation despite being right next to my twin. I risked a glance at Lanny, whose gold was clouded again, his eyes gazing towards the door where Jackie was- no, where Jackie had been waiting. She was gone and that confused me. I hadn't sensed her cerulean leave.

I closed my eyes and focused, remembering what Ethlon was trying to teach me. I never achieved it under his overbearing command, but in my own time, could I do it? There was only one way to find out. I saw Lanny's gold, tried to decipher his emotion, but he was too conflicted. Fírean was incredibly distressed and my throat tightened with guilt, so I quickly moved on from him. Reaching, searching...

Jackie's cerulean was outside, accompanied by a soft brown, almost a hazel colour. The hazel one was frightened, like me, but also very curious: though what about, I could not tell. Uncertainty rushed through Jackie, her colour flooded with conflict, as if she was trying to make a big decision but didn't really want to. Was she scared of the faery-king? Did she want to leave? And who was the hazel one with her?

"Benji? He's gone now." Atti's voice cut through my searching and I jolted back into my body, eyes squinting as they adjusted to the harsh, natural colours. Turvo's hand was gone from mine, but he was still beside me, stern like a statue.

"What did he want?" I whispered, hoping only Atti would hear. I wasn't so lucky.

"What makes you think it concerns you?" Turvo snapped, his tone frightening me.

Mutti gave him a look that froze him in place. "We should be hospitable, yes? Come with me," she said, her tone soft but the implications of command were heavily interwoven. Turvo relented and followed after her, as I slowly processed their words.

"Still here?" was all I managed, my throat screwed into a tiny hole. Mali whined so I scooped her up, burying my face in her fur.

"Yes, but he will not see you again," Atti affirmed, his orange flickering as he took in Mali, "And where did you get that cat?"

I mumbled my lame excuse about finding her in the gardens, which was somehow accepted. At least, that's what I thought Atti's grunt meant.

"But what did he want?" I asked again. Atti huffed.

"I don't really know, Benji! It seemed like he only wanted to see us as he was passing by - though why the faeries are this far into our territory, I don't know - but you and Ethlon are being paranoid and it is rather irritating!"

"What's paranoid?"

Atti glared at the floor. "Ah, never mind!" he exclaimed, then glanced at Lanny, "Honestly, I don't know why you named *him*, of all people!"

Mali jumped out my arms and I bit my lip. Atti was being mean, his colour was all nasty and he was mad at me and Lanny and it was my fault because I was stupid and not very good at these things-

"Benji, stop," Lanny soothed, his gold wrapping around me. I took a deep breath and clung to his shirt, noticing that Atti and Fírean had both left the room, each headed in a different direction.

"S-sorry," I mumbled into Lanny's chest, struggling to calm my breathing. Kalic awkwardly patted me on the shoulder.

"Come on, Benji. Do you want to see Anatti again?"

"He's still here too?" I whispered, my voice cracking as I peeled myself away from Lanny.

"Yeah, but he's in the library, hiding from the creepy faery guy," Kalic explained. I smiled slightly at his description.

"Would be nice to go," I said, "But I should on check Fír." As I spoke, I reached out, and the blue of my gentle brother was so deep that it caused my eyes to well up. Kalic shrugged, as if Fírean's wellbeing had not even been considered by him, and we agreed to meet in the library. I mentioned to Lanny that Jackie was outside and he was off in an instant, barely pausing to give me a quick kiss goodbye. I tried not to let it bother me too much, though. Jackie had helped save my life. I'd let Lanny see her for another day.

I padded out of the hall with Mali hot on my heels, heading towards the music room, and at once the painful sound of sobbing reached my ears, in rhythm with a hit of overwhelming blue as I passed the door. It was ajar, so I pushed it, wincing at the creaking sound it made.

"Fírean?" I called out tentatively.

His cries were stifled. "What is it, Benji?" he muttered through his hands. I trotted over to him and wrapped my arms around him. Sad people liked to be hugged, that was what Mutti said. And Fírean's blue was a sad blue, so obviously he wanted a hug. He stiffened slightly at first, but relaxed soon after, and I snuggled into the curve of his shoulder blade. Of all my brothers, he was the second most open to my physical affections: the first being my Lanny, of course.

"I'm sorry Fír," I whispered, squeezing my eyes shut so all I could see was his blue mingling with the turquoise of Mali.

"It's not your fault, Benji," he replied shakily, "I'm the one who can't wield a sword, can't hunt, can't ride, can't do anything I'm supposed to..." He trailed off, the thickness in his voice telling me he was going to cry again.

But why? I simply did not understand. Swords were for fierce people and Fírean was not one of those. Hunting and riding didn't matter much either, did they?

"But Fír, you are so talented!" I exclaimed, loosening my embrace so I could look at his face, "You're the best singer I know and you cook amazing pie and I like that you fix my clothes when Mutti is busy and-" I stopped, partly because my brain was all fuddled thanks to the multitude of words I spewed and partly because Fírean's blue was gaining orange. Was that pride I sensed? And a tinge of pink love?

"You really think that?" he whispered.

"Of course! I don't lie about these things," I said quite truthfully.

"But still, I cannot do anything 'masculine'," he sighed, the sadness returning.

I pondered his features for a moment. He was not as beautiful as Lanny, nor as strong and tall as Turvo, nor as skilled in hand as Kalic. His talents lay more in the practical, caring areas, and creativity. *Like mine*, I realised. We both thought ourselves lower for our talents of music and painting, but those were valued, weren't they? Particularly music. I had yet to meet someone who didn't like listening to music.

"So? I cannot do anything stereotypically feminine," a voice said. I jumped, too lost in thought to have noticed Jackie's cerulean slipping through the door.

Fírean sighed again. "And? I suppose people admire you for your bravery and physical ability, Jackie." She cocked her head, slightly puzzled, but he continued regardless. "People look down on me, though, and call me effeminate, or weak."

A flare of red burst through Jackie's blue. "Being effeminate does *not* equate to weakness-"

"Aye, we can debate over gender roles another time!" My heart swelled as Lanny's warm gold joined the mix, immediately calming the fires of Jackie. She scowled slightly but bit her tongue, and he smiled before turning his attention to our brother.

"How are you feeling, Fírean?"

"Useless," came the reply. I wrapped my arms around him again. *Sad people like hugs...*

Lanny sat down on the floor beside us. "Why is that? You have incredible talents, Fír. Just because they don't match up to the expectations of certain people does not mean you are a failure."

"And cooking is *not* a girl thing," Jackie added, still in a bit of a mood. I tilted my head to watch Lanny's response. His colour gained a tinge of vermillion annoyance, but it was quickly vanquished.

"Jackie, listen. You are right: cooking, sewing, and singing are not limited only to females. I don't know how it is in your homeland, but it is the truth that here at least, more females do those things than males. As with hunting and fighting, which are more common amongst males, and rightly assumed so. It is usually the case because females are the gentler gender, and males more protective, which is the way Elohim created us. And those that hunt the food don't cook it, do they?" He paused for breath and we all shook our heads.

"Turvo never cooks," I pointed out.

"Exactly," Lanny smiled, "And Fírean does not hunt. Females like Tulia cook and sew, but males can too, as you do Fír, and that's perfectly okay.

Males typically fight and hunt, like Turvo. Jackie, you are proof enough that females can participate as well!"

He turned then to Fírean, cupping our brother's face so their gazes met, blue eyes on blue. I shuffled back and closed my eyes, smiling at the blissful combination of blue and gold filling my vision. *Their colours work so well together!*

"You can sew, sing, cook, and continue doing all the things you love whilst also being masculine, Fír. I love you that way," Lanny finished, pulling Fírean into an embrace. I wanted to be hugged too, but I knew that it was their moment, so instead I spent a few moments grinning over the beauty of their mingling colours.

Chapter Ten

- Jackie -

I exited the music room shortly after making my appearance, still wondering why I'd followed Benji in. Maybe it was because Arlan had followed me and I really wasn't in the mood for cute apologetic boys. Or maybe I had actually felt some concern for Fírean. It was strange, really. I didn't *know* him very well but, thanks to my dreams, I had a good sense of his character.

If I *was* actually a dream-prophet. The concept still creeped me out.

The pale walls divided neatly, allowing me to pass through the mansion and out to the gardens where I'd spontaneously left Hazel with no explanation. She wasn't alone, though; one of the twins was with her, talking animatedly.

"Zel?" I called out gently.

She looked up, as did the elf, who I recognised as Kalic. *Of course.* Benji was still inside.

"Oh, hey, Jackie. I was thinking about earlier, what you said-"

"Not in front of him," I snapped, shocked at the harshness of my tone. Hazel's eyes flickered.

"I'm not a baby for you to boss around!" she retorted, almost yelling, trying to straighten herself up to full height. But at only 4ft, she had no hopes of being intimidating.

I ran my hands through my hair, trying to keep the stress off my face. Hazel was *definitely* acting different. But then, so was I. Prophet stuff and weird physical reactions around a certain male elf had accosted me since we'd first arrived. What if the same was happening to Hazel? How had I been so self-absorbed?

"Zel, I'm sorry, okay? I need to talk to you though."

She sighed and muttered goodbye to Kalic before following me deeper into the gardens. We wound around the hedges as if they were the barriers of a maze, though to me it felt more like a trap. I decided that the greenery looked less menacing and more beautiful in the alien moonlight than it did in the harsh light of day.

"What is it?" she asked, turning to stare up at me after a few minutes of walking.

I sat down on the helpful bench lying nearby. "I'm really sorry, I've left you almost alone and-"

"Yes, yes you have!" she exploded fiercely, "You left me alone, running off with that elf guy with no explanation! Scaring me! And I don't like this place, there's weird voices and people telling me what they think I am but at the same time I also like it because strangely I actually feel at home here and people are actually nice to me and-" She paused, almost gasping for breath, and I struggled to suppress the wave of guilt threatening to consume me.

"Voices? People?" I managed to say.

"One voice, really. But it's nice and comforting. I think..." Her mouth curled up and her brow creased in that funny expression she did when puzzled, "I think it's the Big Guy that Mum tells us about."

"God?"

"Yeah. Or Elohim. That's what Kal said they call Him."

My mind whirred but I didn't let it drift, not yet. "And the people?"

"Kal seems to think that I'm half-dwarf," she answered matter-of-factly, "And in a way I think he's right. The land here just seems to connect with me, and it just... *fits*, you know?"

Not really, I thought, and said nothing.

"But Kal reckons I'm only half because I'm too pretty," Hazel continued with a grin, and my hands inadvertently clenched into fists. I didn't want to hear any more about 'Kal'. He was too young for her, anyway. More to the point, I did *not* want my little sister to try and start a relationship with someone in this crazy fantasy land.

Hypocrite.

"Zel, we have to get home," I whispered, hating the way my voice broke at the end. Hazel cocked her head.

"You don't want to."

"We left Mum." *And we left her with those creepy cobrai.*

"So go back and bring Mum here, and then we'll be all happy, yes?"

I blanked. "I'm not leaving you here alone!" I snapped, disliking how grown-up she suddenly seemed. If she wasn't so short, I'd have a hard time thinking of her as anything below fourteen, the way she was acting.

"You left me before. Besides, I'll be fine," she smiled, like a deceptive adult trying to convince a child to get into their car.

Well, I wasn't the child. *She* was.

"No," I said firmly, "We both go to the Dryslan forest, and that's it."

I seized her hand, ignoring her protests, and marched her back through the gardens, angrily trampling on various plants. Arlan or another member of his family would probably give me hell for it but right now I just did not care. Hazel was really getting on my nerves with her defiance, and the urge to find Mum was accelerating my blood pressure to dangerous levels. I was so consumed by the rage pulsing through me that I didn't notice the blond elf until we'd nearly careered into him. My first thought was panic, then I realised it was not Arlan, but his younger brother, whose name had completely evaporated from my mind.

"You need to go to Dryslan? I can take you," he said coolly.

I halted and Hazel broke free from my grip as I stared at the elf. Despite being younger than me, he was my height exactly, so our eyes locked with no difficulty.

"You can? No extra conditions or anything?" I enquired sceptically.

Turvo - I remembered his name now - shook his head. "Of course not. But I get the impression this must be done in secret, yes?"

"Preferably," I confirmed, trying to calm my tone to match his. He smirked ever so slightly, though at what I couldn't tell.

"Well, I promised a friend I'd take him hunting tomorrow, and if we ride hard we can make it to Dryslan in six days. Does that work for you?"

"Jackie doesn't like riding," Hazel pointed out, unhelpfully.

"I just haven't ridden much," I corrected.

"No problem," Turvo shrugged, completely blasé about the whole thing, "We'll meet at the stables just before dawn. If you're coming, be there."

He spun on his heel and left, his thin ponytail flying out behind him. I bit my lip, considering. Turvo's offer seemed genuine, but I could not shake the suspicion that arose in me. Then again, I was suspicious of Fírean the first time I met him, but he'd proven to be a butterfly, really. I was probably overreacting.

One day. And six days' travel. Seven more days until we could see Mum again. I sent up another prayer in hope that she would remain safe, though with each day that had passed my concern only grew. Had the cobrai attacked? Did they take her captive, or worse? Were they leaving her alone, but waiting for her to call the police and report us missing? I'd lost track of how long we'd spent in Pylisya. It felt like a lifetime already. Time, I decided, was very messed up here. Sometimes it would fly by, other moments seemed to drag and drag. I suspected what made the difference, and it concerned me.

Hazel spent the rest of the afternoon with Kalic and I spent mine avoiding a certain elf. Both scenarios were to my great annoyance; consequently, I was in a sour mood when nightfall rolled around. Even the blue moonlight couldn't raise my spirits.

I'd managed to scrounge some clothes from one of the servants and a rucksack, as well as an assortment of foods. Camping was not my expertise; at home we were so close to hills and forests, we never saw the point in staying out in them when we could simply walk back to the house and sleep in the warmth. Nevertheless, I had a rough idea of the food we'd need for the next two days, and packed a little extra just in case the journey did take longer.

No words were spoken as Hazel and I slipped into bed, the curtains open so the rising sunlight would shine on my face, hopefully waking me. I had a tendency to get up early, anyway. Not that any of my habits could really be applied to this world.

When my eyes opened again, I knew instantly that I was dreaming. Arlan stood in the shadows of the room, his eyes dark, expression unfathomable.

"You're leaving," he stated, no trace of emotion in his voice.

I nodded slowly. "I can't stay here any longer," I whispered.

"Why?"

As I was dreaming, I saw no harm in telling him the truth. "I've had bad dreams, and I can't just wait for them to become reality. Besides, I really need to get home, to see Mum."

"Have you even considered that you came here for a reason, Jackie?" His alluring voice crept up a pitch at the end, as if it pained him to say my name.

I shook my head, bewildered.

"*Nothing,*" he put far too much emphasis on the word, "*nothing* happens by accident. You came here by the hand of Elohim, with visions that my people have been waiting centuries to hear, and your instinct is to turn tail and run?" Our eyes flickered to the rucksack by my bed, then to each other.

"I have to see my mum," I started.

"Then see her," he snapped, "You're a dream-prophet. Enter her dreams." He turned so I couldn't even glimpse his face. "Or at the very least, get some sleep. You look tired."

I gasped then, as realisation dawned on me that I was *not* dreaming. He'd just snuck into my room. *Whilst I was sleeping.* Surely that was plain creepy, no matter what the culture?

My head fell back against the pillow, mind spinning with all the words. *Elohim. Hazel thinks she hears Him. Arlan thinks He sent me here. But why? And who is Elohim? Should I be believing all this crazy stuff?* I sighed, thoughts wandering back to my Sunday-school days.

"*Why is it that people believe?*" *I asked,* "*What if it's all false?*"

The lady, my teacher, smiled gently and ruffled my hair. "*Well, the way I see it: if God is real, then to have faith is of utmost importance. But if He isn't real, then there is still no harm in leading a positive, moral life, is there?*"

"No harm," I muttered, closing my eyes as I focused, thinking of Mum. Not her appearance, but her mind, or what I perceived it to be. I wondered if she dreamt of the land of her heritage and the gardens of cherry blossoms that she'd never been to. I wondered if she dreamt of the florist store where she worked. I wondered if she dreamt of me.

Suddenly, I was in an alien place; yet it was familiar, in a way. Arrangements of stone surrounded me, accompanied by glorious greens and cherry blossoms almost as vibrant as Pylisya's. In the background stood an oriental red hut, its black roof turned up at the edges. It reminded me of the temples and buildings we'd seen on TV, just on a much smaller scale. And sitting on the doorstep was my mother.

"Mum!" I yelled, forcing my feet to move.

She didn't respond.

"Hana?" I tried, her name foreign on my tongue. She stirred, raising her head, a lot more youthful than I knew her to be. Her slim frame was highlighted by elegant, traditional garments, and her jet-black hair hung far below her shoulders. I knew, then, that I was seeing my mum as she saw herself. Young, and in the culture she believed she belonged.

Her dark eyes lit up as they recognised me. "Jackie!" she breathed, rising to meet me.

I fell into her arms. "Oh gosh, Mum, I am so sorry! This is gonna sound crazy but we fell through this mist-thing and now I'm in this weird world with elves and dwarves and-" I paused, gasping for breath.

"I know."

I stood back and examined her, incredulous. "You *know*?"

"Well, I knew this would happen someday. You didn't think we lived near a realm portal accidentally?" she deadpanned.

"Uh." For some reason, my voice wasn't working.

"Your father warned me you couldn't stay in this realm forever. I just held on to you as long as I could," she added, sadness creeping in.

"So you're, uh, fine with this?" I managed to say.

"You're there for a reason, sweetheart. Stay as long as you need. Of course I want you back," she added, "But I can't take your destiny from you. Just, look after Zel, okay?"

"S-sure," I stammered, still rather bewildered by her response. Where was the panic, the maternal concern?

"But you're safe, right? No-one's attacked?" I gazed into her eyes, my anxiety reflecting in their depths.

"The angels keep me safe. You know this," she smiled, pulling me into her arms again.

I struggled to focus. This *felt* real, though I knew full well we were not in the oriental gardens, and this conversation was only happening in our minds. In her dream. Or was I dreaming the whole thing? *No.* In my dreams, I had no control.

This was different.

Still, it did not explain her lack of concern, but upon further scrutiny I discovered the deep-seated fear in her dark eyes that she was trying so very hard to conceal from me. Evidently whatever she believed about this world, Pylisya, and my so-called 'destiny' was enough for her to want me to stay, to not come back for her. Her calm was simply a facade.

"You mentioned my father," I whispered.

Mum's brow creased, childlike confusion on her face. "Not now. It is not my place to disclose his identity," she responded firmly.

"His identity?" I echoed.

"He will tell you in due time," she said, and then the scenery around us suddenly started spinning, smacked into motion by those seven fatal words. Blossoms and leaves and the temple-like building blurred into a kaleidoscope, growing ever darker by the second. The minor control I had over the dream was slipping through my fingers, replaced with the sensation of knives cutting into my skull. I screamed, the searing pain turning my vision into a blazing white, pulling me away from Mum, away from the beauty of her fantasy...

I gasped and shot out of bed, tumbling onto the floor. The sheets slipped away from me in a damp mess, soaked through with sweat. *Gross*. But I couldn't really focus on that, nor the fact that it was dawn and we were supposed to be meeting Turvo.

Mum's last words resonated in my skull: *he will tell you in due time.*

My father is still alive.

Which only raised the questions: *how?* And why hadn't he ever made an effort to see us? I didn't even know what he looked like! All my life I gave some thought to the mystery surrounding my father, dead before my birth. I assumed him to be Caucasian - to explain my eyes and complexion - but other than that, I had no idea what he looked like, or what his personality was, or even what his *job* was. Did we share any of the same quirks? Likes? Dislikes?

If he was alive, why hadn't Mum told me? Why hadn't he visited? Was he *ashamed* of me?

Was I an accident in his eyes?

I bit my lip, curling my knees to my chest in a effort to stop the sobs from bursting out. It was silly. Heck, *I* was being silly. Clearly this world was getting to me. But inside I knew it was something more.

The story I'd believed for sixteen years had been enough to control the void that my father's absence had left, but now it shattered and the void erupted, threatening to consume me. Bile rose up my throat and trickled onto the floor as my stomach threw itself into a fit, the hole inside me expanding and expanding, wrenching my organs into its abyss.

"Jackie?"

An angelic voice broke through my suffering, but I couldn't speak, gagging on the foul substances that were flooding my mouth.

"Ah no! She's bleeding!"

"Jackie? Oh, gosh, can you hear me?"

"Jackie!"

I forced my eyes to open, coughing up the liquid in my throat so I could at least attempt to speak.

"Give me... minute..." I gasped out.

"Jackie, you're hurt," the angel said again, and I focused on his face. *Arlan.*

"Hurt?" My head was still thumping, though it was just a headache: or that was what I believed until my hand brushed my skull, coming away wet and crimson. *Did I hit my head on something? Or did the dream mess with my body?* I wondered, a little dazed.

"What did you do?" Hazel screeched then, her fists connecting with Arlan's bare chest. *Oh gosh.* My head spun again, and not because of the bleeding.

"I talked to Mum," I coughed, "In her dream. She's fine." I exhaled, my features setting into a smile, though all I really wanted to do was cry. The void was expanding, crushing my lungs, stopping my breathing, as if I'd just had a major collision. Which, in a weird way, I had.

A collision between my long-believed lie and the harsh truths of reality.

Something cool pressed against my forehead, in an attempt to stop the bleeding, I presumed. Arlan's mesmerising eyes bore into mine, distress etched onto his perfect pupils.

"I'm sorry, Jackie," he murmured, "I shouldn't have pushed you to do that."

"It's fine." The lie was heavy on my tongue. "I saw Mum. I'm not leaving yet." That part was true, at least. Hazel's eyes brightened and she smiled, her gaze drifting towards the door. I locked mine back on Arlan.

"It's fine," I repeated, the void squeezing its circumference, retreating just enough for me to breathe properly.

And somehow - despite the blood, the void, the knife of a lie destroyed - when I looked into those droplets of oceanic gems, I believed the second truth I was faking. That it was fine. Everything would be fine.

Chapter Eleven

- Benji -

For the rest of the afternoon I stayed in the music room, listening to Fírean's beautiful, heart-wrenching songs. Lanny was in a strange mood, but I was too exhausted to bother him about it, and ended up dozing off at various points. When I awoke again, the house was quiet- *too* quiet. Fírean was gone, probably up to his bedroom, as the slither of moonlight breaking through the curtains hinted that this was very late indeed. A part of me was a little hurt that I'd been forgotten, but I *had* fallen asleep behind the sofa.

Yawning, I straightened up and jogged out the room, heading to my bedroom, but something stopped me in my tracks. Barely pausing to think, I pivoted and crept up the stairs, tip-toeing towards the library where Anatti had supposedly been waiting for me, but his soft yellow was not present. I shouldn't have expected him to wait until night, so his absence was fine, yet the room wasn't empty. My breath caught in my chest, the greys hovering there terrifying me. Why were the horrid faeries in the private parts of our house? Hadn't they left with the creepy faery-king?

I glanced around, not really knowing what I was looking for, then Mali caught my attention, mewing beneath a shattered frame. Hesitant, I caressed her smooth ginger fur, then seized a shard of glass that lay beside her. The painting above us was indecipherable, obscured by the web of cracks in the glass, the largest of which was now in my hand, wrapped in a strip of cloth I'd torn from my sleeve. Kalic wouldn't mind too much.

Focus, I told myself, staring through the door at the disgusting colours, trying to eke even the slightest emotion out of them with no success. It was then that I noticed the faded yellow thrashing on the floor between them, colour draining with every second.

My mind blanked, teetering between panic and resolve, finally falling onto the latter. Without thinking, I dashed forwards, my grip on the shard tightening so much I felt the glass begin to cut into my skin, bursting through the door into a room of darkness. The stench of blood was thick in the air and I held my breath, refusing to look at anything even remotely red lest I faint again. The faeries glared down at me, all three of them, tall and imposing and horrid.

"Perfect," one hissed, "Didn't even need to bait them."

I followed his gaze to the stained body on the floor. "A-Anatti?" I stammered, dizziness rushing over me. The regal elf I barely knew lay in a puddle of crimson, his white robes stained, colour pulsing very weakly. My eyes darted to the mortal blade in the faery's hand, dripping with the same colour as my grandfather.

In that moment something within me snapped. I screamed and suddenly the faeries were screaming too, their colours flaring white, pain ripping through everyone in the room. I was hurting but I didn't care, I just wanted to make *them* hurt, to hurt worse than the ripples punching through me, worse than the thrashing of my grandfather, worse than Fírean's pain at the nasty horrible things spoken over him-

"Benji! Stop!" Ethlon's yell morphed into a scream as he entered my threshold. A grin spread across my face. I had power and they were hurting, all hurting because of me. *Filthy, wretched urthets.* They deserved it.

"Ahh! Benji, you have to stop this! Listen to me!" Ethlon shrieked, his hand connecting with my face. I gasped and staggered backwards, the colours around me resuming their normal greys and silvers. Someone shuddered and collapsed to the ground. Another lay still, no trace of colour left in them.

"E-Ethlon," I stammered, my voice sounding awfully raw. I couldn't tear my gaze from the blood on the floor, which wasn't just Anatti's anymore.

"Benji," Ethlon managed to gasp out, "What have you-" He stopped and stared at the one faery left standing, their grey darkening to a violent red. A flicker of satisfaction dashed through their colour as well, though why they were satisfied at their comrades' situation I couldn't understand.

"So you tried," the faery said, their monotone gruff and masculine, "You tried to keep another from me. Honourable." His eyes flickered over my body and I trembled, my feet frozen in terror.

"So young, as well. Pity." Colours flashed and he lunged at me, in the same second that Ethlon flared white, gasping and clutching at his chest. My head spun at the dark stains on the floor, their bitter, salty scent causing bile to rise in my throat.

"Look what you did, foolish child!" the faery screeched. I backed up, stumbling out of the door and into another faery, her grey mass impenetrable.

Instinctively I thrust the glass behind me, but she caught it, tearing the shard from my hand with ease.

"Tria should've warned us what she'd picked up," that faery lilted and my pulse accelerated.

"D-don't kill me," I stammered as the male approached with a bloodied knife.

"Oh, we won't kill you. *Yet*," he laughed, and then my vision went dark.

The strange thing was, I could still see their colours. I just couldn't breathe very well and something rough rubbed against my face, chafing the skin. I tried to cry out but a hand slipped up into my dark seclusion and shoved something hard and bitter into my mouth. In my attempt to spit it out I ended up gagging, nostrils flaring with the effort to take in the air I really needed. My feet stumbled against the marble floor, my eyes were useless, as were my hands that were held firmly together; but I could still see the colours, just about. Fírean was not far, though Lanny seemed quite occupied with Jackie and the little brown one, both of which were sleeping.

I tried to scream again, but the thing in my mouth wouldn't let any noise come out. So I snorted loudly through my nose, which only resulted in snot splattering against the fabric and subsequently rubbing against my face. *Gross*.

Someone kicked me in the back of my shin, not too hard, but enough that it made me lose my balance. I went completely limp then, pretending to be asleep, waiting for their grip to loosen, my thoughts wandering. Where were my family? How were these creeps taking me without anyone noticing?

Wait. Kalic was watching from the shadows; I suddenly sensed his metallic red.

Kalic! Help me! I cried out mentally, hoping he was close enough.

Hold on, he urged, and I resisted the urge to fight back against the stone grips, instead choosing to trust him.

"Which way?" one of the faeries hissed suddenly and my twin's colour flashed grey with fear.

"Way to where?" he stammered.

"Out of here, of course." The screech of a sword being drawn sounded loud, even in my covered ears. "Open that passage."

What are you doing? I cried out silently as Kalic slowly trudged forwards, obeying.

Trust me!

We stumbled down a cold, stone passage – rather, the *faeries* stumbled, I simply let them drag me, though my feet were getting sore again – winding down and down so the harsh colour of Kalic was fainter by the second, drifting away so I could no longer hear his thoughts. Yet the colours of my other family members seemed to grow stronger with each step of our descent, the musky air growing strangely familiar, though I couldn't quite place it.

One of the faeries started muttering and I strained to decipher their flowing words. "Can't believe we got so lucky," he was saying, "Both targets in the same place."

"No thanks to our little friend," the one holding me laughed, and I frowned, confused. *Who are they referring to? Mali, perhaps?*

It was then that I realised where we were: in one of the old, hidden passageways that Kalic and I liked to play in, at least up until a few seasons ago.

Thank you, Kal, I thought, though I doubted he could hear me. I took a deep breath through my nose and focused, locking my limbs together, waiting, waiting-

"Ah!" One of my captors tripped over a stone I'd fallen over many times before and I threw myself from his grasp, hitting the floor with a flash of white slicing through me. Instinctively I rolled, knocking the lever to a second, smaller passage I'd discovered completely by accident. I rolled into that as well, waiting for the gentle grunt of stone as the walls automatically slid closed, sealing me in. Now my hands reached for the cloth, tugging it off my head and pulling the gross fabric from my mouth so I could breathe properly again. They were still tied together but I could work with it, especially with my full sight back. I scurried away from the greys, running straight into a room where Atti and Turvo were waiting- though, not for me.

"Benji, what?" Atti exclaimed, then he took in my appearance. I doubled over, breathing heavily.

"Faeries," I gasped out, "There's faeries and Anatti-"

"Shh, Benji," Atti soothed as Turvo hurriedly untied my wrists, "It's alright. You're safe now."

I hugged Turvo and my brother returned the embrace somewhat awkwardly, patting my curls. "What in Pylisya happened?" he asked, agitated.

"There were faeries, they got me, and Anatti he was hurt," I stumbled over the words, tears welling in my eyes and threatening to fall.

Atti stiffened, his orange flashing. "Hurt? How bad?"

My fists clenched in Turvo's shirt as the vivid image of Anatti's fading colour rose unbidden, pushing the moisture from my eyes.

"R-really bad," I cried, pressing myself against my brother. Turvo's arms encompassed me fully, his green fading to blue.

"It's okay," he started, "He'll be okay-"

"No he won't!" I exclaimed, pushing back and rubbing my eyes, "It was *really* bad, Turvo!"

He bristled, flaring red.

"I'm not stupid!" I continued, voice rising to a yell, "I know he's badly hurt! Stop trying to pacify me!"

I kicked a random breakable object over, grimacing as it hit the floor and shattered, then set my face firm and stormed out of the room, almost colliding with a stone-faced Ethlon in the process. To my surprise - and relief - he ignored me, instead occupying the space I'd just left, his usually placid silver displaying tinges of blue.

"King Myranis is dead," he whispered.

Silence descended so heavily that I froze, my brain slowly processing the horrific realisation that *I was right.*

He's gone.

"Long live the king."

Atti bowed his head, blue flooding his colour. I stood like a statue in the doorway, struggling to comprehend the finality.

"D-dead?" I stammered, my scarlet completely evaporated.

"Yes," Turvo said harshly, "He's dead."

My expression must've been blank because he huffed rather loudly in exasperation.

"Dead! Gone! How am I supposed to explain it?"

"I know what it means," I whispered, "His colour was fading... I..." I choked off, turning away as tears started to fall again.

He's gone. Anatti is gone, he's never waking up, his colour is all faded and it's my fault...

"Who?" Atti hissed, pain so heavy in his words that the crimson blazed into me, though I didn't understand what he was asking.

"A faery assassin. He was dead too, though." Ethlon's eyes flickered to me again and my gut twisted. *Was that my fault too?* I wanted to ask the question, but something was locking my mouth shut.

"Cause of death?" Turvo, ever the gore-lover, presented the question rather eagerly.

"Not in front of *him*," Atti muttered, so low I doubted anyone else heard.

Ethlon tensed up. "Unknown. But it appears the faery's insides have... *imploded*."

"Imploded?" Turvo echoed, inappropriate delight seeping through him.

"Imploded?" I also repeated, confusion lacing my tone, "What's that?"

No-one would answer my question. Instead, Atti's hazy eyes drifted to my face. "Go and get Arlan," he commanded, "Turvo, you find Fírean. Then Benji, just... go and see the new girls or something." He waved his hand dismissively and I bit my lip before running out of the room again, my emotions thrusting themselves into complete turmoil.

Now away from the solemn atmosphere, the fear in me resurfaced. I was *terrified*, not that I'd openly admit that to anyone. The faeries had tried to kidnap me! Only then did the true gravity of that settle and I ran faster, as if I could get away from the situation. But no amount of running could change the fact that the faeries were after me and they'd *murdered* my grandfather.

Why? Why did they want me? And if they wanted *me*, why had they murdered *him*?

I stopped suddenly as a shot of crimson burst through me, coming from someone else. Glancing around, I noticed that I'd completed a full circuit in the house and was outside the guest's room. Lanny's gold flickered near the door, accompanied by the nice brown, and crimson-streaked cerulean.

Jackie is hurt? Why?

Cautiously I pushed the door open, slipping through the gap and tugging on Lanny's robe.

"Benji? Are you alright?" he asked, without even glancing down to look at me.

"Atti needs to see you," I said, "It's Anatti, he... he's gone." My voice broke as Lanny looked down at me, his face unusually pale and tight.

"Gone?" he echoed.

I nodded and he frowned, turning back to Jackie. "I won't be long, I promise," he whispered, before running out the room. I let the door shut behind him and stared curiously at Jackie, whose expression almost matched mine.

"What do you mean by gone?" she enquired gently.

"Dead. Anatti is dead." The words were so heavy on my tongue and I burst into tears again, half-collapsing into Jackie's arms. She stiffened at first but pulled me near, her heart labouring against my ear.

"Shh, Benji, it'll be alright," she soothed, rocking us back and forth like Mutti used to do when I was a baby. For once, I wasn't bothered by the childish treatment as it calmed me, stopping the crying.

"I'm so confused," I mumbled into her tunic, which smelt a lot like Turvo.

"I'm pretty confused too," she confessed, the crimson slowly receding from her colour.

"About what?" I asked, looking up into her peculiar green eyes that were wet like mine, the pale skin beneath them glistening. Above them, a thin, darker line broke her brow, tracing from her scalp down to the bridge of her nose, which I was pretty certain hadn't been there before.

She sighed. "A lot of things, I'm not sure you'd understand. Not because of your age," she added quickly, as if she knew my response, "but... well, I'm from another world, Benji. And recently so much has changed, I don't know what's real or not anymore..."

"This," I said, touching her hand, "This is real. And this." I pointed to her chest, then at mine. "Our colours, emotions. They're real."

A trickle of a smile crept across her face. "Arlan had a similar response to you," she whispered, emeralds glazing over.

I looked down at my hands, the skin on my wrists red from the restraints, but that wasn't what concerned me. Specks of reddish-brown were dotted across the backs of my hands and my left palm, which I realised now was leaking crimson liquid. I curled my hand into a fist, staring with fascination at the trails seeping through my fingers. It should hurt me to do that, and I waited for the flash of white pain, but there was nothing.

I was entirely numb; that realisation frightened me.

Jackie remained silent, her colour clouded in thought, so I squirmed out of her arms and just sat on the floor, my body feeling too tired and *weird* to do anything properly.

"Is God real?" she mused suddenly, staring at something past me. I blanked.

"Uh?"

"Elohim. Is He real?"

I mouthed the name, shimmers of pleasant white and orange and yellow coming over me, temporarily cutting through my numbness. "Well I think so. Tastes real. And Lanny says He is."

Her eyes widened. "Tastes? Wait, is Hazel real?"

"Hazel," I muttered, soft brown touching me, "That's Hazel?" I pointed to a short, pretty girl sat on the other side of the room. Jackie nodded, her mouth agape.

"Whoa. That's kinda creepy," Hazel commented, pink creeping into her colour. I turned my attention fully to her then. Straight hair so dark it was almost black flowed down to below her shoulders, resting only a handspan from her waist. It complimented her coppery complexion, which darkened over her rounded cheeks, gaining a reddish tinge. She was shorter than me, but had a stockier build, and her brown eyes were lighter than mine, very similar to the colour of her name.

"But very cool!" Jackie exclaimed and I tore my gaze from Hazel. Her eyes and colour both lit up as she continued, "Thanks, Benji. You really helped distract me... but, oh gosh, your grandfather! I'm really sorry, I-"

"It's okay," I shrugged, "I... I'm not too upset over him. More shocked, I think," I replied, trying to put a name to my emotions.

"Oh. Still, I'm sorry... Wasn't he the king?"

"Yeah."

"So your father is now the king!" She smiled at me enthusiastically, but could not hide the dread seeping through her colour. I frowned, not really understanding, but quickly controlled my expression so she'd stop talking at me.

"Gonna find Kal," I mumbled, backing away and slipping out of the room, a strange grey-blue settling over me. Atti and Lanny were hurting - I could sense the blue in them even from this distance - but why was *I* hurting so bad? What was this strange feeling crashing down on me?

As my mind wandered so did my feet, taking me circling around the house. Every trace of faery was gone, but still I was not at all at ease. Something had shifted. Atti's colour was more resolved. Jackie's and Ethlon's words seemed to claim that Atti was-

I gasped, halting suddenly and almost falling over in the process. *Atti is the king now. Is he going to leave us? Do we have to move? What's going to happen to my family?*

No answers entered my mind.

Chapter Twelve

- Jackie -

I stared blankly at the wall, my mind struggling to process the severity of the situation. King Myranis was dead.

It had happened sooner than I'd expected.

"Argh!" I screamed, punching the pillow beside me and making Hazel jump. *Why* hadn't I said anything? I knew this was coming, yet, somehow...

You haven't accepted who you are, Jackie. I can't work with you until that happens.

I froze and glanced around the room, searching for the source of the voice, but found only Hazel staring at me, confusion etched on her dark face.

"Jackie? Are you alright?" she enquired gently.

"I... I need a minute," I replied lamely, standing and slowly walking out of the room. Once I was clear of the doorway, I broke into a run, bounding down the now-familiar steps and out into the crisp air. My lungs expanded, inhaling as much of the freshness as they could, and as I stared at the beautiful greenery it started to rain. Fat droplets pounded against my skull, running trails down my skin, soaking the thin tunic I wore until I was shivering, yet I could not bring myself to move. How could this world still look perfect, when clearly it was falling apart?

Everything was falling apart, really. Including me. Who was I, really? Just a silly, pathetic girl whose weird dreams got her caught up in a crazy world and made her feel *guilty* for the murder of someone she barely knew.

Jackie, my child. Stop thinking of yourself like that. You are more than just a girl.

I resisted the urge to glance around and instead whispered, "Who are you?"

I am who I am. People call me by many names. In this world, I am-

"Elohim," I breathed, in the same moment that He said it. A wave of dizziness flooded over me, but it was accompanied by warmth, and despite the pouring rain I felt as comfortable as if I'd been sitting by a slow-burning fire. *Whoa. Big Guy is talking to* me? *This is crazy!*

Jackie, listen. I have called you to a greater purpose here. The heir of Zeraphin spoke correctly: this world has awaited your coming. And now you must explore the gifts that I have bestowed on you.

"So what I saw in my dreams was real? It's going to happen that way?" My gut twisted as the memories started to play, but I suppressed them.

That is one possibility, yes. Ultimately it is up to him, and whether he chooses to accept his destiny or not. Still, do not let the fear of the future stop you; rather, know that all will go according to My plan, and you can help set it in motion.

"Set it in motion? But I don't want-"

Things will turn out for the best, Jackie. Listen to me.

"I'm listening," I said, my heartbeat accelerating.

Then do not fear. Your mother is safe and your sister will be too. As for you, my child... stop running. Come to me. Learn how best to use your gifts and help this world I have brought you to.

"I won't run from this," I vowed, "I still don't understand it all, but if I can help set things right... then I'll try my best."

A whisper brushed against my ear, then the dizziness evaporated, but the warmth I felt remained. I hugged my chest, gazing out into the rain with a newfound sense of peace. *It is going to be alright. I wasn't lying to myself then.* Miraculously, the void inside me wasn't straining or expanding; rather it seemed to be shrinking, enough that it wasn't occupying my mind and emotions. Instead my mind drifted, wandering through the dreams that I now knew were visions, perceiving them with clearer eyes, more understanding-

"Jackie?"

The voice pulled me back to reality and I turned slowly. There stood Arlan, his angelic features twisted into a heart-stopping grief. My breathing hitched as he drew closer, his eyes dull, like in my nightmare.

"Arlan," I blurted out, "If... if you knew something was going to happen, would you let yourself get close anyway? Even though you knew the outcome would be a tragedy?"

"This *is* a tragedy," he replied dimly, then his brow furrowed. "Are you saying... you knew?"

Oh gosh. I could barely breathe as I nodded slightly. "I- I didn't know it was going to be this soon..."

"Why didn't you tell me?" he exploded, his eyes igniting. I took a step back, the torrential rain forming a curtain between us.

"I knew but I... I wasn't certain... Arlan I'm so sorry," I gasped, tears streaking down my face to blend with the rain, "I don't think I could've stopped it though..."

His jaw set firm as he looked over me with a cold expression that froze all the warmth. "I don't know what to think," he hissed, "You absolutely infuriate me, Jackie."

I blanked. *Infuriate? Where did that come from?*

"One moment you're my friend, next you're sneaking out behind my back... and now you're hiding more things from me. Why are you doing this?" he yelled, his voice paralysing me.

"I'm staying now," I managed to whisper.

"Not here. We're moving to the capital," he said harshly, the rain seeming to chisel his expression.

I almost choked on thin air. "Y-you can't," I stammered, "The faeries, they want you dead. All of you."

One delicate eyebrow arched. "That's nothing new. Besides, we will be safer in the capital."

"Send Benji away." The command in my voice surprised me, but I retained the sudden cool.

"Why?" Arlan's voice crept up a pitch, as if distressed by the notion, and the harshness faded from his expression, replaced by a child-like vulnerability.

"If you take him to the capital, your enemies will find him. He has to be sent away." My confidence surged, fuelled by what I'd realised were not just mine and Benji's fears combined, but possible futures.

Futures that I could prevent.

"I've seen it," I continued, "I've seen what they will do to him. But if you send him to the Northlands with Ethlon, then he will be safe."

Arlan regarded me more calmly. "I see," he murmured, "but why the Northlands?"

I shrugged. "It's what I saw. Listen, Arlan, up until - well, a few minutes ago - I didn't have control. Not really. But now I know. I talked with Elohim," I explained, excitement creeping in, "and now I understand part of what I'm here to do. I couldn't save your grandfather, but I *can* save your brother. Please, believe me."

"I do," he whispered and then he was right in front of me, his scent intoxicating me. I inhaled the air he'd just exhaled - our faces were that close - and nearly fainted.

"Don't do that," I complained, with the little oxygen I had left. The rain was still falling and I knew my hair was a soaked, matted mess, but his was still heavenly wavy.

"Do what?" he murmured, moving even closer so all I could look at was his beautiful eyes, returned to their dazzling blue. I'd forgotten what we were even talking about.

"Thi-" I started to say, then his lips were on mine, silencing me.

It was like nothing I'd expected, or even dreamt about. At first I was stiff, my lips granite, but his kept pressing until I relented, my body seeming to know exactly what to do, despite having never kissed a boy before. *Not that Arlan can be called a boy,* my fuddled brain noted as his scent, his *being*, entirely overwhelmed me. I was breathing him in, my hands reaching up and tangling in those beautiful curls. Passion ignited within my chest and I knew I should probably stop, but I was so deep in his eyes that I simply couldn't find the strength. It didn't help that he was kissing me with an equal fury, his hands in my hair, trailing down my back, pressing the damp tunic against my skin-

Gasping, he suddenly tore his lips from mine and clamped his hands behind his back. I swayed and stared at him, breathless and dizzy all at once. My heart screamed for me to glue my lips to his again, but I managed to restrain myself.

"I'm sorry," he panted, a delicate blush spreading over his cheeks. I nodded and focused purely on breathing, my lungs desperately replenishing oxygen.

"I mean, I'm not sorry I kissed you," he added, "I just... well I... I probably should've asked first."

I continued staring at him, amused to hear him stammer over his words. His words about *me*.

"It's alright," I mumbled, still in a daze, "I didn't mind." *Actually, I really liked it. Kiss me again.*

No! one part of me screamed, *Danger! Don't get attached! You know you'll have to leave-*

I promptly ignored it, watching the trickles of rain highlight the contours of his face and wishing that my fingers could copy that motion.

"I went a little far," he was saying, partly to himself. I tensed up, trying to stop the hurt that darted through me.

"I've never kissed anyone before," I confessed.

"Me neither." He took a step towards me again, hands still behind his back. "In my culture, a kiss is sacred. Each one is to be treasured, and only shared with someone you deeply love." His eyes locked on mine and my heartbeat accelerated, pounding so fast I thought I was going to have an attack.

"Truth is, I love you," Arlan murmured, "And I know it sounds crazy, or irrational, but I'm falling. From the moment I set eyes on you, I started falling, and I can't stop."

I couldn't breathe. "You said I infuriate you," I stupidly reminded him, as my vision blurred.

"Ha!" He threw his head back, staring directly into the rain, then turned back to me. "I said it wrong. I'm more infuriated with *myself* and how I react around you." His voice lowered, as if this was some sort of confession. "I've been trained my whole life how to talk to people. Diplomacy is key. But with you... Everything just goes out the window. My emotions make me say things wrong. I don't have the right words and I just... I'm so *confused* by this. The only explanation I have is that I love you."

"The feeling's mutual," I whispered, leaning in closer to him. He reached out a hand and caressed my cheek gently.

"Which one?" he asked, his breath warming my cheeks.

"All of them," I replied, locking my eyes with his. He smiled and pulled me close again, our lips connecting as I drowned in those glorious blue oceans.

This was falling, and it was beautiful.

When we returned inside, the atmosphere was cold and solemn as servants bustled around silently, preparing for a funeral, I guessed by all the black drapes and pale flowers. Yet something *was* different. My perspective had shifted, like I was viewing the world with a different lens. Suddenly these elves, these *people*, were *my* people. I felt a swell of responsibility for them, for the future of their world. Not only that, but I was all warm and fuzzy inside. Whether it was Elohim or Arlan or a combination of both, I didn't care; I was glad to not be hurting from the void anymore.

My hand was entwined with Arlan's, a move that I'd explained to him was romantic in my culture. I guessed we were 'dating' now, though the term didn't seem right. Our declarations of love had come so early, yet it didn't feel that way. Maybe because I'd dreamt it, seen us together many times over. Or maybe that was the way the gears of Pylisya ticked. Whatever the reason, I was *not* looking forward to explaining to Hazel that yes, I was in love with an elf prince, and he reciprocated it: a fact I still didn't fully comprehend.

"Lanny!"

Benji ran over to us then, tears streaming down his freckled face. Arlan released my hand to embrace his brother, cradling him gently.

"Shh, Benji. We'll be alright," he soothed.

I stepped away awkwardly, feeling like an intruder in their situation. My eyes darted across the hall and fell on Kalic, standing near a large dresser. Hesitantly I approached him, observing his tense stature.

"Kalic, what's wrong?" I enquired softly.

To my surprise Kalic started crying as well. "I hurt Benji," he sobbed, hands balling into fists.

I knelt down so we were eye-to-eye. "Hurt Benji? How?"

"We were supposed to meet Anatti but he never turned up, I waited and waited and then faeries came," he explained, his voice shaking, "and they were going to kill me unless I helped them to get out, which I did, but I sent them on a path that Benji knew so he could escape and-"

"Wait, Benji got kidnapped?" I exclaimed. *How big a target does he have on him?*

Kalic nodded. "But afterwards he asked me what happened," he continued, "and I got really mad and hit him. I didn't mean to!" Distress etched itself into his voice and I opened my arms. He paused but let me hug him, stiff at first, but after a few moments he relaxed and cried into my shoulder.

"I'm sure Benji will forgive you, Kal," I whispered, "He'll be okay."

"No, that's the issue! Benji is *not* fine. I know he's weird but he's been getting weirder and that Ethlon guy isn't helping, if anything he's making it worse! And one of the faeries died, Turvo told me he thinks Benji did it, and I'm scared, Jackie! What's happening to my brother?" Kalic pulled back and stared at me with large, dark eyes: which, I noted, did not have the silvery lids that Benji's did.

"I don't-" I began, but something strange happened. A rush of light surged through me and more words were suddenly flooding out of my mouth in a melodic torrent that I couldn't stop.

"Benji will be fine. His powers are growing as he ages and they are nothing to worry about at the moment. Ethlon will train him to master them, and become the greatest Chroma that Pylisya has ever seen. His destiny is bigger than you could imagine, but he will still need you, Kalic. Your bond is one that can never be broken. Stay by his side and do not be afraid: not of him, nor for him."

I gasped as the heat evaporated, the words that were not mine still hovering in the air. Kalic nodded mutely, serenity settling over his face, making him seem more like Benji than before. Blood rushed to my cheeks as I realised that Arlan's family were all watching me, processing the curious words that I myself did not understand. What was a Chroma? How 'big', exactly, was Benji's destiny? I suspected I'd seen parts of it, but not enough to piece it all together. And what about this 'bond' between Benji and Kalic? Was it simply a twins' relationship, or something more?

Elohim, there is so much I don't understand... How can I ever help these people?

"- coming with us," Arlan was saying, and I frowned at him in confusion.

"I'm sorry," I mumbled, "I didn't catch a word of what you just said. Any of you."

Arlan smiled ever so slightly. "It's alright, Benji told us you were lost in thought."

I blinked and stared at the small elf, looking more frightened and young than I'd ever seen him. His dark eyes reflected my confusion and his lips moved as if he wanted to ask me something, but the words wouldn't come out. I thanked him, but all he could manage was a tight smile as he clung to Fírean.

"When do we leave?" that elf asked. His expression was melancholy on the best of days, but now Fírean looked like he was about to have a complete breakdown. I knew that feeling all too well.

"Hang on," interjected Turvo, "I want to know what Jackie meant. What exactly is a Chroma? And Benji-"

"First, do not *ever* use that word unless you want to draw the cobrai's attention," Arazair scolded, "and second, it is not your business what words are spoken over Benji."

Turvo clamped his mouth shut, rather embarrassed at being reprimanded by his father in front of many onlookers.

"As for your question, Fír," Arazair continued, turning to his second son, "We will leave after the first funeral." His voice barely wavered, but his eyes, dark like Benji's, betrayed his true emotion. I bit my lip, unable to imagine what it was like to be in his shoes. To lose your parent and then have to take on the responsibility of ruling an entire nation...

"First funeral?"

I shot a glare at Hazel for her rather unsympathetic questioning, but Arlan answered smoothly.

"We have our family funeral here, then the second one is in Torindell. That is for the public to attend as well," he explained.

She and I both nodded our thanks, then all eyes turned to Arazair, the new king. I wanted to ask when his coronation would be, but the topic was far too sensitive, so I left it unsaid. He didn't say much else, dismissing everyone to go and start packing, but as he walked away his shoulders lowered and he leant into Kalia, the very picture of grief.

I turned back around and found that Arlan was the only one left in the hall. "Are you alright?" I asked, then realised what a stupid question it was.

He grimaced. "No, but I will be, in time." He sighed, eyes drifting across the room. "I'm the heir now, Jackie. It's a lot to take in, especially with the target on our heads."

"You won't be assassinated," I said firmly, which generated another small smile.

"Thanks, but I'm worried that it'll be my father next. I'm not in any way prepared for the throne. Anatti ruled peacefully for nearly two centuries. He had Arazair well into his prime," Arlan added, taking in my startled expression, "but how am I supposed to live up to that? How is my father supposed to live up to that? The faeries don't like him, that's why we don't live in the capital!"

His voice pitched at the end, anxiety replacing the grief on his face. "I-I'm sorry, Jackie, I-"

"Arlan, you don't need to apologise!" I exclaimed, "It's perfectly normal for you to worry, given this situation, okay? I'm sure your father will be fine."

"Are you? Are you actually sure?" His blue eyes locked on mine, hard as steel. "Can you look at me and say with absolute certainty that my father will survive the next five years?"

I squirmed under his gaze, my throat knotted too tight to speak.

"I thought not," he murmured, then he turned to walk away.

"No, wait!" I cried, "Stop! I don't know for certain but I also don't know if something bad will happen or not. I haven't seen anything like that," I finished, fumbling over the words.

"I'm just going to pack my things," he said coolly, without looking around.

I glared at the waves of blond cascading down his back. "No! You said I infuriate you, but you... you do the same! Stop going all cold on me, Arlan! I thought our walls were down..." I trailed off then, because he was gone, my words falling on thin air.

So much for romance, I thought sarcastically, before I, too, turned my back, headed into a pit of uncertainty.

Chapter Thirteen

- Benji -

The world rushed past in a flood of colours, some warm and vibrant, others bleached and cold. Mali curled up against my feet, having reunited with me after the terrifying encounter with the faeries, which I didn't blame her for. Her purr was soothing and the flow of her turquoise helped a little to calm the churning of my stomach.

I clutched a few small pots of lifeless colour in my hand, the only paints Mutti said I could take with me initially. The rest of our belongings would follow in a subsequent carriage, due to arrive after the main funeral. *Funeral.* It was a strange word, because there was nothing 'fun' at all about the event. I'd decided very early on that I did not like funerals. Everything was black and smelly, the colours of dying flowers gave me a small headache, and Ethlon seemed to drone on forever about resting places and heavenly souls. Or was that resting souls and heavenly places? I really hadn't paid enough attention.

Kalic sat opposite me in the confined carriage, refusing to meet my gaze the whole of the journey so far, blocking me from his mind as well. My chest still hurt a little from where he'd hit me, but I was definitely 'over it', as Turvo would say. We rode with Mutti and Fírean, whereas Atti and my other brothers were on horses of their own, instead of a carriage. I could sense Jackie and Hazel as well, sharing a horse that travelled closely to Lanny's. But worse was the second carriage, where Anatti's lifeless body lay. It was shut in a wooden box, but I could still *see* the faded colour, a slight yellow-grey. Why they couldn't just bury him in the ground, I didn't understand. That was what Turvo had done with his old horse. But according to Atti, the 'public' had to see him before we could do that. Another thing I didn't understand: why would anyone want to see a dead body? They were absolutely horrid.

I shuddered and stared out of the window again, watching as the forests turned to fields which then became marked with cold, colourless paths. Those stone paths cut through the green landscape, multiple trails linking up to the path that we were travelling on. I craned my neck, stretching to catch my first glimpse of our destination: Torindell.

It wasn't what I'd expected. For some reason my mind had conjured up a beautiful city with wooden huts and large trees and elegant architecture that thrummed with the colours of a thousand little insects. But in reality, Torindell was cold. White-washed stone walls rose many spans high, turning the city into a fortress that was almost impossible to break in to. Various angles of slanted roofs conjoined to form a mosaic of false colour that surrounded the masterpiece at the city's heart. It was an elegantly adorned castle, painted in the same pearl white as the walls outside the city. The turrets appeared to be fashioned from gold, giving the castle an elaborate yet vulnerable finish. Its gold wasn't warm like Lanny, though; it was cooler, harder, and made me feel uncomfortable.

Beside me Kalic gasped, his colour pulsing as he took in the view. I studied his reaction.

"Wow! That's incredible!" he exclaimed, and I frowned. *Incredible* was not the word I was thinking of. More like rigid. Imposing. Unfriendly.

I wanted to go back home, but apparently *this* was going to be our home now.

The carriage stopped just inside the city walls and a dwarf opened the door, bowing his bearded head as Mutti and Atti stepped out. Kalic moved to follow, but I hesitated, staring down at the creamy stones. They'd been white once, but the sun had tarnished their fake colour, making it even more disgusting.

"Come on, Benji. It's alright," Mutti said, her blue eyes encouraging. I took a deep breath and stepped out, immediately wrapping my arms around Kalic, who didn't seem to mind for once. Mali trotted out behind me, rubbing against my legs with another soothing purr, and my twin returned the embrace. His red was clouded as he continued to absorb our surroundings, clearly mesmerised. I hadn't really been paying attention, so I decided I should try and focus, too. And then the colours hit me.

Red, yellow, green, blue, brown, grey, purple. Every tone and every shade in between. They surrounded me, advancing, blurring into a harsh mess of all the wrong combinations. I screamed as the colours were accompanied by unfamiliar noises. Voices and clanging and more voices and a loud buzzing that was making me *really* dizzy...

I swayed, clamping my hands over my ears to try and block out the horrendous noise. Closing my eyes didn't help the colours, it made them worse, because then I couldn't see my family and their presence helped me a little. Mutti tried to talk to me but I only saw her lips moving; the words she spoke were lost in the air, mixed up with the buzzing and other talking and the screaming, the latter of which I thought was coming from me, but I wasn't sure anymore.

Lanny ran over and scooped me up, his gold only succeeding in dulling down the other colours. I buried my head in his chest, sobbing, my fingers caressing the smooth folds of his tunic. He, too, was speaking to me - I felt his vocal cords vibrate - but, like with Mutti, I couldn't hear him. I think I must've voiced that because he stopped trying and then we were running through the streets, as we had done in Kikarsko. Colours whirled past us, completely overwhelming, and I screamed again, for them to *go away*, please just *go away...*

Eventually the colours stopped, but I didn't release my grip on Lanny's tunic.

"Shh, Benji, it's alright. You're safe here," he soothed.

"Too many colours," I choked out.

Jackie approached, her cerulean tinted, the turquoise of Mali right on her heels. In the rush, I hadn't noticed them following us.

"I told you," Jackie stated, the unspoken 'so' hanging thick in the air.

"Aye, and I should've listened." Lanny gentled untangled my hands from his clothes and set me down on the soft grass. I glanced around, trying to get my bearings. The only colours were those of Lanny, Jackie, and Mali, all of which calmed me. Torindell's harsh white walls sat on my left, far enough away that I couldn't sense the horrid mulch of colours.

"Thank you," I whispered, my voice breaking. Clearly I'd strained it from all my screaming.

"Benji... We need to talk." Lanny's gold was suddenly far too serious for my liking and I tensed up instinctively.

"Wh-what?" I stammered, gazing into his bright eyes.

"Benji, you need to leave. Wait, hear me out," he interjected, as I started to protest, "You know that Torindell is not safe for you, I just didn't realise how badly it would affect you... I should've known, with all the colours and-" He paused, struggling to phrase it.

But as much as I hated to admit it, I knew what he was trying to say, and I knew that he was right. My family were in danger. The creepy faeries had wanted *me* and Anatti was dead because of it.

All this... it was *my* fault.

Just as I'd feared.

Mali trotted over and jumped into my lap, and I immediately concentrated on running my hands through her fur, a lump forming in my throat.

"Not alone, of course," Lanny continued, "Ethlon will go with you, to teach you how to better use your powers. Jackie – I mean, *I* – was thinking, perhaps the Northlands?"

And Jackie was involved, I should've known. Yet I didn't feel threatened by her anymore. She and Lanny had a connection I didn't understand, but it was different to what linked me to Lanny. Both of them wanted me to be safe, so I decided to trust her. For now.

"Northlands," I repeated, then it dawned on me, "Thorn?"

"The dwarf!" Jackie exclaimed, "Of course! Arlan, remember that young dwarf? I'm sure Benji would be welcome with him. Wow," she continued, now muttering, "Elohim really does have things figured out..."

"Elohim?"

All gold and white and yellow and *nice*.

Jackie's colour flushed with embarrassment. "Uh, yeah, Elohim spoke with me. About you, Benji."

My heart swelled. "He spoke? About me?" I grinned at Lanny, yellow rushing through me. "You were right, Lanny! He does care!"

"Of course He does, little one," Lanny laughed, ruffling my curls. I reached for his hand and hugged it tightly to my chest, part of me never wanting to let go. My emotions were going haywire; one moment I wanted to run, then stay, then run again. Now I really wasn't sure of anything, other than three things.

First, this 'power' that I had was dangerous, to me and to those I loved, because people were after me.

Second, Lanny only ever wanted the best for me. Torindell was horrid: I wouldn't survive there and he knew it.

Third, Elohim *did* care for me. How much, or what that meant, I did not know; but if He was talking to me through Jackie, then I should listen.

My mind drifted and I suddenly remembered Jackie's strange conversation with Kalic, about me and Ethlon. I honestly hadn't paid much attention at the time, but now I considered it again, it made a little more sense. Big words like 'destiny' and 'Chroma' scared me, but words like 'bond' offered comfort. Kalic would be with me; I was much stronger with my other half.

"I'll go," I said then, loosening my hold on Lanny. He blinked and stared down at me in shock.

"Really?"

I nodded, trying very hard to hide the fear that was suddenly erupting in me. "But only if Kalic comes too," I added.

Lanny's face paled further. "Kal, too? I don't know if I..." He trailed off, crimson lacing gold.

"Arlan. Remember what was said," Jackie murmured and I strained to hear, "Elohim spoke through me, somehow. Kalic and Benji have a bond, you can't deprive them of that. Besides, dwarves like to make things, don't they? Kalic would be happy there."

"Onta Baelthar has always wanted to return to the Northlands," Lanny mused, the crimson receding, "I'll see what I can do."

"Onta?" Jackie echoed, confusion clouding her cerulean.

"My mother's brother," he explained.

"Oh, like an uncle," she muttered in understanding, though I had no clue what an 'uncle' was.

I leant over and tugged on Jackie's tunic, wanting them to stop all the boring grown-up talk. She glanced down at me, slightly surprised. "What is it, Benji?"

"You said lots of big things. What's Chroma?" I asked. The word tasted rather familiar - a soft, gentle silver - with a deeper undertone that I didn't like.

Jackie shrugged. "I'm sorry, Benji, I don't know. This is all strange for me too," she confessed, "But I assure you, everything's going to work out. I'm not sure how, yet, but in due time it'll be revealed to me."

"Okay." I hesitated, then climbed into her lap and put my arms around her neck, ignoring Mali's mewl of protest as the cat tumbled off into the grass.

"Look after my Lanny," I whispered in Jackie's ear, "And Fír, please."

"I will," she replied, her cerulean surrounding me.

"Promise?"

"Promise," she affirmed, returning my hug.

"Jackie? Can we, uh, talk?" Lanny asked gently, his colour pulsing with grey. I wriggled out of Jackie's arms and stared at my brother quizzically.

"Alone, or-?" Jackie didn't finish the question, but I guessed what she was asking.

"No, Benji can stay. He needs to hear this too."

I settled into a more comfortable position, Mali snuggling against me again, and tilted my ears so I was most alert to whatever Lanny was about to say. He took a deep breath: not for nerves, but for *fear*, which confused me greatly. My brother wasn't afraid of anything! Was he? And out here, what was there to be afraid of?

What if he was afraid of *me*?

"Jackie, I feel I need to apologise," he started, but was interrupted swiftly.

"What for? I thought we were all squared-out," she said.

A speck of irritation flashed in Lanny's gold. "Hear me out. The first time we met, when I rode Brina... I was mad. At my father, at Ethlon, for what they wanted to do. They wanted to take Benji away."

My pulse accelerated as I recalled the conversation in the gardens, which seemed so long ago now.

"And I didn't let them. I convinced Atti otherwise; I begged Ethlon to train Benji at home, a decision he had already made, unbeknownst to me. When Benji ran, I started to question if I was doing it *right*. If I'd messed up. I thought it was because Benji was jealous of me and you spending time together, but I realise now that we weren't the only factor." He turned to address me, then. "You knew you were in danger and you tried to protect us by leaving."

I could only manage a little nod.

"And here is where I should've *seen* it. But then I carried on and the faeries came and I should've been there to *stop* things but I was so caught up with my own feelings that I didn't make the right judgement," he gasped out, his usually controlled mannerisms utterly absent. My brow furrowed.

"Lanny, it's not your fault," I interceded, "It's mine." I couldn't quite say the words that were buzzing around my brain. *The faeries wanted* me. *They came to the house and they murdered Anatti because of me. And I made it worse.*

"What? Benji, no!" Lanny exclaimed, "What I'm saying is, I should've let you go. I should've let you *both* go. Jackie, I-"

"I don't want to leave now," she whispered softly, "I understand just enough for me to stay."

I hopped up and threw myself into Lanny's arms, feeling the gold pulse with grey and blue, colours it did not belong with.

"Don't blame you," I mumbled into his shoulder.

Lanny sighed and some of the grey subsided. "Still, I am sorry. Really, I am."

"That's great and all," quipped Kalic, making all of us jump, "but when are we leaving? The funeral's soon and people are coming from *everywhere*. The faeries are irked that we're blaming them, and I don't want to unpack all my stuff if I have to take it with me soon."

"Kal, what-!" Lanny spluttered. I pulled away from him, very startled: Kalic's red had completely escaped my notice. And how much had he heard?

Benji, your thoughts are really loud. And I can hear you from further away. Great, isn't it?

I stared at my twin, incredulous. *You heard everything? Even from that distance?*

Yup! He grinned at me, his mouth curling in an expression I could never quite mimic.

Wow, I breathed, my head starting to spin. Since *when* could we hear each other's thoughts so clearly? And from a distance, too?

"The bond," Jackie gasped, "It's strengthening!" Her peculiar eyes gleamed as she stared at the gap between us, as if something was there. *Our bond?*

Kalic's thoughts wandered to what Jackie had said to him and the mention of the bond that we shared. It seemed our natural, thought-flowing ability had become stronger, but why? Why now? My brain didn't like all this weirdness. It was getting a bit too much and my head was pounding, like my heart had jumped into it.

"It is time," Jackie murmured, her colour growing paler.

"And not too soon," Lanny hissed, his gaze settling on something over the horizon. "The faeries will be here momentarily," he practically spat, with a malice that did not suit him.

"Lanny? We have to go?" I asked, my voice breaking.

"Aye." He leant down and kissed my forehead gently. "I wish we had longer for goodbyes, but we don't," he whispered, his breath tickling my skin, "This isn't permanent, though. I promise you, we'll see each other soon."

"But Fír," I gasped out, "And Mutti and Atti and Turvo and all our stuff-"

"Ethlon and Onta Baelthar will bring your things and meet you in Grayssan," Lanny instructed, "You just need to get there alive." He whistled harshly and from out of nowhere Brina appeared, galloping fast towards us. "Take Brina."

"What?" Lanny loved his horse! He forced a smile at me as he grabbed her reins, then set Kalic upon her back before I could even blink. I scooped Mali up and hugged her to my chest, my thoughts cascading into a whirlpool.

This was too *fast*. I knew I had to go, but this *soon*? I thought I'd have time for goodbyes, for making last memories. A part of me even hoped that Lanny would come with us. But now we were forced to and I was in no way ready.

"Lanny..." I tried, but he silenced me again.

"No. Benji, just stay with Kal, okay? No matter what, stick together." He reached further and I relented, letting him scoop me up and set me behind my twin, the cat still in my arms. "I love you," he murmured against my ear, "Never, *ever* forget that."

I tried to echo him, to tell him how much *I* loved *him*, but the words stuck in my throat, knotting themselves round and round until a little squeak was all that could emerge. Lanny stepped back and whispered lowly to Brina in a tone I didn't understand; then we were off.

Brina galloped as if her life depended on it, but really it was mine that was. Mine, and my brother's.

Not the brother in front of me, but the brother who was standing, his gold shrinking until he was barely visible, lost amongst the sea of grey faeries.

I let out a sob and tightened my grip around Kalic's waist. He grunted as if my actions hurt him, but I didn't check his colour to confirm. It thrummed red beneath my fingers, usually soothing, but I was far too panicked to make any sense of anything. Not even Mali's soft turquoise, sandwiched between us, could do anything to help. All I could think was how *sudden* this was and I wasn't ready and Lanny was alone with the horrid faeries and-

No. He wasn't alone; he had Jackie with him.

I hadn't mustered up the courage to ask *what in Pylisya* did she mean by everything she said to my twin and I wished I had, because would I ever see her again? Lanny was sending me away – it would break my heart if I wasn't so sure that he did it in my best interests – and I had no clue when we would return.

Another sob wracked my body, almost in time with Brina's thundering hooves. *Lanny,* I cried silently, my slow brain unable to think of anything else.

It is fine, Kalic was chanting mentally, *it is fine, it is fine, it is fine!*

It is not. Everything was falling to pieces; *how* could it *ever* be deemed as 'fine'?

Even my witty twin had no response to that.

Chapter Fourteen

- *Jackie* -

The palomino mare disappeared over the horizon, all traces of her and the precious cargo she carried vanished amongst the spongy grass. I turned slowly to my boyfriend, whose jawline seemed firmer, *harder* now, the babyish shape I first loved almost completely gone.

"How do you know they'll make it?" I whispered, then winced immediately after. *Dang it.* What I wanted most, in this moment, was to offer him some sort of comfort, but clearly that part of my brain wasn't functioning.

"I don't," he replied, his melodic voice flat and dull. Unbidden tears rose in his eyes and he blinked furiously in attempt to destroy them.

I couldn't help myself. "Then why...?"

"I trust you, Jackie."

Every muscle within me tensed. "You... you did that because of what *I* said?" I gasped out.

"Not you. Elohim." He met my gaze, somewhat reluctantly. "I trust that when you say it's from Him, it is."

"I still don't know why He chose *me*, of all people," I muttered, partially thinking aloud. It baffled me still; there was so many other people with faith greater than what I had. Mine was no larger than a mustard seed. Where was the logic in choosing me?

The babble of faeries drew nearer and in that second I suddenly wanted *out*. It was far too much. I didn't deserve Arlan's trust! This wasn't *my* world. Turvo would still take me and Hazel to the Dryslan forest, I just had to ask.

And I really, really wanted to.

But something stopped me from turning tail and racing to find him.

You're there for a reason, sweetheart. Mum believed in me, like she believed in the angels who protected her. She believed in me enough to trust me with looking after my sister, and to tell me to *stay,* of all things, and embrace my destiny.

Have you even considered that you came here for a reason? Arlan's words were harsh, but caring, too. In some crazy spin of this world, he actually *loved* me. And he believed in me enough to put his brother's life in my hands, trusting that what I spoke was true.

Reason. Reason.

Nothing happens by accident.

I exhaled and opened my eyes, straight into those bright blues.

"Are you alright?" he enquired gently, entwining his hand in mine. I continued breathing steadily, determined to keep my calm.

"Yes," I managed a smile and this time I *did* mean it.

We spoke nothing of Benji and Kalic's departure during the funeral, Arlan simply suggesting that the twins were far too upset to participate. Kalia wasn't buying it – she knew that there'd been something severely wrong with Benji and not just because of their grandfather's death – but I sensed she didn't want to question with all the faeries there.

Not only the faeries, but the other humanoids I'd never seen before.

Fairly unusual were the dwarves, as short as their name implied. Most of them were stocky in build and very tanned, something I didn't expect, from a species that lived in caves. I dared to voice this to Arlan and he almost laughed, explaining that these dwarves were native to Torindell and preferred working outside to being cooped-up underground. Hazel had latched on to a gaggle of younger dwarves and I was quite amused by how *tall* they made her look. What was weirdest, though, was the facial hair already present on dwarves as young as Benji. Again, I asked Arlan, but this time he actually had to stifle a laugh whilst trying to explain that the rates of growth vary for different peoples. Arazair shot us a look after that hushed conversation, so I resorted to guessing at the nature of the others.

In comparison, the faeries were so *ordinary* I wouldn't have thought much of them, if I didn't already know their cruel nature. Most of them were silent and hard-eyed, as if they really didn't want to be here. None had the wings typically associated with their name. Strangely, some of them possessed characteristics of the other species, but I didn't really think much of it, because my attention was utterly stolen by the elves.

Pale-skinned, tall, and slender, they seemed to glow under the waning light, smooth faces of perfection framed by elegant hair. Most wore it below shoulder-length and straight, though a few had waves: none as long or curled as Arlan's, though. Their androgynous features made it incredibly difficult to determine gender, especially as they were clothed in dark, elaborate robes. Of all the people present, they were the most melancholy, but the expressions of grief seemed artistically sculpted on them. I was increasingly fascinated by their large, pointed ears, most drooped in an animalistic sadness, but it was so much more ethereal on them than any mammal. As more and more people shuffled forward to pay their respects, the elves hummed, so quietly that my poor human ears could barely make out the tune. I sensed that it was something of great significance, though.

The funeral *did* drag a bit. I was itching to talk to Arlan – there were so many questions I wanted to ask – and my eyes kept darting to Ethlon and the tanned elf standing next to him, who I guessed, from the toolbelt strung around his waist, was Baelthar. Both grew increasingly agitated as time advanced, even Ethlon, who was usually as expressive as a highland cow. They wanted out as much as I did, but for a much more pressing issue.

Eventually I grew so frustrated that I briefly excused myself, slipping past the other important figures to reach Ethlon and Baelthar.

"What are you doing here still?" I hissed, making Baelthar jump. Up close, I realised that he was very akin to Fírean in appearance, but almost opposite in demeanour.

"It is rude to leave the funeral of a best friend," Ethlon murmured, "Especially if that friend was the king."

"But Benji-"

The two elves exchanged a look I didn't quite catch the emotion of. "As we speak, servants are readying our horses," Baelthar whispered, "It will not be long. You don't have to stay here for the last prayers, but we do."

I sighed. "I'm sorry," I muttered, acknowledging the pain in their eyes.

"It is alright." Ethlon put a cold hand on my shoulder and I started in shock. "Thanks to you, Benji has a chance. I will look after the little one, I promise."

"Thank you," I breathed, then he released me and I walked back over to Arlan. As I did, one elf stepped forward, towards King Myranis' casket – but there was something *different* about him. He moved more elegantly than Arlan, with a grace I'd never seen before, his flowing, white garments gathering in a way that made him appear to float. His hair was a rich, dark red, almost like blood, beautifully contrasted against his lightly tanned skin. I continued staring, following his every step, until he stopped by the casket, bowing his head and touching it. A gasp escaped my mouth; it was *forbidden* to touch the casket, Arazair had warned me! Yet no-one commented, or made a move to stop him.

"It's almost over," Arlan muttered, his hand seeking mine. I entwined my fingers with his, managing to tear my eyes from the strange elf to focus on *another* elf that came forward. She stood in front of the casket, completely ignoring the male crouched there, and began to recite something in a rich, flowing language I did not understand. Beside me, Arlan echoed her words, his voice more musical than I thought possible. All around us, the elves lifted up their voices, each placing a hand over his or her heart, in a universal sign of love and respect. But the strange elf did not move his lips to join in the song, his expression unreadable, green eyes locked on the casket before him-

Wait. *Green eyes.*

I gasped, far too loudly, and his head snapped up to meet my gaze. We stared each other down for a few seconds, green blazing against green, then I looked away, my heart thundering.

When I risked a glance back, he was gone.

"Jackie, are you alright?" Arlan whispered, tugging on my hand as the ancient, lyrical words faded.

"I think so," I lied, setting my eyes on the older, female elf standing by the casket. I didn't know where else to look.

"-and now, King Myranis will rest in the Heavens, after the nine-hundred seasons that Elohim blessed him with," the elf finished, bowing her head. I should've bowed my head too, but instead my mouth flew open, brain struggling to comprehend the time scale.

"How *long* do you live?" I muttered under my breath: probably a little too loud again, as Arlan frowned.

"My grandfather died too young," he murmured sadly.

"Nine-hundred is *young*?" I spluttered, causing a few elves and faeries near us to shoot daggers with their eyes. Arlan caught on to this and tightened his grip on my hand, pulling me away from the crowd and the sombre funeral.

We continued marching in this fashion, through the rest of the castle gardens and back into the grand building itself, until we were alone in a room

that reminded me of my old head-teacher's study. Wooden shelves holding mostly scrolls, and a few book-like objects, lined three of the walls, and a large desk filled the centre, so big that I doubted I could squeeze round to the elaborate chair behind.

Arlan's hand fell from mine and I turned just as he shut the door.

"Vaznek! You really have no concept of this, do you? I mean, have you *ever* been to a funeral?" he whisper-shouted, eyes blazing suddenly. I tensed up.

"Yes!" I hissed back, "And I'm sorry for interrupting, there's just so much I don't understand, and, and I..."

Why was *I* apologising?

"Why do you go off on me every time I do something *different*?" I exploded, staring him down, trying to ignore the mesmerising effect I knew his eyes had on me.

He froze. "Go... off?"

Curse these stupid cultural barriers.

"Get mad at me."

"I know what it means," he huffed rather indignantly, "I didn't realise I was acting in such a manner. I'm sorry, Jackie." His voice dropped to a soft whisper at the end, coated in the melodic tone that I adored. *Dang it.* I couldn't stay mad at him.

"It's alright," I sighed, "But please, stop. Everything's going all crazy, I don't want you going crazy on me too."

He nodded slowly, a few curls falling across his face. My fingers twitched, desiring to reach up and tuck them behind his long ears, maybe pull his head down towards me-

No. Focus, Jackie.

"How long do elves live?" I asked gently. He grimaced, though for what reason, I wasn't sure.

"On average? About two thousand seasons."

All the blood rushed out of my head, flooding right down to my feet, leaving me very dizzy and light-headed. "Two... *thousand*?" I squeaked as the world started to spin.

"Aye! A year is four seasons, Jackie. It is not that long," Arlan exclaimed, grabbing my arm, and I suddenly realised how *pale* and weak my skin looked against his healthy tan.

"Five-hundred years. So your grandfather was 225," I whispered, my brain somehow managing to do the math, "and that is...?"

"Too young," he finished with a heavy sigh.

"But he had Arazair too old?" I queried, still trying to make sense of the elven culture.

Arlan smiled dubiously. "Well, most elves start families before they reach thirty. And why wait? Having them sooner means we'll see more generations."

"That's the same for humans, though it's more because our lives are shorter," I said, trying to keep the sadness from creeping into my voice at the fact that Arlan would outlive me, probably by a few hundred years. Which was silly, really: he was only my *first* boyfriend, not necessarily the last. But something in me just wanted to be with him forever.

Too soon, too soon, I chided my silly little heart. To make matters worse, we were technically discussing the optimal ages for child-making. Brilliant.

"So you've, uh, stopped aging?" I blurted out, to stop my mind from wandering to bad places. "Physically," I added, when confusion flashed across his sculpted face.

"Not entirely. Once we reach adulthood, our aging just slows so it is barely noticeable."

"Right." I stared down at my hands, fighting the urge to look at the face that didn't look a day over eighteen, now I considered it.

We sat in relative silence for a while, myself desperately thinking of everything *but* the elf standing across from me. When I did look up again, he'd removed a few scrolls from the shelves and was skimming through them, examining the strange texts with a light of understanding. I shuffled a little closer and peaked over his shoulder - suppressing the irritation that I had to stand on tip-toe in order to do so - following his finger as it traced over the elegant illustrations surrounding the unfamiliar symbols. The elves painted there seemed to be holding a sort of energy in their hands, and another question rose unbidden, quickly making its way from my mind to my mouth.

"Do elves have powers?"

Arlan quickly rolled up the scroll and I stepped back, heat flooding to my cheeks. *What a silly question,* I scolded myself. I knew full well that elves weren't the mischievous, magical beings that human culture suggested them to be, and that Arlan was likely to correct my thinking.

But to my relief, he chuckled lightly. "Not all. We have the potential, I suppose; it depends what the elf's gift is. So Benji's gift happens to be a form of power. Kal's is the same as Onta Baelthar's, which is a gift of hands and forge work."

Wait, so they do *have powers? Just called... gifts?*

"Fír's is his music?" I guessed.

"Yes. And Turvo's is his ego," he laughed, "Actually, Turvo is a fantastic hunter. He just doesn't use his gift enough."

"What about you?" I asked softly. Arlan's humour faded.

"Some of the elders believe it to be intellect," he said, blushing slightly, "But if so, I'm rubbish at applying it. So I honestly don't know what mine is."

"I'm sure you'll find out," I encouraged, managing a smile, which he returned.

"*You* definitely have a gift, though," he murmured, "The abilities that come to you from being a dream-prophet."

I frowned. "But humans don't get gifts like you do," I protested.

"I find that hard to believe," he breathed and suddenly he was right in front of me, his face almost touching mine. My pulse spiked, earlier fantasies invading my mind, and I wasn't strong enough to keep my hands from caressing his cheeks, his ears, his curls...

Our lips met and I closed my eyes, relaxing into his strong embrace, all my worries momentarily forgotten. There were no cruel faeries, no disapproving elves, no peculiar dwarves. No shelves of scrolls, no walls of stone, no gardens of death.

Just me and the elf prince I loved.

"Prince Arlan- oh!"

I fumbled as Arlan pushed me away, his movements uncharacteristically disorganised, both of us startled by the sudden appearance of a younger elf. A blush rose to my cheeks, as I was consciously aware that the manner in which I'd pressed into my boyfriend was probably inappropriate for anyone else's eyes.

Whoops.

"Ah, Your Highness, I am sorry," the elf rushed, trying very hard not to stare at me and utterly failing at it.

Arlan sighed as he attempted to untangle a few of his curls. "Well, what is so important?"

"Ethlon and your onta are leaving," he explained, "And they wanted to know if you would come with them."

Immediately the flushed embarrassment drained from Arlan's face, replaced with features made of cold stone. "No. Now, leave us."

"Of c-course," the elf stammered, bolting out of the room within seconds. I turned to my boyfriend, scrutinizing his sudden change in emotion.

"You're not going?"

"No."

"Not even to say goodbye?"

He hissed and the sound was so inhuman it frightened me. I stumbled back, watching as his lips curled up in another animalistic tone, before he took a few deep breaths and calmed himself.

"I'm sorry, Jackie." He seemed to say that a lot lately. "I just can't see him again, not yet. If I do, I won't say goodbye. I'll take him with me, or worse, I'll run off with them. I *have* to just let him go."

"Not even a small goodbye? We did just leave in a whirlwind..." I trailed off at the pain flashing through Arlan's eyes.

"I can't do it," he muttered, blinking furiously as he bowed his head. Moisture blossomed amidst his sapphires and his entire body was shaking. Tentatively, I took a few steps forward, until I could place my hand on his shoulder.

"Benji will be alright," I whispered, "And so will we."

Arlan's fists clenched. "Why? Did you 'see' it?" he almost spat, his voice breaking at the end.

"No. I just believe it," I replied firmly, and I didn't know if it was my words, or my touch, or something else ticking away inside of him, but Arlan broke down and sobbed.

I pulled him into my arms, letting him rest against my chest, feeling the chill as his tears soaked through my tunic.

There were no words to say.

All I could do was run my hands through his curls, in an attempt to soothe him. I found myself caressing his drooped ears as well, their texture against my skin calming my own fears and nerves.

"They're going to be okay. Oh, Elohim, please let them be okay," I murmured, so quiet I doubted even Arlan heard it.

But what you saw-

Shut up, I commanded the voice of doubt.

"We're all going to be alright," I said aloud, trying to reassure myself. It felt like I had to say that a *lot* lately. Yet deep inside my heart, a warmth burst forth, surging through my veins. Sure, I doubted. I didn't really know what the future held, even with my 'gift'. My emotions were a mess, my world flipped over so many times I couldn't tell which way was up.

But I had hope. More than that: I had *faith*.

As Arlan straightened up, his hand slipped into mine, the touch already familiar. We turned towards the door, where the remaining members of his family waited beyond. He inhaled deeply and I squeezed his hand, smiling reassuringly as our eyes met.

He was broken. The loss of his grandfather had seen to that, as had the realisation that he could no longer protect his youngest brothers. He was broken and the near future promised anything but healing. He was broken, but so was I.

"This all happened for a reason," I declared, setting my jaw firm as I turned forward.

Arlan's tears ceased and we stepped into the new season, *together*.

- END OF PART ONE -

- PART TWO: NIGHTMARES -

Chapter Fifteen

- Benji -

Northlands, Pylisya. Autumn's Rise, 5966 PY

The sun's rays flashed across the horizon, temporarily illuminating the mountain peaks a brilliant red, before the moon slipped in and turned them purple. I sighed, catching the last waves of warmth, but did not move from my position. Out here, the air was clear. Not like the mugginess of the mountain caverns, where Ethlon insisted I spent most of my time.

"Benji?"

Kalic approached and I knew immediately that he was not alone; my onta's colour was pretty distinctive, and if he *had* been alone, then there would be no need for verbal communication.

"The night is falling," Onta Baelthar said, "You should be inside."

I didn't move, though I mentally shifted my perspective to get a better view of his colour. Purple-brown, deeper than his sister's: and now, speckled red with annoyance. *Good.*

Benji, come on, Kalic pleaded mentally, *I don't want them to put us on rations again.*

"Benji."

"Fine," I grumbled in response to both, seizing my cloak and throwing it over my shoulders. Kalic's soft *thank you* did nothing to change my mood. Evening was the only time I could truly get alone, but now even that was being checked.

In the eight seasons we'd been here, there hadn't been even a sniff of an attack. Lanny wanted me somewhere safe and he'd achieved it.

Would've been nice for him to visit, though. At least once.

Instead, I had lessons with Ethlon, focusing on my supposed powers, and subsequent classes with Thorn and the other young dwarves: to learn about trade, culture, various 'life-skills', and – to my embarrassment – speech therapy, which was tailored to just me and one young dwarf. Everywhere I went, someone had to accompany me, even if it was to just go and get something to eat or drink. It took ridiculous to a whole new level.

And I didn't like it, not one bit.

When the red had started to creep in, I wasn't entirely sure. Perhaps it was as far back as when we'd left, waiting with Brina in Grayssan for three days before Ethlon and Onta Baelthar finally turned up. Though I was scared, then, mostly. Grey was my companion for a few seasons. Grey, and blue, and now red.

I could *feel* it in my veins, tainting whatever my original colour was meant to be, deep as the dying sun, lacking the warmth of Kalic's. I felt it and I despised it, but I couldn't weed it out. In all honesty, I couldn't really do *anything*.

The Northlands were just too monochrome for my liking.

I followed Kalic inside, heading to the room that was my own: he'd decided two seasons ago that he no longer wanted to share a room, and I didn't mind. It gave me time alone, to work on the sketches and paintings that I probably wasn't ever going to show anyone. My eyes fell on the latest work I'd completed. It was primarily silver, but the largest figure had eyes specked with an ugly, jealous green, and stood looming over another figure, this one originally blue, but coated with so much red it was more of an ugly purple.

Just like the mountains.

"Argh!" I let out a scream of frustration and kicked the nearest object, which happened to be a painting. My foot went straight through the canvas, destroying another horrible failure of art. Mali, the orange-furred, turquoise-coloured cat I'd adopted seasons ago, let out a surprised hiss and jumped from her sleeping spot on the bed as I glared at the ruined artwork. The colours just weren't *nice* anymore. Everything was too red, too grey, too ugly.

I missed the vibrant colours of my family. Heck, I just missed *them*. Mutti, her lilac soft but stiff at the same time. Atti, his orange too tainted for my liking. Turvo, his green frequently unreadable. Firean, a constant source of blue. And Lanny...

Gold. Beautiful, warm, loving gold. But I wasn't sure I knew him anymore. Things the dwarves said... and his lack of contact... was Lanny really the brother I thought him to be?

Benji, you're super loud. Tone it down, Kalic moaned.

Stop eavesdropping, I snapped back, and sensed his red recoil.

I don't mean to. Listen, Onta Baelthar still promises me we can go to the village tomorrow. Are you sure you don't want to come?

I paused, considering. Going to the village of Lidan meant I'd get to spend time outdoors, interacting with the occasional non-dwarven being, but I'd also have Ethlon constantly breathing down my back, which would make the whole experience utterly constricting. He was as strange as when I'd first met him and I suspected he knew how intimidated he made me feel, but I neither voiced it nor gave him any reason to stop. There really was no point in me going to Lidan if Ethlon was to be there; I would be more free if I simply stayed inside.

A swift knock on the door and the presence of silver stopped me mid-thought. "Ah, Benji, I hope I did not wake you?"

"No," I said, quickly kicking the ruined canvas aside, barely avoiding Mali.

"Good. I have a few errands I need to run, so there will be no lessons for a few days. Jasmine will look after you, though, so just–"

"Be inside by nightfall, don't go out without a companion, and don't talk to anyone about colours. I've got it," I sighed, struggling to keep my tone of voice from sounding rude. At least the words came easier than they used to.

Ethlon managed a faint smile, before closing the door. I kept my emotions muted until I could no longer sense his colour, then I excitedly called for my twin, my earlier fears now gone. *Kal!*

Yes?

Ethlon's away for a few days. So yes, I will come with you.

My twin cheered with such volume, I heard it aloud as well as in my head, despite his room being across the hall from mine.

So, do you think we can lose Onta Baelthar? I asked, my thoughts already running away from me. Jasmine would be easy to escape – she was guaranteed to be distracted by any fabrics out on sale – but our onta was another matter.

Hey, since when are you so sneaky? Kalic retorted.

I sighed, because he knew full well the answer to that. *Since we left. Since my world was flipped upside down. Since I've been stuck in this darn hole for seasons.*

Kalic didn't bother to reply, and as I focused his red faded, signifying that he'd entered the land of dreams. His ability to go from fully awake to fully asleep was one that I rivalled; unless I was seriously exhausted, I couldn't sleep. Especially not these days.

Instead I focused on clearing up the mess I'd made of the canvas, organising my paintings by date and my paints by their colours. Mali watched me work, her bright eyes glinting with curiosity as I sorted the supplies. All the reds together, then the blues, then yellows, and every shade in between slotted into place. Apparently I had done it *wrong,* but almost everything I did was wrong in somebody's eyes, and Lanny wasn't here, so I'd stopped caring.

Lanny. I *needed* to see him. Part of me didn't want to – I was *mad,* so mad at him for leaving me and not coming back – but *mad* and *Lanny* did not seem to go well in a sentence together. The part of me that did want to see him was more worried for his safety. *What if he hasn't come to see me because he can't?* That wasn't a scenario I was willing to even risk.

After all, I'd agreed to leave to keep *him* safe, as well as me. And I was safe enough. No-one was after me now, so surely it would be alright for me to return?

My eyelids drooped then, suddenly growing heavy, Mali's purring lulling me towards unconsciousness. *No,* I protested, but the drowsiness of Kalic's mind was starting to seep into my own; surely it would be fine, if I just closed my eyes, rested a while –

I jolted out of bed, except I wasn't *in* bed anymore. *No.* Immediately I pinched myself, silently willing my mind to wake me *up,* get me *out* of this dream before it could start: but there was nothing. Only a sharp twinge in my arm where my fingers had squeezed the skin.

I never really understood *why* pinching yourself was supposed to snap you out of a dream: it still hurt me, even when I *was* dreaming. And I knew full well that I was dreaming, because no-one had any colours.

I couldn't see the colours when I dreamt.

The darkness surrounding me slowly evaporated, revealing a city square writhing with people. They were *everywhere.* Elves, dwarves, even other humanoids with odd features, but most prominent were the faeries. And, though I could no longer see their greys, I could feel it, cold and cruel, pressing against my skin as they slowly surrounded me.

"You killed him," five hissed in complete harmony.

I shuddered. "No," I managed to gasp out, feeling all tongue-tied again like I used to.

"Yes." Their dirty hands elongated, morphing into swords that all twisted and pointed at my throat. I imagined the red in their colours. Anger. Accusation. Condemnation.

"I never meant to." My words were pathetic, weak, the tone coating them equally so. I didn't believe it myself.

And the faeries knew it.

Their eyes flashed red, faces distorting into expressions so horrendous, 'monster' was on the tip of my tongue. But they hadn't sent a person into the afterlife without even *touching* them.

If anyone was a monster in this instance, it was *me*.

I gasped and tumbled out of bed, the echoes of the dream still resonating in my mind. *Vaznek*. I'd had enough of the stupid nightmares but they just *would not* leave me alone! Sleep was becoming increasingly less appealing, though my body still longed for it. In the rare occasion that I did manage to fall under, it always came accompanied by the evils that seeped into my mind, and there was nothing I could do to stop them. Except for stay awake, that was.

For three days I had gone without fully resting, and the little I'd managed to claim that night was nowhere near the amount I needed, but I could not face the dreams, not again. The only reason I'd drifted off in the first place was because my mind had been connected to Kalic's as he slept: or that was my theory, anyway.

Mali meowed then, as if to say that it was *her* who had helped me to sleep, but I didn't want to blame her. She started purring again, the sound a mere comfort and not enough to send me to sleep again, thankfully. I busied myself with the task of tidying up the rest of my room, gathering anything that could be of some use on my journey. Anything too large and my onta would be suspicious, so I stuck to essentials only: a spare tunic and breeches, a sketchbook, charcoal stick, a few pots of paint, enough coins to afford food and drink – if needed – and some oatcakes for the road. All fit neatly into my smallest bag, though the clothing was incredibly creased in a manner that would've made Mutti scream, if she were here to see it. I shook my head, not allowing my mind to trickle down that path again, instead wondering about my twin. I'd advised Kalic against taking all his tools – like my paints, they could be replaced – but as usual, he wouldn't listen to me.

It was like I was still a scared little child.

Well, I had been, but I certainly wasn't now. I'd grown a lot in the last two years.

"Benji! Are you ready?" Kalic hammered on my door as he yelled, though I knew full well that he already had the answer; he was simply keeping up appearances. Why he was yelling at me this early, I had no idea-

Wait. My eyes flew to the small window, noting that the light seeping through was the soft amber of the rising sun and not the moon's blue glow.

Did I seriously sleep through the night? I sure didn't feel like I had.

"Benji!"

I grunted my response and shouldered my cloak. "Yes, nearly!"

Did you pack everything? I added.

Yes.

Including the tools?

Not all of them!

I groaned and Kalic laughed, then quickly failed to cover it with a cough. At that moment, Onta Baelthar's deep mulberry entered my field of vision, talking to Kalic about something. I retreated from my twin's mind because, though connected, we both respected each other's privacy.

At least, *I* did.

I shouldered my bag, then paused, glancing down at Mali's small form. "I'm sorry, girl," I whispered, "But you can't come with me."

Mali mewed her protest.

"I know, I know. I'll miss you," I murmured, scooping her up for one last cuddle. She nuzzled against my cheek, her damp nose cool and comforting, and I threaded my fingers in her ginger fur, memorising the smooth texture. "You have to stay here, though. Promise me you'll be good for Thorn?"

She huffed, but nodded after a moment, letting out another small mew as confirmation. I set her down then, reminding myself that she *had* to stay, because bringing Mali with me would only cause further suspicion.

"I'll see you again," I promised her, before closing the door on the room I'd been forced to call my own.

In theory, going to the village with Onta Baelthar wouldn't arouse any suspicions. In reality, it was much different. The second I entered the Hall – a large cavern near the entrance, where people greeted and said goodbye – a young dwarf made a beeline for me, his warm brown almost as familiar to me as Lanny's gold had been.

"Benji, where are you going?" Thorn exclaimed, rather loudly. I sighed. Twice before he'd intercepted my attempts to leave, and now took to *yelling* his greetings to me, in case I was to try something again. In the years we'd known each other, he'd changed more than me. I was taller than him now, but only by a little: Thorn was set to be one of the tallest dwarves, ever. His dark hair helped add to his height, spiked up in an attempted mohawk that liked to flop on one side, missing the effect he was striving for. His tan skin was now defined with muscles, and everyday more stubble grew on his rounded chin, something which I, as an elf, would never experience, and was very relieved for that to be the case.

"Pylisya to Benji!"

I huffed. "I'm just headed into Lidan, Thorn. With Kal and Onta Baelthar."

"And Jasmine?"

I scowled at the glint in his grey eyes. "For Zeraphin's sake, stop mothering me! Yes, she's going."

Thorn laughed, which only made my brows furrow further. "It's so weird hearing *you* curse your ancestor like that," he chuckled and I rolled my eyes.

"It's not cursing exactly. Besides, I'm not-"

"Do you even know who Zeraphin was?" he interjected, a smile lighting his face.

"Some old elvish guy who started my family."

"Almost. The legends say-"

"The legends are not legends but history, Thorn. And Benji, you really should know your family's history," Onta Baelthar said, suddenly coming up behind us. Instinctively my fists clenched, my whole body tensing, frustrated and confused that I hadn't sensed his colour.

"Relax," he added, taking in my posture, "That's a lesson for another day. Are you ready?"

I shifted the bag on my shoulder, hoping my onta wouldn't question what it contained. "Sure. Ready when the rest of you are."

"Any chance I can tag along?" Thorn enquired brightly. I groaned inwardly. Getting away from Onta Baelthar would be hard enough, but to escape Thorn as well... *No chance.*

"Yes!" Onta Baelthar exclaimed cheerfully.

No, I groaned internally. *There go my escape plans.*

Kalic's dark eyes met mine and I knew he'd heard me. *Why don't we let Thorn in on it?* he proposed.

No. Thorn was far too stubborn; he wanted to stay with us, it was evident in both his colour and mannerisms, but he would not go south again. The faeries had taken him captive – when and how, he wouldn't disclose – but the fear of its repetition denied him the opportunity to leave this dreary, monochrome habitat. Caves and mountains were fine for dwarves, but I was an *elf*. My blood pulsed and called for the colours of other living creatures, longing for nature: to feel grass underfoot, the yellows of insects buzzing around, the sky so incredibly blue like my brother's eyes-

I stopped the thought in its tracks before I became too sentimental. *Vaznek.* After this long I thought I would've gotten over it but I knew, deep down, that I still missed him. I missed him terribly. I needed my eldest brother; even though he hadn't always been there for me, I still knew he'd only be a couple of day's ride away. That if I was in deep trouble, a messenger could ride out and return with my gold.

But I had no clue how far away he was and no real means to even try and find him. Part of that was his fault – he should've come to visit – but what if he couldn't? What if Atti was keeping him trapped like Ethlon did with me?

The only way to find out for certain was to leave the Northlands and succeed in reaching Torindell.

My jaw set firm, then I scrambled to hide the determination on my face as I realised that Onta Baelthar, Kalic, and Thorn were all staring at me.

"Uh, sorry," I said, without really knowing why I was apologising. It just seemed the right thing to say.

"If you're tired, Benji, you shouldn't go!" Jasmine fretted and I sighed at the pinky dwarf. Her brown was coated in layers of care and maternity – probably because she had eight dwarflings, the crazy female – which both comforted and sickened.

Three versus two.

Two versus two, really, Kalic corrected, *Jasmine's not really one.*

But Onta Baelthar counts for more than one, I pointed out.

I guess.

I sensed discomfort in his red, probably at betraying his mentor. Kalic idolised our onta, and they were the only elves I knew who actually liked being in the caves with the fires of forges scalding their skin and the sound of hammers and anvils shattering their ears. Well, I didn't really know that many elves anyway, but my twin and my onta did seem to be of a different breed.

So says the one that sees colours, Kalic huffed.

I shot him a glare, both physically and mentally. *Privacy, please, Kal!*

Sorry. His colour didn't echo the thought.

I continued to glare, the action forming cerebral daggers which fired at him, and to my surprise his colour flared white, physically recoiling from me. Surprise gave way to horror as I realised I'd accidentally *hurt* him, like I had with the faeries-

Stop. I'm fine, Benji, Kalic urged, turning grey with anxiety. He knew how the library haunted me, how even Ethlon didn't know what to do about it, how this 'power' absolutely terrified me...

Kal. Out of my head, I snarled, careful to not put too much force in the words lest I hurt him again.

Fine, he huffed, retreating, but his eyes wouldn't meet mine.

The others surrounding us were blissfully unaware of our silent exchange and had been chatting amongst themselves: something about what they wanted to purchase in the markets of Lidan. Adults, so boring.

Thorn was giving me a funny look, his colour sceptical, so I forced a smile in an effort to calm him. *I'm not going anywhere,* my eyes lied, as I silently willed him to believe me. I didn't know if it would work but he did not act as if he was on to us, not even commenting on how obviously full my bag was.

"I'm ready to go," Kalic said aloud, lacing an undertone that only I would understand.

I took a deep breath, taking one last look around the caves that had been my surrogate home. *No,* I corrected myself, *this has never been my home.*

"Me too. Let's go."

Chapter Sixteen

- Jackie -

Torindell, Pylisya. Autumn's Peak, 5966 PY

The sun rose over the city of Torindell and it was still a sight I'd never grow sick of. Its rays stretched out, gently caressing the roofs of houses and turrets of towers. White washed walls cascaded into gold, elegant amber and scarlet threading over them as well. In the quiet of the morning, the city I'd grown to call home was the second most beautiful thing in my world.

The first was sat beside me, on the hilly outcrop that had become our watchtower.

I knew why he'd brought me out here again. The view was breathtaking and so incredibly romantic, especially after a night spent camped underneath the multicoloured stars. He hoped these factors would melt away my stone heart. What he didn't realise was that I'd never been stone in the first place.

I turned, then, just as the sunlight tangled in his hair, sandy-blond becoming even blonder, his chiselled yet youthful face positively glowing. Our eyes met, blue on green, but I broke the connection before he could enchant me further.

"We should probably get back," I whispered, failing to hide my reluctance.

Arlan's beautiful smile faded slightly. "Jackie, I-"

I stood up, not even letting him start. "I'm serious. Hazel's got more lessons in Ancient Dwarvish today and that is something I do *not* want to miss," I grinned. My adopted sister had settled in better than I, but the worst thing for her was the learning of a new culture, and that included the dwarves' old language, too. Most I'd encountered spoke the common tongue, but their language was still taught to all young dwarves – and, at thirteen, Hazel was still classed as young enough to begin the lessons.

Arlan sighed as he stood too, and I was brought out of my thoughts. The question was in his eyes – one that I would not allow him to ask again, not until I was ready – and I turned away, not wanting to see the inevitable hurt that would follow.

We walked in silence back into the city; since Brina left, Arlan hadn't bothered to get another steed, so we took to walking pretty much everywhere. It wasn't that hard, really, as we always had to keep the city in our sights.

People were just beginning to wake: dwarves, mostly, bustling around the streets and making preparations for the market. Colourful banners already started to appear, advertising pottery, fresh fruits, clothing, and-

I stopped and felt Arlan stiffen beside me, too. In front of us was an artist's stall, full of colourful canvas paintings; beside it was a blacksmith's stand, adorned with intricate jewellery and painfully familiar stone carvings. My mind immediately flew to a certain pair of elves: that was what had stopped me in my tracks.

The twins.

"It's been over two years," Arlan whispered. I moved to face him, watching as his blue eyes flickered with anguish.

"How are you still going on?" he continued, "It *kills* me that Benji is gone... and Kal... I miss them so much! I can't even walk through the streets without missing them!" His voice rose a pitch in agitation, "Your mother-"

"I still see her, in dreams!" I exclaimed, cutting him off.

"That's not the same-"

"No no no," I interrupted again, placing my finger on his lips, "*No*. I'm fine. And I'm not missed, believe me."

His eyebrows arched.

"Hey, everyone thinks I went to college abroad. No idea what I'm supposedly studying, but Mum had a plan in place, to explain my absence. She knew this would happen someday," I shrugged, "and besides, after I left school, most my friends moved away: off to various colleges and world exploration. I don't miss them." That was true; I'd stayed to help Mum and gain some experience with the children's home, but I didn't really have any friends. Not in the interim between school and my new life in Pylisya, anyway.

"A plan? That sounds too easy," Arlan commented sceptically.

I frowned. Here he was, bursting my little bubble, because I didn't want to admit that I was hurting. That, actually, I *did* miss Mum like crazy. I wanted to go back, but I also wanted to stay, and neither desire was strong enough to conquer the other. So I didn't answer, instead choosing to resume my walking, barely holding in a sigh as he followed me.

"Jackie, you're changing," he murmured, once we were out of the growing crowds.

My brow furrowed further and I struggled to keep the blood from rushing to my cheeks. "Puberty hit me and went, Arlan."

"No. Your ears."

"What?" My hands flew to the appendages, tracing their outline. Arlan watched me, incredulous, and gestured to our reflections in a nearby window. I stared. My ears seemed normal at first, but they were longer than I recalled, and ended in a slight point.

"How?" I breathed.

Arlan shrugged. "I don't know. It's been gradual, but... Do you have any other changes?"

I paused, considering. "My back's been pretty sore," I confessed, "but it's probably nothing. Maybe just muscle strain?"

"If Pylisya is hurting you-"

"How many times must we have this conversation?" I huffed, "If I was to have a reaction to this world, it would've happened when I first came! I. Am. Fine. And I want to stay here, I do."

"Then why won't you say yes?" he whispered, his breath like honey against my lips. I gasped, my lungs suddenly lacking oxygen.

"I-I..." I stuttered, words failing me. My eyes fluttered around, trying to avoid his, and ended up settling on my left hand. I visualised a ring on the fourth finger, toying with the idea. It *would* make sense to accept. We'd been dating for over two years now and I knew that I didn't want anyone else. I only wanted him.

But I just couldn't commit.

Accepting his proposal was agreeing to stay in Pylisya forever. At this current point in time I was fine with that, but the way my fickle brain worked lately, that soon wouldn't be the case. Plus, the visions that plagued me at night all pointed to me staying being a bad idea. Yet I couldn't leave. I *loved* him. It was quite a conundrum and I couldn't see any obvious solution.

Thankfully I was saved by an over-enthusiastic Fírean, who bounded over waxing lyrical about the new composition he'd dreamt of. Arlan was immediately whisked away and I exhaled, sending my thanks to Elohim.

Stalling him was only hurting him, I knew that, but he was so moral, he didn't even consider asking someone else. It was flattering, really, and I hated having to let him down. I suspected there was some pressure on him to marry and beget another heir to the throne – especially with the rising tensions between faeries and elves - but he never pursued me more than I was comfortable with.

"Hello? Pylisya to Jackie?" A dark hand waved in front of my face and I started, glancing down to see my adopted sister staring right back at me. "You *majorly* zoned-out there," she continued, the Earthly colloquialisms she used becoming less and less familiar to me. *It's what happens when you spend a couple of years in a different world.*

"Sorry, Zel. I've got a lot on my mind."

She rolled her eyes and frowned slightly. "You've *always* got stuff on your mind, Jack."

Now it was *my* turn to scowl. "It's *Jackie*. You know that," I huffed, folding my arms. The stupid nickname had started when one of Hazel's dwarven friends mistook me for a male elf, thinking 'Jackie' was a term of endearment. It had quickly become a running joke amongst the young teens, much to my annoyance.

"Aren't you supposed to be in lessons, anyway?" I asked. Hazel shook her head, pigtails bouncing with the motion.

"Nah. The lesson got cancelled. Guess *why*," she responded in a sing-song voice, dragging out the last word. It took all of my self-control to not send her flying into next season; unfortunately, she was one of the children who became more annoying during puberty, not less.

"I told Arlan I was attending the lesson with you!" I exclaimed, "And no, I don't know why."

"Hmm, refusing him again, are you?" She cocked an eyebrow and tilted her head mischievously, and a blush rose unbidden to my cheeks.

"No! Not exactly, I just... I..."

"Ha!" Hazel laughed, "Knew it!"

"Look, we're *not* having this conversation right now, alright?" I sighed, running a hand through my hair.

"Vaznek, Jackie, you're so *awkward,*" Hazel chirped and I frowned at her use of the Pylisyan curse word.

"I'm not that awkward," I protested, "And you need to watch your language."

"Sure, sure, whatever. But first, you can't avoid him forever, and second, the faeries are coming to visit," Hazel announced coolly.

I blanked. "The faeries?"

"Yeah. Apparently they're still irked about the whole blaming-them-for-killing-the-king thing and they want the restrictions to be lifted. It's all boring grown-up stuff, really. But I thought I'd let you know, seeing as your night-"

"Okay, okay, enough said," I interjected hurriedly, glancing around to ensure no-one else had been listening to my blabbermouth sister. The only other person within earshot was an elf, but he was so absorbed in tending to a cluster of bright orange plants that I sincerely doubted he'd heard a word.

"Well in that case, I'm off to hang out with Carrie and the gang. See you!" she exclaimed, before turning and bounding down the main street. As she left, so did my energy and I gasped, feeling as though a plug had been pulled on my reserves. Immediately I staggered over to a stone bench and half-collapsed onto it, all my remaining energy converting itself into nausea. I turned to retch, but the motion caused my back to flare up with sharp daggers that shot between my shoulder blades, just as the world around me started to grow dark. *Great.*

First it was the nausea. Then the pain. And now, predictable as ever, the vision.

I found myself in a large plaza, but the body I observed from was not my own. Many people crowded the area, elves and faeries mostly, all straining to catch a glimpse of something at the centre. Fighting my way forwards, I was suddenly hit by salty air, tainted with the music of the sea, and it was then I realised the plaza was actually a pier. On its edge stood three figures.

The first was tall and dark-skinned, with black hair skimming just past his ears. A thin beard adorned his angular chin, but he was far too tall to be a dwarf. Perhaps a faery? I couldn't get close enough to determine that. His clothes were a deep crimson, decorated with a peculiar, splotchy pattern of slightly deeper red, as if the robes were covered in various stains. Beside him stood a much shorter figure of undetermined gender, slight in body, with tanned skin, and deep, chocolate-brown locks that fell straight to chin-length.

Their robes were a similar style to the man's, but grey instead, and they lacked the stain-like pattern.

I knew who the third person was, but at the same time, I didn't. His face was marred beyond recognition, bloodied and bruised with the marks of a thousand attacks. The hair hung in matted clumps, much shorter than mine, and so dirty I could not distinguish its colour. His robes, too, were torn and bloodstained like the rest of him, but the insignia on his tunic was as familiar as the back of my hand.

The glistening, golden, six-pointed star of Zeraphin.

I wanted to throw up. Before me stood – or rather, knelt – one of the sons of Arazair, though which I could not tell. He wouldn't open his eyes and I couldn't get close enough to see if the hair had any blond or black, or if it really was brown in colour. My judgement was skewed, too, by the fact that I didn't know how tall his captors were: if the tanned one was a dwarf, then the elf could very well be one of the twins, a thought I couldn't bear to dwell on. Heck, I couldn't bear to think of *any* of the brothers, bruised and broken, held in place by a chain around his neck like he was a wild animal on a leash.

But the unknown brother was there, he was hurt, and I couldn't do anything except watch as the dark-haired man advanced on him, drawing a dagger from his belt, pulling back his arm to deliver the strike and-

I screamed and jerked back, accidentally banging my head on something hard. Gasping, it took me a few minutes to realise that I was back in *my* body, in Torindell, with the only red in sight being the blood that dribbled into my eyes from the blow I'd just given my skull.

"Well done, Jackie," I muttered under my breath, wincing as fingers caressed the tender wound.

"Ah, do you need any help?" The previously-distracted elf scurried over, not waiting for my reply as he pressed something cool and wet against my forehead.

"Yes, thanks," I grimaced as the wound began to sting.

"Sorry," he muttered, but he didn't move his hand. I sighed and glanced around as best as I could, trying to recollect my surroundings more. It appeared that I'd somehow fallen off the bench and then fallen forwards again, knocking my head on it. *Confusing...*

"How long was I out for?" I mused, partially to myself.

"Not long. Maybe ten minutes," my helper replied, and I recoiled suddenly. His deep red hair fell in a fringe over his eyes, hiding them from me, but I could feel the weight of his stare.

"What is it?" he asked, nervousness creeping into his tone.

"You said minutes." It came out as an accusation, but I was astonished. Pylisya did not have the same time measurements as Earth: there were no clocks, so everything was done according to the brightness and position of the sun, with undefined 'moments' in place of the usual seconds, minutes and hours. So to hear someone other than myself or Hazel speak of minutes was unnatural.

The strange elf did not respond immediately, so I examined him more closely. He seemed familiar somehow: I had certainly seen him before, but where, I was not certain.

Then it hit me, the very second that the wind blew, revealing bright eyes set in a tanned face.

Bright, *green* eyes.

"You," I gasped, "You were at the funeral! I saw you! But, but Arlan said no-one else has green eyes, *ever*, and-"

"I have to go," he roughly interrupted, standing. I copied the motion, though it made my head spin in the process.

"No! You can't just leave without an explanation!" Our eyes met and my stomach churned, but I refused to let nausea overcome me again. This was too important for me to pass out with another random vision.

"I... I can't give you one. Not yet," he said hurriedly, "I just wanted to make sure you were alright."

"Well, I'm not," I huffed, folding my arms. He tilted his head, eyes blazing.

"You are, actually. Here." He reached into a bag – *since when did he have a backpack?* – and handed me a small jar of what looked like green slime.

I took it gingerly. "I hope this isn't medicine," I muttered, feeling my gut twist again.

"It's cream. Should help with your back," he explained. My fingers ran over the engravings on the lid, failing to decipher the symbols depicted.

"How did you-" I stopped, then, realising that he was gone. Disappeared as if he'd never existed.

No. The jar in my hands was proof enough that our conversation *had* occurred and so was the cut on my head-

Wait. My hands flew to the bandage he'd tied there and I pulled it away, tracing the smooth, perfectly healthy skin underneath. I frowned; had I imagined that? The bench beside me did have a few specks of crimson on it, though. Perhaps I had just... healed. But wasn't that impossible?

So wonders the human girl who has crazy dreams and now lives in a fairytale world.

"Ugh, this is making my head hurt," I grumbled, shoving the bandage and the jar into one of the pouches on my belt, before heading back to the castle. In hindsight, I probably should've noted how *quiet* the road was, that no-one else travelled on it, not even castle servants headed down to the market. So lost in my head was I that the rustling in the crates outside the guard-tower didn't worry me, even though the city was free of rats and wooden crates most certainly do not *rustle.*

I supposed in one weird sense I *was* noticing those things, just not reflecting on them until much later, too busy puzzling over the strange elf. I wasn't entirely sure he even *was* an elf. Arlan wasn't lying about the 'no green eyes' thing, I knew that, but what if this male wasn't an elf, or dwarf, or even a faery? What if he was some other creature that travelled through a portal like I had? It wasn't unreasonable to presume that there were other portals scattered around Pylisya, or other worlds that they opened to. Seeing as lots of strange fantasy creatures were now, in fact, my reality, who was to say that other 'myths' weren't real as well? Could the green-eyed stranger be a pixie, goblin, or troll? He was too human-like for the latter two, though. Perhaps he was something more sinister, like a werewolf or a vampire?

Jackie, you're going nuts, I mentally chided myself.

Right before I found myself face-to-face with a navy-skinned monster.

I screamed, in shock more than fear, and immediately drew a dagger from my belt, brandishing it out in front of me with a better stance than I'd adopted last time I met a beast like this.

"Get back, cobrai," I spat and the humanoid visibly recoiled. He soon composed himself, dark lips splitting to reveal the sharp teeth, glistening with the gory remains of his last victim.

"Ah, so you know what I am now. Flattering," he hissed, raising his sword. I tensed up, trying to remember the moves Turvo had taught me. *Go*

for the stomach, or even just the arms, anything to distract or hinder them. The sooner you can land a hit, the sooner you can get out of there.

"But do you know what *you* are?" the monster continued, starting to pace. I mirrored his steps, so we found ourselves circling, neither letting our guards down.

"Yes," I replied firmly, refusing to let his words do anything to me. *I'm a human and a dream-prophet. No more, no less.*

"No." His smirk grew, the reds of his eyes flashing with malice. "How sad, he still hasn't told you."

"Who's he-" The words evaporated as the breath was suddenly knocked from my lungs, by a roundhouse kick straight to my left side. I stumbled and wheezed, irritated that I'd allowed the cobrai to distract me in that manner.

"Hah, not so strong now, are we?" he jeered, spinning his sword as he advanced. I raised my dagger again, ignoring how my arm was shaking, a couple of ribs screaming their protests.

"I won't go down that easily," I snapped, but my voice was trembling. The cobrai opened his mouth to make some sort of snide comment in response, but a sudden gust of wind silenced him, the warm air pushing me back with such force I almost fell into the red-head standing there.

"Leave her alone, Zaro," he snapped, positioning himself in front of me. His eyes were so bright they practically glowed, trails of green light snaking over the lids and dancing across his face, illuminating previously hidden tattoos. I gasped, still struggling to reclaim my breath, but backed away on instinct.

Zaro's eyes glowed a brighter red in response. "Ah, Sachiel. And here I was, thinking we wouldn't meet again. I have *so* missed you," he purred, stroking his sword in a manner that was disturbing in the least.

"Go," Sachiel whispered to me, but my muscles were frozen. This was the guy who'd been name-dropped back in the woods! Why was he here, now? Why was the cobrai here?

What had I gotten myself into?

"You should return to us, Sachiel. It's not too late to come back home," Zaro continued, "Of course, we won't take you as our leader again, but you can be our comrade, hmm?"

Sachiel tensed up and the wind howled louder, droplets of rain falling on the ground around us. "Never," he growled, "I was done with that life years ago."

"Pity. I guess we'll have to do this the hard way, then." Zaro flung a dagger in my direction and I barely dodged, the attack snapping me out of my frozen state.

"Run!" Sachiel yelled as a blade materialised in his hand, meeting the sword that Zaro thrust at him.

I didn't waste any more time, spinning on my heel and sprinting towards the castle, ignoring the screeches of battle and pounding of bruised ribs as I poured all I had into just getting away from that situation.

It was only when I was back inside the castle that I realised there were no clouds in the sky.

Chapter Seventeen

- Benji -

Our journey to Lidan didn't take long and for that I was glad. The longer I spent with Thorn and Onta Baelthar, the more guilt seeped into my colour. I told myself that deceiving them was the only way I could let them go, but still, it was hard to keep up the lie. Persuading them to let us ride Brina there was hard enough, especially considering the majority of dwarves disliked riding with a passion. But Brina needed her exercise, I'd pointed out, and it would enable us to spend more time in the main town. Thorn's cocked eyebrows implied he was on to us and I knew we didn't have long to make our escape. Kalic would focus on getting Thorn alone, whilst I was to evade Onta Baelthar and Jasmine. It seemed I had the tougher end of the bargain, but Mutti hadn't nicknamed me 'little shadow' for nothing.

And so I found myself wandering through a bustling marketplace, Jasmine hot on my heels. Her rounded cheeks were flushed with the effort of keeping up with me – Onta Baelthar was already lost in the crowd, distracted by a blacksmithing friend of his – and I just needed to lose the dwarf. It was easier said than done, though. As if she had a sixth sense, Jasmine was hyper-alert with me that day, ensuring I was no more than four handspans away from her.

This is going to be tougher than we thought! Kal? Any luck?

Thorn's drinking, so we should separate soon, Kalic responded.

Drinking? I shouted, barely able to refrain from yelling it aloud, too.

Hah, only fruit juices. When he heads off to relieve himself, I'm running for the paddock.

I'll meet you there, I responded, turning my focus back to the produce on the stall in front of me. Kalic's plan wasn't that elaborate, but if it worked, who was I to protest?

"Want some, kiddo?" the dwarf behind the stall asked me. I blanked for a split second, then nodded, a plan forming in my head. He grinned and passed me one of his little wooden carvings – a horse, I guessed – which was decent, but nowhere near as good as my brother's handiworks. I pulled the bag from my shoulder and started to rifle through it, then frowned.

"Vaznek," I cursed under my breath, loud enough that Jasmine heard. Her dark nose wrinkled.

"Benji, what have I told you about your language?" she chided, though her colour lacked the confrontational crimson.

"Sorry," I sighed, "Just remembered, Onta Baelthar has my coins."

"Oh! Ah! Okay!" she fretted, rubbing her hands on her apron nervously, "Ah, I'll go find him, but don't go anywhere!"

"I won't," I replied, making a show of sitting down on an empty barrel. Jasmine scurried off, her pink flushed, and I jumped up as soon as she was out of sight.

"Thanks, but no thanks," I said to the stall's owner, handing him back the carving, along with a couple of silver coins. He eyed up the money sceptically.

"But kiddo-"

I put my finger to my lips and twitched my ears like I'd seen Turvo do. "You didn't see me, alright?"

His reply might've been no, but I didn't hear, because I was already gone, crawling on hands and knees underneath the various stalls. *I'm on my way,* I called out to Kalic, following the trail of blue paint I'd been dropping as I walked. Sure enough, it led back to the paddock, where Brina was already loose, my twin seated on her golden back.

"About time!" he exclaimed, as I darted around, freeing Onta Baelthar's horse and the dwarves' ponies.

"Sorry," I managed to gasp out, adrenaline churning through my veins, leaving me breathless and energised all at once. I hauled myself onto the mare and kicked her into action in the same fluid motion. "Come on, let's go!"

Brina whinnied and bolted, her hooves drumming against the grey paths, dislodging any loose stones and sending them flying behind us. It wasn't the most subtle escape, but speed was our ally now, more than anything else.

Kalic asked something, but his voice was lost in the wind, so he resorted to our telepathic bond. *Do you know where we're going?*

Just as far away from here as possible. Once we're sure they've not followed, then we can figure out a route. For now, just head south, I instructed, my mind flying back to the map I'd seen many times on Lanny's bedroom wall.

South. Sure. Without the cloudless sky, all sense of direction would've been lost, but the sun was our ally now, its position giving us enough clues to identify which way was south. Kalic took the reins and gently steered Brina whilst I tried not to hold on to him too hard, struggling to find the right balance of a grip strong enough to stay on the mare's back, but not so strong that I would appear scared. I *was* a little grey, but the adrenaline's neon orange helped to drown it out.

I couldn't help but glance behind, but the dust generated from Brina was forming a smoky cloud, one that I was unable to see through. Closing my eyes, I concentrated on searching for colours – Onta Baelthar's in particular – but he was still in Lidan, surrounded by a mass of brown. Satisfied, I tried to tell Kalic we could afford to slow, but he either didn't hear me or didn't want to, because Brina accelerated.

Kalic! I yelled, louder this time.

What if they catch up to us? My twin was suddenly panicked, his colour flashing grey as he questioned me, and I felt from the vibration across his back that he'd voiced his worries, too.

We have to keep going, I replied, *Find somewhere to rest, hide, and get a map.*

Planned this out well, didn't we, Kalic thought back sarcastically, and I sighed. He *was* true in his thinking, but until last night I hadn't thought of escaping so soon. My plan was simply to get to Torindell as quick as possible; it was as detailed as my first 'real' plan, where my goal had only been to leave. Now, at least, I had a destination in mind, but as my twin so *helpfully* pointed out, that wasn't good enough. Two young elves on the road were bound to draw attention, especially as we were near-identical. If Onta Baelthar or Jasmine followed and enquired about two young elf twins, we'd be very quickly identified.

My eyes darted from my clothing to Kalic's, noting that we were dressed far too similarly: it was a subconscious thing, I knew. Even if we wore different colours, which we did so less and less now, our clothing was always of a very similar style. Kalic would be loath to change his clothes, or his hair, but I cared much less. My hair had grown so long over the past seasons, and I did *not* want any dwarves with their shears coming near it, so I now had to tie it back like my brother's. That could easily be changed, though, and I couldn't help but grin at my new plan.

We did not stop for ages, though Brina slowed a little, and the sun gained much height before we came to another village. It was lesser than Lidan in both size and population, but large enough that we wouldn't instantly become the talk of the town. I urged my twin to stop; he wanted to carry on, but we were both tired and hungry, and I couldn't implement my idea without the help of a few older dwarves or elves.

I dismounted as soon as I could, ignoring the white aches in my legs, and took Brina's reins from my brother, whose colour pulsed faintly with fatigue. As I led them through the town, over cobbled streets of fake colour that were near-identical to those in Lidan, it suddenly occurred to me how out of my element I was. I'd never been anywhere by myself! No, that was a lie; I had gone to Kikarsko and Grayssan, but both of those had ended in utter disaster, with my family and friends having to step in and save me. Now *I* had to be the responsible one. Brina was exhausted, Kalic was struggling to keep his eyes open, so the only one of us awake enough to find what we needed was the one least capable of it.

I doubt Brina could buy us food, Kalic commented sleepily.

I didn't chide him for listening in, for once.

You can do it, Benji. I would help but I... so tired...

I quickly pulled out of his head before he fell unconscious, not wanting to sleep myself. *How* he could sleep, I didn't know – it was only a little past midday – but I let him rest. Clearly, he needed it.

"Little ones! How can I help you?"

I looked up as an elderly elf stopped by us, both relieved and apprehensive to see another of my kin. She was healthily tanned, her brown hair gaining a few white streaks that betrayed her age, but her eyes and colour were warm and friendly.

"We are travelling to see our mita," I lied quickly, "But my brother lost his bag. Do you know where I can get some clothes for him? And a map?"

The elf peered closer at us. "He's got a bag," she pointed out.

"Ah, those are mine," I corrected, "His had clothes for him and the map. But they are lost." I struggled to suppress my annoyance, focusing on letting my ears droop and my eyes grow wide. It had stopped working on Jasmine long ago, but a newcomer...

Her yellow buzzed and gained a sudden patch of grey-blue. "Of course, I'll sort you out what you need," she smiled, "This way."

I followed, sending a little more pity towards her, then stopped as I felt her yellow curl around me. Her hands were resting on the belt of her cream dress and no other skin was near me. Yet I could *feel* her yellow, calling to me, wanting to be a little warmer – it liked the pity, she did not experience that enough, but it was most pleased when she felt *joy* – and I recoiled fully, my mind trying to dart back to its source of nightmares.

No. I steeled myself; I was *not* going to fall asleep right now, not when I was so close! It was really important that I stay awake and *focus*. I couldn't let the nightmares come. Not now.

The lady led me to a tailor's and I busied myself with looking through the various clothing, trying to find something small and plain enough for me. There were a few pieces in a deep green, not my usual colour *at all*, but I didn't want it to be 'usual', did I? I grabbed two tunics, a grey cloak, and some dark brown breeches, then brought them to the owner of the small shop, fiddling in my bag for enough coins. My companion stopped me.

"No, no," she said, "I'll pay." Then she handed the dwarven tailor more than enough coins to cover the cost, the blue of pity in her colour more prevalent than ever before.

"Thank you," I smiled, though it was forced.

"It's no problem, really. I just want to help," she replied, as we left the shelter of the tailors. Brina stood outside, head hanging, and I moved to grab a bucket of water from the well at the town's centre before the lady elf could. She took it gratefully, lapping up loads whilst Kalic slumbered unawares. Then I spun on my heel to face the elf, her yellow incredibly irritating me now.

"I can do this by myself, okay?" I snapped, feeling the red start to pulse through me. She visibly recoiled.

"I just-"

"*No!*" I yelled, startling Kalic awake.

"Whaa?" he asked, still half-asleep.

"Vaznek!" I cursed, then quieter, "Kal, it's okay. Go back to sleep."

Thankfully my brother mumbled something and obeyed, so I was left to handle just the over-friendly elf lady.

"Show me where map buy," I blurted out, then mentally cursed as some of the words got stuck in my throat and didn't form. *Vaznek! I thought I was over this!*

"Are you-"

I shot her a glare that may or may not have been laced with a shock of red to her colour, and her face paled, her words cut off like some of mine had been. We stood there for a moment, neither moving or making a sound, before she closed her mouth and turned abruptly, heading for a large building adjacent to the town square. I read the runes above the door, then my steps faltered.

A library. Oh, for Zeraphin's sake...!

I was having far too much fun using the various 'forbidden' curses, both verbally and mentally, but even they could not detract from the situation in front of me.

I have to do this. It's not a private library. This is a public one. Just scrolls and maps and more scrolls. No faeries.

I closed my eyes; no grey made itself known.

Definitely no faeries.

Barely composing myself, I looked back up to thank the lady elf like Lanny would, but she was already gone. So I tethered Brina outside, took a deep breath, and stepped over the threshold.

Immediately the scent accosted me, all wood and paper and ink but surely there was *blood* too, blood and sweat and death, sweet, sickly death...

I cried out as faeries approached me, pouring out from behind every shelf, every desk, some of them walking confidently, others crawling on hands and knees, their limbs oozing crimson and ochre. Nausea ignited within me and I stumbled back, but the door behind me was blocked by one faery, more hideous than the rest of them combined.

The faery king.

It was not his appearance that was ugly – he carried the same arrogant beauty that my middle brother did – but his *colours*, which I could not see but I could *feel* them, feel the way that they stretched out towards me, not asking for manipulation, but probing as if to manipulate *me*.

I pulled away from him, looking all around for an escape route, but there was just faeries and scrolls and faeries and scrolls and faeries and-

Wait.

There were faeries, but no grey.

It wasn't real.

I slapped my cheek, hard, and fell to the ground with the force of it, grunting in pain as my arm hit the floor at an awkward angle. White laced up through my wrist, but I was strangely elated, because I *saw* it. I *saw* the colour of my pain, as I saw the blue-brown of three dwarves nearby, none of them knowing what to make of me.

And no faeries. There were *no faeries.*

I got to my feet, a small laugh escaping my lips, and I felt rather fey in that moment, but did not think much of it.

"Where are the maps?" I exclaimed, turning to the nearest dwarf. He pointed with a shaking hand and I bounded over, relishing in the fact that I was in a *library* and that *no-one* was going to die on me. Of course, those that *were* with me were rather freaked out – it was evident in their colours – but I really didn't care. I managed to locate a map that covered enough land to show our route to Torindell, then left as quickly as I could, before the dwarves recovered and started asking me questions.

For the final aspect of my plan, I found a younger elf sporting bright green hair and persuaded her to cut and dye mine in exchange for one of Kalic's least favourite carvings. Lanny was on my mind throughout the whole exchange, as I tried desperately to remember how he dealt with strangers in a polite manner, so much so that I almost asked for blond hair. But at the last moment I decided on light brown, as it was more subtle. She was rather disappointed that I didn't want anything more radical, but I was trying to hide, not stand out. And so, as the sun began to set, I peered into the illuminated waters of the well, unable to recognise the elf staring back at me. His hair was lighter than Fírean's and it hung in curls just below his pointed ears, which were perked in anticipation. The green tunic fit him very loosely, its lack of embroidery or detail signifying that he was no-one of any importance. He looked older, too, a light tan on his face making the freckles less noticeable.

He was me, and that was both exciting and frightening.

I gave my thanks to the elf who'd helped me, not pausing to see if she was happy with the little carving of an urthet, and made my way back over to Brina and Kalic.

"Are you rested?" I asked my brother, as he yawned and took in the rising moon.

"I slept all afternoon?" he gasped, sitting bolt upright and almost falling off Brina, who had been dozing herself.

I grinned. "Yes. But I entertained myself."

He took in my appearance, then his eyes widened. "Benji! What happened to you?"

I shrugged, but the grin refused to leave my face. "Twins are too obvious," I whispered, "so I changed a little."

Kalic's red suddenly lit up with yellow. "You *genius!*" he exclaimed, half-falling off Brina as he embraced me, his colour thrumming against me. I froze, but returned the gesture, holding my brother close to me, like he was my entire world.

He was half of it, actually. The other half resided where we were headed.

I produced the rolled-up map from my rucksack, brandishing it in front of my twin. "I know where we're headed, too," I announced proudly.

"Great!" Kalic looked like he was considering embracing me again, but he stiffened suddenly, noticing something behind me.

I think it's best we leave now, he said, then quickly added, *Don't act alarmed.*

I nodded slowly, hauling myself up onto Brina's back. *I'll steer this time. Be stealthy.*

I suppressed a laugh. *That, Kal, is why* I'm *taking the reins,* I retorted as he settled down behind me. The map I tucked back into my bag, its image still at the front of my mind, so I knew enough about where we were going. Then I lightly spurred Brina on, taking her through the rest of the town, so we emerged on the eastern side. Blue moonlight morphed the natural colours of the world around us, which was still barren of the greens and yellows of plants and insects, but I could sense the forests calling. Brina's rhythmic canter threatened to make me sleep, but I took a sip of some ale I'd borrowed from the last village, the sweet, fruity taste rejuvenating me enough to last the rest of the night.

We passed another village, though it was more of a town, and Kalic recommended I sleep but I lied, saying that I'd rested during the afternoon too. I didn't want to stop, not until we were far enough away that Onta Baelthar and Jasmine could not easily find us.

I didn't consider quite how *large* the land was, though.

Chapter Eighteen

- Jackie -

"Arlan!" I gasped, running through the corridors as if my life depended on it, "Arlan!"

The prince emerged from the music room so quickly that I nearly bowled him over.

"Aye, Jackie, what is it?" he exclaimed, as I tried to catch my breath, wincing at the pain shooting through my side.

"Fight," I gasped out, "cobrai, and this guy, with green eyes...!"

Arlan froze and pulled me into the music room, swiftly shutting the door behind us.

"Are you certain?"

I nodded rapidly.

"I don't understand," he muttered, at a loss for once.

"Neither do I."

He took in the way my hands curled protectively around my side. "Are you hurt?"

"The cobrai kicked me. It's not bad though," I protested as he moved in closer, his hands gently pushing mine away. I winced at the tentative prodding and his brow furrowed.

"Definitely a little bruised, but I don't think they're broken," he assessed.

"That's a relief," I sighed.

"Why didn't you come back with me?" he asked then, changing the subject, and I sensed he wanted to ponder my happenings later. My chest ached at the worry in his eyes.

"I was accosted by Hazel, and then..." I trailed off, not wanting to think of the vision I'd had. They were getting worse, showing me more and more horrific scenarios, but that last one had been the worst, by far.

"Then?" he prompted, but how could I tell him the truth?

"A vision, I... I don't want to talk about it," I sighed lamely, turning away as my face burned, partly at my inability to lie to him. Instead, I scooted around the question, leaving it unanswered, but I doubted he'd be satisfied with that. Suddenly, I noticed that Fírean was in the room with us, scribbling something down as he sat by the grand piano. His pale cheeks flushed as he caught my eye.

"Just trying to finish this composition," he muttered, in an explanation I hadn't asked for. I smiled slightly, then turned back to the older brother, managing to cool my own expression.

"Should we go elsewhere?" I asked.

Arlan paused. "I suppose I should get ready for the faeries' arrival," he commented bitterly.

"Why this again?"

He did not answer immediately, but placed his hands firmly on my shoulders, our eyes locking, and I could not turn away.

"Jackie," he then whispered, in the low, melodic tone that melted my insides, "I need you to tell me. Have you seen anything of this encounter?"

"I'm not sure, I..." I trailed off, gasping and staggering backwards as a wave of nausea hit me. Arlan called my name, but when I turned to reassure him, he was not there. My surroundings had shifted to the great hall, where the throne lay, and I knew then that this was *another* vision.

Two in one day? Lucky me, I thought sarcastically.

My child. You have been given this because he asked for it.

I froze. *Elohim?*

Yes.

I walked forward, as if pushed by an invisible force, close enough to the throne that I could easily make out the faces of those kneeling in front of it. One of the faeries, a young male, glanced up and met my gaze. I shifted. His crimson eyes were strangely familiar and they bore into me with a passion.

"Who is he?" I whispered, rather unnerved by his presence and apparent awareness.

One you must talk to.

"About what?"

That, you will discover when the time comes.

The faeries and the hall faded, giving way to Arlan's beautiful face.

"Jackie?"

I rubbed my head as he helped me to sit up. "Another vision," I groaned.

"Did I cause it? Jackie, I'm sorry-"

"Don't apologise," I interrupted, "I'm fine. And I can answer your question: yes, I have, but I cannot see anything ill happening. If it does, then don't blame me; Elohim did not permit me to see that."

"I'm sure if something truly bad were to happen, you would've seen it," he replied, with much more conviction than I possessed. I wanted to believe him, but I just couldn't. Had I seen the old king die? Yes, but I didn't understand it then. Had I seen Benji leave? No, though I had been told where to send him. I'd have to be on alert the whole time that the faeries were visiting, in case any other clues or visions came as warning before they attacked. That they *would* attack, I had no doubt. It was simply a matter of when and where. The faeries wanted retribution for us rightly accusing them of a crime! I was certain that if they killed one Zeraphin, they would not hesitate to kill the others. Part of me wondered if I was being a little too rash and unforgiving, but it *was* hard to see reason with a race that I had only witnessed doing evil.

Especially in my penultimate vision.

The more I thought about it – try as I might, it still hung heavily on my mind – the more I was convinced that the two foreboding figures abusing someone I loved were, in fact, faeries. At least, the bearded one certainly was.

But now, I was supposed to actively seek one out? *Elohim, are you crazy?* I doubted the faeries would take too kindly to me. I wasn't an elf, but – my hands gently touched the pointed tips of my ears – I wasn't entirely human anymore, a thought that both scared and excited me. Mostly scared, though.

The cobrai was adamant that there was something I did not know about myself, but what? Was Pylisya changing me? That, I knew the answer to. But *why* had he suggested my... differences... before? Could cobrai have visions too?

"Um, Jackie?"

I jolted back to my peculiar reality, smiling sheepishly at Fírean. "Sorry, I was-"

"Lost in thought?"

"Yes."

Fírean nodded and smiled in return. "I get the feeling. Arlan said he's left some clothes in your room – you didn't hear that, did you?"

I shook my head, feeling heat rise again to my cheeks.

"I thought not," Fírean continued, but his tone was understanding, rather than condescending. I gave him my thanks, then quickly left the room, hurrying along to my own. The deep green tunic I wore had served me the majority of yesterday, including the night, and I was keen to freshen up, now the mention of clothing had crossed my mind.

The wooden door opened smoothly, soft pine giving way to the warm, yellowish colour of the walls I could call mine. Directly ahead sat a large, oval window, the outer panes of glass stained a brilliant blue, almost identical to the colour of Arlan's eyes. The few rays of sunlight that trickled through the coloured glass cast everything they touched in a near-turquoise glow, as if the moon was risen and dancing in, rather than the sun. Over the year I had expanded my personal belongings; what had started as bare shelves now housed various trinkets. The centre shelf I'd dedicated to everything that Arlan gave me, or items that reminded me of him, such as a polished sapphire-like stone and an elegant bracelet he'd given me for my seventeenth birthday. On the shelves above sat a collection of scrolls, the majority written in the elegant script of the elves, which I was slowly but surely learning. Below them, a few other treasures had accumulated, including the key to the back door of my old home on Earth.

The bed lay adjacent to the shelves, a grand piece of furniture, far too big for me but I wouldn't complain. Some nights, when Hazel did not want to be alone, she would join me, and the bed was more than large enough for the two of us. She did that less and less now, so the sheets beside me were often cold and empty, but I didn't have the heart to get it changed.

On the light, downy covers lay a dress of a glorious emerald, and as I approached my eyes fell on a little note by one of the sleeves. Written in delicate script, it declared;

"Reminds me of your eyes. Wear it for me. ~ A."

A blush rose unbidden to my cheeks and I pocketed the note, turning to inspect the dress closer. There was a significant lack of lace, which I was extremely glad for, and in the places where such material would usually be – the cuffs, collar, and hem – there was instead intricate embroidery, tiny leaves and flowers stitched in threads of copper and gold. The sleeves themselves were long, but quite loose, as with the rest of the dress. It was quite high-cut, though still shaped at the waist, and the skirt of the dress flowed smoothly down so it would not hug my legs. I swiftly drew the curtains and undressed, washing with the cloth and bowl of warmed water that sat on a table at the bedside, before slipping on my undergarments and then the dress itself. It fit perfectly, shaped enough to highlight the few curves I did have, but not so fitting that I could still easily move and breathe in it. I wondered when someone had measured me: probably when I first arrived, though I had only been fitted for tunics and breeches then, as this was the first dress I'd worn the whole time I'd been in Pylisya.

A knock on the door snapped me out of my thoughts and I quickly tied my hair back, not wanting to bother with tidying it up immediately. Kalia entered before I'd given her permission, but as the queen she had full rights to, so I didn't complain. Her dress was in a similar style to mine, an elegant lilac complete with gold lacing; it was beautiful, but certainly not to my tastes.

"Jackie, you look lovely," she smiled, her bright eyes darting over my appearance. I resisted the urge to squirm under her scrutiny, which even then made me feel rather insignificant. It wasn't completely Kalia's fault, though. She hardly ever had time for her sons, let alone me, so I rarely saw her. Becoming queen so young – in elvish terms, at least – took its toll, forcing the already-regal lady to increase her skills tenfold, becoming the perfect companion to her royal husband. With that was bound to come an aura of superiority.

I dipped my head to her in thanks, conscious that my hair was starting to fall out of its lame ponytail. The ebony locks were difficult enough to control when I used specialist conditioner, instead of whatever plant oils Turvo had recommended to me. In recent weeks, I had taken to simply slinging it back out of the way, especially as it fell below my shoulders: an issue I would have remedied, if it wasn't for the silly elven culture that insisted the longer the hair, the better. To cut it as short as my old style would be almost criminal, despite that obvious fact that I was *not* an elf. Still, I lived with them, so I accepted their peculiar rules, making a mental note to have Hazel 'accidentally' cut off my ponytail in a failed prank, sometime in the future.

Kalia, of course, noticed the state of my hair and immediately offered to brush it for me. I was tempted to decline, but the creasing around her eyes and tightness of her cheeks implied that not all was as good as she'd like it to seem. So I relented, letting her tackle the wavy mess, whilst trying to think of conversation. Thankfully, she saved me from speaking first, but not in the best way.

"I hear you won't give my son a straight answer," she commented, a little too casually for the topic in question. I stiffened instinctively, glad she couldn't see the blush on my cheeks that seemed to be my body's immediate reaction whenever Arlan was mentioned.

"Sorry?" I muttered, unsure of what the appropriate response would be. But to my surprise, Kalia chuckled, the sound very unusual coming from her.

"Thrice I declined Arazair before finally accepting his proposal. I am pleased you're not rushing into things," she said, gently working my hair into braids.

"You declined him?" I exclaimed.

"Why, yes. The first time we were only children, so it would not have been official anyway. The second, I was in a relationship with another at the time, though we separated shortly after. And the third time... I wanted to accept, but Baelthar had a lot of problems then, so the timing was really inappropriate. It made me think, though, and realise that I truly did love him. So the fourth time he proposed, I accepted," she explained.

"Didn't he give up?"

Kalia laughed again, "I am glad he didn't! Arazair is ever so stubborn, and unfortunately, he's passed that onto four of our sons. Arlan is stubborn too, not as much as his father, but enough that he won't stop until you give him a definite answer. If you decline," her tone sobered at this, "then I have no doubts that he will leave you be and cease his pursuit. But if you *do* want to officiate things, then I suggest you accept soon."

I stared down at my hands, pondering her words. "I do love him," I confessed, my voice barely above a whisper.

Kalia finished the central braid and gently smoothed the rest of my hair down. "Then what is stopping you?"

I hesitated. "If I... accept... then there's no going back. I don't want to leave, but to say yes... finalises things," I finished lamely, taking the bracelet off my 'Arlan Shelf' and slipping it on to my left wrist.

Kalia stepped back and moved so we were facing one another. "You must do what your heart calls you to do," she advised, "And listen to the spirit of Elohim. Personally, I think that Pylisya needs you. *Arlan* needs you. But of course, it is your decision, whether to stay or not."

"I *am* staying," I quickly interjected, though the words felt rough on my tongue. If one of the Zeraphin brothers were to die like my vision implied...

could I stay in Pylisya still? Knowing that I could see it, but not prevent it? Unless I *could* prevent it –

Hope arose in me then and I sensed that, if there was even the slimmest of chances that the events I saw could be prevented, then Elohim would show me and I would do all in my power to stop it. I didn't want another death on my hands, albeit indirectly.

"Lady Kalia?" I asked carefully.

She tutted, her blue eyes softening. "Please, drop the formalities. I'd like to hope we are close enough to be family," she said gently.

Our definitions of 'close' were certainly rather far apart, but I didn't comment on it.

"I would like to be present at the faeries' meeting," I continued, keeping my expression calm.

"That may be a little complicated. Arlan was hoping to introduce you as his fiancée, you see," she explained, "But as that is not the case, I am not sure how we could explain your presence."

"Please, I need to be there in case I *see* something," I pleaded, putting extra emphasis on the word. She seemed to catch on, then, her brow furrowing.

"And have you 'seen' anything?"

"No, not yet," I confessed, "But there is a chance I might."

She scrutinised me then, with more vigour than when she'd first entered. "Hmm. You're a little young," she mused, "but I suppose you *could* pass for an adviser. Just stay quiet and don't take the role too seriously. It would not be good for you to give inappropriate advice."

"Of course not! Thank you," I breathed, both relieved and nervous all at once.

Kalia managed a smile. "I expect you to be there soon. We don't have long before the faeries will arrive."

I nodded in acknowledgement, then she left me with much to ponder over and not enough time. Sighing, I resorted to checking my appearance over one last time and abruptly halted in shock at the mirror. My hair had been styled in a way that was so typically *elvish*, I looked like I could belong in this world. It didn't help that my ears already seemed more pointed than when Arlan had drawn my attention to them, so much so that I could almost pass for an elf. *Ridiculous*. I was just a human, nothing more. What was this world doing to me?

My eyes fell on the small jar of cream, in the same moment that a searing pain ripped across my back. I gasped and cried out, half of me expecting to see a hooded attacker, the other half awaiting a vision. Neither proved true, though, and the pain spread up to my shoulder blades, the shock of it forcing me to my knees. Vision blurring, I fumbled with the ties on my dress and pulled it off, surprised to see no bloodstains or marks of any kind on its back; it certainly felt as if my skin was being split open. I seized the jar, almost dropping it as I was lulled towards unconsciousness, but managed to scoop some of slimy cream out and awkwardly smear it over the screaming areas, twisting my arms in the process. Nothing happened for a few minutes, and I was just giving in to the calling darkness when a soft numbing spread through the bones and muscles, relieving the pain. Shakily, I set the jar down, wiping furiously at my cheeks in an effort to tidy up my appearance.

"Vaznek," I cursed under my breath, "How long is that going to keep on happening?"

Someone knocked on the door and I hurriedly rinsed my hands of the cream before attempting to redress myself.

"Jackie? Are you ready?" Arlan called.

"Not yet!" I yelled back, "Give me a moment – ah, stupid dress!" One of the sleeves had somehow become tangled with the ribbons by the waist of the dress and I struggled to free it without causing any damage. Arlan entered then, despite my words, and smoothly took in my predicament.

"Having a little trouble?" he asked, his left eyebrow twitching. I rolled my eyes and fought the urge to cross my hands over my barely-clad chest, silently praying that my cheeks would remain pale.

"Some help would be nice," I admitted, letting him work the fabric free. He did so nimbly, as if he'd done it before, and I realised that he probably *had*; not with a dress, but the robes and tunics of his four younger brothers. I moved to finish dressing as soon as he'd finished, but Arlan beat me to it, gently pulling the garment the rest of the way.

"I can do it," I protested, as he moved to tie the back.

"No, I've got it," he replied gently, true to his word. I sighed, but let him, slightly unnerved by how *natural* his hands felt close to my skin, lacing the back of the dress, his breath warm and soft against my neck.

I could have this most days, I realised, *if I did accept his proposal.*

"Jackie?"

"Um, thanks," I mumbled, turning to face him. Arlan's cheeks were crimson, to my surprise, and he wouldn't meet my gaze at first. "What is it?" I then prompted.

"I... Jackie, you, uh..." He blushed harder, both ears flopping down and darkening at the tips as he gazed at me with an expression of... adoration?

"Yes?" I asked gently, feeling my own cheeks heat up.

"You look amazing," he commented, the words almost slurring as he blurted them out.

"Th-thanks," I stammered, "And for the dress, I-"

"Jackie! Arlan! They're here!" Fírean announced suddenly, bursting into the room with Turvo hot on his heels. We both blushed and stumbled back away from each other, as the two brothers realised what they'd walked in on.

"Sorry," Fírean added quickly.

"But the faeries *are* here," Turvo continued, before giving Fírean a pointed look. They left as abruptly as they came and Arlan flashed me a small smile.

"Later?" he whispered, offering his arm to me. I took it and nodded.

"Later," I echoed, knowing exactly the conversation we needed to have. We just had to make it through the faery meeting, which was much easier said than done.

Chapter Nineteen

- Benji -

We covered a lot of ground over the next few days, pausing only for necessary breaks. Kalic and I took it in turns to sleep in the saddle, and we steered clear of any settlements, living off our meagre supply of food from Lidan and the other village. The journey had taken us over dry, rocky ground at first, but soon the stones gave way to paths of fallen leaves, surrounded on either side by trees whose colours pulsed a fainter green every day. It was beautiful, but desolate too, and though I was glad to be amongst nature again, it was not the nature I knew and loved.

Just over a fortnight since we'd first set out, the remaining bread went stale and the skins of water grew dry. This I discovered one day, as dusk set in and my growling stomach had only a few nuts to sustain it. Tentatively, I prodded Kalic's red, forcing my twin to wake from his slumber.

"What is it?" he grumbled as Brina slowed to a halt.

I showed him what was left of our supplies. "It will take us at least two more days to reach Grayssan," I sighed, "we don't have enough to get us there."

Kalic frowned and rubbed his eyes, trying to get his brain into motion. His thoughts were very sluggish, remnants of strange dreams still echoing in his mind. "So just head to another town, right?"

"No!" I exclaimed, suddenly rather frustrated, "Look!" My finger almost punched a hole in the weary map and my twin struggled to follow. "We're here. Roughly. Grayssan *is* the nearest town."

His eyes narrowed and he tore the map from my hands, scrutinising its complex lines. "*How* did we get lost?" he yelled, startling Brina. She bucked slightly and I had to grab Kalic's shoulder to not fall off.

"Not lost," I complained, but he was having none of it. His pocketed the map, pulling himself from my hold in the same motion, and dismounted, storming towards a slight clearing in the trees.

"Get some sleep," he growled over his shoulder, "I'll figure this out."

"No!" I half-fell off Brina and jogged after him, "Kal, stop! We're *not* lost, just..." I trailed off as his red flared up, the fury pulsing through it physically repulsing me.

What have I done? I wondered, glad Kalic wasn't listening in on my thoughts, *Everything was going fine, I thought he was pleased with me!* Was I wrong in taking the lead on this? Was I wrong for not checking the supplies sooner? The latter I suspected for sure.

Sighing, I settled down on the outskirts of the clearing, wrapping my cloak around me tighter and using my bag as a makeshift pillow. Sleep whilst riding was light and infrequent, enough to replenish me, but not enough for the nightmares to take hold. But lying down on surprisingly soft ground, the crackle of a campfire calming my mind, was the perfect vulnerable moment for those grey claws to reach out and –

I jerked backwards, forcing myself awake as my head collided with a tree trunk. Everything flared white for a moment, fading quickly to a dull throb, and I carefully sat up to not aggravate my new injury. Across the clearing, Kalic slumbered near the fire, despite having dozed throughout the afternoon. His near-constant need for sleep was almost concerning, but I had more pressing things to worry over.

Slowly, I picked my way over to him, hesitantly reaching for his colour before I did his person. It was clouded with dreams again, so I leant over and slipped the map from his pocket, scooting round to the other side of the fire. He didn't even stir and I let out a breath I hadn't realised I was holding in. Unfurling the map, I moved closer to the flames in order to get a better look at its sketchy, squiggled lines that failed to match up to the landscape surrounding us. It was then that a weight slammed into my chest, grabbing my windpipe and squeezing it until I could barely breathe. There were no colours, I knew the attack wasn't physical, but that knowledge did nothing to stop the crushing, or to stop my lungs from screaming for much-needed air. I gasped and fell back, the map barely missing the flames as it slipped from my clammy fingers.

And I realised, Kalic was right. I didn't know what I was doing.

The map made no sense. The paths before us were all open, but none was seemingly better than the other. Kalic suggested before that we head east. The last group of dwarves we passed advised heading south first. One elf instructed me to head west and change our destination completely.

I knew what they saw. Kalic saw me as his brother, only as able as he was: so, not good enough to lead us onwards. East was logical to him. He didn't understand the sense of foreboding surrounding it.

The dwarves saw two young elves, far away from home. To them, if you kept heading south, you'd end up somewhere. They disliked the folk in both the east and west, and as we came from the north, south is what they thought to be the only viable option. But what was best for them was not necessarily best for us; though we'd headed that way, I now wasn't sure I trusted their judgement.

The elf saw us for what we were: lost, frightened children struggling in an adult's world. She'd told me to go west, because that was where the majority of our kin lived. She wanted us to go somewhere safe and secure, far away from the harsh reaches of the other races. She thought our future lay there, in a land we could grow up in, learn trade in, become successful yet oblivious to the surrounding world.

But they didn't know my heart.

I couldn't shut their voices out, they were screaming, screaming at me to make a decision, and they all thought that what they said was in my best interests but the pathways were all *different* and I couldn't *think* in all this noise and would they *please just shut up* because I needed my space, I needed to decide, I needed –

I didn't really know what I needed. But I *did* know that it wasn't that.

Head bowed, I gazed into the flames, searching for something, *anything* to help me in that moment. The fire flickered, a memory forming in its centre, the words of my brother; *Elohim loves you,* whispered as he cradled me close, and I fell into both of the arms caressing me. Lanny's touch drifted away with the breeze churning up the embers, but the second warmth stayed with me.

"Elohim," I murmured to the starlit sky, "I don't know who's right, and I... I can't do this. Please," my voice dropped so much, almost no sound was made, "I need Your help. Lanny believed in You, I never really understood..." I stopped then, my throat constricting so much I couldn't get the words to form. Something wet fell on my hand and I flared slightly red as I realised it was a tear.

Don't cry, don't cry, I chided myself, then stiffened. *When... when did I start thinking that it's not okay to cry?*

The red faded from my colour as quickly as it had come and for that I was glad. I didn't want it. I didn't want the red of anger and frustration to have a hold on me. I needed it to be *gone*. Examining my colours, I found reams of blue and grey, but those could stay. No matter how hard I tried, I doubted they would leave: not with what had happened in the library. They were stains that I just accepted. But the red was of my own making – my *wrong* making – and it had to go.

Tendrils of sleep clawed at my mind, urging it to rest, but I resisted. There were far too many things for me to figure out; I couldn't afford to go to sleep.

Benji.

I stiffened. "Who... who's there?" I stammered, glancing around cautiously, but the only colour I could sense was the warm, white-gold that had been wrapped around me since staring into the firelight.

My Name is one that you know, but do not concern yourself. Sleep, my child.

"I can't sleep," I protested, "The faeries-"

They will not plague you tonight. That, I promise you.

I tried to respond, but the warmth lulled me into unconsciousness and this time I succumbed.

"Benji, wake up!"

I groaned and swatted at the hand waving in front of my face, blinking owlishly as my eyes adjusted to the bright sunlight seeping through the overarching canopy of trees.

Wait. Sunlight.

"I slept through the night," I muttered aloud, in partial disbelief.

"Yes, and well into the morning too," my twin huffed, "I've been trying to wake you for ages."

"Sorry," I sighed, sitting up and wincing as the bones in my lower back stretched and cracked back into place.

"Eh," Kalic shrugged, his scarlet rather placid, "I managed to get us some supplies, though." He gestured to a pile of faded green by his feet, which, upon further scrutiny, turned out to be a deer's corpse – and not one that had been dead long, judging by its colour.

"That's disgusting," I grimaced, then frowned. "Kal, how did you-"

He shuddered. "Trust me, you *don't* want to know," he replied quickly, and I didn't try to probe into his mind. As horrid as the thought of eating a newly-deceased animal was, I knew we had little choice otherwise. The forest offered many berries, but over half of them were poisonous, and I couldn't differentiate between the ones that were safe and those that would kill an elf. Ethlon had hinted that I would be able to sense it based on the plants' colours, but every plant just seemed *green* to me, and I wasn't planning on finding the creepy, controlling elf anytime soon, so I supposed that was something I just wouldn't know. Thus, I agreed to Kalic's idea of cutting up the deer into more 'manageable' pieces of meat, though I refused to help.

"Benji, please. My tools are for wood, not flesh," Kalic complained.

"No." I replied firmly, staring into the face that was near-identical to mine as I thought of the time I'd sworn to not hurt any living creature.

"The deer is dead*,"* Kalic responded bluntly.

"Only just." I then thought of how doing such an act would be very likely to make me sick, and did Kalic really want to put up with me being ill?

Considering that he set to skinning the deer with no further comments, I presumed the answer was no.

I busied myself with the map, trying to block out the disgusting noises and the *stench* that came with them, finding that the lines made just a little more sense as I looked on them with refreshed eyes. By the position of the sun, I judged where south lay: and from that, where we needed to go to reach Grayssan. A ray of the sun then burst forth and collided with the map, highlighting a faded blue line that I hadn't noticed before, and I jumped up in excitement.

"Kal!" I exclaimed, "There's a small stream not too far away!"

"Really?" His ears perked up and I nodded rapidly before forgetting that he wasn't looking at me.

"Yes!" I answered quickly.

"That's good." He shoved what meat he could salvage into a thick leather bag, then slung it over his shoulder. I packed up the rest of our meagre camp in silence, about to mount Brina when Kalic's hand brushed against mine.

"Benji, I'm sorry for getting annoyed at you yesterday," he said gruffly, his colour spotting with unfamiliar pink. I turned and smiled at him.

"It's okay, I was annoyed at me too," I laughed slightly, and he returned the smile, "Ready?"

"Yes." I clasped my brother's hand and pulled him close in a quick embrace, like I'd seen the dwarves do, before the two of us scrambled onto Brina's back: and this time, I let him lead.

The journey to Grayssan was relatively uneventful; the promise of a river proved true, so the meat, nuts, and water sustained us enough to reach the small city. The skies were kind to us too, letting the sun shine through and holding off the threat of rain. But Kalic and I grew closer than we had the past two years, even since setting off on the journey, as if some sort of barrier had dissolved from between us, allowing our connection to grow even stronger. His thoughts flowed with mine, not obtrusive, but in complete synchronisation, and I understood his reasoning even as he understood mine. If he wondered at the change, he didn't voice or think it, but I did, searching our colours and pouring back over memories in an attempt to decipher the reasoning *why*. Before I could, though, Grayssan was upon us, displaying a stronger variety of colour than that which I'd been exposed to in a long while. Nausea churned within me and I struggled to press it down, refusing to let myself freak out like I had at first in Torindell. *Vaznek*, that was an embarrassing memory.

"You alright, Benji?" Kalic asked gently, bringing Brina to a halt. I took a deep breath – all wood and horsehair and *Kalic* – then nodded as I exhaled, forcing myself to look at the colours of the village as a whole, rather than trying to examine each and every colour. That would only result in an amalgamation of multicoloured brown that overwhelmed my senses and made my head burst.

"Yeah, I'm okay," I replied, adjusting the bag slung across my shoulder.

"We'll only stay a night or two, I promise," my twin said firmly, clicking Brina into a steady trot. I nodded, toying with the unfamiliar curls that had already grown past my chin again. They were still brown, Kalic had reassured me, but I needed to find some more dye soon in order to keep up the appearance.

By the time we entered through the northern gates of the city, it was nearing dusk, so most of the inhabitants were indoors. Still, Kalic slipped on the fake beard he'd made from moss, leaves, and some of my black paint, as I adjusted his natural hair to hide the tips of his ears. My hair was far too short to even try to cover my elvish ears, so I simply pulled the hood of my cloak up and hoped that no-one would ask me to remove it.

"Greetings," Kalic called out, deepening his voice, "Can you direct us to an inn where my friend and I may stay?"

The elven guard he addressed looked us both over rather quizzically. "What are two dwarves doing so far south?" he asked.

"Visiting our kin in Torindell," my twin replied smoothly, and I barely suppressed a smile at his perfectly truthful words.

The guard grunted something, then pointed down the street. "The Red Swan inn should allow your kind. Don't hold me to it, though."

"I won't. Thank you, sir," Kalic responded, and we both dipped our heads politely.

'Your kind'? I asked mentally.

Kalic clicked Brina forward again, an ugly ripple seeping through his colour. *It seems dwarves may not be welcome here.*

I could show them I'm an elf, I suggested.

Only do that as a last resort. I doubt word has reached Grayssan of our disappearance, but we must be on guard.

Agreed.

We dismounted outside the inn, a tattered, worn-down building, its walls flaking red paint, the sign declaring its name sun-faded and barely legible. Instinctively my hand slipped into my bag, feeling the few pots of paint that I did have, wondering if I could do something to help.

I've got another plan, I told Kalic, *it could save us money.* Quickly, I filled him in, but before he could respond, a trio of faeries came out of the inn and sized us up.

"Travellers?" one asked and I tensed as their greys flooded my vision. *These are different faeries,* I told myself, *they're good faeries. They won't hurt us.*

"Yes," Kalic affirmed, "We only wish to stay one night." *Benji, will you be alright here?* he added, sensing my discomfort.

I should be. Just need to get away from them.

"That'll be two silvers each. Plus five for the horse."

"Five?" my twin spluttered.

"Yes. Or you go bother someone else," the second faery snapped.

"Wait," I interjected, struggling to keep my voice steady, "What about four silvers for the two of us, and I pay for the horse by painting your sign there," I said, gesturing.

The lead faery's cold, purple eyes fixed on me. "You're an artist?"

"Yes."

"He's excellent," Kalic added, "People pay a lot for his wood-painting."

"It's a good deal," I grinned, "Even brought my own paints."

"Five silvers, plus the painting, and we'll accept," the faery negotiated.

Is that okay? I asked my twin.

A little steep, but better than the original nine.

"Agreed," he answered, counting the coins out and handing them to the faery who I presumed was the innkeeper. He took them and frowned.

"What about the painting?"

A flash of red shot through me, but I ignored it. "It's dusk," I pointed out, "I'll do tomorrow." Then I winced, as a few words seemed to get lost from my brain to my mouth, thankfully unacknowledged by the faeries. They agreed then, threatening that Brina wouldn't be returned to us until the painting was completed, but I didn't expect anything less.

We were shown to a meagre room on the second floor, but soft beds and two mugs of ale awaited us, so I wasn't going to complain about the draught, or the rats scurrying about under the dresser. As soon as I'd locked the door, Kalic tore off his fake beard and furiously scratched his rather red chin.

"I think I'm allergic to something in that moss," he huffed, taking a swig of the ale. I sipped mine cautiously, very conscious of how un-resistant my body was to such beverages.

"You did great, Kal."

"Mmm." He downed the last of his mug in the manner of one who is familiar with the drink and I wondered if Kalic had really been telling the truth about the fruit juices in Lidan. Not that it mattered now, with the two of us fending for ourselves, no adults around to tell us what we couldn't do or say or eat.

"Vaznek," I said then, giggling at the way the curse sounded in my childish tone. The mug of ale in my grasp was emptier than I'd thought and I quickly placed it back on the dresser before I could lose my head even further.

"You sound silly when you curse," Kalic commented.

"I know," I grinned, "For Zeraphin's sake."

"You swine," he retorted and we both fell into a fit of laughter, yellow pulsing through the room, tinged with the rosiness that only came when sobriety was lacking. Yet, I did not care, I decided, as the ale found itself in my hands again, the sweetness tickling my throat and warming my stomach. I laughed again, the sound liberating, then I tossed the mug aside, nearly hitting Kalic in the process.

"Aye!" my twin yelped, followed by a series of hiccups.

"We should sleep," I giggled, flopping onto one of the creaky,stained mattresses. It was softer than the bed of leaves and dirt that I'd last slept in, though, and the peculiar pops generated with my motion were more amusing than irritating, especially in the hazy state of my mind.

"Mmm, not so tired," Kalic protested, echoing my movements. A shaft of moonlight crept in and illuminated his face, the shape and colour that was so alike to mine and yet so *unlike* in the same manner. We lay there for a few moments, myself reflecting on the serenity of our colours, ignoring the ones that drunkenly staggered around in the rooms adjacent to and below our own.

"Love you, Kal," I murmured, as the lightheaded feeling turned into sudden tiredness, the physical demands of travel finally catching up to me. My twin's red flickered and began to cloud over as he ran my last words over in his mind.

"I... love you too, Benji," he mumbled back, "goodnight, I suppose."

I rolled away and smiled, then sent a silent plea up to the skies above. *Elohim, grant me a dreamless night again. Please.*

And as my twin slipped into unconsciousness, so did I.

Chapter Twenty

- *Jackie* -

I stood in the hall beside Arlan, trying my best not to fiddle with the elegant cuffs of my dress. The air was thick and stifling, and for a moment I regretted begging to be let in, but the thought quickly passed. I was tense, alert in mind, yet managed to relax my physical posture enough to not look out of place. However, Arlan's usually smooth face was currently lined, his jaw rigid, a couple of veins on his slender neck sticking out with the stress he was failing to hide. My hand brushed against his and he relaxed ever so slightly, flashing me a quick smile, one that didn't quite reach his eyes. This was the first contact Arazair would've had with the faeries' leaders since the death of his father, and it was crucial. No-one had explicitly said anything of the consequences, but I caught the drift that, if these negotiations were to go wrong, it could result in war.

Taking a deep breath to calm my racing heart, I absentmindedly adjusted my fringe, hoping the angle at which it fell would cast a shadow over my eyes, hiding their unique colour from a distant glance. The elves all had their hair pulled back away from their faces, even Fírean, whose brown locks were slung into a ponytail like Turvo's. All three brothers stood clothed in their best robes: green and copper on Turvo, blue and silver on Fírean, and white and gold on Arlan. The latter's made his beautiful hair stand out, even though it was braided back in an attempt to be less conspicuous. We were lined up in a peculiar formation, with Turvo, Fírean, and Kalia to the right of the throne, and myself, Arlan, and one of the king's lead advisors on the left. King Arazair himself sat grandly on the throne, made from the smoothest stone and carved with the six-pointed star of the house of Zeraphin. Ribbons of gold threaded throughout, so it appeared that colour in appearance, rather than the deep grey the stone originally had been. He was the archetype of royalty: in appearance, at least.

A knock arrested my attention then and I turned as an elven herald pushed the grand oak doors open, bowing low.

"Your Majesty, may I present, King Havain and his company of faeries," the herald announced, stepping to one side as seven figures entered the hall, their muddied boots leaving footprints on the luscious red carpet that ran down the hall's centre, from the door to the throne. I examined each of them briefly, silently asking Elohim for guidance, but nothing came.

The first faery was clearly their king; I recognised him from that visit over two years ago. He sported a small goatee, with chin-length black hair and skin as dark as Hazel's, clothed in deep purple robes that screamed superiority in every fibre. His ears, I noted, tapered to a small point like mine now did, but the majority of his company had rounded ones. In fact, I would have thought all of them to be human aside from the young male closest to me, whose tanned ears were almost as long and pointed as an elf's. He looked up at me and I started, barely holding in a gasp. Crimson eyes met mine and I realised that I was looking upon the faery from my vision; the one I supposedly had to speak to.

"Greetings," Arazair said then, his voice echoing around the hall, utterly domineering. The faeries all bowed, save their king, who only dipped his head in a semi-polite gesture.

"Greetings," Havain repeated curtly.

"I assume you are here to negotiate," Arazair stated firmly.

"You assume correct."

"Speak, then."

Havain's deep, red-brown eyes surveyed the room, gaining a peculiar grin when they settled on me. I kept my face still in a pleasant half-smile, but shot him as large a glare as I could muster with my eyes. He turned back to Arazair, his demeanour darkening.

"The restrictions and accusations you have placed upon my people are false and unjustified. We did not kill King Myranis," Havain began. Beside him, the young, crimson-eyed faery's hands clenched into fists.

Arazair gripped the arms of his throne tightly. "I am certain it was by faery hands that my father was slain."

"Still, it was not by our doing," Havain replied, his shoulders lifting in a minor shrug. Arlan's breath escaped his lips in an angry hiss at the audacity of it.

"You are faeries, are you not? It was some of your race. And so, you are held accountable."

I winced: Arazair's reasoning wasn't at all the best, brought on by his anger, I suspected. *Elohim, help him,* I prayed silently.

"So if one elf is a thief, does that make you all thieves?" came the retort.

"Absolutes."

"You are being hypocritical," Havain scoffed, "You cannot fault all faeries for the actions of a few."

"It was treason!" Arazair roared, standing from his throne. Six of the faeries fell back into their kneeling positions, but Havain straightened up, rising to the challenge.

"*I* am the ruler of Pylisya," our king continued, "as was my father before me. The murder of King Myranis was treason of the highest degree. You forget that the faeries are still under my rule, as they were under his. Did I punish them all? No! I still allow your people to walk in my streets, trade in my marketplaces, travel the land as they wish. My quarrel is not with them but with *you,* Havain. There is far too much suspicion surrounding you. First, you came for an unannounced visit, then my father was murdered."

"I know what happened," Havain snapped, "We assume that the assassins followed us."

"But why did you come to visit me, Havain? At my family's home, nonetheless: not the castle?"

The faery's mouth flopped open like a goldfish, then he abruptly closed it, his dark brow furrowing as he tried to think of a response.

"It was my fault," the young faery spoke up then, his voice surprisingly soft and lilting. Havain glared at him with an expression so fierce that if looks could kill, the faery would be six foot deep, but the brave boy carried on regardless. "I asked if we could visit Kikarsko, Your Majesty, as I desired to see one of my friends who resides there. Father was reluctant, but I then proposed he pay you a visit."

Arazair seated himself, his expression calming. "Thank you for your honesty, Galen."

Havain bristled. "He is as much a prince as your offspring, so address him as such."

"No, Father, it's alright," Galen interjected quickly, his crimson eyes darting around almost nervously.

"Perhaps it would be better for the children to leave us?" Arazair suggested tersely.

"No. I wish for them to hear me out."

"Very well. Finish."

Turvo and Fírean exchanged worried glances, the former shifting closer to his older but smaller sibling, their eyes locked on the intruding king.

"I have good reason to suspect that the actions of the assassins were not unprovoked, but in retaliation for the crimes that your people have committed against mine. Leaders of cities in the Southlands have been targeted, their families or even themselves murdered in cold blood. And ten seasons ago, my own son was targeted." Havain glanced at Galen then, but I struggled to see the resemblance; Galen was far too *elvish* to be the son of a faery.

"And your point is?"

"The murders were committed by elven hands, under the command of King Myranis. You call us treasonous, but he betrayed and targeted us all."

Silence deafened the hall for a minute, before chaos erupted.

"How *dare you* accuse Anatti of murder!" Turvo yelled, the muscles on his arms tensing and showing through his tunic as he prepared for retaliation.

"How dare *you* accuse *us* of murder!" shouted back one of the faeries, lighting fuel to fire. Most of the screaming was done by Turvo and a couple of faeries, but Arazair's advisor joined in and soon even Fírean looked angered by the goading comments and accusations flying between each side. Arazair and Havain glared at each other in what looked to be a power-seeking staring contest whilst their sons and followers moved from violent words to violent actions. Turvo floored two faeries before I could even blink, punching a third who tried to take a swing at poor Fírean. The musician was visibly shaking, thin arms raised to protect his face, a feeble move that was only successful due to his brawny younger brother getting in the way.

"Stop!" Kalia yelled, crying out as a larger faery shoved her aside in his quest to reach Turvo. Arlan spurred into action then, racing towards his mother with inhuman speed and pulling her out of the way with more force than his slim frame would let on. I was frozen, in a state of shocked observation, before something flew towards my face and I ducked, barely managing to avoid the projectile. It clattered to the floor, my eyes focusing upon what I now saw to be a *shoe*, of all things!

This was absolute chaos. Why hadn't Elohim warned me?

I kicked the shoe aside and made my way towards the doors of the hall, away from the fighting, but my path was blocked by the crimson-eyed, elvish faery.

Galen.

"Sorry about, well, this," he commented, gesturing to the scuffle.

I sighed. "It's the fault of my people, too."

His brow furrowed slightly. "You don't seem like an elf."

"And you don't seem like a faery."

The frown deepened. "My mother was an elf," he responded and I winced at the tone behind the past tense.

"I'm not an elf," I confessed, then tensed up, unsure of how he'd react, part of me wondering *why* I had randomly blurted the truth out. To my surprise, though, Galen's expression softened.

"I thought not. You're a faery, then?"

I shook my head. "Actually, I'm something called a human. Not many people have heard of us, though."

Galen's pupils dilated, almost seeming to expand and consume the colour in his eyes. "*Human?*" he hissed, "I... I think you need to come with us." He grabbed my hand before I could protest and hauled us out of the hall, into the safety of the corridors where no-one but two bewildered guards stood.

"Let *go* of me!" I growled, tugging my arm free and abruptly crossing it over my chest, "I am *not* coming with you!"

"Listen," he pleaded, "My father is going to propose that a couple of elves return with us to examine the evidence. He's already eyed you up, you and the brown-haired one."

Firean. I stopped glaring daggers at Galen but did not relax my posture. "Because we look the most vulnerable?"

He grimaced. "In part, yes. But you *know* things. You're not like the others, you can help them understand."

"And why would I help you?" I queried, my mind darting back to the visions I'd had. The majority of them contained faeries doing some evil.

"Because *I* can help *you*," Galen whispered, "If you were fully human, your ears would not be pointed. Nor would your eyes burn with such light. My people, we have science that the elves could only dream of. I'll help you to uncover the truth about yourself, if you at least try to uncover the truth around the assassinations."

Nausea kicked through my gut and I staggered, finding the walls to suddenly be tilting at a peculiar angle. Galen let out a cry of alarm, but I pulled away from his outstretched hand, my back hitting the wall and sliding down it as my legs gave away.

"Not... fully... human?" I breathed, my lungs constricting so hard that black spots began dancing across my vision.

"You didn't *realise*?" he exclaimed, then cursed under his breath. I tried to focus on getting oxygen into my body as my head lurched into a kaleidoscope of human ears and my ears and human eyes and my eyes and humans and elves and faeries and me...

"Jackie! Jackie, breathe!" a familiar voice urged, smooth hands touching my face with a firm yet gentle caress. I couldn't get my body to obey. Something hit my chest, then honey-coated lips were on mine, forcing my lungs to expand. I coughed violently, blinking to clear my vision as moist blue eyes met my dazed gaze.

"Arlan," I whispered, then broke off coughing again.

"Don't do that to me," he half-growled, before turning to Galen. The half-faery was in a state of shock, his twitching hands the only signs of life.

"What *happened*?" Arlan yelled, jolting Galen back into his body.

"I was talking to her and she just... freaked! Started shaking, and collapsed... I didn't know what to do!" Galen exclaimed, backing up. Arlan's eyes darkened and I didn't need to be a Chroma to see the anger radiating off him.

"What did you say?" he demanded fiercely, walking right up to Galen. I noticed then how small and young Galen looked, with my lover towering over him.

"Arlan, stop," I croaked, failing to get to my feet, "I... overreacted."

Neither male moved.

"She's not fully human," Galen murmured, still loud enough for my newly-sensitive ears to pick up, "I didn't realise that she wasn't aware."

Arlan's posture loosened slightly and I knew he was thinking back to the few incidents where I'd panicked upon certain revelations, causing bizarre physical harm upon myself.

"None of us realised. Her mother is human, but she's never met her father. I suppose it *is* possible."

I managed to sit up fully and frowned at both of them. "My father died before I was born! Besides, how would someone from Pylisya get to Earth?"

Galen stiffened almost imperceptibly.

"The same way you came to Pylisya," Arlan deduced, and I recalled then the mentions of portals on some maps of Pylisya that I had seen. Of course, it made sense that the system wasn't one-way, but I had never thought of it like that before.

Now it felt like the truth was smacking me right in the face.

I forced myself to my feet and looked Galen solidly in the eye. "I'm coming with you."

"Jackie, what-" Arlan started, but at my raised hand he stopped.

"No," I interjected, "Havain wants some of us to return with him, to assess if his accusations are true or not. If I go, I can try and figure out *what* exactly I am."

Arlan glanced up rather pointedly at Galen, who abruptly hurried back into the hall. He then locked his gaze with mine, a few curls escaping his braid and falling to frame his angelic face.

"Are you *sure* about this?" he murmured, the closeness of his lips almost intoxicating me. I almost forgot to breathe.

"Yes," I whispered back, "I'll find out the truth, clear their charges against you and your family. And maybe I'll find out who my father was."

Arlan sighed, reaching a hand into a pouch on the belt around his waist. "Before you go, let me do something. Please."

I stepped back a little and nodded, waiting.

He took a deep breath, fiddling with the contents of the pouch. "This isn't how I wanted to do things, but the unexpected always happens with you involved," he commented, shooting me a crooked smile, then his expression sobered. "I am in love with you, Jackie. I thought it would be impossible to find someone that warms my heart, my soul, in the way that you do. Before we met, I'd resigned myself to the arranged union that was bound to come from politics and the fact that I seemed incapable of falling in love."

He paused, then, and my heart clenched. *Arlan?* Beautiful, intelligent Arlan, had never found love before? *Never?*

As if reading the question in my eyes, he cheeks heated up. "It wasn't that I didn't get the attention," he confessed, "I just didn't see it. I didn't understand the signals that girls were giving me. I didn't have any feelings beside friendship, or the appreciation of a pretty face. I wasn't attracted to *anyone*. Until I met you."

Elegantly, he fell onto one knee and I choked back a cry.

"Jackie, you are my world. I loved you from the moment we met. Everything about you just draws me in, and I want to spend the rest of my life with you. I know this is a huge ask for you – you've denied me all my ideal proposal opportunities – but I can't let you leave without knowing. I want you to be my wife, Jackie. Will you do me the honour?"

I couldn't breathe, my heart pounding way too fast in my ears. Arlan knelt before me, everything gorgeous and good and *right* in this world, and my fears drained away.

I wouldn't leave him. I *could not* leave him, not even for my family back on Earth.

"Yes," I cried, and with one fluid motion he swept me into his arms, our lips meeting with a passion that set every nerve in my body on fire. Somehow he managed to balance my weight with only one arm, as I felt the other slip something over my neck, when we parted for air. I glanced down, fingering the sapphire pendant that was no larger than my thumbnail. It was as deep in colour as Arlan's eyes, with the only blemish being a small, golden, six-pointed star somehow set in the centre of the gem.

The star of Zeraphin.

"I don't know what your Earth traditions are, but here, a pendant is a sign of engagement," he explained and I kissed him before he could say any more.

"I love it," I whispered against his lips, "Much more beautiful than our rings."

We melted into each other for a few blissful minutes more, before the awkward cough of a guard brought us back to reality and the chaos that had erupted in the throne room.

Arlan looked mildly annoyed that the guard had interrupted us, but the poor elf was redder in the face than I was, frantically muttering his apologies.

"Your Highness – ah, I *am* so very sorry, I did not mean to, ah, sorry!" he rambled and my now-fiancé sighed.

"Has the situation calmed down?" he asked coolly.

"Yes," the elf replied with a funny jerk of his head, "The faeries are trying to form a conditional treaty with us and His Majesty requires your presence."

"We're not-"

"We will be there," I cut in and Arlan stiffened.

"Jackie..."

"We'll have time later," I whispered to him, "but we must resolve this situation."

His mouth quirked up into a melting side-smile. "Already speaking like a princess," he murmured softly, sending my heart into faster palpitations.

Arlan laced his fingers with mine and we followed the guard back into the hall, myself very conscious of the pendant around my neck and what it symbolised. Thankfully, the occupants were rather busy nursing their wounds and giving each other loaded glares. Turvo's face was bloodied, his nose at a slightly crooked angle, but his fists were stained crimson as well from the blood of his enemies. Four of the faeries were heavily bloodstained and a fifth cradled his right arm awkwardly. The elven advisor appeared to have a small bald patch, where the skin was red and raw, but was otherwise unaffected. Fírean, despite being the least injured – I could only make out a couple of bruises on his cheeks and exposed arms – appeared the most shaken up by the whole ordeal. Fortunately, Arazair, Kalia, and Havain were physically unharmed, though the two kings had barely been able to subdue their subjects. My eyes scanned the room for Galen, but he was absent.

"We are striking a deal for investigation," Havain announced, though I could tell from his tone that he was only talking for the benefit of me and Arlan. Everyone else was already in the loop.

"And what are the terms of that deal?" Arlan enquired, keeping his voice level as we strode towards the faery.

"Two elves accompany us back to verify our claims, and we leave two of our most valuable members with you."

"Which two elves do you propose?"

"The girl," Havain replied, gesturing to me almost dismissively, "And Prince Fírean."

A gasp rippled through the surrounding elves, signifying that this was the first time Havain had directly named the ones he wanted. Predictable as ever, Turvo spiked into life.

"No," he growled, "You are *not* taking Fírean and Jackie. No."

Fírean put a hand on Turvo's arm in an attempt of restraint; not that it would do much good, with Turvo possessing at least double Fírean's strength.

But the action itself seemed to calm the blond enough that he didn't make another move towards any of the faeries.

"I will go in Fírean's stead," Arlan offered, straightening up as his hand slipped from mine. Abruptly Arazair stood, his face stern as he shook his head.

"No. Arlan, you are the heir and I need you here with me, in Torindell. Jackie, what do you have to say on this matter?" the king asked.

"I am willing to go," I said, "But I am not as weak as I may seem. Don't let this be a trick."

Arlan sighed, even though he *knew* what my answer would be, but Turvo wasn't pacified.

"There is no way in *hell* that I am letting you *filthy* maggots take Fírean with you. If he goes, I go," Turvo spat, folding his arms aggressively.

"Language!" Kalia chided, but Havain's dark face twisted into a smirk.

"Very well. Nimfel, Vondri, and Yaroc; you will stay here in their stead," Havain commanded, and three faeries stepped forward, two males and a female.

"Are they worth the same as two royals and one soon to be?" Turvo hissed, receiving a harsh glare from both his parents.

Havain stiffened slightly. "Yaroc is my nephew, and as I do not have multiple children, I have selected my most beloved advisors, Nimfel and Vondri. I would not wish harm upon them, so I will ensure that the princes and the girl are not harmed in my lands. As I believe that you will ensure their safety in yours?"

"Of course," came the reply from Arazair and he extended his hand. Havain took it and I stared at their clasped hands, the elf's pale, near-flawless skin against the darker, more weathered hands of the faery.

The motion of their handshake sent a shudder through me and a deep sense of foreboding twisted in my gut, as if I'd just sealed my fate.

Chapter Twenty-One

- Benji -

I surveyed my handiwork in the midday sun, feeling oddly proud at the boldness of the colours leaping off the Red Swan's sign. Of course, the colours were not as vibrant as *real* colours, but they were attention-grabbing enough. The fresh paint glistened as rays bounced against it, immediately blessing the inn with a friendlier appearance. It wouldn't do much to change the worn-down insides, but it was a start.

"You finished?" the faery innkeeper asked gruffly, walking over with his hands shoved firmly in his pockets.

"Yes," I responded, in as deep a voice as I could muster.

"Mmm." He stepped back a span, tilting his head as he examined my handiwork. "Not bad," he said in a monotone, but I could see the flicker of yellow in his colour; he was pleased and that was good enough for me.

I'm done. You ready? I asked my twin, extending my mind to his.

Yep. I'll be down in a moment. Get Brina ready?

Sure. I turned my attention back to the faery, packing away the rest of my paints as I did so. "Where is my horse? We will be leaving now."

"This way." He headed off towards some dingy stables and I winced at the state of them. Brina seemed happy though, her honey colour flushed with a pinkish-yellow, and she was clearly well-rested. I wasted no time in getting her ready for travelling, giving the faery my thanks before meeting Kalic in the street adjacent to the inn, Brina trotting along behind me. There were far too many people around in Grayssan and, though I doubted any would recognise us from our visit over two years ago, I didn't want to take any risks.

"We need to leave," I hissed.

"Supplies, Benji," Kalic sighed, "That *is* the reason we came here, after all."

I fished in my bag and pulled out a handful of coins. "You get the supplies. I'll meet you outside the town."

"But-"

"No. Kal, just go," I commanded, shoving the coins into his palm. He sighed and adjusted his fake beard, grabbing the bag we used for supplies as his forehead creased.

"I don't like us separating."

"Kalic," I snapped, sending the rest of my warning mentally. *There are too many faeries here. I can't risk having an episode, and you're better disguised than I am.*

Fine. But don't go far, and any trouble, you call me, okay?

Of course.

I mounted Brina and urged her towards the outskirts of the town, heading towards the gates where we had once entered as young, frightened elves, torn away from our family with no real warning. It was rather poetic, that we would exit through the gate that marked our exile, retracing our steps to reunite with our family once more. Torindell was no more than a week's hard ride away; it was *so close,* closer than I thought we would get. In fact, I never thought I'd be excited to return there. The walls were so white, the colours so overwhelming... but I was older now. I had better control. Sure, Grayssan had made me feel a little nauseous, but that was because of the grey faeries present. Not because the colours started to become a kaleidoscope.

Concentrating on my breathing, I let the colours of life fade: watching them all at once, still, but letting each colour lose some of its vibrancy so it was less overwhelming, as Ethlon had taught me. They blurred together to form a pastel tapestry, which did not make my head hurt as much as the original brightness had; or as much as it would've if I'd let them mulch into a horrid brown. Brina's honey colour thrummed against mine and I closed my eyes, turning away from the town as I slumped forward on her back. Despite the decent sleep the night before, exhaustion still trudged through my bones, brought on partly by the exertion of my painting. I could afford to just rest a little while...

"Benji?"

I froze, just as the silver crept into my vision, and sat bolt upright. "...Ethlon?"

"Thank Elohim I've found you!" he exclaimed, surging forward, and I started as a wave of grey slipped out from his usually monochrome silver. *He was... worried about me?*

He stopped, barely two handspans away, and examined me with his grey eyes, an unfamiliar warmth creeping into them. "Why did you run off like that? You scared your onta, and you scared me."

"You weren't even there!" I protested.

"No, but Baelthar and I crossed paths when I headed back. So I then set out to find you."

"Why?" I asked, the question blurting out before I could think it through.

The harsh lines of the elf's face softened slightly. "It is my duty to look after you, Benji. If you wanted to return to Torindell that bad, you could've asked."

I blanked. *Ask* to return? That didn't make sense.

"I thought you'd say no. That you'd try and stop me," I said, folding my arms and suddenly finding the patch of dirt on my tunic to be very interesting.

"Benji. Look at me."

I did so reluctantly.

"You were sent to the Northlands for your own safety. Torindell is far too unstable at the moment. But I cannot keep you from your family. It does trouble me that we have had very little contact and I was intending to return there in the next season. All you had to do was ask, and we could've arranged something! I would send a messenger ahead, to ensure that you would be safe there. If it were too dangerous, we would wait until that was not the case," Ethlon explained, and my brain sluggishly processed the words.

"You would let me return? Why didn't you *tell* me?" I asked, feeling red flare up in my colour, but making no effort to stop it.

"I..." For once, Ethlon was lost for words and I didn't have the energy to press him.

"Don't stop us," I hissed, fiddling with one of the straps on my bag.

"I won't, but I *will* accompany you."

"Fine." I slid off Brina, completely turning my back on Ethlon as I sat down on a slightly-crumbling wall, seizing the sketchbook and charcoal stick from my bag, before aimlessly doodling whatever came to mind in an effort to be antisocial and calm down at the same time. It worked to some extent; Ethlon didn't bother me further, though his impassive silver didn't stray far, and I was glad to feel the remnants of red disappear from my colour. Having my emotions go crazy again was the last thing I needed.

Kalic, I gently called out after the sun had traversed a great deal of the sky, *how are you doing?*

I'm headed back now. Wait, is someone with you? he asked.

I sighed. *Ethlon found us.*

Vaznek, Kalic swore, both mentally and verbally from the volume of his words. *How?*

I don't know, but he's not stopping us. In fact, he'll be joining us.

Fantastic. My twin's sarcasm was so strong, I cracked a smile.

It's that or he marches us back to the Northlands, which I'm not *doing. And if we run into trouble, he can handle it.*

I can't believe you're trying to defend Ethlon, Kalic grumbled before retracting from my mind. I stood and gathered up my few art supplies, ignoring the grey eyes that stared out at me from the pages of my sketchbook.

"Kalic should be here soon," I told Ethlon bluntly, "Do you have a horse?"

He nodded ever so slightly, then stared at me, as if he expected me to make some sort of move.

"I'm not going anywhere," I reassured him, unable to keep all the attitude out of my voice. Ethlon didn't react, his usual stone expression taking over his face, and he walked towards a company of trees about five spans away: to retrieve his steed, I presumed. Not a moment later, Kalic returned, with two bags bursting with supplies and a new chisel clipped to his belt.

"Is that what took you so long?" I asked cheekily, gesturing towards the tool.

My twin's cheeks heated up. "No," he grunted, concealing his thoughts from me when I tried to probe, so I left it at that.

Ethlon rode back over to us on a soft dapple-grey mare, rather fitting considering his colour, and greeted Kalic formally. I promptly ignored the older elf, focusing instead on securing the bags of supplies and getting Brina ready for the last leg of the journey. We wouldn't stop in another town, if I had my way. I wanted Torindell to be the next piece of civilisation I laid eyes on, and Ethlon would *not* stop me.

We travelled in relative silence, Kalic and I choosing to communicate telepathically to deliberately exclude Ethlon. It was rather awkward, linking our minds for so long, but neither of us had any desire to converse with our unwanted companion. Thankfully, Ethlon wasn't feeling very conversational, so he didn't try and press it on us, only suggesting the times at which we could stop for refreshments or a rest. The fact that Kalic and I were accustomed to sleeping in the saddle didn't register until the third day since we'd left Grayssan, when Kalic dozed off as I took control of the reins. Ethlon, unable to do anything to get us to stop, was exhausted, the lack of sleep showing clear on his face.

"Benji, we really should take a break," he urged, slowing his mare.

I kept Brina trotting briskly and shook my head. "No."

"You haven't slept in days," he pointed out, which wasn't entirely true. I'd caught a little bit of sleep the previous day.

"Kal is asleep now," I countered in a whisper and Ethlon glanced at my twin as if seeing him for the first time.

"Oh," was the only response he had, and we carried on in silence for the next hundred spans or so, until the flash of orange in his colour was the only warning I had for his questions.

"Benji, what did you do to your hair?" he asked, and part of me wondered why he hadn't brought it up sooner.

"I had another elf change it, to disguise myself. It's not permanent," I added. According to Kalic, the roots of my hair were back to their natural black and the colour was spreading.

Ethlon merely shook his head. "Unbelievable," he murmured and I considered him carefully. Had something *changed* in the weeks that we'd been gone, to turn Ethlon from his usual stone to someone a little more expressive? He wasn't just monochrome to me anymore, which certainly was a source of confusion. Could it be that my abilities were growing stronger? Or was Ethlon simply letting down his shields?

Benji, shut it with the internal monologuing. Please. I'm trying to sleep, Kalic protested, making me jump slightly.

"You're always trying to sleep," I grumbled under my breath, then added, *get out of my head if you don't want to hear it.*

I try, but you're so loud. *Seriously.*

Sorry. I tried to focus on nothing but the sound of Brina's hooves bouncing off the well-trodden path, creating a melody of sorts with the pace of Ethlon's mare. *Melody.* My heart clenched as the thought of my second eldest brother slipped into my mind, the beautiful songs he would sing now faded memories that I needed to rejuvenate. The desire to see the rest of my family drew stronger with every span we rode, every day that passed, bringing us closer and closer to that possibility. I'd completely lost count of how many seasons it had been since I'd seen them last, only that it was *too many*.

I *needed* to see my family again.

"Elohim, please," I whispered, slowing Brina slightly so I was out of Ethlon's earshot, "Let me see my family again. Let them all be okay, please."

I wasn't sure why the prayer sounded so *desperate*; after all, we were closer to the rest of our family than we had been in years. But I couldn't shake the sense of wrongness that tainted my desire to reach Torindell, the little voice in the back of my head that urged me not to set foot anywhere near the city.

I ignored it, but I could not silence it.

Ethlon forced us to make camp two days' ride from the city, and I relented, only because sleep deprivation had gifted me with a steady pounding in my skull that I was eager to be rid of. After whispering a quick prayer, I fell into a relatively deep sleep, one that carried me through the night and did not plague me with any nightmares or dreams, much to my relief.

Dawn brought with it a strange mix of apprehension and excitement, along with the mutual understanding that this was the very last stretch of our journey. Kalic and Ethlon indulged themselves in a hearty breakfast, but I could not bring myself to touch the food, my stomach deciding to perform somersaults instead. No words were exchanged as we packed up the camp, distributing nuts, berries, and water-skins evenly so we wouldn't need to have any more stops. Ethlon had reassured me the day before that he could go without sleep until we reached Torindell and I knew the same applied to me. Kalic I instructed to sit in front of me, so that when he inevitably drifted off, I'd be there to stop his fall.

I can't believe we're so close, he mused as we set off on the last stretch.

I know! We've come so far, we have to make it now. I refused to listen to the cynic in me who was convinced that something would go wrong before we could reach the city, because my twin was right; we were *so close*. Kalic's good mood rolled off him in yellow waves and I found myself smiling, his colour rather contagious. Brina seemed to pick up on it too, her trot bouncier than normal, as if the thought of returning home had given her a surge of energy. Only Ethlon's mare seemed subdued still, her rider actually showing a hint of a smile on his usually impassive face.

We did not break speed once, choosing instead to face the challenge of picking the shells off nuts whilst riding a horse without dropping the edible parts, a task that Kalic was brilliant at, but myself not so much. I ended up satisfying my hunger with the berries, letting my twin have the nuts so they wouldn't go to waste. As the penultimate dusk drew near, Kalic began to doze and I quickly drew myself away from his mind so the tiredness would not creep into me too. Then came the awkwardness of taking the reins whilst keeping my twin seated comfortably on the horse, which I had partly mastered over the course of our journey.

As the moon's blue light washed over us, Ethlon finally decided to break the silence.

"Will you be alright with Torindell, Benji?" he asked, and I knew it wasn't the thought of seeing my family that he was enquiring after.

I nodded, before remembering that it was dark and he wouldn't have seen the motion. "I have a better handle on it now. Grayssan was manageable," I replied softly, so I wouldn't wake Kalic. Not that my voice could stir him, anyway. He slept like a log.

"I'm glad to hear that." Ethlon slowed his mare slightly so we could ride side-by-side, the moonlight illuminating his grey eyes and giving them a warmer, bluish tinge. "I am proud of you, Benji," he added and I almost halted Brina in my shock.

"What?" I spluttered, heat rising to my cheeks, "You...?"

"Yes. I know I am not the best teacher, but I am proud of how far you've come," he said, the corners of his mouth creeping up a little more.

"Th-thanks," I stammered, then we fell into a comfortable silence once more.

The next time dusk came, it brought with it a sight that I never thought I'd be glad to set eyes on.

Torindell.

Its white walls carried a rosy tint in the dying light of day, and I began to see some of the beauty that Kalic had marvelled at when we first went there. As we drew closer, I braced myself for the onslaught of colour; it came, but it was nowhere near as ugly or overwhelming as I'd remembered it to be. Like in Grayssan, I let the thousands of shades fade into soft pastels that tickled the edge of my vision, taking the nausea and chaos with them. Exhaling, I shot a grin at Ethlon, who nodded his approval.

"We're here!" Kalic yelled loudly, kicking Brina into action before I could stop him. I yelped and clutched at the folds of his cloak, the muscles in my legs aching with the strain of gripping on to Brina. Shock soon gave way to exhilaration and joy as we galloped through the gates, Brina's hooves echoing on the cobbled stones of the quiet streets, the yellow buzzing through Kalic soon enveloping me as well.

And then we were staring up at the grand, gold-turreted castle that the rest of our family called home.

I slipped off Brina's back, climbing up the first few steps before I froze, tasting the colours of those around me: silver, red, gold –

Gold.

My limbs kicked into action and before I could think I was surging forwards, colliding with a colour so beautiful it made me want to cry. The gold flashed with orange surprise, then gained a rosy tinge as my embrace was returned.

"Benji," Lanny whispered and the tears fell. His voice was so much softer and more lyrical than I recalled it being, possibly because I had become too accustomed to the huskier voices of the dwarves.

"Lanny," I sobbed, suddenly aware that I came up higher on his chest now, an observation which simply didn't matter because *Lanny was okay*, we were both okay, I was in his arms again and that meant everything was alright –

Though why couldn't I sense any deep blue, vivid green, or curious cerulean?

I pulled back from my brother and we both had a good look at each other, Lanny's brow furrowing when he took in my shorter, coloured hair. I examined the curves of his face, which almost matched up to the one I had committed to memory, except his eyes were drawn tighter, a deep-set anxiety present in their oceanic depths.

A flash of grey darted through me at the absence of the three colours.

"Lanny? Where are Jackie, Fír and Turvo?" I asked cautiously, keeping an eye on his colour: which, sure enough, gained splotches of grey and blue.

"They had to leave on a... diplomatic matter," Lanny answered after a momentary pause, "I'm sorry, Benji, you just missed them. They left yesterday."

You just missed them.

Fír, his beautiful songs that always calmed me... Turvo, his strong arms that made me feel so safe... Jackie, who I'd strangely come to think of as family, though I barely knew her...

They were gone.

"How long until they return?" I choked out, fighting to keep back more tears.

Lanny shrugged, "Not too long, I pray," he murmured, and I wrapped my arms around him again, wanting to hug away all the grey and blue and negativity that mottled his colour. As our colours touched, though, I sensed a sickening darkness in the very corners of his gold, as if he knew something that was fated and was trying his best to conceal it from the world.

He couldn't hide it from me, and I wondered if Jackie knew something of it too.

Not that I could ask her anytime soon.

My thoughts were interrupted by a loud cry from my twin, accompanied by a soft rush of amber and lilac from the other two elves I had longed to see.

"Atti! Mutti!" I exclaimed, Lanny barely releasing me before I was sprinting over to them, clutching Atti with a fervour I didn't know I possessed. Kalic's red mingled with Mutti's lilac, and I lost myself in the warmth of Atti's orange. Lanny's gold joined us a moment later and I closed my eyes, letting myself drift in the beauty of the mingling colours, the love and security embracing me for what was far too brief, but enough time to satisfy me.

For one moment, almost everything was perfect in my world.

Chapter Twenty-Two

- Jackie -

I rested my head against the carriage's window pane, thankful that it had not been a requirement for me to ride a horse on the journey. Turvo had taken that option, but Fírean rode in the carriage with me, humming softly under his breath. He hadn't made any effort to converse, so I gladly let my mind wander back to the ones I'd left in Torindell.

Hazel had been more irritated at my leaving than anything else, but after promising to make more of an effort with her studies, she'd embraced me tighter than we had for seasons.

"Stay safe," she whispered, "I need you to come back, okay?"

I ruffled her hair gently in response. "I will. Love you too, Zel."

An unspoken query sung in her eyes, but I did not press her to voice it; I already knew what the question entailed, but that was one thing I could not promise her.

The thought of promises brought me to what had happened with Arlan and, to my embarrassment, a few tears slipped from my eyes at the memory.

"Jackie, I know you are set in this, but listen to me. Don't go," he pleaded, his blue eyes in the process of turning my insides to mush.

"I must," I replied as firmly as I could, "I told you, I need to resolve this. And I need to find answers."

"Do you? You are not as human as you thought, but does that matter? Nothing's changed about the way I think of you!" he exclaimed, "I thought you were satisfied here!"

"I am! I love you, I don't want to leave Pylisya," I cried, "But-"

"That's the first time you've said that," he murmured, interrupting me. I froze.

"That I love you?" *Haven't I told him that many times before?*

"No. That you want to stay."

Heat rose to my cheeks and I nodded slowly. "Arlan, I couldn't ever leave you. Earth isn't my home," I said, realising both the finality and the truth of my words. I knew that, even if I wasn't so madly in love with Arlan, I still wouldn't be able to return to Earth. Pylisya held my heart in a grasp almost as firm as Arlan's and I simply wasn't human enough to return to my old home.

It was strange, thinking of myself as not-human, because for all my life I'd thought myself relatively ordinary. Sure, I had weird dreams and I'd ended up in an amazing, fantastical land, but I put that down to powers greater than myself. I didn't even consider that my DNA wasn't entirely that of homo sapiens. The pointed ears should've clued me in – and before that, the 'gift' of dream-prophecy that all the elves claimed I had – but I was blind to it all, far too caught up in the wonders of the land to process the fact that my identity wasn't what I'd believed for eighteen years.

My fiancé – it felt so strange and yet so *right* to refer to him like that – then breached the subject of my only connection to Earth.

"What about your mother?"

"I've come to terms with that. She... she'll be safer with me gone," I confessed, my voice pitching slightly.

Arlan frowned. "You're not a danger, Jackie."

"Maybe not, but I'm a magnet for it. The cobrai have attacked me twice now. I need answers – for that, and for *these*." I gestured at my ears, not as long or flexible as Arlan's, but certainly not human.

"You heard what Galen said," I continued, "My father wasn't human. *I'm not fully human.*"

"And what makes you so sure that Galen and the faeries have the answers?" he snapped.

"Elohim told me to speak with him!" I yelled, "And I just have this... *feeling*... Arlan, I already said I have to go. You can't change my mind now."

He sighed and deflated, all the anger disappearing as quickly as it had come. "I had to try, because I love you." His hands gently cupped my face and I didn't pull away, my frustration diffusing too.

"Come back to me. Soon," he breathed, all honey and sweetness against my cheeks.

"I will. I promise," was all I managed to say before our lips met and I melted all over again.

The memory faded and I roughly wiped my eyes, already missing Arlan though it had only been a day since leaving. Fírean met my gaze, then, and shuffled over to sit beside me.

"I miss them too," he whispered with his arms extended, and I curled into his chest without a second thought, letting him embrace me. Fírean's hold was nothing on the strong, beautiful comfort of Arlan, but it was satisfying in its own way, like I imagined the hug of a brother to be. In a way, I supposed, Fírean *was* my brother. He was the type who'd hug you and let you cry it out, whilst Turvo would storm off and beat up whoever caused you upset in the first place. I considered both of them – no, *all* of them – my family.

"Fír? Are you scared?" I asked gently, after I'd calmed down, tugging myself out of his arms but still sitting close to the elf. His eyes, a darker shade than my fiancé's, were wide and slightly moist around the edges.

"A little," he confessed, "I'm really not the person for this job. I worry that I'll just mess it all up."

"Hey, I'm a little worried about that too, but we'll be okay," I soothed, "Besides, I have no experience in investigation, but I think we're here more to witness and determine if the faeries are lying or not."

"Do you think they are?" Fírean enquired, his voice dropping in volume.

"I'm not sure," I admitted in a whisper, "I don't think they're being completely honest, but there might be a little truth involved."

The elf let out a little hum of acknowledgement, then lazily turned his head to gaze out of the window. I fiddled with the cuffs on my sleeves, worrying about Fírean's lack of reaction; had what I said upset him? I wasn't accusing Myranis of being a murderer, but had it appeared that way?

Fírean gasped loudly all of a sudden, shooting out of his seat and pressing against the window.

"Vaznek!" he breathed, "That... that's...!"

"That's what?"

"We just passed the city of Vonyxia!" he exclaimed, "That's impossible!"

I wracked my brain, trying to bring up the mental image of Pylisya's map. "Vonyxia? Isn't that over three-hundred miles away?"

Fírean turned back to me, his brow furrowed. "Miles?"

Ah. Earth terms. "Um... very far?"

"Yes. It should take us ten days riding, maybe eight at a push, to reach Vonyxia," Fírean explained and a chill went through me.

"This isn't natural," I murmured, finally able to recall Vonyxia's position on the map. It would take a day to reach in a car, if driving on a motorway with no stopping, but this was Pylisya. They didn't have cars, relying solely on horsepower for long-distance land transport. To have passed Vonyxia already...

It *really* wasn't natural.

"How have we travelled so far?" Fírean was ranting, his thoughts in tune to mine, "It's ridiculous, there's no animals that fast – well, maybe dragons, but there hasn't been a dragon sighting for seasons – and we're not exactly moving quickly, are we?"

I shook my head, barely concealing my bafflement at our situation and Fírean's rambling reaction to it. The trees outside seemed to be moving by at a steady pace; a little faster than what I'd expect from a horse-drawn carriage, but not fast enough to cause concern. Certainly not fast enough to justify the distance we'd covered.

"You're sure that you saw Vonyxia?" I asked.

"Positive. No other city has red walls with silver peaks. It's a weird combination," he pulled a face, "But it's unique. Definitely Vonyxia, I have no doubts."

"Where is the faeries', uh..." I struggled for the word, finally settling on, "base?"

"Syndekar. It's only fifteen kilo-spans from Vonyxia, so we should be upon it soon," Fírean noted, sitting back down with his arms folded. I scrutinised him slightly, curious about this new side of him that the second Zeraphin brother was revealing. His knowledge of the land was greater than Arlan's – my fiancé was more interested in histories than geography – and guilt trickled in my gut as I realised I'd severely undermined Fírean without really meaning to. We were close, but I knew him for his soft heart, beautiful voice, and delicious cooking. The learned, intellectual side he'd never shown to me before now, and I reckoned it was due to the absence of his brothers. Arlan was the intellectual, Turvo the master of the land: why would he compete with them? I made a mental note then to not undermine the brown-haired elf again.

Soon enough, the carriage slowed to a halt and I peered out the window for my first glimpse of Syndekar, home to Havain and the higher-ranked faeries. The walls around the city were lower than those of Torindell, and a soft grey in colour, but I could barely make out the shapes of buildings past those walls. The few that dared to peak over the top were made of stone the same monotone shade of the walls themselves, and even the largest building in the city's centre – the castle, I presumed – was grey, with the barest smudges of red on its roof the only marks of colour. Torindell was white, but that was strangely warm and serene. Syndekar was grey, as if all the colour had been drained from it.

The irony that Benji saw faeries as 'grey' was not lost on me.

The carriage was opened by a faery clad in deep orange uniform, with Galen stood beside him, the younger faery shifting on his feet.

"It is tradition for us to walk our guests to the city, if that is alright with you?" he asked somewhat awkwardly.

Fírean and I exchanged a puzzled glance. The city, though close, was still a while away, and I predicted it would take us about an hour to reach the centre, if that was our intended destination. It was a peculiar ask, for sure, but relations were already tense with the faeries and ignoring their tradition would do nothing to help.

"Yes, that will be fine," I replied steadily, meeting Galen's crimson gaze. We exited the carriage and Turvo immediately ran over to embrace his brother, whispering some sort of promise that I didn't quite catch. Then the blond elf turned to me, the healing wounds from the ordeal in the throne room marring his face in a way that was frightening, but oddly comforting at the same time. Turvo disliked the faeries more than any of us and I knew that he would do anything to keep me and Fírean safe.

We walked along the cobbled path to the city in relative silence, Turvo choosing to walk beside Galen – a move that I knew was deliberately threatening – so I was partnered with Fírean, whose expression had moved from apprehension to a peculiar excitement. A dozen other faeries walked with us, though there was no sign of Havain, something which only added to the sense of unease I had about the faeries.

Once inside the city, conversation resumed somewhat and Fírean exchanged places with Galen so that Turvo could talk with the former. The half-faery was giving me strange looks, but I ignored him, instead focusing on where we were headed. Every street seemed the same, the only colours being those of curtains hung in thin windows. No flowers sat outside houses or below windows and the whole absence of colour created a very noir-esque, urban atmosphere. Torches hung from doorways, but on closer look I could see no flames and the light was far too monochrome.

"You have electricity?" I gasped.

"No, it's magic," Galen corrected without a hint of sarcasm, though his face drew taunt.

Magic seemed a more logical explanation in this fantastical world, but I wasn't convinced. The lights behaved exactly like bulbs did on Earth. That was either a crazy coincidence, or the faeries were hiding something. Come to think of it, Galen *had* known what a human was, unlike Arlan, who'd thought them – *me* – a myth.

"Where will I find information on my heritage?" I asked then, keeping my voice low.

Galen tensed up. "First you need to investigate-"

"Turvo is handling that, and I will bear witness when required, but I agreed to come on those terms," I replied smoothly.

"Alright. I will take you to the archives, but please, rest with the others this evening. We have rooms prepared for you at the castle."

"Of course." We fell into silence again and I busied myself with committing the layout of the streets to memory, though the dull, greyscale buildings all looked the same. It was much harder to map Syndekar than it had been to map Torindell, despite the latter being larger. Perhaps that was one of the faeries' defence tactics; to make every road look so much the same that it was very easy to get lost.

Hardly any faeries walked the streets, those that did making an effort to keep their heads low and hurry past, and I wondered if there was an event or something happening. It was the only explanation I could think of for the lifelessness of the city.

"Felicia!" Fírean cried out suddenly and I glanced up to see him break away from Turvo and run towards a young female faery, clothed in a soft pink dress. Her pale face lit up in a bright smile that extended to her lilac eyes and she frantically moved her hands before Fírean embraced her, kissing her rosy cheeks lightly. They stepped back quickly, both twisting their hands in peculiar ways, more than a friendly greeting. I sped up to stand next to Turvo, whose brow was deeply furrowed.

"I didn't know that Fírean had a, uh," I paused, not knowing the term.

"A lover? He writes her often. They met after the funeral," Turvo replied, keeping his voice low, "She only visits twice a season."

"I see. I just thought he-"

"He what?" Turvo's eyes darkened and I shrugged.

"Eh, it doesn't matter. I was wrong, anyway," I swiftly corrected. I then made my way towards Fírean and the faery, eager to get away because *dang*, Turvo could be scary sometimes. Upon further scrutiny, I guessed the faery to be at least half-elf like Galen, from the way her ears pointed and the ethereal grace she carried. She was very pretty, the cheerleader-type, with hair as blonde as Turvo's and lilac eyes that shone with joy, especially when they settled on Fírean. But those eyes also held a deep intelligence and awareness of everything they saw, and I tore mine away before she could catch me staring.

"Hello," I smiled in greeting, but only Fírean turned to look at me.

"Ah, Jackie! This is Felicia." He turned back to the girl, "Felicia, this is my friend Jackie. She's engaged to Arlan," he spoke at a slightly slower pace, his hands moving in the same manner as before.

My sluggish brain began to connect the dots as Felicia grinned and gestured something at me, but made no noise.

"She offers you her congratulations and welcomes you here," Fírean said.

The final dots joined together.

"Is she deaf?"

Fírean nodded slowly and my eyes widened on instinct. Felicia gestured – *signed*, I realised – but my thoughts were all jumbled. Fírean, master of music, with the most beautiful voice I'd *ever* heard, was in love with a *deaf* girl? It didn't make any sense to me.

"Jackie? Felicia is curious about your eyes."

"Tell her-"

"You can tell her yourself," Fírean interrupted softly, "She can read lips."

I turned back to Felicia, quickly rearranging my expression so that the varied emotions would not slip through. No doubt she received looks of pity and judgement from people; I didn't want to contribute to them.

"I'm curious about them too," Galen noted, intruding on our conversation. I suppressed the urge to glare at the secretive half-faery and instead explained that I wasn't an elf, or faery, I was a being called a 'human' and that was why my eyes were a different colour to everyone else's in this land. Galen scowled at my response, as it wasn't anything he didn't already know, but I wasn't going to give him the satisfaction of more information. No, if he wanted to know more, then he had to answer *my* questions truthfully. Felicia, on the other hand, seemed rather enamoured by my short tale and made me promise – through Fírean – that I would tell her more about Earth, when I had the time.

We eventually reached the castle, then, and I was rather disappointed by it. My expectations of Pylisya's architecture were high: first from Arlan's old home near Kikarsko and second from the majesty of Torindell. But Syndekar's castle was as bland as the rest of the city and hardly worthy of the title of 'castle'. It was more like an industrial-inspired mansion, all grey walls and slanted windows, though there were a few splashes of colour in the flowerbeds in front of the building. Turvo, a lover of the outdoors, muttered his distaste, but Fírean was rather unfazed, probably because he was far too engrossed in a signed conversation with his girlfriend.

All of this stopped when we entered the castle's main hall, and I blanked for a moment at the sight of Havain sitting grandly on a throne that looked to be made of steel, because hadn't he been travelling with us? Dismissing my confusion as tiredness, I bowed my head in respect, Turvo and Fírean echoing my movements.

"I trust your tour through our city was satisfying?" the faery's king asked.

"Yes," Turvo answered smoothly, which I knew was a blatant lie, "Thank you."

"My servants will show you to your quarters and you may begin your investigation tomorrow," Havain said, "Though I would like to have a moment alone with the lady, if that is alright."

It took me a few seconds to realise that he meant me.

Turvo tensed up, the muscles on his arms bulging against the fabric. "My brother would not want her to be alone with you," he hissed.

"Turvo, it's okay," I urged. Diffusing the situation with the faeries was going to be a *lot* harder with Turvo around, but we would also be much safer, so it wasn't much of a disadvantage.

"Fine," the blond grunted, ignoring the servant assigned to him, instead storming out of the hall. Fírean muttered an apology then followed with Felicia, Galen and two other faeries.

And I was alone with Havain.

He wasted no time with formalities. "Galen has informed me of your mixed heritage and I am curious to find out more. As are you, I assume?"

I silently cursed the half-faery. "Yes."

"Then walk with me." He stepped down from the throne and headed for a side-door in the hall. I hesitated – it felt *wrong* to trust the words of this man, to follow him without question – but my feet acted before my head could figure it out and I traced his steps with caution.

"Galen said he'd show me the archives," I piped up, after a minute or two of walking down a narrow corridor.

"Galen doesn't know what he's dealing with. He is still a child, and a foolish one at that," Havain retorted, stopping before a steel door. He placed his dark hand on a slab beside the door, which lit up blue and granted access to the room. *More magic,* I thought dryly, but the blue light was peculiar; manufactured, almost.

The cold tendrils present since we'd passed Vonyxia wrapped themselves further around my mind and I tensed up, glad for the dagger hidden in the folds of my dress. Havain entered the room, lights in the ceiling brightening at his presence, and I knew for certain that they weren't the lights of natural fires.

This is wrong.

I have to get out of here.

But I stepped over the threshold, glancing around the room with the stupid curiosity that was keeping my sense of self-preservation at bay. The walls were all made of steel, two covered in shelves of various containers, all dark or tinted with neatly written labels. In the centre of the room stood a long table, also metal, covered in paper and wires and various other small oddities that I couldn't identify. It was all very peculiar, but what arrested my attention was the display on the wall opposite the door. Havain stood aside as I approached it, dread looming in my chest.

The wall showcased a large map of Pylisya, lying next to another familiar map that I hadn't seen for years.

"That's *Earth*," I gasped, my hand reaching out to trace the outline of Europe.

How... how did the faeries get their hands on a map of Earth?

Heart pounding furiously in my ears, I pivoted to stare at Havain, searching for an expression, an answer, *anything.*

He smirked and my blood ran cold. "I know. I used to live there."

CHAPTER TWENTY-THREE

- Benji -

Blue moonlight filtered through the windows of the castle and I paced the unfamiliar corridors, unable to sleep despite the demands of my exhausted body. Kalic and Ethlon had both slipped into the world of dreams with hardly any effort, but my mind was keeping me awake. It was a struggle to withhold all the colours of the people living in Torindell, not that I'd admit it, because I had to adapt. I had to hold them back. I *wouldn't* leave – no, I *couldn't* leave.

I was home, but it didn't quite feel right.

Lanny was hiding something from me, again, like he'd forgotten that I wasn't a silly little child anymore. I'd grown up in the time we were apart, a fact that he had yet to see.

Atti's orange, though normal at first glance, now had many more layers, stained with far too much grey and blue, so it was almost brown in places. Mutti's lilac was tainted, too, and for some reason I felt *guilty* for it. When we left, all those seasons ago, I hadn't even given them a proper goodbye. I wanted to, but I couldn't, and that had hurt me: but only now did I consider how it might've hurt my parents, too.

Then there was the issue of the greys in the castle, which I knew to be three faeries. They were guests, that was all Lanny had told me, but why were there *faeries* and no Fírean, Turvo, and Jackie?

It was all so very wrong.

So I found myself unable to sleep, despite having not done so for at least two days, walking the castle halls and letting the colours of its inhabitants flicker past me in a soft kaleidoscope. Red, silver, gold, orange, lilac, grey, brown, pink, copper –

I froze. *Copper?* I'd never encountered anyone with a *copper* colour before, it was different and weird and I couldn't quite place the source. It wasn't as clear as the other colours, more transparent, with an underlying yellowish tone that was strangely familiar. I'd seen something like it before, but I didn't remember the copper...

Frowning, I closed my eyes and reached out with my senses, focusing on pinpointing the copper's location. It was very hazy, drifting in and out of my view, before finally settling in one of the castle's towers: in the southern wing, if my sense of direction was right. Satisfied, I opened my eyes and jogged towards the copper, taking care to ensure that my footfalls were soft and wouldn't wake up anyone else in the castle. At a few of the corridors I encountered guards on a night-patrol, but their colours alerted me before I even saw them, so I was able to creep past them with relative ease. Only one guard spotted me, but I sent a ripple of grey-blue confusion in his direction and he quickly muttered something about needing more sleep.

Eventually I made it to the southern-facing tower, creeping up the stairs that were illuminated only by a few trickles of blue moonlight, not wanting to light a torch as that would immediately alert the copper-person to my presence. But when I reached the room at the top, I froze, suddenly uncertain as to what to do.

A figure sat on the broad window-ledge, gazing out at the stars, the copper rippling out from them. Their hair was a deep red, almost coppery itself, and cascaded in waves down to the figure's shoulder-blades. It was almost as long as Lanny's, but much straighter, and neater, too. Their face was hidden, turned as it was towards the night sky, and I wasn't close enough to determine gender. So I took a step forward and instantly grimaced as the wooden floorboards protested.

The figure stiffened and slowly turned to face me, the lines of their face distinctly masculine. Green markings curled beneath eyes of the same shade and I gasped. Wasn't Jackie the only person with had green eyes? And what were those peculiar markings? I'd seen dwarves with black marks on their skin – *tattoos*, Thorn had said they were – but never markings that seemed to glow.

"What are you?" I blurted out before thinking, taking a tentative step forward. The male's green eyes narrowed.

"Who are you?" he asked in response and I swallowed nervously.

"Benji," I whispered, and his eyes narrowed further before softening completely.

"Ah, the Chroma," he noted, his whole form relaxing as he leant against the window, adjusting his position so he was facing me. I tensed at the word –

it was a *bad term*, Ethlon said it would bring too much attention – yet the strange male spoke it without fear.

"You're not an elf, or faery, or dwarf," I said, "So what are you?"

He rested a hand on his knee casually. "What do you think?"

I closed my eyes, examining his colour further. The copper leapt out at me, a few other shades huddled within it, but I was most curious about the faded, yellow tone that I'd seen before. It was *familiar,* I just couldn't place it. There was something... *something...*

My mind flashed back to the meeting with the faery's king, over two years ago, when I had cowered in his shadow, fear threatening to consume me. But there had been a yellow presence, soft, yet protective.

It held no copper, but it was the same yellow.

I opened my eyes again to find that he hadn't moved a handspan. "You're someone ethereal," I answered, "I've felt your kind before. You... you're connected to Elohim, aren't you?" My voice jumped a pitch at that realisation. The yellow was that of the presence, but also that of Elohim, part of the tapestry of colours that made Him so warm and comforting and *beautiful.*

"Smart boy," the male commented, standing. The air behind him rippled, his colour distorting, and I gasped as a pair of feathered wings fluttered into existence, sprouting from his strong shoulder-blades.

"You're an *angel*," I squeaked and suddenly it made so much more sense. The ethereal presence, part of Elohim's colour...

He was one of Elohim's messengers.

I moved to bow, but the angel stopped me, his hand gently resting on my shoulder. I blinked; *how did he get over to me so fast?*

"Benji, I am not to be bowed to," he murmured softly and I nodded.

"Okay," I whispered, still in shock and awe. When my fuddled brain had recovered, I opened my mouth to voice my question, but the angel raised a hand to stop me.

"I know what you're going to ask, and I can't disclose that. Not fully. All will make sense, in time," he said, then added dryly, "I hope so, anyway."

"But you're an angel. Don't you know these things?"

The angel laughed, almost bitterly. "I wish! But I am not one of those privy to such information. It took me a lot of effort to even be allowed here, and I wasn't going to push my luck."

My brow furrowed. The angels in the few legends I'd heard were always *good* and pure. This angel was good, I could see it in his colour, but his past was tainted. He hadn't always been good, I realised, but he was trying his best to make up for whatever wrong he'd once committed.

Like me, a small part of my brain noted, and I ignored it.

"Can I at least ask your name?" I enquired gently.

His expression relaxed. "You just did," he chuckled, without bitterness, "It's Sachiel."

Sachiel. I ran the name through my mind, it tasted *familiar* somehow: someone I knew once had mentioned his name, at least in passing, but I couldn't place the memory.

"Pleasure to meet you," I responded, extending my hand to him. He stared at it for a few seconds, but made no move, so I awkwardly lowered it, clenching my fingers around the fabric of my tunic.

"It's best I don't have any physical contact with you," he murmured in a sort of explanation that only left me more confused.

"Why?"

Sachiel sighed, exasperation leaking into his colour. "You ask too many questions! Must I explain everything?"

Yes. "No," I responded, moving my gaze from his intense eyes to the feathers arching behind him. They were a pale, bluish-white, the tinge of colour strong enough that I knew it was not just a trick of the moonlight. His hair was a startling contrast to his lightly tanned skin, only a little darker than mine, and if it hadn't been for the obviously angelic wings, I wasn't sure I'd place him as an angel. Some sort of heavenly being, yes, but not an *angel*. The term brought up images of fair-haired, pale-skinned beings clothed in white, with pure, colourless wings, and warm auras of yellow.

Sachiel not meeting my expectations didn't mean he *wasn't* an angel, it just made it harder to grasp the concept.

Though, what was an *angel* doing in the castle in the first place?

Was somebody going to die?

Panic curled its clawed hand around my throat as I recalled the three greys I'd felt, sleeping in the guest rooms. There were *faeries* in the castle, they were coming for me, or Atti, and it wasn't safe and I was putting them in danger-

"Benji, breathe!" Sachiel commanded, his copper brushing against me. I gasped, chest heaving as I struggled to get in the air my body needed.

"The faeries won't hurt you, or your family, not on my watch. I promise," he said then, the words managing to calm me to some extent.

"Okay," I breathed, rubbing the corner of my tunic between my finger and thumb, the soft texture grounding me, "Okay. Sorry."

Sachiel's fingers twitched as if he wanted to touch my shoulders, but he didn't, choosing instead to rest them against his belt. I closed my eyes and inhaled, letting everything wash away until all I could see were the colours of those in the castle. Honing in on the greys, I examined the for any trace of malice, but they were as monochrome as ever, if not a little clouded from their slumber.

"The faeries. Why are they here?" I asked.

"It is not my place to tell you," was Sachiel's rather infuriating response, and red flashed through my colour.

"Fine," I grumbled, folding my arms. Sachiel's gaze drifted out the window again, silence descending upon us for a few painful moments, and I fiddled with the fraying cuffs around my wrists. The travelling clothes were showing obvious signs of wear and I had yet to change out of them, but I probably should've. As if sensing that, Sachiel stirred, his unnerving green eyes settling on me once more.

"You should get some rest," he noted.

"Yeah. Probably should," I agreed, turning towards the door, then hesitated. "Are you staying?"

"Yes. I will keep watch over the castle."

I relaxed further, the red fading, stress I didn't realise was present lifting from my shoulders. "Thank you," I murmured, exiting the room and slipping through the castle halls as silently as I'd come. I barely made it to my new room before collapsing on the bed, its soft, cushioning texture unfamiliar but very comfortable. Dimly I noted that I should remove my boots and dirty outer-garments, but the darkness rushed to claim me before I could take any action.

Benji? Benji, are you alright?

I groaned at Kalic's presence in my mind, trying to push away the tendril he offered, like a hand.

Benji, wake up!

Reluctantly I forced my eyes open, blinking owlishly at the harsh sunlight flooding my room. A second later, the colours assaulted me and I instinctively cringed backwards. Gold, red, lilac, silver, all coated in a shivering grey anxiety.

"Thank Elohim you're alright!" Mutti exclaimed.

"Vaznek, Benji!" Lanny huffed, much less eloquent, "You gave us a scare!"

I yawned and stretched casually, feeling more refreshed than I had in weeks. "M'sorry," I mumbled, not really certain what I was apologising for as I pulled myself into a sitting position. Lanny immediately gathered me into his arms and I soaked in his gold, letting it embrace every fibre of my being.

"You didn't wake up, Benji," he murmured, "You've been asleep for almost two days."

Oh. That explained the refreshed feeling, but also the concern rippling off them.

"I did tell you he hardly slept on the journey," Ethlon noted, his silver as stiff as always. Lanny pulled away, only for his arms to be replaced by Mutti's, the sheer volume of pink emitting from her making me gasp in surprise.

It was then that I realised, people *cared*. Mutti cared, Lanny cared, Kalic cared, even Ethlon cared.

They all cared about me, Mutti and Lanny especially; they cared about me and it *had* hurt them when we'd been forced to leave.

Suddenly, the bitterness and anger I'd harboured towards them for seasons felt awfully foolish and I was thankful to Elohim that He'd enabled me to let it go before I returned home to them. Embracing Mutti back, I let her lilac wash over me, silently vowing that I would *not* take my family for granted again.

Then I remembered my conversation with Sachiel the night before and the questions he'd refused to answer. Pulling away from Mutti, I swung my legs round the side of the bed, preparing to get up.

"Why are there faeries here?" I enquired, tilting my head as I glanced at Lanny.

"How did you know?" Mutti asked, rather startled, and I was again reminded of how long I'd been gone; they didn't know the extent of my abilities.

"I, err, sensed them," I explained lamely, looking to Ethlon for support.

He sighed. "Benji's power has grown stronger, and he is more attune with it, as I am," the stiff elf said in a monotone.

Mutti blinked, then her brow furrowed, taking in my different hair and tattered clothes in the daylight. "What happened to you?" she gasped and I couldn't help but giggle a little.

Trust Mutti to fuss about the clothes.

She threw a head fit at the state of mine, Kalic groaned mentally, briefly recalling the memory.

"Your *hair!*" our mother continued to lament, "Kalic's was short enough, but you...!"

"Lanny's the long-haired one, not me," I pointed out, a light smile showing her I was joking. Well, partially joking.

"You need to get cleaned up and have someone tidy up that hair. What did you cut it with? A blunt knife?"

"I wasn't the one who-" I started, but Mutti had seized my arm and pulled me off the bed, down the corridors to a room that was unmistakably a bathing room. She immediately ordered a servant to start heating water, and the thought of getting clean was suddenly a lot more appealing than it used to be, especially since I hadn't bathed in weeks. Sure, I'd washed my hands and face whenever we'd had access to flowing water, but taking the time to bathe would only have delayed us further. Now I stopped to think about it, I realised that I *was* actually a little on the smelly side and would definitely benefit from a bath.

Mutti reached out as if to undress me and I swatted her hand away, nimbly undoing the ties myself. Her colour trembled and I sighed.

"I'm sorry, I-"

"No, *I'm* sorry," she interrupted, "Benji, I am *so* sorry. I should've been there for you, but I wasn't, and I know things can't go back to how they were before... There's no excuse for my absence," she sighed, "Sending you away for so long wasn't the right decision, we should've thought it through, it should've only been temporary..."

I gently placed my hand on her shoulder, conscious of the fact that I didn't have to reach up as high to do so. Her colour throbbed beneath my fingers, trickles of blue turning it into a soft indigo.

"I don't blame you," I whispered, and the words were so true. If I was to blame anyone, it would be myself.

Her shoulders started shaking and she lowered herself to the ground, the volume of grey increasing. Guilt shot through me, because it was *my* absence that had left Mutti like this. She blamed herself, but it was *not* her fault, it was *never* her fault.

I crouched down beside her, throwing my arms around her. "I love you," I declared, embracing her tightly, "I love you, Mutti. Don't blame yourself. I'm here now, aren't I?"

She hugged me back, then her nose wrinkled and she pulled away. "Yes, and you smell," she noted, to which I laughed.

The servant chose that moment to come in with heated water, pouring it into the basin. Mutti stood and turned to leave.

"I will get some clothes for you," she said, her voice quivering again, but she left before I could try and offer more comfort. Sighing, I kindly asked the servant to leave then stripped, climbing into the basin and letting the water wash over me. Almost instantly it turned a muddy colour and I grimaced, seizing the bar of soap and scrubbing at the grime on my arms, a mix of paint and dirt and crusted berry-juice breaking off and dirtying the water further. After that was dealt with, I lay back and washed my mangled locks, staring when the soap stained brown.

Guess that dye wasn't permanent. Not that it mattered now, anyway.

Your hair is back to normal? Kalic exclaimed excitedly.

Kal! I yelled, *Get out of my head! I'm bathing!*

So? It's not anything I haven't seen before-

Get. Out. I growled, sending a shock of red his way.

Okay, okay, he grumbled, but retreated, his warm, metallic presence fading from my mind.

I finished up quickly then, eager to return to my family and try to make up for the time we'd lost together. The tunic and breeches Mutti had laid out for me were relatively plain, dark blue and beige respectively, and they were a little too large, so I suspected that I was not their intended owner. But they were better than the green travelling clothes, and certainly less worn than the other tunic I'd brought with me from the Northlands, so I wasn't going to complain.

Lanny's gold greeted me when I headed back to my room, placing my paints and sketching materials on a few shelves, in an attempt to make the room less bare. I approached quietly, squinting at the paint pots. *Didn't I leave my purple paint behind?*

"Benji!" he exclaimed, pivoting suddenly, "You look much better now!"

"Are those new paints?" I asked.

Lanny's colour flushed. "Yes. Well, sort of. They were from your bags when we moved from Kikarsko," he admitted and I blinked. Of *course*, Ethlon and Onta Baelthar hadn't brought all of our belongings, but it had never crossed my mind that my family would keep them. A flutter of warmth crept into my colour and I hugged my eldest brother, wishing that I could embrace green and blue, too.

"Thank you, Lanny," I breathed.

His arms held me tight. "I missed you so much," he murmured into my hair.

Then why didn't you come to visit me?

I shoved the thought away, instead focusing on the moment. "You and Mutti didn't answer my question about the faeries," I said rather pointedly as we both pulled away. Lanny's expression flickered, as if he was surprised at the fluidity of the words flowing from my mouth – which, I supposed, he *would* be. Two years ago, I'd struggled to form coherent sentences.

It was yet another reminder of the time we'd had stolen from us.

"Ah, the faeries." Lanny's colour grew darker, but he didn't elaborate until I prompted him.

"What about the faeries?"

"They're here for... diplomatic reasons. Three faeries here, three elves-" he seemed to stumble over the word, and I sensed a lie – "visiting the faeries' home."

It didn't take me long to piece things together. "Fír, Jackie, Turvo. They've gone."

"Yes," Lanny sighed rather dejectedly.

I frowned. "They've gone to the faeries... Lanny, you *sent them* into the home of the *faeries*?" I shrieked then, panic surging through me at the realisation, because faeries were cold and grey and cruel and they would hurt

Fírean and Jackie and make Turvo work for them because he was big and strong and-

"Vaznek," I swore and Lanny visibly recoiled at my use of the word. I didn't care; who was he to chide me on my language when he'd let three of the closest people to him walk into an obvious trap?

"The faeries hurt me," I reminded him, "They murdered Anatti! And you let them take our brothers and Jackie too?"

His blue eyes grew pained, the agony shooting through his colour sending an ache through me as well. "I didn't want them to go. Benji, believe me, I *tried*, but Jackie... She needed to go. And we're on shaky ground with the faeries already, we *had* to agree to their terms. I'm not happy with this, but if it goes wrong..." He trailed off, fists clenching.

"Goes wrong, like, they die?" I snapped.

"No! Well, yes, but that's not what I mean!" Lanny exclaimed, "Benji, if the faeries continue to be like this, an attack is imminent."

I blinked at him in confusion.

"War, Benji. If the negotiations fail, they will declare war."

Chapter Twenty-Four

- Jackie -

Havain's words echoed in my mind, the sheer volume of them making me feel dizzy. *He... lived on Earth? Did the faeries originate from there? Or...*

I stared at his only slightly-pointed ears and dark complexion, my mind flashing back to the other faeries I'd seen, some with characteristics of other species, others looking so *ordinary...*

Oh, vaznek.

The faeries were *humans.*

The realisation must've shown on my face, because Havain smirked, folding his hands coolly behind his back. "You are not as alone here as you thought," he said, "Though, I *am* rather annoyed that you told them the term 'human'."

"Why?" I exclaimed, "Why do you lie, why do you hate the elves, why- *how* did you get here?"

"You came through a portal. As did I, long ago. Is that so hard to believe?" He cocked a dark eyebrow and I glared in response.

Of course that was a logical explanation, and I knew it, but the whole idea just... didn't sit right. The fact that humans had masqueraded as another race, taking their stand in a world that shouldn't have even been *touched* by them, was sending my stomach into a nauseating whirlwind.

"You shouldn't be here," I hissed, "You should leave."

Something dark flickered in his eyes. "I can't leave. Purebloods get trapped when they cross over to other worlds. Half-breeds like yourself, though, can cross over freely."

I took a subtle step back, processing this information, suddenly reminded of the time Arlan had offered to return to Earth with me and how I'd felt strongly that he should *not* follow me. At the time, I hadn't understood it, but if 'purebloods' would get trapped, then Arlan would've been stuck on Earth.

I sent a silent *thank you* to Elohim for putting that feeling in my bones.

"What am I half of, though?" I asked, crossing my arms and trying to stare him down, which was a difficult task when he was at least four inches taller than me.

"Half-human," he responded with a smirk.

"The *other* half," I spat, clenching my fists.

"I'm not entirely sure," he mused, "Not merfolk, that's for certain. Or dwarf. Maybe an elf, though the development in your ears has only been recent, am I correct?"

"If you don't have the answers, I'll leave. I came here to find out about my heritage."

"No, you came here to witness my claims," he corrected.

"On the terms that I could uncover my heritage," I shot back, conscious of the tiredness creeping through my body and the increased pounding of my heart. But I couldn't afford to be weak here. Havain was *dangerous,* that I was certain of, and I knew I'd seen him in one of my visions but I couldn't quite place which one.

"We can run a DNA test," he said, suddenly brandishing a needle, and I took another few steps backwards. Blood wasn't needed for a DNA test, I knew that.

"No," I murmured, shaking my head as the sudden need to *get away* escalated.

"But don't you want to know?" he purred, "Don't you want to know where you came from, to understand?"

I clenched my fists, scanning the room for my escape route, when my eyes settled on a worn, leather-bound notebook. A picture flashed before me – the hooded executioner, leaning over the pages, gloved hands running over unfamiliar runes – and I quickly catalogued a path that would take me past the table.

"Yes," I hissed, "But not your way. I'll find out by myself."

Spinning on my heel, I ran for the door, deliberately knocking the table and scooping the notebook up, clutching it to my chest as I bolted from the room. The corridor was straight, and though the path was not lit by torches, there seemed to be a glow coming from somewhere behind me, illuminating it for me to see enough to not careen into walls as I hurtled away from Havain. My heart pounded in tune with my footsteps and as I re-emerged in the throne room, I realised that I had no idea where I was supposed to go.

Pausing only long enough to grab a lantern from the wall – a lantern which lit up with the flick of a switch on its base, very clearly powered by *batteries* – I headed off in the direction that Turvo had gone.

I'd never really sought him out before, but now, I needed to feel *safe* and Turvo was the only one in Syndekar that could help me achieve that.

"Elohim," I whispered, "Please, guide me."

The lantern illuminated the halls, all bare and void of colour, eerily reminding me of a hospital. I just ran, still clutching the notebook, trusting that my feet would lead me to where I needed to go. Soon I stopped abruptly, outside of a door that seemed like every other door I'd run past, but I did not hesitate before knocking.

"Seriously, stop *bothering* me already, you-" The door opened to reveal a bleary-eyed Turvo, his straight blond hair falling loose, not in its usual immaculate ponytail. His frown of annoyance faded into one of concern when he recognised me. "Jackie? What are you doing?"

"Can I come in?" I whispered, my voice shaking. He blinked.

"Uh, okay?"

I slipped past him and set the lantern and notebook down on the dresser, trying to calm my breathing, but all I could feel was Havain chasing me, trying to get my blood, fangs glistening in his mouth-

"Jackie?"

I let out a sob and threw myself into Turvo's arms, the sturdiness of his chest instantly comforting. His heart beat strongly beneath my cheek and I focused on its rhythm, pushing the stupid images of Havain away. Turvo stiffened for a second then his arms encircled me, one hand gently stroking my hair.

"Sorry," I mumbled into his shirt after I'd finally managed to calm myself down. He gently pushed me away, crouching slightly to look into my eyes.

"What happened?" he asked, concern flooding the chocolate irises.

"Havain, he... he scared me," I confessed, ducking my head.

Instantly Turvo stiffened. "Did he hurt you? Are you alright? I *knew* we shouldn't have left you alone with him...!"

I couldn't help but grin slightly at his brotherly over-protectiveness. "No, I'm fine, just a little shaken. Um, I should probably find my room," I added awkwardly, taking a step towards the door. Turvo reached out and grabbed my arm before I could even blink.

"No, you can stay here. If you want. I mean, there's room," he gestured towards a very plush-looking sofa, with velvety purple cushions, and my resolve wavered.

"Okay," I accepted, "Thanks, Turvo." Making a beeline for the sofa, I flumped onto it gracelessly, a small hum of satisfaction escaping my lips as I finally allowed the tiredness in my body to pull me under.

Far too soon I opened my eyes, but it was not to the dimly lit bedroom; rather, I found myself in a courtyard of sorts, surrounded by cold stone columns. The ground at my feet was fresh grass, dancing in the light breeze, but it faded to a sickly yellow in seconds. I stepped on a few grey slabs hidden amongst the grass, then froze.

I remember this place.

It was the first dream I'd had in Pylisya.

Turning slowly, I wasn't surprised to see Arlan walking up to me, the curves of his face as familiar as my own. He looked a little tense, but his eyes still shone when they met mine. I ran to close the distant between us, greeting him with a fervent kiss.

"I miss you," I breathed against his lips.

"I miss you too," he murmured, "but I have to go."

Something cold pierced my heart. "Go?" I echoed.

He nodded slowly, the gems of his eyes growing pained. "I'm sorry, Jackie. They've left me with no other choice."

"What... what do you mean?" I stammered, "What choice, there's always a choice, Arlan! Don't go, please! I've given up everything for you!"

"Not quite everything," he muttered, the sandy curls of his hair brushing against my cheek, and I stood frozen. "I love you," he whispered, then he faded away, and I was left in the sunburnt field, surrounded by freezing stone.

"No! Arlan, come back!" I screamed, breaking into a run, and suddenly I was not in the courtyard, but on the pier, where the three figures stood from before. I wanted to stop, to turn away before I could see the suffering written on the Zeraphin brother's body, but my legs kept moving, pulling me towards the two clothed in fine robes, until I was close enough to see their faces.

Oh, no.

I swore colourfully as I found myself staring into the reddish-brown eyes of Havain, wondering why I hadn't seen it before. The same skin-tone, beard, hair...

Havain was the one who I'd seen murder one of the brothers.

My fists clenched and I turned to look at the smaller figure, but their face was blurry, like I was looking through an unfocused camera lens.

"No, I need to see!" I cried, "Elohim, why won't you show me? Please, show me who it is, I have to stop this...!"

A warm breeze tickled my hair. *Do you?*

What kind of question *was* that? "Of course I do!" I yelled, "I can't let them die!"

Why are you so certain that this will happen?

I frowned. "Are you saying it's not going to?"

No, I am not saying that. Jackie, you must trust Me. All will be revealed in time.

"Why now," I murmured, staring at Havain's frozen face, "Why have you shown him to me now? Why not before?"

You needed to come here and see for yourself the troubles of this land. Humanity I treasure, but it was never My intention for them to walk in this world.

"And what am I supposed to do about that? I'm human too," I grumbled.

Half. You are half-human.

"Then what is my other half? Please, at least tell me that!" I turned away from Havain, the bloodied elf, and the mystery figure, glancing around for any visible sign of Elohim, only to witness the pier and gathering crowd fade away into nothing.

Ask your father, He whispered in my ear, before I gasped and sat up, back on the sofa in Turvo's room.

"Ask my father. Brilliant," I muttered, "It's not as if he's missing and I have *no clue* who he is."

"Who?" Turvo asked sleepily and I yelped, quickly moving to cover my eyes.

"Turvo! Put a shirt on!" I squeaked, mentally shoving the image of his tanned, very muscular chest from my mind.

He laughed slightly, the rustling of fabric implying that he'd heeded my request. "Didn't realise it would freak you out so much," he teased, causing my cheeks to flame up.

"I'm engaged to your brother," I pointed out, removing my hands from my face. Turvo only grinned and shrugged – thankfully clothed in a tunic – as if he didn't see the problem with it. Well, I probably was overreacting a *little*, but Arlan-

Oh, vaznek. *Arlan*. My dream.

"Turvo, I want to go home," I said, instantly chilling the mood in the room.

"What?" he spluttered, "But Jackie, we only got here yesterday!"

I crossed my arms, trying to make myself look stern, which I doubted was possible with the bed hair I likely had.

"I know, but I want to leave. Havain is bad news, we... we have to stop him," I said lamely, my mind whirring as I tried to figure out a way of persuading Turvo without revealing my vision. Sure, it would be easy to say, 'we need to leave or someone in your family is going to die, maybe you,' but I sensed that I shouldn't reveal the vision's contents to anyone, just as I'd kept quiet about the first pier scene.

Words had power and if I spoke of it, it may be more likely to come true: something which I was *not* willing to test. Not with the lives of my new family at stake.

"Turvo," I began again, forcing urgency into my tone, "Trust me. I've seen things, and I *know* we need to leave. We have to get back to our family."

"No," he argued, "We have to stay here and look at the faeries' claims so they don't declare war on us!"

"War is coming anyway!" I yelled, and Turvo's face paled.

"What?" he exclaimed, "Where did that come from?"

I took a deep breath, trying to calm my racing blood. "I don't know, I just blurted it out. I'm sorry," I sighed, though the sentence wouldn't leave my mind. *War is coming? Why did I say that? Is it me being silly or... something more?*

"You can't just 'blurt' something like *that* out," he snapped, his expression darkening, and I took a step back instinctively, placing the sofa between us. *Vaznek,* Turvo was terrifying, the broad arms of safety suddenly flexing their muscles, becoming much more intimidating.

It was ridiculous. Turvo was my *friend*, he wasn't an enemy; a simple fact that my body clearly hadn't received.

After a few tense minutes, Turvo seemed to realise what had transpired and he relaxed his posture, concern replacing anger. "Jackie, I'm sorry," he apologised, ashamed.

I grit my teeth. "And I'm leaving, whether you come with me or not," I stated. He ran a tanned hand through his hair, pulling it up into its usual high ponytail.

"A day. Give me a day, and I'll sort out everything with the faeries, then we can go."

"No-" I started to say, then a shot of pain ignited my spine and the words morphed into a choked scream as something in my back *broke*.

"Jackie!" Turvo yelped and I tried to look at him, but my vision was fuzzy and the floor was rushing up to meet me. The elf growled then, an inhuman tone I'd heard Arlan make on occasion, and ran past me with a sword suddenly in his hands. Forcing my muscles into action, I crawled away from him just as the clang of metal on metal resounded, the fire in my back increasing exponentially. Gingerly I reached behind with a hand, ignoring the pain fluttering down from my shoulder, expecting to find blood or something embedded in my skin, yet there was nothing. With a grimace I prodded the skin, determined to identify the source of the sudden pain – it was so much *more* than the aches of my visions – and froze when my fingers knocked something hard and slightly jagged.

Bone.

Promptly I gagged and threw up a bunch of stomach acid, barely managing to turn my head to one side. There was *bone* sticking out from my shoulder blades, that was what had broken, but *how*?

Strangely, my arms were still functioning and I grit my teeth, gathering all my resolve as I pushed myself up to standing, mainly using the strength in my legs. My eyes darted towards the fight, just as Turvo let out a small cry, our assailant's sword catching his cheek. Then I took in the stretched, navy skin, and glowing red eyes.

Another cobrai? How...?

There was no time to ponder over that, or the extent of the injuries on my back, and I was very grateful for the adrenaline pounding through my veins that was numbing some of the pain. Before I could think, I was gripping my dagger and adopting a battle stance, fighting against my shoulder's protests. Turvo was a skilled swordsman, one of the best I'd ever seen, but I also knew the cobrai were formidable themselves. The two blades danced in a mesmerising way as the cobrai went on the full offensive, leaving Turvo to block and dodge, the latter of which he wasn't so good at. I calmed my breathing, focusing on the cobrai's movements, waiting for a opening...

Turvo stumbled and the cobrai lunged, leaving their stomach exposed in the motion. The dagger left my hand, shooting through the air and making contact with unnatural flesh just before Turvo was impaled. Instead the sword went wide, grazing the elf's arm, and the cobrai let out an unholy screech, falling to their knees. Turvo spun and stared at me, eyes wide.

"Good shot," he breathed, and I grinned, then grimaced as another spark danced over my spine. His eyes widened even further when they made contact with my back.

"That bad, huh?" I grunted.

"I guess we're leaving after all," he muttered, "Come on, hurry." Turvo seized a cloak and slung it over my shoulders, then took my hand and marched us out of his room, not bothering to grab his bag of belongings. I snatched Havain's notebook from the dresser as we passed it, shoving it into the largest pouch on my belt. The adrenaline was starting to wear off, but my legs were still functioning perfectly fine, so I was able to keep up with him.

"Fírean?" I asked, though it came out more as a gasp.

We rounded a corner and Turvo hammered on the nearest door, which quickly opened to reveal the older brother. "Turvo, what-?"

"We need to leave. Now," he ground out in response, echoing my words from earlier- the irony of which was not lost on either of us, I saw in his eyes.

Fírean took one look at me and nodded, darting back into his room only to emerge a second later with his bag in one hand and Felicia's arm in the other. Turvo raised an eyebrow, to which Fírean hastily murmured that she *didn't stay the night, obviously*, and then we were running through the grey corridors, my back now screaming its protests.

"Which way do we go?" Fírean asked, waving his hands about – asking Felicia the question as well – before a signed response from the half-elf caused him to abruptly pivot and start jogging down a different passage. I tried to follow, but the fire in my shoulder-blades was almost hitting the agony zone and I stumbled with the force of it.

"Turvo, I can't," I gasped out, touching his arm before he could race away from me. His dark eyes lit up with an odd mixture of concern and understanding.

"Can I?"

I nodded and he lifted me up, resting my torso over his shoulder so that my back wasn't in contact with anything. It was quite vulnerable, my arms and legs hanging loose and exposed, but Turvo's grip was firm and I trusted that he wouldn't drop me. Dimly I wondered how we'd make it out of the city, but I was in no state to try and problem-solve.

Our escape, as it now had become, was entirely in Turvo and Fírean's hands, and I prayed to Elohim that we could succeed before faeries or more cobrai came after us.

I must've passed out at some point, as I had no recollection of reaching the carriage we were now in. The seat beneath me was plush and I was lying on my stomach, the throbbing in my back still persisting. Someone's hands caressed my head, fingers untangling my hair, and as much as I wanted to relax under the touch, I couldn't.

Because my ears were working again and they were picking up a sound I never thought I'd hear.

Fírean was *shouting*.

"-can stop pretending now!" he yelled, "You're urthets, all of you! Absolute swine!"

"You're breaking the terms of our agreement," a male replied smoothly. My fists clenched instinctively as I recognised the voice and the hand in my hair stilled. *Havain.*

"You broke them first, when you attacked Jackie," Fírean retorted.

"I don't know the attacker-"

"Like you didn't know who killed my grandfather? Right." Sarcasm as well as anger laced the elf's tone, a combination that didn't suit him. "Why in Pylisya should I believe you?"

"Enough of this," Turvo interrupted, his tone furious, "We're leaving, Havain. The negotiations are off."

My blood ran cold, due to two things. First, if Turvo was now so willing to stop the investigation, what had happened to change his mind more than I could? Second, if both brothers were *outside* the carriage, then whose lap was I lying across?

"You will destroy the peace!" Havain screeched, "We won't let you get away with this!"

"Vaznek," Fírean spat out in response, then boarded the carriage, slamming the door shut behind him. His entire face was crimson and his ears were pinned back against his skull, their tips red as well.

"Sorry about that, Felicia," he added in a calmer tone and I exhaled; it was Felicia who had been taking care of me, and though I didn't know her, she was close to Fírean and that was good enough for me.

The carriage lurched beneath us and I tilted my head to get a better look at Fírean, alerting him to the fact that I *was* awake.

"Jackie!" he exclaimed, "How are you feeling?"

"Rubbish," I groaned.

"We'll be back in Torindell soon, I hope – Turvo seems to think he's got the stupid faery magic worked out. That's how we got here so fast. Magic," Fírean practically spat the word, the anger not leaving his face.

"I'm not sure it's magic," I mumbled.

"What else could it be? Not that I care, anyway. Those faeries are filthy maggots," he ranted, "Oh, not you, Felicia! Of course not!"

"You certainly gave them what-for," I managed a smile. Heat rose again to Fírean's cheeks, this time due to embarrassment.

"You heard?" he asked, and Felicia paused in finger-brushing my hair to sign something that only deepened the elf's blush.

"Impressive," I commented, then let out a cry of pain as the carriage jolted, aggravating my back.

"Turvo, steady!" Fírean yelled.

"How bad is it?" I whispered.

"Turvo's driving? Terrible."

Felicia sighed rather loudly.

"Oh, your back." Fírean rubbed the back of his neck awkwardly. "Sorry. It's okay, we don't think it's an injury. Not exactly."

"Not exactly?" I echoed, the words hissing past my gritted teeth, because *vaznek,* it sure stung like a gory wound.

"Ah, no? It's more like a," he floundered, trying to think of a word, and from the absence of Felicia's touch I guessed she was helping him out.

"A what?" I prompted.

"Like a growth," he said and I stiffened. *What...?*

"Well, two growths, really."

"*Two?*" I squeaked.

Fírean nodded, his fingers grasping at the hem of his tunic. "I'm not a biology expert, at all, but that's what it looks like. Felicia says they're..." he trailed off as I raised my head enough to meet his gaze.

"They're what, Fír?"

He took in a deep breath. "Wings. Somehow, you're growing wings."

Chapter Twenty-Five

- Benji -

Soft fruits gathered on my fork as I stabbed the little pieces repetitively, my stomach, though empty, cringing away from the sweetness in the bowl set before me. Although it was very appetising, there was something in the room putting me off my food.

Well, three things, really.

The faeries.

Their greys had made me freeze when I entered the dining hall with Lanny, but I'd quickly recovered, focusing on the warm colours of my family instead. That didn't do anything to help the sudden lack of appetite, or the nausea rising within me, because faeries were *bad*, they wanted to take me and kill my family and-

Lanny squeezed my hand gently and I let out the breath I didn't realise I'd been holding in, his soft touch and fluttering gold grounding me.

"So, Vondri," my brother started, trying to make conversation, "I heard you enjoy reading the works of Balerin?"

The female faery paused in her eating, setting her fork down with a poised mannerism that sent red streaking through me. "Enjoyed is not the right term," she responded prudishly, "I read his works primarily for research purposes."

"Right," Lanny said awkwardly, the room proceeding to descend into an uncomfortable silence. After a few more moments of me ruthlessly stabbing my fruit, Atti cleared his throat and stood.

"If you'll excuse me, I have business to attend to," he announced, "Benji, will you accompany me?"

I shot up faster than was acceptable, eager to get away from the stifling greys of the faeries, and kept up easily with Atti's smooth pace. We walked through a few cold corridors, stopping outside a grand room adorned with towering shelves, filled to the brim with scrolls. A pair of large, cushioned chairs lay in the centre and it was to those that Atti was headed so I followed him, taking a seat when he motioned to do so.

"Benji, you know that was not acceptable behaviour, yes?"

"You know that I can barely breathe around faeries?" I shot back without thinking, then froze, shame washing over me. "Sorry, Atti!"

To my surprise, yellow rippled in his colour and a small chuckle escaped his lips. "Ah, Benji. How much you have grown." His hand gently touched my cheek and I leant into it instinctively as his orange clouded with blue. "And how much I have missed," he murmured.

"I'm here now, though. We can make up for it," I smiled, "Atti, I know you're busier now, but we can still make up for the time lost, right?"

He pulled his hand away and nodded. "Yes. In fact, that's what I wanted to talk to you about."

I rested my hands on my knees, trying – and failing – to keep my legs from swinging in anticipation. "Really?"

"It's not what you think." Atti took a deep breathing, orange clouding as he considered his words carefully. "I would like you to accompany me with some of my duties as King."

My brain slid to a halt. "Isn't that Lanny's role?"

Atti nodded, his dark eyes trying to gauge my reaction as he continued, "It is, but I am extending that to you, as my father let Arlan take on some of *my* roles, when I was the crown prince."

I folded my arms and frowned, the whole proposal not adding up. "But shouldn't that be Fírean's role? He's next after Lanny, right?"

"That's not quite how it works, Benji," Atti sighed, "You see-"

"Your Majesty!" An elf burst into the room, the soft pink of his colour brightened with urgency, and my father groaned, annoyance flashing across his features.

"Is it an emergency?" he asked, unable to keep the frustration from his tone. The elf looked between us then, as if only just noticing my presence, and his pale face flushed red.

"Yes, Your Majesty, please forgive my interruption," he answered with a hurried bow. Atti raised an eyebrow, waiting, which caused the elf's cheeks to darken further.

"Your sons have returned from the Southlands, the lady with them, but she is injured," the elf reported. I immediately closed my eyes, pushing past the brimming excitement to focus on extending my mind. A flicker of blue caught my attention, standing with familiar green and not-so-familiar lavender. The latter was almost greyish in colour and I suspected that person had faery blood; but they were elvish, too, and had a close connection to Fírean, if I was reading the colours correctly, of course. Frowning, I searched for Jackie's cerulean, then gasped and recoiled immediately. Her usually-soft colour was harsh and streaked with the burning whites of physical pain, so intense that my own back flared up momentarily.

"Jackie's really hurt," I gasped out, returning to my own body. Atti nodded, surprisingly cool about the whole thing, though I sensed his irritation at having our conversation cut short. Clearly he was about to say something important, but it could wait. We had plenty of time to discuss it at a later date.

The interrupting elf ran off, presumably to go tell Mutti and Lanny, and I nervously fiddled with the cuffs on my sleeves, waiting for Atti's instruction.

"Come on," he urged, "We should greet them." Anxiety clouded his colour and I frowned, gently easing the pink of love and comfort his way.

"They weren't supposed to return yet, were they?" I asked lowly as we walked.

Atti stiffened ever so slightly. "I should give you more credit," he muttered under his breath, not really answering my question, but his words sent a warmth through my colour that was unfamiliar, but certainly welcomed.

Suddenly, blue and green burst into my vision and I yelled out the corresponding names, all other thoughts forgotten. Turvo froze, startled, but Fírean reacted instantly, running to close the gap between us.

"Benji!" he cried, scooping me up, and I buried myself in my brother's chest, breathing in everything that was *sweet and pretty and Fírean...*

But there was a spot of red staining his usually placid colour and other emotions that were new to me. Fírean set me down then, his cheeks flushed, and I blinked a couple of times. Had Fírean shrunk?

No, you grew, silly. We both did, Kalic pointed out and I barely suppressed a sigh. Fírean wasn't tall – Lanny and Turvo both towered at least a handspan over him – but somehow, I now came up to his shoulder. It was yet another reminder of how much time had passed.

"Wow, you're so tall now!" Fírean commented, as if reading my mind, and I grinned at him.

"Your hair is long," I responded, "Are you trying to copy Lanny?"

My gentle brother gaped. "Um, no? Benji, you..."

"Can form articulate sentences without stumbling over every word?" My smile grew, earning an astonished laugh and another hug from Fírean, love seeping from his blue into me, adding to the fuzzy feeling in my chest.

"I missed you," he whispered, placing a kiss on my forehead.

"I missed you too," I admitted, turning just as Turvo finally decided to walk over.

"Benji, how did you-"

"Kal and I rode here," I answered quickly, "It's good to see you again, Turvo."

The shock in his colour and expression was less than Fírean's, but still present, and he only embraced me briefly, his green clouded with worry and concern: mostly directed towards Jackie, I realised. Lanny and Kalic finally joined us in that moment, my twin playfully punching Turvo whilst Lanny bolted towards Jackie. Curiosity got the better of me and I followed silently, focusing entirely on their colours. A thread ran between them, ribbons of a rosy hue, and I tensed slightly when my eyes caught the pendant hanging around Jackie's neck.

A betrothal gift. They're getting married.

I exhaled, relieved that no crushing panic was encroaching. If Lanny was happy with her, then that was good enough for me. He still loved me, as I loved him, and I knew now that connecting with someone on *that level* wouldn't do anything to change our relationship.

"How bad is it?" Lanny was asking her, and I winced as the white pain made itself known to me again.

"A mess," Jackie whispered in response, "I need to rest, there's a cream that should help, but you should know that..." Her words faded on the air as she and Lanny moved out of my earshot, and I no longer had the desire to follow them. Their connection was intimate and I had no right intruding on it. Especially when Jackie's cerulean was clouded with doubts and fears, the swirling mess of tones starting to make my head hurt.

"Benji?"

I turned to face Turvo, noting from the spikes in his colour that he'd been trying to get my attention for quite a few moments.

"Sorry," I mumbled, but a small smile crept onto his face.

"It *is* good to see you again," he said, and I grinned, "Though I'd rather it have been in better circumstances," he added as an afterthought.

My grin faded. "Better circumstances?" I echoed, then the lines began to connect.

We're on shaky ground with the faeries already, we had *to agree to their terms.*

If the negotiations fail, they will declare war.

They weren't supposed to return yet, were they?

I should give you more credit.

"Vaznek," I swore as the pieces fell together, ignoring all the harsh looks the surrounding elves gave me. I'd been so caught up in my elation at seeing my other two brothers again that I'd completely overlooked the horrible downside to their return. They'd come back far too soon.

And that meant *war* was coming.

I swallowed, a hand running through my short hair as I tried to process the scale of that realisation. Pylisya had been at peace for centuries, no mentions of war in the history scrolls I'd reluctantly read. But I knew enough to understand what war meant.

There would be bloodshed, colours draining everywhere, staining the grass and destroying both the large and small life-forms in the land; one would die by the blade, the other would die as a result of the former's destructive end.

Surely there was another way? Jackie was hurt, so they'd returned early, but surely, *surely,* the negotiations could still happen? Surely the faeries wouldn't be so stupid as to declare war?

My mind drifted back to the faery-king, a horrid, muddy blemish in my memory of what had been happier times, then floated to the cold, grey faeries who'd murdered my grandfather. *Yes,* I decided, *those faeries would be stupid enough to condemn thousands of lives.*

I abruptly pivoted and stormed towards Atti, not bothering to calm the red churning through me. "You have to stop it!" I yelled, starling him.

"Benji, what-?"

"You have to stop them, the faeries! Stop them from fighting us!" I continued, my hands curling into fists.

Atti's orange darkened with grey. "Benji, that was why Jackie and your brothers left, but I fear-"

"NO!" I screamed, "No! Thousands will *die,* Atti! And what for?"

He was silent, colour clouded as he struggled to find an answer.

"It's not *right*," I hissed, "The faeries have no right to do something like that, they... Why would they do that?"

"Because they're conquerors," Fírean said softly, the greyish-lavender half-elf standing beside him.

"Conk- what?" I asked, the red starting to trickle away.

"Conquerors. They dominate everything they can, seek to understand and rule over anything and everyone," Fírean answered, though his eyes were set firmly on the half-elf, whose pale hands were forming a flurry of symbols.

"Do you know Havain's goal?" Atti asked, looking at the half-elf directly. She nodded, then quickly moved her hands with a practised fluidity, her expression and colour grim.

Fírean stiffened, a small gasp escaping his lips, and Atti turned to him. "Well?" he prompted and I realised that my brother was translating the girl's gestures.

"He... he wants the throne," Fírean stammered and Atti's face paled considerably.

"Who's Havain?" Horrible colours came to mind as soon as I spoke his name, answering my own question. *He's the faery-king.*

"But he already has a throne," I then pointed out. Turvo huffed loudly, having suddenly joined our little gathering.

"Benji, you don't get it. Havain is the king of the *faeries*, but he wants Atti's throne, because Atti is the king of Pylisya. He's the king of *everyone*," Turvo explained, not without a slither of annoyance entwining with his tone.

"Oh," was all I could say, because suddenly, that was a lot harder to resolve. How could my father come to an agreement when the opposition wanted what he had? It made my head hurt just thinking about it.

Don't think about it then, Kalic unhelpfully advised.

Kal, this is bad. This is really bad.

Relax, Benji. The dwarves used to joke about war all the time. It's not going to happen.

I frowned. *Kal, it's not funny.*

I'm not saying it is, he retorted.

You said 'joke', I pointed out, *War isn't a joke.*

Vaznek, Benji, don't be so pedantic.

I pushed him from my mind, ignoring the raging colours of the people around me, abruptly turning back towards the castle in a search for one person I trusted wouldn't lie to me. Taking a deep breath, I reached out, brushing against every colour in the area before I connected with the strong silver, situated in the gardens behind the castle, amidst a flurry of yellow and green insects.

"Benji, where-"

"For a walk," I snapped, immediately setting off at a brisk pace that hopefully told Turvo I didn't want him to follow me. Thankfully, he obeyed, exasperation flashing in his green as he turned to converse with Fírean. I focused solely on the silver, slipping through a gap in the castle wall that I knew was a shortcut to the gardens. The path was narrow and ridden with armed plants, their thorns digging trails over my boots and tearing into my breeches, but I pushed past the discomfort and soon emerged out into the fresh green area. Inhaling deeply, I let the colours of life wash over me, the scents of grass and a multitude of brightly coloured flowers tickling my nose, the soothing joy forming moisture in the corners of my eyes. *This* was what I'd missed, what the cold, rocky Northlands had deprived me of. Nature had surrounded us on our journey home, but in that moment, in the gardens, my colour finally felt at peace with the land.

It's just a shame there can't be peace with its people, I thought dryly, the serenity shattered.

"Ethlon?" I called out tentatively, sending a small ripple of orange his way so he would sense my presence. The elf stirred, moving from his seated position to glance my way.

"Hello, Benji," he greeted and I took that as an invitation to approach.

"I need to ask you something, but can you promise me you'll be completely honest?" I asked.

Ethlon's brow furrowed. "Benji, it depends-"

"Will you be honest with me?" I asked again, crossing my arms and keeping my tone firm. He sighed.

"Yes, I will answer honestly," he replied, and I smiled slightly.

"Good. Ethlon, will the faeries go to war against us?"

He froze, all the colour draining from his face, his usually-impassive silver flickering.

"Where... where did that come from?" he stammered.

I sighed. "Ethlon, I'm not blind. Can't you see the concern in their colours? Atti's acting like everything is falling apart and I don't want there to be a war."

Ethlon grimaced. "The faeries tend to act irrationally, and they *will* use force over negotiations."

"Then how can we stop them?" I pressed.

"I'm not sure if they can be stopped," he admitted.

"But Atti could talk to them-"

"He already has! Havain won't be reasoned with!" Ethlon exploded, a flash of red igniting his silver. I reached out and gently placed my hand on his arm, feeling the ribbons of blue and crimson hurt churning beneath.

Ethlon inhaled deeply, attempting to collect himself. "My sister, she was younger than me, and such an optimist. She'd see the good in everyone and gave an endless amount of second chances. But some people took advantage of her kindness." He clenched his fist and I remained silent, my entire focus on listening. I hadn't known anything about Ethlon's family; until now, he'd made no mention of if he even had any siblings.

"Edwyn – my sister – believed that there was good in the faeries. Tensions were present between our races even when I was young, and the faeries had a bad reputation, almost worse than the one they have today. But Edwyn was adamant that they were good at heart and made it her mission to ease the tensions between faeries and elves. Havain was quick to take advantage of her kindness." Ethlon paused and I sensed this was difficult for him to tell, but before I could suggest he stop, he carried on.

"Eventually they fell in love, though I suspect he manipulated her to feel that way. She stopped visiting us soon after Arlan was born, and as the king's first advisor, I was not permitted to visit Syndekar. Seasons passed with us only exchanging the occasional letter. But a year after Turvo's birth, Edwyn finally visited; she was so pale and thin, I could immediately tell she was pregnant. She wanted to have the child in Torindell, to raise him with the elves. 'He's special, like you,' she told me, and I knew what that meant."

"Her child could see colours?" I gasped.

Ethlon nodded. "He can see colours, yes."

Ethlon and I aren't the only Chroma! "But who-" I held my tongue, suppressing the question, and perked my ears up to show Ethlon I was still listening.

"I wanted her to have the baby in Torindell, too, but Havain wouldn't allow it. He returned for her, absolutely furious, and demanded that we 'released' her, as if she was a prisoner! If we wouldn't, then he threatened to take one of Arazair's – sorry, your father's – children in his son's place. Turvo happened to be in the room and Havain seized him as proof of his motives. My sister stepped forward and agreed to go. She sacrificed her freedom to save your brother, Benji. And without the facilities we have in Torindell, she also sacrificed her life. The child survived, but my sister died. With her last breath, I am told, she named her son Galen."

I repeated the name, tasting the silver on my tongue. "Galen is like us?"

"Yes. He's a Chroma, and my nephew. But he is, unfortunately, loyal only to his father."

I nodded solemnly, slowly processing the story as Ethlon then sighed loudly.

"Now you understand why we can't trust faeries," he commented bitterly.

I frowned. "I never trusted them in the first place and I don't like them one bit. But you can't let the past events define the future. We have to try, don't we? We have to try and avoid war."

Ethlon fell silent, his colour settling back into its usual monochrome, expression becoming placid. His grey eyes were glazed, still lost in the past, and I moved to leave when an accidental yawn slipped from my lips and broke our serenity.

"You should get some rest," he commented.

Though he hadn't given me a set answer to my original question, the exhaustion from weeks of restless nights still hadn't faded, reminding me of its existence with another yawn.

"Yes, okay," I agreed, turning and heading back inside, leaving Ethlon alone with the quiet I knew he needed.

Turvo then greeted me and my cheeks flushed, suddenly remembering the frustration I'd directed at him earlier.

"I'm sorry-" I started, but he cut me off with a sudden embrace, scooping me up like I was a small child again. Startled, I yelped, which only made Turvo laugh as he carried me through the corridors towards a room where familiar red and blue waited.

"There you are!" my twin exclaimed as Turvo set me down. I blinked, staring at the sight before me.

Blankets spread across the floor, all different shades and textures, mixed with a multitude of soft cushions. Fírean was snuggled beneath one heap of blankets, already half-asleep, and Kalic leant up against him, using Fírean's torso as a pillow.

"What is this?" I asked, utterly confused.

"It's a human tradition that Hazel told me about. Something called a 'sleepover'," Kalic explained, popping the 'p', "We haven't all been together in seasons, so I thought it would be nice."

The soft blankets *did* look very inviting, so I wriggled out of my outer tunic and kicked my boots off, stepping over the scattered cushions to rest against Fírean's other side. Turvo lay down next to Kalic, taking care to not squash my twin with his bulky frame.

"Where's Lanny?" I mumbled, so I wouldn't wake Fírean.

"Here," my brother answered, entering the room in that moment. His gold was tinged with greys of concern for Jackie, but he manoeuvred his way to my side, pulling me close against him.

"How is she?" I enquired gently. Lanny stiffened almost imperceptibly.

"She's still pretty hurt," he whispered back, "but she told me to come and join you in this, and stop fussing over her."

I curled into his embrace, shifting so my head rested on his chest. "M'glad you came," I mumbled sleepily.

"I'm glad *you* came home," he responded, "I love you, Benji."

"Love you too," I breathed, before I finally went under, the peace and security from my brothers' presence promising me a dreamless sleep.

Chapter Twenty-Six

- Jackie -

I staggered back towards the castle, eyes bleary, struggling to focus on anything but the pain tearing through my back. Someone darted past me – Fírean, I presumed – but I was too out-of-it to really pay attention. Then my fiancé rushed over to me, his blond hair an uncharacteristically tangled mess, and I forced myself to look at his oceanic eyes, brimming with concern.

"How bad is it?" he asked, his voice shaking.

"A mess," I managed to reply, "I need to rest, there's a cream that should help, but you should know that the faeries... they're not who they say they are."

Arlan's hand rested on my shoulder, gently guiding me away from the others as I spoke, hissing when another dagger of pain tore through my back.

"Steady, we're almost there," he soothed, and my vision refocused just as we stopped in front of the door to my bedroom. Dimly I realised that I was in Arlan's arms – *when did he pick me up?* – but I didn't dwell on it as he sat me down on my bed, immediately glancing around for the cream I mentioned.

"There," I whispered, pointing weakly to the jar sitting on one of my shelves next to a few scrolls. Arlan's nose wrinkled at the smell of it, but he quickly rubbed the cream into the sorry mess of my back. I grit my teeth against the sting, waiting for the relief to set in, which it did after a few torturous minutes.

"Jackie," Arlan murmured then, "This... isn't normal for humans, is it? To grow wings?"

I inhaled shakily. "Wings?" I echoed, still struggling with the notion.

"It's the only thing that makes *sense*, unless they did something to you?" He knelt in front of me, taking my hands in his, forcing me to look into his eyes.

"M'not sure," I mumbled, suddenly feeling rather drowsy again. My body lurched forward without my consent, muscles turning to jelly, and Arlan quickly manoeuvred me so I was lying stomach-first on the bed.

"It's okay, we'll talk later," he said, gently running a tender hand through my hair, and I let the exhaustion pull me under.

My eyes opened to a familiar setting, though I'd only ever seen it a few times in my dreams. My mother sat on the doorstep of the hut, just as she had been the first time I'd dreamt of her from Pylisya.

"Mum!" I exclaimed and she stood, smiling at me with tears in her eyes. "I'm sorry," I continued in the same breath, "I don't know why I haven't been able to dream of you; everything is going crazy and I-"

She raised a hand in the universal gesture and I stopped, taking in precious air.

"It's been months, Jackie," she whispered, causing guilt to swell up in my stomach. *Has it really been that long?*

"I'm sorry," I repeated, pouring all my truth into the words.

"I miss you," she breathed, gently caressing my cheek, and I leant into the touch.

"I miss you too, Mum," I confessed.

She arched an eyebrow, her dark eyes unreadable. "Do you? You're not coming home to me, are you?"

Mutely I shook my head, guilt squeezing my throat closed.

"It is as I thought," she murmured, "You and your father, both short-lived blessings from Heaven. He never came back, and now you won't, either."

"You... You could come here!" I exclaimed, "Mum, I can leave, I can come and bring you here and then we can be a family again, you and me and Hazel, and then you can meet my fian- uh, Arlan," I quickly corrected, but the damage had already been done.

Mum smiled weakly. "See? You have made a life for yourself there. As I have my life here. I can't leave Earth forever, Jackie," she said and I frowned, Havain's words echoing in my mind.

I can't leave. Purebloods get trapped.

"Oh," was all I could manage. Of course, she still had her parents – though they were never that close – as well as her friends and the community she'd built up. Hazel and I weren't the only people in her life; not that we'd been there for the last two years.

"I'm sorry, Jackie," she sighed, "I should never have kept this from you. I always knew that you'd be taken from me one day, I just *hoped* that maybe it wouldn't be the case, that we would have more time."

My eyes narrowed at the words I'd heard before, knowing what was coming next.

"You said my father would tell me, but I've never met him," I snapped, before she could say it again, "And I don't understand how you can just let me go like this!"

"I've *had* to let you go!" she yelled back, "I won't cope otherwise! I know you're still alive even though you can't be with me, and that has to be enough for me. Jackie..." Her voice softened and she crossed the distance between us, "My darling, I love you. I love you and that is why I'm letting you go, and why you should let me go, too."

"No," I whispered, anger deflating, "Mum, I can't-"

"You already are. You haven't dreamt of me because part of you is letting me go. Hazel has already let me go, she did so months ago. She found her place, didn't she?"

I nodded slowly, biting my lip as I recalled how my adopted sister never spoke of our mother anymore. I'd dismissed it as a teenager thing, but now... Now I wasn't so sure.

"Then let me go, Jackie." She gently touched my cheek again, "Let me go, and live your life in this world. Don't feel guilty about me."

"Mum," I choked out as she stepped back, reaching out to grab her hand.

"Let me go, Jackie," she repeated, but it was a plea rather than a command.

A strangled sob broke through my mouth and my fingers loosened, allowing her to pull away, skin turning translucent.

"I... I love you," I cried, crumpling to my knees as my mother and the scenery blurred and faded away into an endless void, tearing through my chest as I realised that she was *gone*, our tentative connection wasn't there, I was alone and-

"Jackie!"

Gasping, I jerked away, crying out as the motion aggravated my back.

"Vaznek, don't do that!" Hazel swore, peering down at me, "I've been so worried!"

I didn't have the heart to chide her for her language, especially as I'd adopted the word too, and awkwardly pushed myself up so I could wrap an arm around her.

"I had a bad dream-" I started to apologise, but she swiftly interjected.

"No, silly, I mean your back! It's cool that you've got wings now, even if they are all gory and blood-covered," she frowned disapprovingly, "But really, you scared me, coming in all unconscious. I can't lose you."

I managed a weak smile. "I can't lose you either, Zel," I whispered.

"Jackie!" Arlan exclaimed then, entering the room; he'd obviously left me alone when I was sleeping, something I was glad for. "How are you feeling?"

"A bit better. My back's not on fire anymore," I reassured him.

His eyes darted in the direction of my back and instantly widened. "Wow. Those are definitely wings, Jackie."

I craned my head to try and see, but the action sent a spark through my spine and I hissed.

"Steady," Arlan fretted, moving to step towards me, but Hazel blocked him.

"Nope," she said firmly, "Mister, you are going to the sleepover with your brothers. Jackie is fine now."

I raised an eyebrow. *Sleepover?* I mouthed, and my sister shrugged.

"Bonding time needed," she whispered, as if that explained everything.

Wearily I turned my gaze to Arlan, absorbing the anxiety reflected there. "I'll be fine, like Zel said. Go on, join your brothers. You don't need to fuss over me constantly," I added with a smile.

"Okay," he agreed rather reluctantly, before Hazel practically shoved him out the door.

"Brothers?" I asked, "Why-?"

"Oh, the twins returned, shortly after you left actually," she replied casually. I blinked, my mind still a little groggy. *Benji and Kalic are back? But why now? Isn't this more dangerous for them?*

Sighing, I dismissed the thoughts and instead concentrated my energy on moving. I forced myself to sit up, gasping as I became increasingly aware of the extra weight on my back.

"Zel, can you get me a mirror?" I asked, "I... I need to see."

She frowned. "Yeah, but you gotta get cleaned up first. Like I said, they're all blood-covered. It's gross."

"I can help with that."

Both of us jumped at the sudden appearance of the red-headed elf that I wasn't sure was actually an elf. He stood casually in the doorway, clothed in a loose, toga-like garment that barely covered his chest, green markings on his cheeks seeming to give off a soft glow.

Yeah. He's definitely not an elf, I decided.

"Sachiel," I greeted, blushing as I suddenly became aware of my own state of undress. The dress I wore was loose and only came down to my knees, as well as being backless – for ease of treatment, I knew, but it didn't make it any less uncomfortable.

"You know this guy?" Hazel spluttered.

"We've met," I answered calmly.

"I need to speak with the lady. Alone," he stated, no traces of malice in his voice. Hazel's gaze flickered between us, suspicion growing.

"It's fine, Zel," I whispered, "He gave me the cream in the first place. I think... I think he might know something."

"Alright. Well, I'll be back in an hour, okay? Not giving you any more time than that." She moved to leave, then paused, and quickly pivoted back to give me a quick kiss on the cheek. Her own face darkened before she left the room and I gently touched the damp spot, treasuring that rare display of affection.

"You grew wings."

I frowned at Sachiel for just stating the obvious. "I don't know how that's possible."

He let out a small hum, crossing the room to stand beside me, his hand reaching towards my back. "May I?" he asked and I nodded. Immediately a rush of cool air brushed over me, tickling the two appendages that I was only just becoming aware of, and I stared at Sachiel's hand in disbelief as he pulled it back. A bubble of water sat in his palm, streaked with the crimson of what I knew to be blood, the liquid dissolving into his skin as I watched, astonished.

"You're not an elf, so what are you?" I asked, receiving my answer as I looked up at his face.

Because there, towering above him, was a pair of bluish-white wings.

"Oh, my gosh," I squeaked, "You're an *angel?*"

"Yes," he answered tentatively, his green eyes watching mine for some sort of reaction. Slowly, he twisted his hands and as his arms pulled apart, a shimmering, reflective veil appeared between them. "Look," he urged, so I did.

Feathers. Very pale blue – so pale they were almost white – feathers met my curious gaze, hanging from thin, sturdy curves of bone, that erupted from just below my shoulder blades.

Oh, vaznek.

I actually had *wings*.

It was one thing being told that, another to actually *see* them, rising at least a foot above my head, curving elegantly like Sachiel's did.

Cautiously, I shrugged my shoulders, wondering if the wings would obey: they did, not just with the motion of my shoulders, the muscles stretching and unfurling seemingly on their own accord. The tip of the left wing twitched in some sort of twisted wave and my head started spinning again.

"How is this possible?" I spluttered, glancing up at Sachiel. He let the reflective veil disappear, giving me a better view of *his* wings, which were the same colour as mine.

Same colour. I locked eyes with him, the vibrant green so familiar to me because it was what I saw every time I looked in the mirror. Heart pounding faster, I scrutinised his face for any other similarities, finding the nose to hold the same gentle slope as mine, the elegant arch of his eyebrows almost matching my own, save the difference in colour.

"You're my father?" I exclaimed, though it came out more like an odd mix of a whisper and a screech.

Sachiel's eyes widened in surprise and I held my breath as he nodded almost imperceptibly.

"Oh gosh," was all I could manage, a thousand questions racing through my mind. I could feel the wings behind me fluttering slightly and the motion was so *natural* that I wasn't too surprised at my lack of freaking out. Honestly, with all that had happened, me being part *angel* actually served to explain a lot of the madness.

But how was that even possible?

"You're my father," I said again, staring up at the man I'd been longing for my whole life, then blurted out, "Why didn't you tell me?"

He shifted uncomfortably. "I wasn't sure it was appropriate."

"*Appropriate?*" I exclaimed, "I've been wondering where you were my *whole life* and you decided to make me wait a little longer? Are you serious?"

Sachiel – I couldn't yet call him 'Dad' – sighed loudly. "Jackie, listen. More than anything I wanted you to have a normal life. I would've stayed with you, but due to my... *actions*," he almost hissed the word, "I was no longer allowed to be on Earth. It broke my heart, having to say goodbye to you and Hana."

"Hold on," I interrupted, "I thought you died before I was born?"

Sachiel's eyes grew sad. "That was the story we agreed on, but the truth is, I was there at your birth. The an- *others* didn't come for me until shortly before your second birthday."

"So, I... I knew you?" I breathed.

"I suppose. But *I* knew *you*, Jackie. And even though it had been many years, I recognised you at Myranis' funeral. But how could I reveal myself to you? It was not an appropriate time and you already had enough to worry about. My daughter, a dream-prophet," he smiled and my heart warmed at the pride in his tone.

"I know this won't be easy. We're strangers, at least, I am a stranger to you. But Jackie, I want to build that relationship with you, to restore what we should've had."

My eyes welled with tears and before I could stop to think my actions through, I had thrown myself into his arms, breathing in everything that just felt so *right*.

"I want that too," I whispered as he returned the embrace, his wings brushing against mine and sending a peculiar sensation through them. We stayed like that for a few precious moments, familiarising ourselves with each other, and as I listened to his steady heartbeat a sudden thought occurred to me.

"How are you alive?" I asked, pulling back.

Sachiel frowned down at me. "What?"

I blushed. "Um, aren't angels, like, supernatural beings?"

"Yes," he replied slowly, dragging out the word, "But that doesn't mean we're dead. When I am in my flesh form, I still have a heart that beats, lungs that respire, and all the other human organs."

"Right. I mean, I should've guessed human and angel anatomy was compatible, because, well," I gestured awkwardly to myself.

"I didn't know that would happen," he confessed, "The only other angel-mortal born from love was part elf. But I am glad that we were granted you."

"Even though you had to leave us?" I asked gently.

"Jackie, leaving you was the worst thing that happened to me. But having you was the *best,* so I would *never* take it back," he said firmly, gently brushing his smooth hand against my cheek.

"Thank you," I whispered, placing my hand over his and squeezing it gently, relishing in the fact that I had a *father* and he was *here* and he *wanted* me.

I'd let my mother go, but I'd found my father; though I'd rather *both*, I could work with it.

A knock sounded at the door and Hazel's voice crept through. "Jackie? You okay in there?"

"More than okay," I responded, a huge grin splitting my face, and Sachiel moved to open the door. My adopted sister entered, her eyes widening as she took in both our wings.

"Oh, wow. *Wow,*" she exclaimed, "Jackie, is he your long-lost brother or something?"

"No. He's my dad," I said, still smiling. Hazel's eyes widened in a comical manner.

"Oh, my gosh, Jackie you're part *angel?*" she squeaked, "That's...that's crazy awesome!" She ran forward and hugged me, and I laughed, returning the embrace. Sachiel smiled down on both of us.

My left wing jerked suddenly, knocking against a shelf and eliciting a squeak from Hazel.

"It's going to take a while to get used to these things," I grumbled. Sachiel chuckled and I watched as his wings simply disappeared. "How did you...?"

"I can change my form to fit in with my surroundings," he explained, "You should develop the ability to hide your wings, too. Your body has only now developed them because of your choice to stay in Pylisya. As with your ears, it would not have been safe for you to have your true form on Earth," he pointed out and I shuddered to think of what would happen with human scientists.

Humans. Scientists. Faeries.

"Oh no," I whispered, then louder, "I have to talk to Arlan! It's urgent!"

Sachiel frowned. "How urgent?"

"The faeries, they're actually humans," I exclaimed, "Havain told me. I *know* they're up to no good, I saw it in a vision, one of the brothers is in danger and I have to warn them!"

"Steady, slow down, Jackie," Hazel urged, just as Benji ran into the room.

"Turvo's missing!" he yelled, then stiffened as he took in my appearance. "You're an angel too?"

"There's no time for that," Sachiel said firmly, "If your brother is missing, and Jackie's visions prove true, he may be in danger."

But why Turvo? Of all the brothers, he was the *last* person I would've thought the faeries would take. *Though he did start a massive fight with them.*

"Jackie, come on," Benji urged, pulling me from my musing.

"Just a minute!" I quickly slipped on some breeches underneath my short dress, fastened my belt, and secured my betrothal pendant. Then, I tried to pull my wings in behind me, sighing with relief when the new muscles obeyed, tucking close to my back in order to prevent knocking things over.

Benji kept glancing at me, confusion etched onto his less-familiar features; his hair was shorter, his cheeks and jawline had lost some of their childish roundness, and his silver-lidded eyes were tainted with a weariness and understanding that didn't belong on a face so young. He didn't move to express his thoughts and I sensed that he knew something was amiss, more than just Turvo's absence.

"Elohim," I muttered under my breath, "Please, if there is anything to see, show me."

No visions graced me in that moment, but a warmth flooded throughout my body, a whisper of a promise echoed by the hand that my father placed on my shoulder, anchoring me. As we rounded the corner to the corridor with the lounge and music room, Arlan froze midstep and ran over to us.

"Jackie, you're alright!" he exclaimed, then he looked me up and down, eyes widening as they settled on my wings, a blush spreading over his cheeks. Kalic popped up behind him, taller than I recalled, and exchanged a look – along with a thought, I suspected – with his twin, causing them both to snicker. I watched them curiously, absorbing how much they'd grown, Benji especially. Then I frowned, a thought crossing my mind.

How exactly did the twins return here? Was it planned? I wondered, turning to ask the question.

"Who are you?" Arlan then enquired of Sachiel, interrupting me before I could begin, his brow furrowing in suspicion.

"I am Sachiel, Jackie's father," he introduced himself and the elves' mouths flopped open, "Soon to be your father-in-law, I suppose."

Arlan's face grew redder in a manner that was completely adorable, melting my heart into a little puddle despite our circumstances. He awkwardly tucked a stray curl behind his ear, then extended his hand in greeting.

"It is a pleasure to meet you, Sachiel, and as much as I'd like to get to know you, I'm afraid we don't have the time. Turvo is missing, as are the three faeries from Havain's company."

"Humans," I corrected automatically.

Arlan frowned. "Jackie, what-"

"The faeries are actually humans, from Earth. All they want is to conquer this place, and one of you," I nodded to the Zeraphin brothers, including a bleary-eyed Fírean in nightclothes, "is in grave danger, I've seen it. I just don't know which one."

Benji's eyes narrowed and Arlan grit his teeth. "Then Turvo is in danger," my fiancé deduced, "Come on, they can't have gone far." He took one look at my dress and shrugged off his cloak, shoving it in my direction.

Is he really just going to ignore the fact that faeries *are* humans? *That, according to the laws of this world, I'm technically half-faery?*

Apparently that was the case, as Arlan adopted the tone of voice that truly showcased his status as the crown prince. "There should be boots by the back door. Benji and I will lead. Kal, Hazel, Felicia," I suddenly noticed the quiet presence of the deaf half-elf, "you stick close. Same to you and Fír, Jackie. Hurry," he urged.

I gratefully pulled the cloak on, then fell into step behind Felicia and Kalic, the latter of whom was dressed in a reddish-brown tunic and grey breeches combo identical to that of his twin. Fírean paused beside me, looking down at the fabric of his nightshirt.

"I'm going to change quickly," he announced, signing the message to Felicia, "I'll catch you up."

"Careful," I whispered, receiving only a small nod of acknowledgement.

My father brought up the rear as Fírean darted off, though watching him leave only filled me with more foreboding. I grabbed Hazel's hand, keeping her as close to me as I could. We navigated the dimly-lit corridors, torches and the trickles of blue moonlight our only visible guide, at a relatively brisk pace. Arlan and Benji lead the way, the latter clearly trying to use his soul-sensing gifting to locate their missing brother.

I paused only to mechanically shove my feet into a pair of oversized boots, my instincts yelling at me to hurry up and *get outside*, though for what reason I wasn't sure. As soon as I stepped out on the turquoise-tinted grass, a knife of pain split my skull, unleashing a sharp cry as a vision seized my eyes.

Smoke. Fire. The city, burning, burning, burning...

"Vaznek," I choked out, "Arlan, where áre your parents? *Where is Fírean?*"

Arlan turned around, tensing up at the panic in my tone. "Jackie, what did you-"

"Fír's in the halls, coming towards us now," Benji answered surprisingly eloquently, "But our parents are still in their room."

A very human curse word escaped my lips, met with confused looks from all but Hazel and my father.

"We have to get them," I gasped, pivoting to run back into the castle, "We have to get them out of there!" Alarm bells were clanging in my head, my every instinct screaming for me to run away, but instead I shoved Hazel towards Sachiel, my fists clenching.

"Jackie, what are you doing?" Arlan yelled as I strode back indoors, "Turvo is this way!"

"But the faeries aren't," Benji stated anxiously, "They're in the castle."

My heart sped up, wings flapping to propel me through the corridor as my family faded out of earshot, dread seeping through my bones. I rounded the second corner and nearly barrelled into Fírean, a small laugh escaping my mouth out of relief.

"Go," I urged, "You have to get away from here, but I have to-"

The words died in my throat as a bright light burst behind Fírean, accompanied by a sudden rush of heat that washed over us as the elf pushed me to the ground.

Someone screamed, and the walls around us shattered.

Chapter Twenty-Seven

- Benji -

Fire lit up the night sky, reds and oranges swallowing the soft azure of moonlight. White flooded my vision, tearing through my colour and ripping a scream from my throat as part of the castle exploded, taking the faeries and dozens of innocent servants with it. Their colours faded almost instantly, the backlash heading towards me and I desperately pulled away, retracting until I could feel the blues of Jackie and Fírean. Both were stained with white, but my brother's even more so, and I cried out as I felt him begin to fade.

"No!" I yelled, "Fír!"

Lanny helped me stand, gold streaked with panic. "Is he-?" he choked out.

"Not yet," I responded, breaking into a run. Someone else shouted my name, but I didn't listen, running towards the damaged walls as fire raced from the centre towards us. Fírean was fading, but I wouldn't let him go.

I *couldn't* let him go.

The doorway was crumpled, but not entirely, with a gap in the crying stone just big enough for me to slip through. Immediately smoke hit me and I gagged, but forced my feet to move further in.

"Jackie! Fír!" I screamed, before the smoke flooded my lungs and I doubled over, coughing.

The answer was faint, but it was enough to guide me through the hazardous corridor, not wanting to reach out to find their colours as I knew I'd only be met with pain. Rounding a corner, I could just about make out Jackie's prone form, lying at an awkward angle, her strange new wings crumpled on the ground. Fírean was on top of her, blood trickling from a head wound, his left arm trapped by a block of stone. The fire was fast approaching – I could see it in the distance – and the threat spurred me on.

"I'll roll Fír off you," I told Jackie quickly, "Can you move?"

"Yeah," she croaked, her wings twitching. I gingerly stepped around them, shoving my arms beneath my brother's unresponsive form and pulling him towards me, trying not to aggravate any of his injuries further. Jackie managed to wriggle out of the way, grimacing as she stood, favouring her left ankle.

"We've got to get Fír out of here!" I exclaimed, letting him roll back on the ground again. Jackie knelt down, trying to get my brother to respond, whilst I struggled to roll the stone off his arm.

"Come on!" I grunted, "Elohim, help me!"

I didn't know why I said that plea, but a warmth suddenly surged through my limbs and with a cry I pushed the stone aside, freeing Fírean. His pale arm was extremely discoloured, an array of purple bruises blossoming, but we didn't have time to examine him.

If we didn't move *now*, the fire would consume us.

Jackie seemed to be on the same path of thought, as she awkwardly scooped up my brother, using her wings to help her carry the extra weight. I pointed her in the right direction and we set off, though I quickly remembered how narrow the corridor now was.

Kalic! I called out, *I've got them, but the exit is too tight.*

Already on it, he responded, showing me what he was doing in that moment: working with Lanny, Hazel, and Ethlon to clear some of the rubble away from the doorway, making the gap larger. And it was not a moment too soon, as I felt the rush of heat behind me.

"Jackie!" I yelled and she moved faster, practically flying out of the ruins. I ran out behind her, immediately pulling my twin away from the line of fire.

Run! I screamed internally and he obeyed, sprinting with the rest of us. Jackie passed Fírean over to Sachiel and Ethlon scooped Hazel up, carrying the half-dwarf with ease. I ignored the protests in my legs, not stopping until Lanny gave the signal, all of us collapsing just outside the walls of the castle grounds. I crumpled down beside Fírean, gently touching his wrist to feel for a pulse, his blue brushing against my fingertips but still holding on to his body.

"What... happened?" Kalic broke the silence, his cheeks flushed with exertion.

Sachiel stepped back from Fírean, and the lavender-grey elf-faery immediately took his place on the other side of my brother. "The faeries set off a bomb," the angel said.

I frowned at the unfamiliar term. "Bomb?"

"Explosive," Hazel explained, wriggling out of Ethlon's arms, "Caused the fire, made the walls break apart."

"Wait," Jackie gasped, green eyes darting over all of us, "Where... where are the others?"

Lanny's face paled and as I tentatively reached to examine his colour, all the white from earlier came back to me.

"Colours f-faded," I stammered, "They... they're gone..."

Jackie inhaled sharply and Ethlon's cold expression crumbled, the piercing blue of grief spreading across their colours. Lanny fell to his knees, tears streaming down his face, but I sat frozen, looking around in confusion. The faeries were dead, but Fírean was still breathing, so why was everyone so upset?

Then it hit me. *Oh, vaznek. Please, no...*

Our *parents* had been in their room.

In the wing of the castle that exploded.

"No," I murmured, then screamed the word, reaching out with my mind to find the lilac and the amber because they *couldn't* be dead, they couldn't, I just got them back they couldn't leave me now-

"Benji," someone said, tugging on my arm, but I ignored them, squeezing my eyes closed against the growing fire as I desperately searched. Faded, lifeless greys met me, along with the drained colours of the servants, but I kept looking, because they *had* to be there, they *had* to be okay...

Two faded shades greeted me, remnants of white clinging to them, lying near the heart of the explosion.

No.

I punched the ground, a raw scream escaping my throat as reality slammed into my chest, knocking the breath from my lungs. *Dead. My parents are dead. They...they're dead, but they can't be... Please, let this be a nightmare...*

"This is real," Ethlon murmured, and I realised I'd said that out loud.

No no no no no...

I turned and buried my head in Lanny's chest, sobbing into his clothes as his tears dampened my hair, clinging to each other with all that we had.

"Wh-why," I stammered, "Why, *why* did they do this?"

No-one needed to ask who I was referring to.

"We have to move," Ethlon said gruffly and I pulled away from Lanny long enough to glare at him.

"I c-can't," I half-growled, "Mutti, Atti... th-they..."

"I know," he whispered, his voice cracking slightly, "But we have to move. The faeries..."

I sensed the greys the moment he mentioned them: cold, solid colours striding through the wreckage of the castle, their monochromes completely unaffected by the carnage that three of their own had caused. Upon a closer look, I noticed the dark red, almost black, that speckled the majority of their greys. It was the deep, wine-colour of hatred and desire for bloodshed.

They called me a monster, but I'm not *one.* They *are the monsters.*

Slowly I let go of Lanny and he stood, turning to help Jackie up. Sachiel gathered Fírean in his arms again and Hazel quickly edged away from Ethlon. The lavender-grey female hovered near my injured brother and though she had the blood of my enemies, I knew she wasn't one. A thread of pink ran between her and Fírean, and the warmth in her colour was one I'd never seen in faeries before. I knew that I could trust her.

Ethlon stiffened suddenly, then his hand was on my shoulder, urging me onwards. I rubbed my eyes roughly, shoving the crimson hurt deep inside, where I could let it consume me later. We didn't have time to grieve; Fírean was injured, the faeries were coming, and from the flickers of wine-red I sensed, they were out for blood.

We headed through narrow streets in the city, every step taking us further and further from the faeries, closer to the place Kalic and I had run from. Crowds of people were gathering, the majority elves and dwarves, and I ignored their colours, my sole focus on not losing sight of my family. The urgent need to *get away* was never voiced, but we all felt it, struggling through constricting passages in an attempt to avoid contact with the growing masses. As I helped Jackie and Lanny to navigate a particularly tight alleyway, another colour brushed against my mind and I instantly froze.

It was *green*.

Not the warm, confident shade that I usually associated with my brother, but a darker, sickly tone, marred with a conflicting mix of guilt and thirst for blood.

Lanny glanced back, noticing my hesitation. "Benji? What is it?" he asked gently. I slowly met his gaze, both our eyes still damp with unshed tears.

"Turvo," I whispered, "He's all *wrong*, his colour's changed, why has it changed?"

"I don't-" he started, but stopped suddenly, ears flickering at a sound I couldn't catch.

"Get down," he hissed and I panicked, not seeing any obvious place to hide. The alley was so *narrow* and everyone else was ahead so there was nowhere to run if the faeries had caught up to us, we were trapped-

Lanny huffed in frustration and grabbed my arm, pulling me down just as two faeries walked past, their voices drifting to my sensitive ears. The night was on our side as we crouched there, turning us into silhouettes that could simply be crates or piles of rubbish in the narrow alley.

"Sounds like the bombs didn't get them all. The princes escaped."

"Vaznek!"

"They can't have gone far, though."

"True. Well, if you see one of the little swines, make sure to-"

Lanny clamped his hands over my ears, drowning out the rest of the faeries' words, but he was trembling, fear staining his gold. I squeezed my eyes shut and huddled close to him, tears carving sorrow down my cheeks. The faeries took Anatti, and then Mutti and Atti... and now they were coming for me and my brothers?

It's as if the faeries want my whole family dead.

A small gasp escaped me then, as I realised that it was *exactly* what the faeries wanted. I thought they'd be stupid enough to start a war, but maybe they *weren't* quite that stupid. Maybe they could actually see that sending thousands out to fight and die to solve a petty argument would only cause sorrow and loss. Maybe they thought they'd solve the 'problem' by just taking out the lead opposition.

By *murdering* my *family*.

Lanny's hands fell away from my ears, moving to grab my arms instead, and I let him haul me to my feet, still rather dazed.

"Come on, Benji, we have to keep moving," he urged, and my body obeyed as my mind wandered, stuck in the realisation of the faeries' motives. How could they be so *cruel*? Why couldn't they just resolve the conflict with discussion rather than bloodshed?

More importantly, why was Turvo's colour so *different*, bold against a sea of grey?

One answer sprung to mind, but I threw it away with passion. *No.* My brother was *not* a traitor. He would *never* help the faeries, especially not after what they'd done.

My feet slipped on a loose stone and I stumbled, the action jolting me back into my body. I noticed then that we'd caught up with the rest of my family and friends.

"Where are we going?" I whispered to Ethlon, as Lanny left my side to assist Jackie.

"I'm not sure," he confessed, "We just need to get out of Torindell."

"Can we stop soon? I'm tired," Kalic whined, but I sensed from his colour that it wasn't his only reason for wanting to stop. We all desperately needed a respite, a moment to grieve and let the tears of reality fall, but it had not yet been granted to us.

Ethlon glanced to Sachiel, the two oldest adults exchanging a knowing look.

"There is somewhere," Sachiel announced gruffly, "Follow me."

"I'll take the prince," Ethlon quickly offered, cradling Fírean to his chest in order to free Sachiel's hands. I walked apace with Ethlon, my left hand brushing against my gentle brother, checking that he was still holding on. His blue flickered, a small wisp trailing up my arm, but I forced it back with a shot of pink.

"Hold on, Fír," I whispered, "I love you – we *all* love you – so you... you can't go yet." My voice broke slightly, but I swallowed, forcing the words out, "You can't go. I can't lose you too. You've got to stay with us, you hear me?" As I spoke, I poured the soft pink of affection into him, letting his blue absorb the colour, each drop keeping him anchored.

Sachiel lead us, followed by Lanny and Jackie, the two girls, my twin, then finally myself, Fírean, and Ethlon bringing up the rear. The sun began to creep over the tops of the various buildings in the city, but I found no joy in its golden rays, striking cruelly on a sorrowful day. Our path was better lit, though that also meant we couldn't travel in the shadows. For the first time, the daylight had become my enemy.

When the streets turned to narrow alleys, I let Ethlon walk ahead as I kept alert for any signs of grey. The ruins of the castle were slowly filling up with that horrible monochrome, and the streets surrounding it were a headache-inducing mix of grey and the panic-streaked colours of elves, dwarves, and some other beings I didn't recognise. Sachiel was headed east, taking the lesser, dirtier streets, the parts of the city that no-one would expect to find us. A few bleary-eyed people stared at us with mouths agape, some displaying colours and features that didn't look to be elven, dwarven, or fae – just like the strange ones near the castle – and I briefly wondered how much about my homeland had been hidden from me, especially since a few curious faces didn't seem surprised at the wings clearly visible on Jackie and Sachiel. The latter then stopped in front of a low tunnel, the sun's cold rays barely lighting a span of the stone structure.

"This will take us out of the city. It is tight to get in, but it does widen, I can assure you," Sachiel explained quietly, his bright eyes darting around nervously.

"How can we trust you?" Kalic asked sceptically.

"He's my father," Jackie answered, her tone weary. I glanced over her colour, alarmed at the volumes of white shooting through the cerulean. She was clearly hurt, but trying her best to hide it due to the danger we were in, and admiration for her fluttered in my chest.

My twin blushed at Jackie's response and ducked his head. "Sorry," he mumbled, to which Sachiel smiled in response. However, the brief turn up of his lips faded when he refocused on our situation and the task at hand.

"It's a bit of a drop," he warned, "So I'll go first. Ethlon, pass Fírean down to me." The coppery angel nimbly slipped into the dark passage, descending until he was only visible from the waist up. Ethlon did as he'd commanded, then followed down after, to help Jackie and the other girls down. Just as Kalic entered the tunnel, sudden greys made themselves known, only a few streets away.

"Hurry," Lanny hissed, practically shoving me down after Kalic. I bit back a scream as I fell, the lavender-grey girl somehow managing to catch me. Flustered, I wriggled out of her arms, but shot her a grateful smile. I was about to ask her name when I remembered the faeries – and my brother still out there.

"Lanny!" I called out as loud as I dared, darting away from the passage's entrance as his high boots appeared, greeting the ground with an elegance I wished I possessed. He took my hand and we set off at a jog after the others, new determination flashing through everyone's colours now we were no longer so exposed.

Sachiel led us through the passage and, though being surrounded by everyone's positive colours was fuelling me, I couldn't stop the advancement of the aches and exhaustion in my bones. Kalic quickly caught onto it, his whispered protests to Hazel growing increasingly louder by the moment. What also concerned me, though, was the lack of response from Fírean. His colour was steady, but he had yet to wake, and I knew that this worry was gradually spreading through the group at a rate rivalling that of exhaustion.

Eventually the angel gave us the signal to stop and we all did so gladly, most of us collapsing rather gracelessly. Sachiel made some comment about scouting ahead, but I didn't bother to listen, adjusting my cloak so that it became a blanket between my body and the cold stone ground. I was about to fold my arms to use as a pillow when Kalic's red brushed against me, the warmth of his body already seeping into mine. Gratefully I turned and snuggled into my twin, letting out a low hum of contentment.

Thank you, I whispered through our bond.

It's cold, you're warm, so thank you, came his response, and as he drifted off, so did I.

As the vast expanse of a dreamless sleep slipped away, I slowly became aware of voices around me, colours growing ever darker with concern.

"-not far," the coppery angel was saying, "We need to get him to a healer."

"It's too dangerous," Ethlon argued, "The faeries are out there, and from the sounds of it, the cobrai are with them too."

"So?" my eldest brother exclaimed, "Fírean is really hurt! If we *don't* take him to a healer, he might not make it!"

A frost fell over all of us and my heart clenched.

"I can't lose anyone else," Lanny whispered, his voice breaking, and the pain lacing his colour was too much for me to ignore. Sitting up, I gently untangled myself from the cloaks I'd shared with my still-sleeping twin and crept over to Lanny, wrapping my arms around him. He jolted, surprise flashing through him.

"Benji? I'm sorry, did I wake you?"

I shrugged, scooting round so that I was facing him. "No, I woke up by myself. Don't apologise." The rest of the words were on the tip of my tongue – *how bad is Fírean?* – but for some reason, they didn't form.

"I'm going to check if the coast is clear," Sachiel announced, standing as straight as he could in the confines of the tunnel.

"I'll come with you." The sentence was out of my mouth before I could think; both Ethlon and Lanny's colours flickered in disapproval, but Sachiel nodded and smiled. I released my hold on Lanny and took the angel's gloved hand instead, pushing aside my concern for Fírean for a moment. There was something that had made me answer so quickly and I tentatively reached out with my mind as we walked, before recoiling abruptly a span from the tunnel's exit.

"Faeries," I hissed at the touch of the greys, "And there's something else with them." It was a dark presence, the colour completely black, lacking the thrum of life that everything else did.

"A cobrai," Sachiel growled, letting go of my hand to push me behind him, "Stay back."

I obeyed, the presence of the new black making me rather nauseous, but curiosity would not let me wander far from the tunnel's exit. The ground outside was bathed in soft moonlight, turning it a gentle turquoise shade, but the beauty was marred by the three figures waiting there. Two I instantly recognised to be faeries; the third, the source of the black, I'd never seen the likes of before. It was similar to the faeries in size and figure, but its eyes glowed an unholy red, and its skin was blue-black, like a mottled coat of bruises.

"Ah, Sachiel. We meet yet again," the black one spoke, gruff and masculine, exposing white fangs that flashed in the moonlight.

Sachiel's copper darkened and his right arm flashed, a sword suddenly forming in his hand, which he proceeded to brandish at the black one.

"I'll give you one chance to leave, Zaro," he spat, "Or I'll kill you."

The threat made my gut twist and I staggered back as bile rose in my throat, a few drops leaking into my mouth. *Kill? Why would Sachiel kill someone? Isn't he supposed to be a good person?*

"Don't," I whispered, swallowing back the rest of the bile, then repeated the word again with more force.

Zaro's fiery gaze settled on me. "Oh, a little Chroma? How very cute. Come here, child," he cooed and I stiffened, but my legs were somehow moving towards him, not of my own accord. Sachiel reached out and grabbed the collar of my shirt as I passed him, thankfully not letting me cross over into the open.

"Leave Benji alone," Sachiel commanded.

"Let him hear my proposal, and I will," Zaro retorted.

Sachiel sighed, but nodded and released my collar. The urge to move disappeared and I found myself reluctantly locking gazes with Zaro again.

"You don't want war, do you, little one?"

I clenched my fists at the condescending term, but nodded slowly.

"You can stop it, Benji, you or your darling brother. Arlan, is it?" A small smirk crept across Zaro's dark face and I swallowed the churning fear and nausea.

"All I need is for one of you to surrender, and then I ask the faeries to stop their attack on the rest of your family," Zaro continued, a slight flicker of red in his colour.

My eyes narrowed. "It's not that easy, is it? You don't just want surrender."

His grin faded. "Smart boy," he hissed, "No, I want one of you to surrender – and *die*."

"I'll do it."

Chapter Twenty-Eight

- Jackie -

My back ached and I rolled onto my side, suddenly becoming aware of the lack of warmth where Arlan had previously been lying. Slightly disgruntled, I sat up, rubbing the sleep from my eyes as I noted who was missing. Sachiel, Benji, and Arlan were all gone; Ethlon was awake and standing to one side, his arms crossed in a rare show of irritation.

I got to my feet, ignoring the slight twinge in my ankle, realising as I straightened that the ache was not in my back but rather in my new wings, a discovery that only served to muddle my brain further. Ethlon made no move to stop me as I ventured towards the tunnel's exit, stopping abruptly when I saw the dark figure waiting outside.

A cobrai. But not just any cobrai; the one that Sachiel had fought outside the castle. *Zaro.*

Fear spiked in my chest, the blood pounding through my ears loud enough to drown out Zaro's toxic words, but the elf's response was crystal clear.

"I'll do it," Arlan said firmly, causing Benji to jump and turn around, eyes wide.

"No!" the younger exclaimed, "Lanny, you can't!"

I frowned, trying my best to focus on the conversation and *not* the creepy monster lurking beyond. *Can't what?*

"Benji, listen to me," Arlan urged, grabbing his brother's arm, "I can't let you do this. You have far too much ahead of you." His voice dropped to a whisper that I could barely make out, "They want you for your abilities, and for that, they'll keep you barely alive. But the faeries won't stop. There's someone they want more."

No.

My heart was suddenly struck by lead, ruthlessly tearing it down through my organs until it rested in a bloodied pile at my feet.

No.

"Arlan," I cried out and he brought his eyes up to meet mine, their depths swimming with an agony anchored in painful conviction.

No.

"I'm sorry, Jackie," he murmured, "They've left me with no other choice."

I choked, the words spiking through the air so brutally familiar, and it was all I could do to shake my head, no sound able to pass my lips. Benji's expression mirrored how I felt; all the blood had drained from his face, making his freckles and silver eyelids stand out more than ever, and his eyes were wide open, irises seeming to shrink in terror.

Arlan turned to Zaro, the sight of his back making me freeze up even more. "I will come with you," he said steadily, "But none of you – no cobrai, no faeries, *no-one* – must lay a hand on my family. Understood?"

Zaro grinned, his fangs flashing. "Of course. Those are the terms, after all," he hissed, "We will leave you be for the next day, but on the second dawn, we will come. Do not stray far." He backed up swiftly, melting back into the dying shadows, and I gasped in a breath, suddenly aware of the ache in my lungs.

Arlan's face as he looked back at us was firm, but his hands were shaking and those oceans were brimming with so much hurt and fear that it increased the pain in my own heart.

Puzzle pieces finally fell into place, though at this point in time, they were more of a fractured mosaic. The cold, bitter hand of fate laughed as I realised the truth of my visions.

Him leaving was not just a fear, but a future. And the one I'd seen die wasn't Benji, or Turvo.

It was Arlan.

All along, it had been Arlan.

I clenched my fists and cursed every force in the known universe, all the pain inside twisting in to sudden anger. *How? How could this happen? I've given up everything for him, he can't just leave me now...!*

I opened my mouth to confront Arlan before Benji could, but a sudden movement from Fírean distracted both of us. He sat bolt upright, pupils blown, gasping in pain and clutching at the haphazard, bloodied bandage wrapped over his forehead.

"Fír!" Benji exclaimed, shoving roughly past Arlan to get to his injured brother.

"What happened?" Fírean croaked, moving to rub at his discoloured arm, which Felicia had put in a makeshift sling.

Arlan inhaled sharply, tears glistening in his eyes. "Fír, we had to leave the castle. There was an explosion and... our parents..." His voice shook, unable to finish, and my anger faded as I realised that Fírean didn't yet know the truth.

He didn't know that his parents were dead.

But from the tears welling in his blue eyes, I saw that he'd already figured it out.

"No," he whispered brokenly, and Benji immediately moved to gently embrace him, mindful of his wounds.

I bit my lip and looked away, accidentally locking gazes with Arlan in the process.

Talk. Now, I mouthed, hoping the message was conveyed in my eyes as well. He sighed, but nodded, and we discreetly stepped past the still-sleeping forms of Hazel and Kalic to walk back down the tunnel. I stopped once I thought we were out of earshot, but he continued a couple more metres, forcing me to follow.

"Jackie-" he started, but I raised a hand, cutting him off.

"No. Arlan, how could you?" I hissed, struggling to keep my voice calm, and failing.

"I *have* to do this. If I don't go, the faeries will declare war, and our situation will only get worse. Then they'll just come and kill us anyway," he said, far too placid.

I folded my arms, fists clenching against my ribs. "Fight back! You can't just let them kill you, you have to at least try-"

"They have Turvo," he murmured, interrupting me.

I froze. In the heat of the moment, with everything that transpired the day before, I'd completely forgotten about the third eldest brother.

"Turning yourself in won't make them release him," I started to argue, then stopped, realising how cold it sounded.

Arlan shook his head slowly, blond curls falling to partially conceal his expression. "I know that. But I might be able to save him."

I frowned. "How-?"

"They have Turvo," he repeated, "No, let me rephrase that. *Turvo is with them.*"

The gears of my mind spun, settling on a conclusion that I didn't like one bit.

"Voluntarily?" I whispered, dreading the answer.

He nodded.

"Vaznek," I breathed, running a hand through my hair. *Turvo* – strong, caring, dependable Turvo – was a *traitor?* Surely that couldn't be true? He'd been with us right until the night before the explosion and I'd never seen him shown anything but anger towards the faeries. *Why* would he *join* them and betray his family?

"Why? How do you know this?" I exclaimed.

"Elohim told me," Arlan answered lowly, ignoring my first question, "Now, come on, we need to get to Ignaro and find a healer for Fírean," he continued in a louder voice, before I could press him further.

I pursed my lips and nodded, the anger returning. "Fine. But we're not done," I snapped, pivoting to stride back towards the rest of my newfound family, fists clenched tightly as I tried to hold on to the life I'd made here.

But I could feel it slipping as its centre was willingly leaving in the worst possible way.

"Jackie?" Hazel mumbled sleepily, wrenching me from my thoughts.

"Get ready, we're going to a village," I told her, "I think so, anyway."

She nodded and obeyed, running a hand through her sleek, dark hair in an attempt to brush it. Something else broke in my chest as it finally registered that we'd lost every physical marker of our home in Pylisya; all our belongings had perished in the fire.

Not everything, I reminded myself, fingers brushing against the pendant around my neck, grateful that I'd decided to wear it.

But a small piece of jewellery was no real conciliation.

"If you could go back, would you?" I blurted out suddenly.

Hazel frowned. "Back to where? Torindell?"

"No. Earth," I whispered.

Her brow furrowed further. "No, not a chance! Everyone I care for is here, and I finally feel like I belong somewhere. It was never like that on Earth. Plus, now you're engaged to Arlan, you're not going to go back. And there's no way I'm leaving you," she added, cheeks flushing in embarrassment at the confession, and I smiled weakly in response.

"Everyone ready to move out?" Sachiel asked then, "If we move quickly, we'll reach Ignaro before midday."

Everybody nodded, so we set off, Kalic and Hazel ambling tiredly near the back. Ethlon carried Fírean again and Benji hovered by him, refusing to make eye contact with Arlan, who walked in stride with Felicia somewhat reluctantly. As we exited the tunnel to the soft amber dawn, Sachiel fell into step beside me, letting Felicia take the lead.

"What's wrong?" he enquired gently. I couldn't stop the harsh laugh that bubbled in my throat.

"How about everything? Arlan, he-" I choked off, unable to say it, unwilling to admit it.

"You don't know for sure," Sachiel whispered.

I stared up into his bright eyes, so alike to mine. "But he's planning to-"

"No," Sachiel interjected, "Listen, Jackie. The future is *never* set in stone. There is always time for change. You can't let your heart become clouded with the worries of something that might not happen." His gaze drifted up to the sky and a smile spread over his face. "We just need to trust in Elohim. His plans are greater than any of us can fathom."

Sachiel's hand rested gently on my shoulder and I leant into his touch, falling silent as I wrestled with his words. *Elohim has plans... but why hasn't He shown me them? What if His plan is for Arlan to die? He didn't save Myranis, or Kalia, or Arazair... Is He just going to let Arlan be taken, too?*

No answer came to mind.

Part of me desperately wanted to confront Arlan again, but I couldn't bring myself to face him. Not when he was seemingly set on leaving me.

I resorted instead to walking in silence, ignoring everyone else as we trudged east towards Ignaro, the small village coming into sights after a couple of hours. It was less civilised than Kikarsko: most of the buildings were made of simple wood, and the boundary was a mere fence with a five-metre gap serving as an opening. Dirt paths wound through the streets, a jumbled mosaic of grass, stones, and mud. A few people meandered around – mostly elves, though a few dwarves were present – but none of them seemed fazed at our presence, despite the way we looked. My wings stubbornly refused to disappear, but, like in the backstreets of Torindell, the inhabitants paid no notice to them.

Guess there really is some weird stuff in Pylisya, I thought dryly.

Ethlon picked up his pace, taking Fírean to find a healer, with Felicia hot on their heels. Benji and Kalic hovered together, the intensity in their gazes hinting at a private conversation; I suspected that Benji was making his twin aware of Arlan's stupid agreement with the cobrai. Hazel, to my surprise, walked beside Arlan, but dropped back to me once we'd entered the village.

"Okay, you two need to talk," she declared, "I don't know what's going on, but he's hurt, and you're hurt, so you need to sort it out. Okay?"

I sighed. "Zel, it's not that simple-"

"Oh, really? He said something that you don't like. You're mad at him. Or am I wrong?" She put a hand on her hips and cocked an eyebrow, daring me to challenge her. I huffed, unable to do that.

"Fine, I'll talk to him."

She grinned.

"Alone," I added quickly, and Hazel nodded.

"Good. And *I'm* going to have a talk with your dad, because technically he's mine too. I need to get him to adopt me!" My sister giggled and grabbed Sachiel's arm, dragging him off further into the village. I glanced around, noting that everyone had left; everyone, that was, except the one I loved the most.

Arlan stood in the shadow of a rundown shack, arms folded, expression unreadable from this distance. Steadying my breathing, I made my way over to him, trying to adopt a casual walk rather than the confrontational stride that my body wanted.

"Zaro won't keep his word," I said abruptly, barely holding back a wince. *Nice one, Jackie.*

Arlan sighed heavily, his head slightly bowed so that his fringe covered his eyes. "I know," he murmured, "But as I said before, I have to try. I have to get Turvo-"

"Forget Turvo!" I yelled, "If he's a traitor, that's on him! *He* made that choice! Arlan," my tone dropped to pleading, "you have to stay here, stay with us. We can think of a plan together, find a way to stop Zaro and Havain and the faeries. Please."

"I wish there was another way, truly, I do. But I *feel* this, Jackie. I feel it in my soul that I must go," he answered softly, his voice far too melodic and beautiful to be speaking words that were tearing up my organs.

"Why? You giving yourself up to them won't achieve anything good! They'll just come after Fírean and the twins anyway!" I exclaimed, clenching my fists as my eyes stung with moisture.

"They'll only try for Benji," he muttered.

I frowned. "How can you be so sure of that?"

"Because Benji's a Chroma. And I named him as my successor," Arlan sighed.

"Not Fírean?"

"No. Fír never wanted the responsibility." His mouth crept up in a ruthful half-smile. "I could've named Turvo, but he was too reckless and strong-willed. If I had, I suppose he would only be targeting me. But Benji... I don't know why I did it, he was only three years old at the time. I just saw something within him, I suppose."

"Does he know?" I asked gently.

Arlan shook his head. "Turvo knows, but I never told Benji. We were waiting until he was older: that is, me and my father," His voice shook, but he carried on, "I never thought it could come to this. At the time, I was third in line to the throne. I figured I'd be married with children of my own before I would take on the crown. But now..."

My eyes widened in realisation. "You're the king," I breathed, feeling rather stupid for not recognising that sooner.

He laughed shakily. "Technically, but I don't feel like it. I mean, I ran from my own castle, didn't I? From my own *city*. And now the faeries are threatening war, my father was willing to take arms and stand up but I *can't*," he cried, "I can't do it, Jackie! I can't condemn thousands of lives just because we can't come to an agreement. If I surrender, then I can try and talk to Havain, try and come to terms of peace. If he wants the restrictions lifted on the faeries, I'll lift them. If Turvo wants some land to rule, I'll give it to him."

"But they killed your parents!" I exclaimed, "Are you just going to give in to them?"

His fists clenched, and he looked at me through his curled fringe, blue eyes dangerously dark. "It's not giving in, Jackie. I will never do something that compromises what I believe. And what I believe in is *peace*. We weren't created for violence and war, and I *won't* resort to that."

"But they will. The faeries are humans," I reminded him, "And humans are violent. Wars are always happening on Earth, some affecting the whole world, others confined to a small country. They'll still fight, even if you don't."

"Then I'll take the beating," he said in a resigned voice, looking away. A sudden pain dashed across my skull and I gasped at the memories of that cursed vision.

The third figure, baring Zeraphin's star, bloodied and bruised, marred from a brutal beating...

"No," I whispered, then louder, "No! Arlan, don't! Please, I can't lose you!"

He jumped slightly, brows furrowing at my sudden change in tone. "I'm not going to let them kill me, Jackie. I won't-"

"No, you don't understand! I *saw it*!" I cried, then abruptly clamped my hand over my mouth.

His eyes widened. "You saw...?"

I shook my head, tears starting to blur my vision. "I-I saw you leave, before we started dating," I stammered, "but I, I didn't think it would happen, I-"

"And you let us happen anyway?" he exclaimed, concern blossoming across his face.

"Yes! I used to have hope that the future wasn't set, Arlan! I tried to stop myself from loving you, but it was futile. I... I love you," I wept, tears falling steadily now, "With every fibre of my being, I love you, Arlan Zeraphin. I love you even though my heart will break when they-" I choked, unable to continue.

He closed the gap between us, a hand reaching to gently wipe away the rivers carving down my cheeks. "They won't kill me," he tried to soothe me and I forced myself to turn away, not wanting to see his face when he realised.

"Jackie?" he asked then, trying to tilt my face back towards his.

"I saw one of you die, but I didn't think it would be you... Oh, Elohim, why did it have to be *him*?" I screamed at the sky as my knees gave way and I crumpled. Arlan knelt beside me, cradling me close, and I sobbed into his chest.

"I love you, I love you so much, don't leave me," I pleaded.

"I'm sorry I led us to this," he murmured back.

Momentarily enraged, I pulled away. "No! No, don't apologise for this! Falling into Pylisya was the best thing that happened to me, because it led me to you. It's as much my fault as it is yours. And I wouldn't change it for the world."

I fiddled with the pendant strung around my neck, the mark of our engagement, a crazy plan forming. "How long do we have?"

"They'll be coming at dawn."

I glanced up at the sky, where the sun hovered in its midday position, counting the hours left. There weren't many, but there were enough.

"Find the others," I commanded, roughly drying my eyes, "I'm going to get the girls and head to a tailor's."

"Why?" Arlan asked softly, "Can't we just spend this time together?"

"We will," I responded fiercely, "But first, I want to marry you."

His ears stiffened, stunned into silence. "...Tonight? Even after-"

"I don't want to be your betrothed," I answered, each word building my resolve, "I want to be your wife. You're the only person I want."

"You're the only one *I* want," he murmured in response, his tone slinking towards seductive. I blinked rapidly and pulled away as a blush spread across his cheeks.

"Ah, sorry-!"

I cut him off with a kiss, our lips brushing gently before the fires ignited, and I clung to him with a passion and fury, desperately committing the feeling of his lips on mine to memory. I wouldn't let this be our last day together. I *wouldn't*.

But just in case...

I pulled away as quickly as I'd initiated the kiss, breathing hard against his smooth skin. "I want to do this the right way," I managed to say, suddenly aware of the way my hands were curled against his strong chest. It would be so easy to let myself go, to give myself to him, but I desired to be his in every way, and spending one night together wouldn't fulfil that.

"You have more self-control than me," he confessed, moving his hands from my hips, and I blushed.

"I *am* half angel, so I suppose that counts for something," I grinned.

He stiffened. "But can you-"

"I'm also half human. So yes, I can." I kissed him again, only a brief touch, then jumped to my feet, my heart somehow joyful despite the horrid situation we faced.

But that was tomorrow. We had to focus on today.

And right now, we had a wedding to throw together.

I ran off to find Hazel and Felicia, the latter in particular, as I needed help in finding a suitable dress in time. Arlan yelled something about Ethlon being qualified to officiate before he took off in the opposite direction with a new energy in his step. My sister was easy to find, making conversation with a few dwarves, but at my sudden announcement she immediately dragged me to the small tailor's shop, stopping briefly by the healer's house to get Felicia to join us. The two girls sorted through clothes like a hurricane, settling on a white dress that was meant for elvish festivals, but was so reminiscent of an Earthen wedding dress that I immediately wanted it. The sleeves were long, cuffs embellished with elegant leaves that curled halfway up the forearm. It was a snug fit, but the collar was fairly high, similar to the one on the green dress that Arlan had requested to be made for me, and the back was low to accommodate my wings. The skirt of the dress flared out beautifully, just brushing the floor, cascading silks that showcased intricate embroidery when the light caught it in a certain way. According to the tailor, elves traditionally wore pale blues or lilacs, but I wanted a piece of my home-world in the last minute, haphazard wedding we were attempting, and the dress was far too beautiful for me to let it go.

Four hours later, I was standing in the entrance of a chapel-like building – the only stone structure in Ignaro – wearing that dress, along with a thin, flimsy veil, and clutching a bouquet of freshly-picked flowers. Sachiel stood beside me, his wings out on show, clothed in a smooth white robe. He extended his arm to me, and I took it, squeezing his hand gently.

"Thank you," I whispered, "For being here with me."

He pulled me into an embrace, kissing the top of my head with a sweet tenderness. "Thank you for letting me be a part of this," he murmured, "I'm sorry I wasn't there sooner, but I love you, Jackie."

I smiled. "Love you too... Dad," I responded, the last word strange yet comfortable on my tongue.

Sachiel – *Dad* – beamed, the markings beneath his eyes seeming to glow, and I was very glad that I'd worked up the courage and asked him to assume the father's traditional role on this day. We stepped back from the embrace and he quickly adjusted one of the cuffs on my dress, before taking my arm again.

"Ready?" he asked. I inhaled deeply, then nodded.

We walked down the makeshift aisle in silence, save for the gentle tap of footsteps; Fírean was well enough to attend, but in no condition to play. The lack of music didn't matter, though, as soon as I set my eyes on the person standing beside Ethlon, the true angel in the room.

Arlan.

He was dressed in white too, his sandy hair braided back in an elegant plait, the curls of his fringe restrained by a thin gold band with a sapphire embedded in its centre. My eyes traced every perfectly sculpted curve of his face, absorbing his beauty and committing it to memory.

This was how I would remember him, if it had to come to that.

A soft blush spread over his cheeks as we met, and I felt the action echoed in mine as Ethlon took a band of gold ribbon and used it to tie our wrists together, my left with Arlan's right. He started speaking words of unity and duty in the same ancient, melodic tongue that had been used at Myranis' funeral.

How far we have come since then, I thought, gazing into the depths of Arlan's dazzling blue eyes, so lost in them that I almost missed the cues.

"I do," he stated, those two words igniting my heart.

"I do," I breathed when it was my turn, pouring every emotion that I had into it.

Ethlon split the ribbon with a ceramic dagger, and I gasped as it solidified into a band of gold, one that welded into my skin with no pain at all, leaving a perfect circlet hugging my wrist. The same happened to Arlan and I felt the gold pulse with the beat of his heart.

"I now declare you husband and wife," Ethlon announced, then suddenly Arlan's lips were on mine, kissing with a passion and hunger that I'd never experienced before, and I tugged away before we could make a scene. He grinned and I beamed back at him before turning to face our small family.

Hazel whooped and Felicia applauded quietly, but Fírean only managed a small smile, eyes glazed from the ongoing battle with his wounds. My father's markings seemed to glow even brighter and I suspected he was almost as happy as I was, which only made my heart swell further. Even the twins were grinning, Benji looking surprisingly satisfied, and he nodded in approval when our gazes met.

I turned back to Arlan then, losing myself to his gorgeous oceans, clinging to the reality that we were united, together, inseparable for tonight.

Zaro and the faeries loomed on the horizon, but I pushed them from my mind, keeping myself anchored in the moment. We had this night, and no-one was going to take it away from us.

Arlan was mine, and as the sun set over the village, I became his.

Chapter Twenty-Nine

- Benji -

The last slithers of blue moonlight faded, giving way to the cold yellow of the sun breaking the horizon and my family. I moved from my night-long perch on the windowsill of a rather grubby inn and immediately headed towards the room where Jackie and Lanny had spent the night, after their rather spontaneous union. Both of their colours were smothered in the rosy tinge of adoration, the threads running between them the strongest I'd ever seen. But neither could stop the blues and greys from creeping in with the knowledge that my brother had to leave.

I clenched my fists, focusing on the pain in my palms as fingernails dug in, rather than the pain in my chest. I'd been up all night trying to think of some way, *any* way, that the looming events of this morning could be prevented.

I failed to uncover a better answer.

The greys of faeries had multiplied in the dark, so they now completely surrounded Ignaro, cutting off any potential escape routes. Deep rubies shone out from their usual monochromes, marks of malice so strong they made me physically sick.

I wanted to be strong, to step up and let them take me instead of Lanny, but everyone – even Jackie – was adamant that it wouldn't work. The faeries would just come after Lanny anyway.

Was it really this hopeless? Was I going to lose my brother like I'd lost my parents? And what about Turvo? Was he alright? Were they going to hurt him too?

A knock on the inn's door jolted me out of the whirlwind of questions in my mind and I grimaced as I sensed the greys, including one that was oddly silver, almost the same colour as Ethlon.

"You have until the sun has fully risen to come out!" one of the faeries hollered. I glanced out the window, where half of the golden beast was already visible.

Vaznek. There's no time.

I knocked on the door of Lanny and Jackie's temporary room, and the former opened it. Immediately I embraced him, as if I could hug all the sadness from his gold.

"Please don't go," I murmured into the soft fabric of his tunic, the star of our house emblazoned on its centre.

He sighed and gently caressed my curls. "I'm sorry, Benji. It's the only way to try and obtain peace," he whispered.

"B-but they want to hurt you," I cried, voice shaking, "I can't lose you-"

"You won't," he interrupted, pulling back so he could scrutinise my face, but I refused to meet his gaze.

"Benji, look at me," he commanded softly. I reluctantly obeyed.

"Can you promise me something?" he asked, grey filtering into his colour. I nodded slowly.

"Promise me you won't stay here. Go with Kal and Ethlon back to the Northlands, as far from the faeries' lands as you can. Promise me!" Lanny exclaimed, his hands falling a little hard on my shoulders as his eyes grew moist.

"I-I promise," I stammered, a few tears falling from mine as well.

"Good," he breathed, pulling me in for another embrace, "I love you, Benji."

I swallowed the lump in my throat, determined to say goodbye properly this time. "I love you too," I whispered firmly, sending a shot of pink into his colour as I inhaled his scent, praying that this would not be the last time I'd hug him.

Elohim? If You're there... Please. Don't take my Lanny away. I don't care if You never answer another prayer of mine, as long as You answer this one. Don't let them kill him. Please! I cried out silently.

Lanny carefully prised my hands from his tunic with a sad smile, turning to say goodbye to the others that had gathered. Fírean leant heavily on the lavender-grey girl – Felicia, I'd been informed of her name – his colour still far too pale for my liking. I turned away as more tears were shed, staring out again as the sun continued to rise and everyone's colours stained blue, even Ethlon's.

"Tell Benji of his naming," Lanny whispered to the older elf, and I frowned, wanting to ask Lanny what exactly he meant by that. But then he was embracing Jackie, tears falling freely as they kissed with such a passion that I was embarrassed to look at them.

Then, Lanny was turning away from all of us, walking towards the inn's door where the faeries lurked beyond like a pack of wild dogs waiting to pounce, all grey and grey and – *green*?

Turvo is here?

A flicker of happiness ignited in my chest, but quickly faded as I absorbed the whole situation. My brother was stood *with* the faeries, close to the silvery one, his green the same darker, twisted shade I'd sensed before, just after the explosion.

Oh, no.

What's wrong? Kalic asked, *Aside from this whole rubbish scenario, of course.*

I shot him the impressions of the colours that I sensed. *Turvo's here, but he's different. Changed.*

You don't think he – Kalic's thoughts halted as Lanny stepped outside, just as the sun cleared the horizon. Jackie, Ethlon, and I moved forwards as well, standing in the wooden porch of the inn.

"Perfect timing," the silvery one commented, crimson eyes gleaming from beneath a fringe of dark brown hair. He didn't look much older than me, but the manner with which he carried himself was rather frightening.

Beside me, Jackie gasped. "Galen?" she whispered, disbelief gracing her cerulean. Ethlon stiffened, his hands twitching by his sides, and I almost gasped myself as the pieces fell into place.

That's Galen? Ethlon's nephew, the other Chroma?

A sickening black appeared then, striding forward with fiery eyes set in unnatural navy skin. *Zaro.*

"So, Benji," he crooned, those unholy eyes settling on me, "You're letting your brother take your place, hmm?"

"Leave him out of this," Lanny snapped, before I could respond.

Zaro laughed, the sound sending shivers down my spine. "Of course, I'll leave him and take you instead. I'm just a *little* disappointed that he's such a coward."

"Don't listen to him," Sachiel urged, stepping out to stand on the porch beside us. Zaro's grin widened.

"My dear old friend, won't you join us once more? It'll be your last chance," he offered in an almost-purr.

Sachiel's copper darkened. "Never," he hissed.

"Shame," Zaro commented, then his eyes locked on a painfully familiar face in the crowd of our enemies.

Turvo, no...

The elf strode forwards, dark eyes focused on the path that was cleared in front of him, his usually-immaculate hair falling loose and tangled past his shoulders.

"Hello, brother," Turvo greeted, as he walked up and kissed Lanny's cheek. Instantly four heavily-armed faeries broke from the gathering crowd, flanking my brothers and seizing the eldest's arms, harshly binding his hands together with coarse rope.

Rage surged within me at the sight and my fists clenched, the red extending from my body and shooting like sharpened arrows towards Turvo's corrupted green.

"How could you?" I shrieked, moving to step forward, but Sachiel placed a firm hand on my shoulder, preventing me from doing so.

"Benji, it's alright," Lanny soothed, turning just enough so our eyes could meet, the pain and fear swirling in his irises telling me the opposite.

"Enough talking," Zaro snapped, "We have who we came for." He flicked his wrist and a shot of white burst into me, taking my breath with it. I gasped and fell to my knees, barely able to send a flicker of the same shade towards Galen, who I figured was the source of the attack. The grimace on his tanned face proved me right.

As I struggled to withhold his curious attack, I failed to notice the other greys slipping around us until my remaining older brother cried out in pain. Their cold hands grabbed at his struggling blue; other cold hands tightened their hold on the increasingly-pained gold.

I stood for a moment, torn, unsure of which brother to go after. Ethlon made the decision for me.

"Come on!" he urged, "Benji, we have to go."

Kalic echoed the request in my mind; I noticed he was already gone, running with Sachiel and Hazel towards the winding path that would lead us north. Felicia struggled against her kin to reach Fírean, whilst Jackie stood frozen, her colour completely clouded. The two girls, along with Ethlon, were close enough to help Fírean.

They weren't close enough to Lanny.

I'll see you later, I told my twin, before turning and sprinting after the disappearing backs of the faeries, who had gained much ground during my hesitation. My family and friends called out after me, urging me to turn back and go with them, but my steps did not falter, locking on to the sight of the gold in front of me. The faeries set a steady pace, a sea of greys separating me from my dearest brother, yet I was slowly gaining on them. My genetics lent me more speed and stamina than they had; though as I rarely had to tap into that ability, I was not as physically able as Turvo.

The thought of my treacherous brother sent ribbons of red steaming through me, but I would not take my focus from the gold to peer into the depths of his darkened green. *Why* he was siding with the faeries, betraying Lanny, I didn't understand, and I doubted that I ever would.

As much as I wanted to be angry at him, to attack him both physically and emotionally, I couldn't afford for that to happen. Anger would cloud my mind, just as grief from my parents' deaths would cloud it too. I couldn't allow myself to feel either of them.

So, as I ran after the enemy, I let my emotions dissolve away, blue and red melting into the surrounding atmosphere. If the bees buzzed with increased fury and the flowers drooped in sadness behind me, then I did not bother to care. Instead, I cleared my mind so that all I could see were the colours in front of me, driving me forwards.

But the taints in their greys shifted and they sped up, moving with such velocity that I knew they were no longer relying on just their feet to carry them eastwards.

Frustration crept in, despite my intentions, as I was forced to slow down, the thin trees and fields giving way to a thicker cluster of forest, producing obstacles of tree roots and stumps, hoping to trip me up. My gut twisted when I glanced up at the horizon, no longer sensing the gold, and came to the sickening realisation that the faeries hadn't come this way.

I was lost.

Panic sped past the frustration, eagerly throwing its grubby hands around my neck, restricting my airways and leaving me choking for air. I closed my eyes, lungs screaming, desperately reaching out again, stretching my mind for any sign of gold, or twisted green, or even the horrid greys.

There was nothing, except for the steady hum of the small lives in the grass and trees around me.

"Vaznek," I hissed, punching the ground, then grimaced as I felt a small beetle die beneath my fist, its yellow draining in an instant. Slowly I raised my hand again, nausea building at the greenish liquid smeared across my knuckles.

"I'm sorry," I whispered to the remains of the beetle, then stiffened. What was I doing, apologising to a bug, when my *brother* was in danger? I *had* to get to him; the faeries' intentions were dark, but nothing compared to what the cobrai had in mind. I *needed* to get to Lanny, needed to save him, needed to, to...

My thoughts spiralled down into nothingness as the tightness in my throat and chest only increased, the pressure causing tears to slip from the corners of my eyes.

"Elohim," I gasped out, "You took him, but, I need to get him back... Please, help me... get back... to Lanny..."

I was hyperventilating now, the hurricane of panic failing to slow as the trees drew closer, branches twisting and mocking me, the harsh laughter of wind tearing carelessly through the leaves, reminding me that I was a failure; I couldn't save Anatti, or my parents, and now I wouldn't be able to save Lanny either-

Benji, calm. Another voice came through on a different surge of wind, much warmer, playing with the leaves instead of ripping them from their home, restraining the movements of the cruel branches. Slowly, panic released me from its chokehold and I took in a few larger, steadier breaths, replenishing the air in my lungs.

A yellow warmth surged into my chest then, taking up the space that the panic had occupied, serving to help my breathing rather than hinder it. I closed my eyes again, drawing on the yellow, but I still could not find my brother. Before the panic could rush in again, the yellow nudged something in my conscience, bringing to mind a faded memory of the lakeside town I'd only visited once, on a rare holiday with Kalic and our parents.

"Ekizsan?" I murmured, "Why Ekizsan?"

The nudge happened again. *Go,* it seemed to say. I frowned, trying to make sense of this weird instinct.

"Go to Ekizsan? Is that-" I gasped as realisation hit – "That's where Lanny is!" As I spoke the words, I tasted the truth within them and immediately glanced around, trying to figure out which way was east. A blur of ginger fur caught my eye and I stared in disbelief at the small cat emerging from the thick undergrowth.

"*Mali?*" I spluttered, "How...?"

She padded over to me and mewed, inclining her head to the left. I turned in that direction, another gasp escaping me as I saw none other than Brina standing there, her blonde tail swishing impatiently.

Where... How...?

Mali mewed again, pawing at my leg for good measure. I shook my head, struggling to not be overwhelmed by the overall oddness of the situation, and jogged over to Brina, climbing on the mare's back with practised ease. The cat jumped up after me, settling in my lap, and Brina turned in a direction that I presumed was east, her ears flickering as she waited for my command. I leant forward and patted her smooth neck.

"Go on, girl," I whispered, "Let's find Lanny."

Brina whinnied and accelerated into a fast canter, manoeuvring through the forest like it was a welcoming woodland and not the menacing mess of untamed roots and thorns that had threatened to trip me up only moments earlier. The branches still mocked us, some whipping out and striking my bare skin, but I ignored those small flares of white, crouching down on Brina's back to help her speed. The yellow still lingered within me: it, accompanied by the soothing nature of Mali's turquoise, kept the anxiety away and allowed me to focus once more on locating my brother.

Eventually the darkness of the forest gave way to cobbled paths, the musky scent of decomposing leaves replaced by the sweetness of freshwater ahead. Sure enough, Lake Ekiz loomed on the horizon, the sunlight dancing on the large expanse of rippling water. The town itself lay a little further east, still on the side of the lake closest to us, a substantial cluster of stone buildings resting on the pebbled shore. As we drew near, I saw the majority of the town's population gathered near the pier on the edge of Lake Ekiz, an unnatural amount of greys lingering in their midst.

And situated there, a hundred spans away from everyone else, was the gold of Lanny.

My joy at finding him again was immediately drowned by concern, as his colour was marred with streaks of agony, both the white of physical and the crimson of emotional. That concern seemed to flow into Mali and Brina, the latter moving into a gallop, hooves pounding out a rhythm of urgency.

Ekizsan drew ever closer, the grey stone of the buildings seeming to blend with the colours of the faeries. The stench of fish assaulted my nostrils and I grimaced, still urging Brina onwards until the crowd began to thicken and my riding on horseback drew a little too much attention. Swiftly I jumped from Brina's back, Mali climbing onto my shoulder, and whispered my thanks before running as fast as I dared through the crowds. It was a thick mass of sweaty bodies, colours trying to overwhelm me, but I placed my sole focus on the waning gold, using my small stature to my advantage as I slipped through the gaps, weaving between people and buildings until I could see the pier up ahead. Two figures stood on the wooden slats: Havain and Galen, I saw from their colours. Zaro was present, too, standing in the shadows, his colour seemingly darker, if it were possible for black to darken. Unable to get any closer, I glanced around for any sign of Lanny and barely held in a cry as he was dragged out onto the pier.

His blond hair was matted and tainted red with blood, the once elaborate curls hacked so the longest strands barely passed his chin. Splotches of purple and crimson littered his face; hardly any traces of the pale skin were present. I observed the way he staggered, bound hands pressed to his abdomen as if to a wound; which, considering the rest of his appearance, was not unlikely. His tunic was torn almost beyond recognition, the six-pointed star of our house dyed with blood and dirt.

There's so much blood, I noted dimly, fighting back against the nausea. It trickled from the corner of his mouth, another bead forming under his nose, more unseen cuts raining their contribution onto the wooden boards with a sickening *drip, drop.*

Ignoring the churning in my stomach, I lifted my gaze to Lanny's eyes: still a bright blue, but their shine was diminished like his gold, which was now so full of grey that it was more of a dull brown. He was trying so hard to hide his fear, to stand tall despite the pain tearing his life from him, and I couldn't be prouder.

I also couldn't be more worried. The flickering edge of his colour was a sign that I was becoming far too familiar with.

If he didn't receive healing soon, he would die.

As panic started to creep in again, I felt hard eyes on me and turned to meet the cold gaze of Galen. His silver pulsed, recognising me, and I immediately sent a crimson threat his way. He winced visibly and I struggled against the satisfaction that I'd hurt him.

He's partially responsible for Lanny's pain. He deserves it, part of me whispered.

I silenced it, ceasing my crimson onslaught.

A flash of white jolted me then, coming from Lanny's gold, as one of the faeries kicked him roughly. My fists clenched and I almost sent crimson to that *swine* too before stopping myself.

I won't be a monster like them. I won't kill and hurt like they do. I won't.

The faery forced Lanny to his knees, pulling him back by the remains of his hair as Havain stepped forward, declaring a list of crimes that my brother had supposedly committed. I didn't believe a word. There was *no way* that Lanny was responsible for Atti and Mutti's deaths; he'd almost been killed with the explosion that had shattered our family. Didn't the people know this?

It seemed that they didn't. To my horror, they were *cheering*, colours flashing red with a hatred directed at my innocent brother. *They believe Havain,* I realised, shock threading through me. There was a drop of hatred, too, materialising in the form of frustration at Lanny for not listening to me, for not letting me go, now he was hurt but it was *his* fault-

"No," I gasped, finally discerning what was happening: Galen was influencing the crowd, like I'd accidentally influenced the elf-lady back when we'd run from Lidan, and others since then. He was manipulating emotions on a larger scale than I thought possible and it was all I could do to keep myself clear of the destructive red.

Another surge of white hit me as the faeries threw chains around my brother, pinning his arms to his sides. His gold grew paler by the second; I suspected the blood loss was starting to become fatal.

No. I reached out for him, biting my tongue to prevent from crying out as our colours mixed. Pain, so much pain of both kinds ripped through me, accompanied with fear and a general lack of anything good. I reached inside of me to find a supplement, but I was running on empty, too.

No.

A slither of pink pulsed at my centre in time with Lanny's struggling heart, and I forced it through the connection and directly into my brother. He was not alone; I would not let this happen to him alone. Our parents had loved him. Jackie loved him. *I* loved him.

I loved him so, *so* much.

My energy returned and I focused every fibre of my being on pouring the love into him, giving his gold a rosy hue, flushing out every trace of fear that could not stand in the presence of pure love. I didn't care that the efforts had brought me to my own knees. I didn't take note of the emotions of the crowd . I didn't listen to the poisonous words spoken over my brother and my family.

There was only love and Lanny.

His eyes met mine as he realised where the sense of love was coming from. A flicker of yellow dashed through his colour – aimed at me, I knew for certain – and I continued my onslaught whilst silently screaming to Elohim for a miracle.

I shouldn't have come alone; if the others were with me, we could've done something, but I was too weak by myself. All I could do was keep up the stream of love, pouring it into my brother, watching helplessly as Havain's colour turned bloodthirsty. His declaration of lies reached a crescendo and the roar of the furious, manipulated crowd joined the cacophony as the faery raised his hand, a dagger glinting in the vicious sunlight. Instantly, I saw what was going to happen and desperately tried to sever the bond, but couldn't.

Havain's dagger sunk into Lanny's chest and we screamed in unison, every emotion streaking through both of us. My brother's outline flickered, his gold fading, and I was barely able to cry out his name before the white consumed me. It tore through my gut, spiking in my chest and cutting off my airway because I couldn't breathe and I was choking on blood and everything was going black–

Come and find me, a voice like Lanny's whispered.

Then his gold faded away, and I lost myself to the crimson shadows.

Chapter Thirty

- Jackie -

Chaos erupted around me, but I stood frozen, my sluggish mind failing to understand the situation. Then a cry from Fírean broke me from the trance and I drew a dagger from my belt, charging into the fray of faeries with a sudden fury streaking through me. Using my wings to gain momentum, I punched the first faery with an adrenaline-fuelled strength, then twisted my dagger to block the blade of another.

"You're not going to get him!" I yelled, desperately fighting through the masses to reach Fírean.

I didn't need to be a Chroma to see the life dimming in his eyes.

The elf could barely stand, weakly swatting at the approaching faeries like they were simple flies, a puddle of crimson forming at his feet. Felicia let out a peculiar yell as she darted forwards, a sword in hand, blonde plaits spinning as she fought with the same purpose as me.

But we were just two against a score of trained warriors, lacking the skills and stamina to prevail, and it wasn't long before I was knocked down, landing hard on my tender ankle. Tears blurring my vision, I could do no more as the faeries bound Fírean's hands, hauling him away like they had done with Arlan.

Felicia screamed, her borrowed sword falling to the ground as she wept, exhaustion preventing her from following. I tried to force my legs to move, but they refused, my weakened ankle amplifying its protests.

"Why?" I cried out, "Why take Arlan, why take *Fírean*? Must we lose everyone?"

A hand settled on my shoulder and I wearily glanced up into the grey eyes of Ethlon, surrounded by worried creases.

"Some of the faeries went east, others went south," he said gently, "We cannot go after both companies."

I stiffened, suddenly becoming aware of the absence of others. "Where are the twins, and Hazel, and my dad...?"

"Sachiel took Kalic and Hazel north, and I'm not sure where Benji went," Ethlon confessed, "I think east, but I'm not sure."

"You're not sure?" I echoed, glaring up at him, "How can you not be sure? You didn't help us in the fight, so what *were* you doing?"

Ethlon sighed, staring at the bloodstained ground. "I'm sorry. Galen's presence distracted me," he answered rather lamely.

"Galen is a jerk," I hissed, struggling to stand, "He tricked me into thinking he was actually a decent person."

"He is my nephew," Ethlon stated, offering me a hand. I took it with a little more force than necessary.

Felicia made an odd noise, clearly trying to get our attention, so I turned away from Ethlon and focused on her instead. Her hands moved frantically, communicating in a language that I just didn't understand.

"I think they took Arlan south," Ethlon answered, signing the response as well: at least, I presumed that was what his hands were gesturing.

"You know sign language?" I asked, both impressed and relieved.

"Of course. Who do you think taught Fírean? But now isn't the time for that; we must decide which way to go. Have you heard anything from Elohim?"

I opened my mouth to respond with the correct 'no' when white light burst into my vision, showing me the haunting image of the pier, of the dagger falling on the bloodied elf-

Just as I was about to pull away from the vision, the perspective shifted, zooming out until I began to see the town as a whole, situated near a giant lake.

"Give me some paper, quickly!" I demanded, reaching out blindly until a stick of charcoal was placed in my right hand, parchment on the ground beside me. Frantically I drew what I could see in the vision, sketching the outline of the town, the proximity to the lake, and the small cluster of buildings I suspected were Ignaro.

"That's Ekizsan!" Ethlon exclaimed as my vision faded, bird's-eye-view turning back to the dreary reality.

"We have to go there," I urged, "As quickly as possible."

The elf nodded. "East it is, then. Give me a moment." He ran off, further into Ignaro, and as I processed his words my heart began to sink. If Arlan had been taken south, but we were headed east...

No, that could be good. That elf might be Fírean, not Arlan. He is going to be okay. I have to believe that, I told myself, focusing on the beautiful image of my husband constructed in my memory, not the bloodied version formed by my fears.

I *was* going to be with him again; I would not let last night be our only night together.

My fingers set aside the charcoal and moved to trace the band on my wrist, the gold pulsing with a rhythm that I knew to be Arlan's heartbeat. *He's alive.* It was a little faster than I would've liked, but it was still beating and that was what mattered.

"Hurry!" Ethlon called out then, suddenly reappearing on a dappled grey mare, two more horses following him. One was a soft palomino, much like Brina, and the other was entirely black, except for a white star on his forehead. My breathing quickened as I realised that *they* were to be our method of transport.

Felicia mounted the palomino with an elvish grace, unfazed by the lack of any tack on the horse. Swallowing my nerves, I approached the black stallion, gently reaching out towards him whilst keeping my eyes lowered. He whinnied softly and pressed his muzzle into my hand, much calmer than any male horse I'd seen back on Earth. Encouraged by the soft gesture, I awkwardly hauled myself onto his back, tucking my wings in and wrapping my fingers in the silky ebony hair of his mane.

"How do we-" The question turned into a yelp as the stallion surged into motion, quickly gathering speed as he ran apace with the other horses. My grip on his mane tightened and I fixed my eyes on the horizon, refusing to look at the dizzying rate of the land moving past us.

"The horses know their way," Ethlon called out, "You just need to hold on." He was seated calmly on the dappled mare, hands rested on her neck as if he were riding at a slow walk, not a near-gallop as we were. On my other side, Felicia beamed with an exhilaration that reached her lilac eyes, the colour of her hair identical to that of her horse's, in a match that was slightly amusing. I matched my horse as well, I suddenly realised – black and black – a thought which would've made me laugh had our circumstances not been so dire.

"Do the horses have names?" I called out to Ethlon, after approximately fifteen minutes of steady riding.

"Of course!" he chuckled, "This is Willow, the palomino is Oak-Wing, and you're riding Stormheart."

"Stormheart," I whispered. The stallion tossed his head, neighed in response, and sped up, which caused a loud yelp to escape from my lips, echoed by laughter from Felicia.

We drifted back into silence then, the only sounds those of the horses' powerful hooves striking the muddy ground, and the soft twitter of birds in the trees above. I relaxed my position, starting to really get a feel for the rhythm of Stormheart's cantering, when a sudden pain shot through my arm, stemming from the band on my wrist. I screamed, the noise startling Stormheart, as flames seared my skin, burning, burning-

"Arlan," I gasped out, "He, he's hurt, we have... have to..."

"Shh, steady," Ethlon soothed, slowing his mare to calm the stallion. I blinked quickly, trying to see through my tears.

"No, *go,*" I ground out, barely holding back a scream as the burning intensified. My skin appeared unblemished, but it felt as if it would be blistered and peeling.

What's going on?

I focused on my breathing, blocking out the pain so I could move again, gently urging Stormheart onwards. He immediately accelerated into a gallop, following in the wake of Willow and Oak-Wing, breaking through the trees to the sight of a lakeside town, the one I'd seen in my vision.

"Good boy," I whispered, leaning forwards to pat his neck with my right hand. We caught up to the others, falling into line behind them, as Willow set the pace of a brisk trot. Suddenly, Ethlon let out a cry, clamping his hands over his ears in a motion of panic that I'd never seen him express. Stormheart slipped around Oak-Wing so that I was beside the elf, able to reach out and place a hand on his shoulder. My wings unfurled and extended towards Ethlon too, gently brushing against his back in a motion than I hoped would be soothing.

"What's wrong?" I asked softly.

Ethlon grimaced. "Galen's manipulating the emotions of the crowd. Benji's there too, but he's badly hurt."

"Physically or emotionally?" I exclaimed.

"I can't tell," he murmured, "It's too much of a mess. The colours are giving me a headache."

I pulled my hand back and curled it into a fist, determination surging through me. "We've got to get down there," I hissed, glancing over at Felicia. She frowned, confusion flooding her features, and I looked to Ethlon for help. He quickly signed something to the half-elf, who nodded in understanding and patted her horse's neck, urging the mare onwards.

"Go ahead," Ethlon commanded, one hand still holding his head, "Don't wait for me."

I nodded, numb now to the pain in my wrist, and Stormheart followed after Oak-Wing, hooves echoing as they fell on the cobbled path. The crowd swirled around us, barely parting to let us through, and I stiffened as I caught sight of another familiar palomino.

"Brina?" I breathed. The mare turned towards me and whinnied, to which Stormheart responded, pawing at the ground in agitation. Seeing that we could go no further on horseback, I dismounted, jogging over to Brina.

"Hey, girl," I murmured, "Where's Arlan? Where's Benji?"

Brina stared at me with dark, intelligent eyes, then inclined her head towards where the crowd was thickest.

By a pier.

My heart jolted in my chest.

No... Please, Elohim, don't let me be too late, I prayed as I flapped my wings, suddenly finding a greater strength within them. They lifted me a few metres off the ground, just high enough to soar over the crowds, and I did exactly that, letting the instincts in my new muscles take over. Eyes scanning for any sign of the elves I loved, I finally caught sight of a familiar mop of black hair, bowed over on the ground.

"Move!" I yelled as I came in for a slightly rough landing, stumbling and pitching forwards as my feet struck stones. The crowd parted, thankfully, and I knelt beside Benji, checking his pulse. It was far too sluggish; his breathing was nonexistent.

"Come on, Benji! Don't do this to me!" I exclaimed, gently rolling him onto his back. A small ginger cat jumped on his chest, pressing her paws over his heart, then glanced at me, her slit eyes screaming for me to do something. My mind blanked, struggling to recall basic first aid, but Felicia came to the rescue, pushing through the last of the gathered faeries to knock the cat aside and start CPR. She pumped his chest, leaning down to blow air into his mouth, then sat back after only a few repetitions. Fifteen painful seconds passed before Benji coughed, his chest heaving as he gulped in breaths, eyes opening to reveal constricted pupils.

"Lanny," he gasped, pain filling his tone.

Felicia shifted so that I could draw closer. "What happened?" I urged.

Benji sat up gingerly, stiffening as his gaze focused on something behind me. "No time," he hissed, "We've got to leave!"

"Who-?" I turned to see the stern figures of Havain and Zaro, Galen trailing behind the former, exhaustion written in his body. I still grappled with the truth that he was a bad person, despite his actions and placing as the mystery figure from my visions of the pier.

Then Benji inhaled sharply as a fourth male walked onto the platform, the green robes and neat, blond hair painfully familiar.

"As the only remaining heir to Pylisya, Prince Hesturvo will become our new king," Havain announced. I froze, only two thoughts forming in my mind.

First: *His full name is Hesturvo?*

Second: *The others are dead? But they can't be,* I deduced, glancing down at Benji, who was still very much alive, *they can't all be dead...*

"Liar," Benji spat, struggling to stand up. Felicia placed a hand on his shoulder, silently urging him to stay quiet and still.

Turvo dipped his head as he passed Havain to stand in the centre of the platform, his face smooth and unreadable.

"It is with great sorrow that I take on this burden. Prince Arlan's traitorous actions have torn my family apart, and for that, I will never forgive him. My first action as your king will be to reunite the faeries and elves. For too long we have crossed swords, but I say, no longer! King Havain and I will work together to make Pylisya a better place, for all peoples," Turvo declared.

"I can't listen to any more of this," Benji growled and I nodded, my blood boiling. How *dare* he call Arlan a *traitor,* when Turvo was the one to betray his family in the first place?

Or Hesturvo. Vaznek, I didn't even know his *name* anymore.

The three of us slipped away through the crowds; rather, Benji and Felicia snuck away, and I took to the skies again, finding that easier than trying to navigate the crowds with a pair of wings stuck to my back. I set down more gracefully beside the horses, my eyes stinging with anger and the pain of betrayal. I had *loved* Turvo, like a brother. He was the person I'd somehow grown closest to in Pylisya: second to Arlan, of course.

Arlan. I traced the gold band that had stopped burning, but still thrummed in tune with his pulse. *He's not dead. He can't be dead.*

"Lanny's gone," Benji whispered brokenly, walking over with the ginger cat clutched to his chest. I shook my head slowly.

"He's not. I can feel him-" I started, but Benji's agonised expression stopped me.

"I *saw* him get stabbed. He was already so hurt... the faeries, they *hurt* him, Jackie! And I connected with him to tell him that you love him, I love him, but I couldn't break free in time and I felt him d-d-d-" he stuttered and broke down in tears, unable to utter that fatal word.

I gripped my wedding band tighter, comforted by the heartbeat within it.

"He's *not,*" I repeated, "Feel his pulse!" I thrust out my hand, and Benji touched the band tentatively, his chocolate-brown eyes widening.

"B-but how, I felt him, he..." Benji gasped, a light forming in his irises, "He just disappeared! Havain stabbed him, then he *disappeared*... Vaznek, he's alive!"

"Disappeared?" I exclaimed, about to enquire further when I suddenly became aware of Felicia tugging on my arm. She pointed to the mass of faeries then made a gesture that was universally known.

We have to leave. The explanation will have to wait.

I climbed onto Stormheart again, pausing only for Benji and Felicia to mount their respective horses before setting off, trotting back to where we'd separated from Ethlon. Confusion and frustration warred on the faces of my companions and I knew those emotions were mirrored on mine, too.

"Where are we going?" Benji exclaimed, "We have to find Lanny!"

I slowed Stormheart until we were apace with Brina. "We need to speak with the others first. Ethlon isn't far," I explained, "This isn't something we can charge into, Benji."

Fury sparked in the young elf's eyes, but he grit his teeth, suppressing the emotion. "Fine. But I remember, Jackie. I heard his voice, asking me to find him. At least, I *think* it was him," he muttered as an afterthought, gaze drifting.

I frowned, turning my attention back to the path ahead as I pondered what Benji had said. *Did he really hear Arlan? Or was it Elohim? Or just a figment of the imagination?*

A loud whinny interrupted my thoughts and I refocused just in time to see Willow tossing her head wildly, nostrils flared. Oak-Wing halted and Felicia slipped off, approaching the frightened mare with an outstretched hand, her slow movements soothing the horse. Stormheart and Brina slowed too, and my breathing quickened as I realised we were past the place that we'd left Ethlon.

Where was he?

Benji slipped off Brina's back, his gaze locked onto a dark patch on the ground. He knelt by it, nose wrinkling into a grimace. "Blood," he commented, turning a little green.

"Is it Ethlon's?" I asked, dismounting as well. The ginger cat padded over and pawed at the liquid before nodding in a very human-like manner.

"Did she just-?" I gasped.

Benji shrugged. "Mali's an odd cat. But yes, that's Ethlon's. I can sense his colour on it." He straightened, glancing around with his eyes closed, light reflecting off his silvery lids. "I can't sense *him* anywhere, though," he sighed.

"Argh!" I screamed in frustration, "First Arlan, then Fírean, and now Ethlon? Can't we get a break?"

Benji's face paled. "They took Fírean too? Vaznek, I should've stayed to help," he cursed, starting to pace.

Felicia caught my eye then, looking utterly bewildered, and signed a series of words that I didn't understand. I turned away, raising my eyes to the sky in desperation.

"Elohim, what are we to do?" I exclaimed, "Everything's going wrong, I don't know where the others are, where we're supposed to go now... I don't know anything. Please, help us," I prayed.

Warmth flooded over me, accompanied by the gentle weight of a hand on my shoulder. I started, glancing up to meet the blazing eyes of my father.

"Please don't say something corny about being the answer to my prayer," I blurted out without thinking. He chuckled, the sound somehow soothing.

"I came because I sensed your distress. But first, Felicia is owed an explanation." Dad approached the half-elf, catching her eye before conversing with her in sign language. I watched, incredulous.

"You too?" I commented.

Dad glanced back at me and shrugged, his wings rustling with the motion. "I know every language, Jackie. It's a perk of the job."

"That's good and all, but when are we going to find La- Arlan?" Benji asked impatiently.

"After we've met with your brother and Hazel. Follow me," Dad commanded, swinging onto Willow's back with an agility that I both admired and envied. We scrambled to mount our horses before following after him at a canter, myself slightly confused as to why he would bother to ride when he could just fly to the location. *Maybe he just wants to set the pace with us?*

The short journey was void of speech, none of us finding any words as we processed the severity of the situation. I was desperate to ask Benji exactly what he meant by Arlan 'disappearing', but I respected him and understood his need for time to think. After all, he'd just lost two brothers, his mentor, and had the third brother turn traitor. Not to mention the recent loss of his parents, too.

I admired him for still going, despite all of that hurt.

My fingers stroked my wedding band, feeling Arlan's pulse, and for a moment I imagined myself back in Ignaro, hands pressed against his chest, his heart pounding steadily against them as his golden locks tickled my face, laughter and joy brimming in his oceanic eyes. He kissed me tenderly, stroking the feathers of my newly-grown wings, and I lost myself in the perfectly carved shape of his body.

But the sting of rain on my cheeks stole that memory away, clouds gathering as the sun's light faded, yielding to the heavy pull of darkness. I lowered my head, unable to tell if the moisture hitting my hands was just rain, or tears, too.

Arlan wasn't dead. Fírean wasn't dead. Ethlon wasn't dead.

I *had* to keep believing that.

After what felt like hours, but was probably only half of one, Dad brought Willow to a halt beside a cluster of trees, that upon further scrutiny were actually just a mound of twigs and leaves concealing the entrance of a cave.

Benji leapt from Brina's back, breaking through the pile of leaves in an instant, much to my father's annoyance. Curiosity urged me onwards so I dismounted too, entering the cave in a less destructive manner.

"Jackie! You're okay!" Hazel exclaimed, her arms wrapping around me in a death-grip. I wheezed as all the air was forced out of my lungs, patting her on the back awkwardly.

"Oops, sorry," she added, releasing me. I glanced over to see the twins embracing, clutching each other like a lifeline. Tears brimmed in the corners of Kalic's eyes and Benji was the picture of exhaustion.

They shouldn't have gone through all that loss.

Felicia entered with Mali in her arms, followed at last by Dad, who attempted to put some of the larger leaves back as a covering. Hazel stared towards the entrance, as if waiting for more, and frowned when no-one else came through.

"Where are Fírean and Ethlon?" she asked.

Dad sighed and leant against the cave's wall, suddenly looking rather weary. "They were taken by the faeries, too."

"And we have to get them back," Benji declared, fists clenched.

Dad pinched the bridge of his nose. "I know, I know. But I don't know *how*."

"You must know something," Benji pressed, "You're an angel! Or Jackie, do you know something? Anything?" His tone was desperate and I hated to disappoint.

So I bit my lip, struggling for the words. "Arlan's not dead, but I have no idea where he is. Hesturvo has claimed the throne-"

Kalic gasped loudly, horror lighting in his eyes. "He has?" the elf exclaimed.

Benji nodded, a scowl forming. "He always despised his full name. I can't believe he's adopted it now," he muttered.

"He will bring Pylisya to ruin," my father commented, his eyes clouded, "The faeries and elves will unite, but it's all a front. Havain just wants to control all the races of the world. Peace is a false promise from him."

"Then what do we do?" Benji asked.

"We're six people against the world. There's not much we *can* do," Hazel pointed out. Immediately Kalic started arguing with her, and when Benji joined in I zoned out, finding myself moving towards the cave's entrance with a will not entirely my own.

The leaves parted, revealing the soft blue moonlight dancing over the grass, a small piece of normality in the chaos that I'd found myself in. I took a step forward, then another, slipping my feet from my boots in the process, letting the moist grass brush against my bare skin. Spreading my wings, I inhaled the cold night air, closing my eyes as it flooded my lungs, anchoring me in that moment.

You're here for a reason, Arlan had told me many times. I refused to believe that my purpose ended in a cave, giving up.

"There's got to be a way," I whispered, "Elohim, show me."

Stars lit up the sky, their multitude of colours expanding until the dots formed images, impressions.

I saw Fírean knelt beside a throne, bleeding but still breathing.

I saw Ethlon surrounded by a mass of grey, bruised but not broken.

I saw a city of stone and a city of coral, both teeming with warriors.

"No," I grinned, "We're not giving up."

I pivoted and briskly strolled back into the cave, my entrance silencing the petty arguing.

"They're still alive," I announced, "They're all alive. Yes, we don't have the strength to face Havain and Turvo and the faeries, not yet, anyway. But we're not just six against the world."

I locked eyes with Benji and understanding rippled over his face. "The dwarves," he breathed, hope returning.

"Yes. We're going north: not to hide away, but to gather our forces and build an army. Then we'll strike Havain with a strength he never saw coming," I declared, direction fanning the flames of determination.

My father nodded, approval written in his eyes. "We leave at dawn," he decided.

The atmosphere of the cave shifted, pessimism fading as hope took hold, promising us solutions to the hurricane of problems.

And as I relaxed, I saw Arlan in the darkness, his blue eyes burning with the fires of life.

Come and find me.

- END OF BOOK ONE -

Pronunciation Guide

Baelthar	BAY-el-thar
Brina	BREE-nah
Cobrai	koh-bry ('bry' to rhyme with 'eye')
Dryslan	dr-EEZ-lan
Ekizsan	eh-KEE-zan
Fírean	fear-REE-an
Grayssan	GREY-zan
Havain	HAA-vain (to rhyme with 'vein')
Ignaro	eeg-NAH-ro
Kikarsko	kee-KAR-su-koh
Lidan	LEE-dan
Myranis	my-RAH-nees
Pylisya	py-LEE-see-ah ('py' like 'pie')
Sachiel	sah-CHEE-al
Syndekar	SIN-deh-kar
Torindell	tor-IN-dell ('tor' like a 'tour')
Turvo	TER-voh
Vonyxia	von-IX-ee-ah
Zeraphin	zeh-RA-fin

Elvish Terms

Family

Atti	=	an affectionate term for father
Mutti	=	an affectionate term for mother
Anatti	=	an affectionate term for grandfather
Amutti	=	an affectionate term for grandmother
Onta	=	Uncle
Mita	=	Aunt

Measurements

Handspan	=	Approximately 15cm
Span	=	8 handspans; approximately 120cm

Thus 5 spans ≈ 6 metres

Printed in Poland
by Amazon Fulfillment
Poland Sp. z o.o., Wrocław